Life had a sense of unreality about it for the next few days, but on Sunday morning a tearful Sarah arrived at Julie's front door.

'Oh, Sarah.' Julie began to cry too. 'We're off tomorrow,' Sarah said. 'I can't bear it.'

'Oh, it's not the end of the world,' Julie said staunchly, although it seemed like that to her. 'I'll come up and see you.'

'You will?' Sarah brightened. 'Really?'

'Promise,' Julie said, 'Come in and say goodbye to Mam.'

Arms round each other, Julie and Sarah walked back to the Lowmans' house.

The next day Ada looked up as a large van went by and recognised the removers. She sighed. That would be for the Lowmans. So they were really off. She would suggest tonight that she and Julie went to the cinema. So far everything was open as usual – they would certainly close if and when the air raids started.

Life would never be quite the same again, she thought.

Rose Boucheron is the author of six novels: *The End of a Long Summer, Pollen, The Massinghams, September Fair, Promise of Summer* and *The Patchwork Quilt*. She lives in Gerrards Cross, Buckinghamshire.

Promise of Summer

Rose Boucheron

Woman's Weekly Fiction

A Woman's Weekly Paperback
PROMISE OF SUMMER

First published in Great Britain 1993
by Judy Piatkus (Publishers) Ltd
This edition published 1995
by Woman's Weekly
in association with Mandarin Paperbacks
an imprint of Reed Consumer Books Ltd
Michelin House, 81 Fulham Road, London SW3 6RB
and Auckland, Melbourne, Singapore and Toronto

A CIP catalogue record for this title
is available from the British Library
ISBN 1 86056 015 6

Printed and bound by
HarperCollins Manufacturing, Glasgow

Chapter One
1939

Spring came early to London that year. In March, a hot dry spell of weather arrived as though the elements had gone mad and were determined to show just how capricious they could be. On London Bridge, the Southern Railway disgorged its passengers who walked across the bridge to their offices, the girls wearing sleeveless summer dresses, the men minus their jackets. Tom Lowman, who went the other way, got up fifteen minutes early, lit the wash boiler, then walked from Charlton to his factory in his shirt sleeves instead of catching a tram to the big engineering factory where he worked. Conscientious mothers wore a frown, everyone knew that you didn't cast a clout until May was out, but what was the sense of wearing winter vests and knickers with the temperature well up in the seventies and eighties?

Old Martin, the newsvendor on the corner, said he had never known a March like it, and he should know for he was over eighty years old. You would have thought it was high summer except that the trees were not in leaf, although the warmth of the sun caused the burgeoning buds to open so that nature itself went haywire for a spell.

How well the year had started, they told themselves, especially since last year had been so fraught, with Chamberlain coming back from Europe waving his little piece of paper – 'Peace in our time' he had said, and the whole world relaxed. Not many had thought there would be a war – it would be a holocaust of such magnitude – and so pushed all thoughts of it to the back of their minds. Others cynically

1

said, if not now, then later. You had to have a war every so often to let off steam for the young ones' sake, and to get rid of flotsam and cut down the number of people in the world. It was logical – it made sense. But now the sun was shining fiercely and London basked in it.

Along Calydon Road, Eva Lowman decided to wash the blankets while Ada Garrett walked up Victoria Road to her place of work without even noticing the hill she had to climb, and the two girls, Sarah Lowman and Julie Garrett, walked to school together – their last term – harmonising the latest Al Bowlly song.

People pushed up their sash windows – you could hear the radios blaring, and the German family at number nine almost smiled after the scare they had had last year with the Munich crisis. Things had not been easy since the last war, and Frau Schmidt wielded her broom with a flourish – she had the cleanest home in Calydon Road. Peggy Vaisey the grocer's wife, brown eyes smiling in her pretty face, exchanged greetings with Dora Gibbons, whose husband kept the shoe repairer's on the opposite corner. Mrs Brown, mother of those three pretty daughters, Lily, Violet and Rose, was out whitening her front step – a thing no one had ever seen her do before.

There was an early heat haze over Greenwich Park where children played and nursemaids pushed their charges in Victoria prams, while on the heights overlooking the river stood the beautiful Georgian house in which lived the Nevilles, descendants of a great naval family whose forbears had built the house. Nowadays Joseph Neville worked in the city where he had an import and export paper business, although today he would play golf at the Royal Blackheath Golf Club – it would be silly to miss a chance like this. Wearing his tweed plus-fours, he left by the front door as Ada Garrett arrived at the back to help with the mending and the sewing, one of the jobs she elected to do in her capacity as a dressmaker.

The sun shone down relentlessly from a cloudless blue sky, you couldn't imagine it would ever change, while down by the river the muddy water slip-slopped against the sides of the wharves, the broken bits of flotsam and jetsam

2

gathering around the tying posts where history had been made as the River Thames flowed on its way to the open sea . . .

Chapter Two

Tom Lowman walked to work on this beautiful sunny morning instead of catching a tram, for on a day like this it was good to be alive. As he walked he toyed with pleasant thoughts of which horse he would place his bet on today, his one weakness being a bit of a gamble, a bob or two a week, though he was careful not to let Eva know. She'd raise the roof if she did; she was dead against gambling. Twice a week he had sixpence each way, sometimes winning a couple of bob but more often not. He had never been really lucky, but then you never knew. The day might come when a rank outsider would win. Captain Coe in the *News Chronicle* tipped Ice Maiden but he had never really fancied betting on a mare. No, he'd go for Old Soldier. That must be a lucky sign. As an old soldier himself he was lucky to be alive on a day like this, not like most of his mates who had rotted away on the battlefields of France.

And now there were rumours of another war, what with the situation in Europe and Germany suddenly on its toes again. They must be mad.

By the time he reached the factory, Old Soldier it was to be, and he knew without any doubt that it would come in first. He told himself this every time. He'd put his money on straight away with Jock Mackenzie who made quite a packet on the side taking bets.

He hung up his cap and put on his working apron. After clocking in, he climbed to the second floor. The one snag with this weather was that the sun played hell with the glass

4

roof and the heat became almost unbearable. Well, it was early yet.

He worked at his bench, a young Irish Mick at his side – young Percy Doyle, newly married at twenty-four, a sunny young joker who kept them laughing when the foreman wasn't around.

'You don't half look a big boy in that pinny, Tom,' Percy said in his strong Irish brogue.

'Get away,' Tom grinned, spreading out the blueprint in front of him.

Back home, Eva Lowman raked the boiler fire and closed the small iron door firmly. The water was heating up nicely and she put on one more bucketful from the tap in the sink to top it up, then covered the gaping hole with the stout wooden lid. The fire made a small roaring and comfortable noise as she took a large block of strong yellow soap and scrubbed Tom's shirts with a stiff scrubbing brush. As each one was done, she lifted the boiler lid and dropped it in the almost boiling water. The washboard on the boiler top was used for scrubbing the sheets and pillow cases and towels with the naptha soap, and once the boiler was full, she dropped in a handful of soda and with the air of a job well done, took off her coarse apron and went back into the kitchen.

It was time the girls were up, and taking down their freshly ironed dresses from the ceiling airer, Eva went into the back room downstairs to see that they were awake.

'Come on, you two,' she said firmly, putting the dresses on the foot of the bed, seeing Sarah's long golden hair on the pillow and Valerie's shoulder-length curls framing her flushed little face. 'Come on, it's almost eight o'clock.'

They groaned a little and sat up, Sarah getting out of bed immediately.

It was a lovely day for March, warm and sunny. Nineteen thirty-nine has started cold and wet, but now there was this lovely warm spell, and the sight of fingers of sunshine across the kitchen floor brought a glow to Eva's heart. She couldn't resist a look at the front room, and going along the dark and narrow passage, opened the door to peep at the new

5

carpet square which had arrived yesterday. The three-piece plush suite sat on the new carpet as though it belonged there. She had bought the carpet with the money saved weekly in Davidson's club. She had three weekly clubs going, one for children's clothes, one for household linen, and this one, which was an extravagance, she knew. The navy plush suite she had bought when she married, and the small upright piano with money she had saved as a single girl when she worked in Woolwich Arsenal at the end of the war on munitions. She could hear Tom's mother now: '"I can't think why you want to spend your hard earned money on a piano – there'll be more important things you'll need, and plenty of them".'

Because I want to learn to play, Eva had thought. Oh, what a misery the old lady had been. Still, she had been widowed quite young, and Eva herself was lucky to have taken over the tenancy of this house at the best end of Calydon Road. Charlton was a lovely place to live after being brought up on the other side of the water. She had always vowed that she would escape from there, and she had done so. In that tiny house backing on to the factories, her mother had reared eight children, six girls and two boys, and they still lived there, most of them. She shuddered. Even Nell, her elder sister, still lived in Silvertown for all she had married an elderly well-to-do Yorkshireman man who spoiled her half to death, and even though she was a leading light in the Conservative Party. North Woolwich was a Tory stronghold, despite being a working-class neighbourhood. They needed the rich in order to become employed. Funny that Nell had never wanted to leave. The others weren't married yet and were all at home except Elsie, the youngest, who had been the only one of them to win a scholarship, which their father had denied her. 'Croft Street School was good enough for the others, it'll be good enough for you,' he'd said. Elsie had threatened to leave home as soon as she left school, and true to her word she had one bleak November morning six months before.

'One less mouth to feed,' their father had said, and her name had never been mentioned since.

They had had it so hard, she thought, no wonder her

father had been strict. Tom was a different sort of man altogether. Amiable and kind, he would do anything for anybody.

She sighed and went back into the scullery to batten down the boiling clothes which threatened to rise over the top. She forced the clothes down with the aid of boiler stick and into the boiling water as they heaved and rose and the strong-smelling water bubbled at the sides. She replaced the boiler lid and went into the kitchen to remove the steaming kettle from the range which gleamed from constant blackleading.

She made a fresh pot of tea and began to fry the children's breakfast of streaky bacon and fried bread. When it was done she placed it in the oven to keep warm.

The kitchen was well steamed up when the girls arrived to wash in the bowl in the sink.

'I hate the smell of washing.' Sarah wrinkled her nose in disgust and Eva looked at her. She was growing so tall, almost sixteen now and due to leave school at Easter. She couldn't imagine what they were going to do with her. Such a funny girl, not a bit like young Valerie who was as transparent as glass and as happy as a sandboy all day long. Sarah lived with her nose in a book, and seemed to dwell in a world of her own. She was tall for her age and thin, with long slim arms and legs – she took after Tom's sisters – and already had quite a little bosom. Eva bit her lip and turned away. The dress pulled tightly over Sarah's chest – she really would have to get her a bigger size. The girl's long thick fair hair hung in a plait down her back, and her narrow blue eyes looked straight at you beneath dark brows.

The table was laid daintily, for Eva approved of orderliness and liked to keep everything nice. She was proud of the fact that she rented the whole house for fourteen shillings a week, for most of the houses in Calydon Road were let off into flats, one up and one down. Tom's mother had long had the tenancy of this house, and when Eva married Tom she let them have the top flat, then when she went off to live with Tom's sister Joan, Eva took over the tenancy.

While Sarah ate her breakfast, Eva took down her bag of

pegs and went outside into the garden. The chickens clucked at the bottom of the garden under the May tree. Tom would already have fed them, and there were three newlaid brown eggs on the dresser. She wiped her clothes line free from dirt and let it down ready to hang the clothes.

It was lovely and warm in the yard. How different you felt when the sun warmed your back. Later she might take a walk up to the top road. She loved it up there.

Having finished breakfast, Sarah put on her navy reefer coat and picked up her satchel, while Valerie stood by the front door ready to go. They were the only girls in the school to have real reefer coats. Oh, Eva knew the proper way to dress them; she had learned from watching the children from the big houses on Blackheath. Valerie ran to give a last-minute kiss to her doll while Sarah waited impatiently.

'I'll go straight to Mrs Mortimer's from school,' Sarah called out.

Eva hurried to the door and kissed each one briefly, watching them as they walked to the gate and then up the road. They were good girls and she watched them proudly, then seeing Julie Garrett, Sarah's special friend, running to catch them up, a slight frown crossed her brow. Julie's luxuriant curls were tied back and danced as she ran along with a quick wave to Eva and a friendly smile. Eva looked after her. Yes, there was something about Julie that disturbed her, but the thought died in mid-stream as she noticed the brass letter box. She must polish that today as soon as she finished the washing – it looked tarnished, and if there was something she disliked more than anything else, it was brass that needed cleaning. You were judged, Eva reckoned, on first impressions.

She went in and closed the door behind her, going straight through to the scullery and picking up the boiler lid, where the water threatened to come over the top. This was the worst part. The clothes were so hot and so heavy, and it took all her strength to lift them out on the boiler stick and drop them into the galvanized bath. The sheets and shirts were tangled and far too hot to unravel. She heaved the heavy bath into the sink, full of cold water, and flushed them about until they were rinsed. Then she put them in the bath, carried it outside and dumped it heavily onto the ground. From over the fence she could see Clara Barton doing the same thing.

'Morning, Mrs Barton,' she called.

'Morning, Mrs Lowman.'

Taking off the heavy rubber sheet which protected the mangle rollers, she wiped them clean and began to insert the clothes, feeding them into the mangle and catching them expertly as they appeared on the other side. With the pegs in her mouth she took each item and hung it on the line. The sun was warm, and she saw with satisfaction that she was one of the first to have her washing out by a quarter to nine. Except Mrs Venning, poor little Mary Venning with the line full of baby clothes and nappies. Oh, Mary hadn't wanted that baby with three small children already and a husband away at sea all the time, but what could she do? They had all felt sorry for her and told her of different things to do, but nothing worked. You were very lucky if it did. It was a shame but that was a woman's lot in life.

By half-past nine the washing was out on the line and Eva began to empty the boiler, using a large saucepan and emptying it one load at a time. With the last lot she washed the scullery floor then cleaned up after herself. By ten o'clock the kitchen and scullery were done, the washing line pulled up high by its prop in the sunshine, the washing up done and the beds made. Then she tackled the brass letter box, taking pleasure in the way it gleamed the more she polished it.

Closing the front door, Eva began to sing as she always did. Of course the songs were different now, with crooners like Bing and Al Bowlly, and Vera Lynn and Elsie Carlisle and Hutch, but she liked the old songs better – 'Pale Hands I Loved Beside the Shalimar' and 'Where My Caravan Has Rested' – songs her own mother had sung, yet goodness knows what she had had to sing about. 'Indian Love Lyrics' they were called; she knew because she had the sheet music.

By twelve o'clock Sarah found Valerie waiting for her at the school gate, and taking her hand walked her down the street until she came to the corner of Calydon Road, then saw her safely across the street.

'Tell Mum I won't be long,' she said, and made her way to Mrs Mortimer's front door. Every day she went to the baker's shop in Church Lane for Mrs Mortimer's cottage loaf, and received threepence at the end of the week. It wasn't just the money, though, she loved the shopping; it was the highlight of her day. She loved walking up Church Lane, carrying a shopping basket. Sometimes she looked in the dress shop window, sometimes in the chemist's, but more often that not in the newsagent's at the magazines and cards on the racks, especially the pictures of film stars: Garbo who was her favourite, Joan Crawford, Gladys Cooper, Gloria Swanson and Rita Hayworth, who reminded her of Julie, her best friend. The funny postcards always made her laugh, although she knew her mother would be annoyed with her for looking at them. There was a second hand shop, too where they sold old books and magazines, and she often browsed in there for the old man didn't seem to mind although she never bought. Then she would race back after buying the bread in Alderton's because she had taken too long and they would ask her where she had been.

Once she had gone to the Co-op for her mother to buy some bacon as well as Mrs Mortimer's bread, and the young man behind the counter was serving the girl in front of her. He was very tall with a thick mouth that really was shaped like a cupid's bow, vivid blue eyes and long lashes and dark wavy hair. He was smiling a great big smile at the girl, and suddenly he reached across the counter and put his finger down her low-necked dress, grinning from ear to ear, and when he gave her the change, he caught her hand tightly and the girl laughed. Sarah didn't know where to look as her face suddenly flared. When it was her turn he scowled at her and said rudely, 'Yes?'

She had felt miserable all the way home, and didn't know why. She thought he was a horrible man and she wouldn't go in there again, not even if her mother asked her.

Today she saw that Mrs Mortimer's eyes were red from crying and her face looked all crumpled. She didn't say anything and didn't have the basket in her hand or the money. Presently she burst into noisy sobs as Sarah stood there, petrified. Then she sniffed loudly and blew her nose.

'I don't want any bread today, dear,' she said, then burst once again into tears. Presently she recovered and stuffed her hankie into her apron pocket.

'Did you know that Mr Mortimer had passed away?'

Sarah was not sure at first what Mrs Mortimer meant. Did she mean he had died? A shiver ran through her and she shook her head.

'I'm sorry, Mrs Mortimer.'

'Thank you, dear.' Her small eyes regarded Sarah, awash with tears. 'He was a lovely man – anyone will tell you. Run along now, dear, and thank you for coming. I won't want any more bread now – there'll be no one to eat it.' And she burst once more into noisy sobs.

Sarah walked slowly down the short path, until she heard the door close behind her, then crossing the road ran as fast as her long legs would carry her, in such a state of excitement and drama that she could hardly bear it.

'Whatever is the matter?' Eva cried when she rushed through the front door and into the kitchen.

'Oh, Mum!'

'For goodness' sake!'

Sarah's eyes were enormous as she waited for her big moment. Her hand instinctively went to her breast in a gesture of anguish as she closed her eyes and assumed a tragic expression, timing her news perfectly.

Eva gave her a quick look then carried on peeling the potatoes.

'Mr Mortimer's dead,' Sarah said simply.

'Who told you?'

'I saw him,' she said.

Eva looked at her sharply. You never knew with Sarah, she had such an imagination.

'Are you telling me the truth?'

Sarah looked at her indignantly and her eyes filled with tears.

'Yes, I am. I did see him!'

Eva went over and put her arms around Sarah's narrow shoulders which quivered beneath her touch.

11

'Oh, she shouldn't have asked you in!' she cried. 'You're only a child. And you shouldn't have gone. Still, it's not your fault . . .'

Sarah relaxed into her mother's arms. It was so comforting to be the centre of attention for once. She closed her eyes. It was like it used to be before Valerie came.

When her father came home at lunchtime, for he came home every day, she heard her mother whispering to him in the scullery, and knew she was telling him about Mr Mortimer.

Her mother dished up the dinner and piled her father's plate with meat and vegetables before serving the children. Sarah frowned as it was set before her.

'And eat your cabbage,' her mother said. 'It's good for you.'

'I don't like cabbage,' she said crossly.

Presently her mother said, 'Mr Mortimer died, Tom.'

'Oh?'

Her father sounded surprised as though he hadn't already been told the news.

'Yes.'

No more was said but Sarah felt herself to be the centre of attention, and she hadn't been made to eat her cabbage.

With her husband back at work and the two children at school, Eva sat down with a pot of tea, her first break in the day. It was a shame about Mr Mortimer, she thought. Still, she shouldn't have asked Sarah in. It was a cruel thing to do to a young girl . . . but she supposed Mrs Mortimer was beside herself and had to talk to someone. Eva stirred her tea idly, staring out unseeing at the house next-door.

What on earth were they going to do with Sarah when she left school? Eva had to admit she could hardly see her in an office, even though she had learned shorthand and typing at the Central School. She hated it anyway had all these fancy ideas – and the school didn't help, encouraging her to be different, praising her performances in the school plays. What good would that do her?

The best thing she could do would be to apply for a job at Johnson's or Siemens – there were usually vacancies there. A nice respectable job, not like she and her sisters had had, going to work in a factory. Eva shivered. Thank goodness those days had gone. Sarah had been educated, and she was quite clever, although it was difficult sometimes to see exactly in which direction.

She rinsed her cup and saucer, and walking along the passage had another peep at the new carpet in the front room, head on one side, approving what she saw. That sofa could do with brightening up. Navy plush was a bit dull. Yes, an embroidered cushion might be the thing. They had some lovely transfers in the wool shop. She would take a walk there this afternoon. She quite enjoyed doing embroidery and it would make a change from embroidering the girls' underwear. For some reason that always irritated Sarah. Basket over her arm, Eva closed the front door, giving an approving look behind her at the brass letter box.

'Less than the dust beneath thy chariot wheels,' she sang under her breath as she made her way along Calydon Road towards the shops.

Chapter Three

Ada Garrett's flat was dark and filled with the assorted bric-a-brac she had acquired over the years. She was a small woman, dark-haired and pretty, with dark eyes; a woman who dressed neatly and well, dressmaking being the trade by which she earned her living.

In the cosy flat there was a cat, a budgie in one cage and two canaries in another – as if, by surrounding her with pets, Ada was trying to make up to her daughter for not having a father.

Alfred Garrett had died when Julie was three years old, a big healthy man who succumbed almost at once to a virulent attack of influenza. Since then Ada had managed to keep them both on her meagre widow's pension and what she earned as a dressmaker. She had trained as a girl straight from school at Debenham and Freebody's, which had stood her in good stead. There was little Ada didn't know about sewing a fine seam, basting a hem, putting in sleeves or even designing a gown, so thorough had been her training.

Despite her widowhood, she was one of the most contented women in the street for when she wanted a new bedspread or curtains, half the fun was trying to see if she could manage to get it. She already had three books of green stamps, and it was a question of whether she would collect more for a candlewick bedspread, which were all the rage, or buy the material and make one. Then again, she paid a shilling a week into a club which soon mounted up. Life was a challenge to Ada.

The canaries were singing in the kitchen as she put the

14

kettle on the hob for tea. Julie would be in soon, and it was wonderful that the nights had grown lighter. Ada hated the winter months. She began to lay the table and get out the cups and saucers for tea. Over the chair hung the fine grey silk of the evening dress she was making for Mrs Neville – she had left it out to show Julie when she came home from school.

Julie left Sarah at her gate and walked on, her dark curls bobbing at the back of her neck and head held high. Many a pair of eyes watched her progress down the road from behind lace curtains. She was considered to be the prettiest girl in the neighbourhood with her lovely complexion and dark eyes which were almost violet. Her hair curled naturally and she had a lovely smile which showed excellent teeth. Everyone liked Julie Garrett. She was a friendly girl, not like some they could name with their stuck up airs and graces.

Julie pulled the key on its string through the letter box and let herself in.

'It's me!' she cried, hurrying down the dark passage and into the kitchen. 'Mmm, something smells nice.'

The kitchen always seemed to take on a festive air whenever Julie came in, and Ada looked up at her daughter with a warm smile.

'Well, I've got to make my simnel cake, haven't I? It wouldn't be Easter without a simnel cake.'

'And hot cross buns.'

'Yes, well, I'll make them next Thursday – I like them to be fresh.' Ada washed her hands at the yellow sink.

'Is this the new dress for Mrs Neville?' Julie put out a hand.

'Wash your hands before you touch it!' Ada said sharply, and making a face, Julie rinsed her hands and dried them on the roller towel.

'Well,' she said, holding the dress out in front of her, and wrinkling her small nose, 'it's not very exciting, is it? I mean, grey. The material's nice, though.'

'It suits her with her grey hair,' Ada said, 'and there'll be a pastel scarf – pinks and mauves and grey.'

15

'It's a pretty style. I love the shoulders.'

'Yes, she likes to be fashionable, does Mrs Neville,' Ada said. Living all her married life in London, Ada had never lost her Yorkshire accent.

'She's jolly lucky to have you on hand to make for her,' Julie said. 'Think what she'd have to pay for that in town.'

'She knows that,' Ada said. 'Besides, what would I do without clients like her?'

'True,' Julie said.

She is such a nice girl, Ada thought. I am lucky to have a daughter like her and she has never been any bother to bring up. Which sparked off thoughts for the future.

'I thought you said you had gas mask drill tomorrow?'

Julie clapped a hand over her mouth.

'Oh – I'd forgotten! Yes, we have. Do you know where my gas mask is?'

'On the top of my wardrobe. Nasty things,' Ada muttered. 'I think it's disgraceful, the idea of children having to wear gas masks. It makes my blood boil even to think about it.'

Very occasionally she was given to sharp outbursts. Now her face was quite flushed.

'Well, I mean, if they did use gas . . .'

'Don't talk about it!' Ada snapped. 'There won't be another war. There'd better not be,' she added darkly, as if she were making a secret threat.

'Shall I put this away?' Julie asked, referring to the grey silk dress.

'Yes, please,' her mother said, 'then I'll get the tea.'

Julie folded the dress carefully and placed it in a large paper bag, putting it on the folded sewing machine. Then she sat down at the table, hands behind her head.

'Oh, I can't wait to leave school, Mam!'

Ada looked at her fondly. There she was, raring to go. Who knew what life held in store for her? If only she could teach Julie not to make the mistakes she herself had made, but everyone had their own life to lead. You could only do so much, teach them the rights and wrongs; after that, it was up to them.

'They are supposed to be the happiest days of your life,

but you'd never think so the way people always want to leave school. What's Sarah going to do, does she know?'

Julie laughed out loud. 'You know Sarah, she's full of ideas. Thinks she is going to be a writer or an actress.'

Ada had been disappointed when Julie had failed to win her Junior County Scholarship at eleven. Still, she had got to the Central School, and Ada consoled herself that her daughter was all there, sharp as a button at fifteen and more than ready to leave school as Ada herself had been at fourteen.

The kitchen glowed with the orange glare from the range, and the kettle was boiling away noisily.

Julie was slicing the bread. 'Miss Wood gave us a talk this afternoon.'

'Oh? What was that about?' Ada poured the boiling water into the teapot.

'She wanted to know what we all wanted to do when we leave school.'

Ada placed the teapot on a stand and covered it with a hand knitted tea cosy.

'Miss Wood wants to see Sarah's mother 'specially.'

'Well, I can understand that. Sarah is a bit different from the rest of you. She's good at words and reading . . .'

'So am I.'

'I know you are, duck, but you know what I mean. She's a good little actress, too. Look how good she was in the school play. But I don't expect Mrs Lowman would like her to take that up for a career.'

'Not likely,' Julie said, spreading her bread with home made plum jam. 'Mmm.' She licked her pointed fingers gracefully.

'Mam, did you ever give any more thought to my working in a hairdresser's – a good one, I mean?' she added hastily, knowing Ada's thoughts on the subject.

She frowned. 'Yes, I did, and that's not for you, my girl. Hairdressing, indeed! You could work in an office like Johnson's, say, just around the corner, come home to lunch . . .'

Julie made a face.

'Mam, you can't mean it! Oh, I should hate it! I don't want to be cooped up all day in an office in a boring job.'

'Well, hairdressing is boring enough, I should imagine. All that steam and washing people's hair. On your feet all day long.'

'Well, *I* would like it,' Julie stressed. 'Couldn't I, Mam?'

'No,' Ada said firmly, a worried frown on her brow. She had hoped that Julie would be a bit more ambitious. She wasn't clever like Sarah but she didn't have to do anything as ordinary as hairdressing.

Julie sat looking rather sulky. She was thinking that if she'd had a father, he might have allowed her to do what she wanted to do.

'You never talk about my father,' she said suddenly.

Ada sighed. 'There's not much to tell, really. We were only married for four years – and we courted for a year before that.'

'Am I like him?'

'I should say so,' Ada replied. 'Same dark curly hair.' She didn't add: 'And beautiful eyes' for fear of making Julie vain. There would be plenty of young men telling her that, she thought. And he had been handsome, a soldier stationed at Woolwich Barracks, a Scots boy from Kircudbrightshire – she remembered how they had laughed every time she tried to pronounce it correctly.

'And my grandmother – my father's mother? I'm called Juliet after her.'

'Yes. I thought it was a lovely name, and she was so nice to me, made me so welcome – it was the only time I ever went to Scotland. One day we'll go back there, Julie.'

Julie's eyes shone.

'I do remember him vaguely,' she said. 'He sat in that chair,' she pointed to the large cane chair, 'and I sat on his lap – he had a moustache, a large moustache.'

'Yes, men wore them in those days.'

Julie sat thinking. How terrible it must have been for her mother when he'd died. Being left a widow so young. As she herself grew older she appreciated more what it meant.

'One day, Mam, we'll move out of here – move to somwhere lovely and green. A little cottage in the country.'

18

'Would you like that?' Ada was surprised. She had never imagined Julie was fond of the country. They so seldom went anywhere.

'Yes, I would. Open spaces – you know, woods, hills, fresh air. I hate the smell of factories.'

And yet she had never known anything else, Ada thought.

'I meant, really get out of here, to move away somewhere nice.'

'Yes, I know what you mean.' But Ada's thoughts were already on something else. She cleared away the tea things.

'I've just remembered,' she said. 'There's a lovely costume on my bed from Mrs Neville. It was Miss Olivia's. She never wears it now and it's too small for Mrs Jenkins' granddaughter.' Mrs Jenkins being the housekeeper to the Neville's at Arkley House.

She looked up to see Julie's scowling face.

'Now then, what's that look for? It was a very expensive costume. Cost ever such a lot of money.'

'It would,' Julie said mutinously.

Ada ignored her. 'From Harrods. She only wore it once or twice.'

'I don't want it.' Julie's lower lip stuck out mutinously. It was so seldom she rebelled against anything.

'And why not?' Ada looked at her coldly.

'I don't like other people's clothes. Besides, she's dowdy.'

'Dowdy? Well! I never heard of such a thing.' Ada was outraged. She had the greatest admiration for Olivia Neville. 'Miss Olivia is a very smart young lady. You'd do well to copy her instead of wanting some of those common things you'd like to wear.'

'I don't like common things,' Julie retorted. 'It's just that she's not my type – she's old-fashioned, for one thing.' She saw Ada's expression and knew she had gone too far. 'Oh, I would like new clothes, Mam. I'm sick of wearing cast offs.'

Ada looked at her, suddenly sympathetic.

'Yes, I know you would. Still, when you start work . . .'

Julie brightened.

'You'll be able to afford new clothes then.'

Julie was smiling again.

'In the meantime, it won't hurt you to wear expensive cast offs. Better second hand good clothes than cheap new ones, mark my words. Why, the costume has hardly been worn, you can tell. So try it on, there's a good girl.'

Despite their argument there was a great deal of understanding between the two, and now Julie, her anger quite forgotten, went into the bedroom to try on the costume.

When she emerged, Ada stared at her, a worried frown wrinkling her brow. What was it about Julie? She had seen Miss Olivia in that costume, and she couldn't have looked smarter.

Oliva Neville had looked tall and elegant wearing the costume with a cream silk blouse and small hat with a feather pulled down over one eye, a fox fur slung over her shoulder. But Julie had a wicked gleam in her eye and had adopted a stance to make herself look her worst. Her feet stuck out sideways, her shoulders were bowed, and the first thing you noticed was her bosom which pushed out the jacket. And although the skirt was too long, she looked so . . . curvy, Ada thought, for want of a better word.

Julie ran into the hall and rammed a black beret from the hatstand to one side of her luxuriant curls. They both burst out laughing.

'See what I mean?' she demanded, happy now that she had made her point.

'Well, I have to admit you're certainly not the tall and willowy type.'

'Thank God,' Julie said fervently.

'Juliet!'

'Sorry, Mam.'

'Anyway,' Ada said, 'it won't need that much altering – it's too long, of course.' She went over and tweaked at the jacket. 'You'll be surprised how nice this will look when I've finished with it.'

Stuffy old clothes, Julie thought. She would rather die than wear the suit. She wanted to wear things like Joan Crawford wore, slinky black satin; really pulled in, with a low neckline. And make up – all that wonderful shiny lipstick, and her eyelashes thick with mascara. One of these days . . .

She took off the costume and bundled it into the wardrobe. Out of sight was out of mind. Perhaps her mother would forget it. She couldn't think what there was about that Olivia Neville that caused her mother to admire her so much. She was tall and skinny like a beanpole – wishywashy, she'd say. Julie had only seen her once, and that was enough.

She stared into the mirror and pouted, liking what she saw. Just wait. Once she'd started work, she would buy what she liked.

Chapter Four

Olivia Neville attended morning service at St Paul's Church on a lovely Sunday morning before Easter. Afterwards she stopped to talk to several elderly friends of the family, explaining that her parents had gone down to Hampshire for the weekend, to their cottage near Hurstbourne.

She cut a pretty figure, and many a masculine eye had settled on the back of her head and shoulders as she sat in the Neville pew. That rich, red-gold hair coiled into a heavy chignon beneath the cream leghorn hat, the slim white neck, the perfect profile. When she stood, it was to reveal a slim figure clad in a tussore silk dress, with a string of amber beads falling to her waist, and those lucky enough to see her walking down the aisle saw the slim silk clad legs in their high-heeled shoes.

Her carriage marked her out, and many women were envious. She would seem to have it all – looks, money, position, breeding – yet despite that most people who knew her liked and admired her.

Walking through the village on this balmy spring day, the streets on the outskirts of South London which still bore traces of an old world atmosphere, she walked past the Bugle Horn and into the shade of the plane trees, making her way down a narrow turning until she came to Arkley Lodge.

Entering the wide gates, she could see the vista stretching way down to the river, a view which never failed to excite her. She was proud of her heritage, and the sight of the sea, or a great river with its ships at anchor, was enough to set her pulses racing.

She could hear the plop of tennis balls from the court at the rear of the house. The front drive was ablaze with daffodils and narcissi, and the wistaria over the front entrance was in bud even though it was early in the season. The great stone urns either side of the front door were full of budding tulips for the warm weather had brought everything on. Even the lawns had had their first cut of the season. She had seen Evans, the old Welsh gardener, mowing the lawn on Saturday.

She found her sister-in-law Peggy in the drawing room, reading the Sunday papers. She looked up as Olivia came in. They kissed affectionately.

'Been here long?' Olivia asked, drawing off her gloves.

'No. Gerald's playing tennis with Andrew. Isn't this weather heavenly? I almost sat outside.'

'Then let's,' Olivia said. 'It's far too nice to be indoors – we don't get enough of this sort of weather. Are you staying to lunch? I believe we have "a little cold" today.' And they both laughed.

Mrs Jenkins' cold collations were a joke in the family, for they usually finished up eating more than they would had they had a traditional Sunday lunch.

'No, thanks,' Peggy said. 'We're due at the Sangster's at past half-past twelve.'

Olivia's brother Gerald and his new wife usually drove over from Chislehurst on Sunday mornings, and had a game of tennis if the weather was fine. They had already played three games this year.

Peggy put down the papers. 'Let's see how the men are getting on, shall we?'

'Yes. I'll follow you.' Peggy went out through the French windows. 'First I'll ask Mrs Jenkins to bring the drinks outside.'

When they had settled themselves in deckchairs on the terrace, Olivia put on her sunglasses.

'You're lucky,' she said to Peggy. 'It must be wonderful to tan like that – I should look like a lobster in no time.'

Peggy laughed. 'Yes, being dark-skinned does have its advantages.'

23

'Doesn't the grass smell divine after being cut?' Olivia said. 'It's almost like summer today.'

They lay quietly for some time then Peggy spoke.

'Is Douglas coming to lunch?'

There was the slightest pause.

'No. Not this weekend.' And glancing at her, Peggy could see that the closed look had come over Olivia's face.

'Viv,' she said tentatively. It was her old name for Olivia from when they had been at school together. 'Look . . .' She felt the slight tension that emanated from Olivia's prone figure, but having started she meant to go on.

'Viv, I hate to see you – '

Olivia wasn't going to be of the slightest help.

'Can't bear to see me what?' Her voice was icy cool.

'Well, you know . . . pre-occupied and unhappy.'

'Who says I am?' Olivia had a small smile on her face, but it was a stiff little smile.

'I've known you long enough to know when you're not happy,' Peggy said. 'That's all.' At her words, Olivia turned and put out a hand. 'I'm all right, Peggy. Honestly,' she said.

'I suppose you're going to say it's none of my business?'

'I could say that,' Olivia said reasonably, 'because it isn't – it's no one's business but mine and there is nothing you can or could do. It's something I have to work out myself.'

'So there is something?'

Olivia didn't answer.

'You're not going to like this but is it anything to do with Richard Bannister?' Peggy wished she hadn't asked as soon as the words left her lips.

She could see her friend's fair skin flush and knew that she had hit on the reason. Olivia gave a weak laugh.

'Really, Peggy! What nonsense. Wherever did you get that idea?'

'I don't know.' Peggy looked quite crestfallen. 'Ever since that night we all came to dinner here, I've wondered . . . I know he's charming but – oh, Viv, don't fall for him!'

But Olivia was standing up now, her face ashen as though all the blood had drained away. She looked across the lawns to the distant birch trees.

'In the first place, Peggy, it's none of your damned business! And in the second, no, you are quite wrong. Now, please leave me alone.' And she rushed inside leaving Peggy cursing herself for her impetuosity.

You fool, she told herself. You and your big mouth. Why couldn't you keep quiet? But her first suspicions were confirmed. She had been right. Olivia was in love with him, that overrated, supercilious, handsome devil who was sure he was the answer to every maiden's prayer. Olivia was in love with him – oh, how could she be? Then she sobered up.

It really was no business of hers. None at all. Olivia's life was her own, and at twenty-three she had every right to do as she liked – and be as foolish as she liked.

Peggy followed Olivia swiftly and found her in the kitchen, talking to Mrs Jenkins.

'I'll take this,' she said, picking up the tray.

'No, Miss Olivia, you hurry along. I'll be out in a jiffy.'

The girls walked outside and as they drew near to the terrace Peggy took Olivia's arm.

'Sorry, Viv. I'm just an old busybody.'

'Yes, you are,' Olivia laughed, and arm in arm they walked towards the men.

'Good game?

'Yes, super,' Gerald said, putting on his white tennis sweater.

They seated themselves as Mrs Jenkins came out with the drinks tray.

'Thanks, Mrs J.,' Gerald said. Then turning to Andrew: 'Did the old man tell you about the problems we are having with the German mills?'

'Yes, he said.' Andrew stretched out his legs and sat back.

'We've got a whacking order to fill for Bowater's – I hope it will be all right. This war threat hangs over everything.'

'Have you?' Andrew's mind was miles away, his eyes were closed.

'I know you've no direct interest in the business, old son, but what's this I hear about your joining the RAF?'

'That's right – if they'll have me.' Andrew grinned.

The girls, who had been lying back quietly now took notice.

'I say, you don't think there will really be a war, do you?' Peggy asked anxiously.

'Olivia should know more about it than we do', Gerald said.

'My lips are sealed.' She laughed. 'Seriously, though, things have been edgy for a while now – long before Munich last year. It's like walking on a knife edge, and one's inclined to get used to it. They will certainly do everything they can to avoid a war, as you might well imagine.'

'Nice having a sister in the Foreign Office,' Gerald teased.

'The PM's right hand,' bantered Andrew.

'Oh, shut up,' Olivia said. They enjoyed teasing her. With two brothers she was well used to it.

'If there is another war,' Peggy said, 'you'll find women will be doing fantastic jobs. After all, they did in the last war.'

'I'm afraid the next war will be nothing like the last,' Gerald said. 'It will be a totally different thing. Everyone will be involved if war comes – women and children.'

'What are you trying to do – scare us?' said Olivia. 'Let's change the subject, please. How is the business really going?'

'Well, you heard what Gerald said. The German mills are having a spot of bother. Hitler has a lot to answer for – it's hotting up all over Europe,' he said quietly.

'Difficult not to talk about it,' Andrew said. 'What does Father think?'

'Well, you know him, keeps everything close to his chest, but he's worried about deliveries.'

'I'm not surprised,' Peggy said. 'With paper and board mills all over Europe and Scandinavia, he's bound to be concerned. Think what he stands to lose – in a business way, I mean.'

There was a sudden silence and then a blackbird began to sing, its sweet musical notes filling the warm somnolent air.

That's the sort of thing you need, Peggy told herself, when you're pregnant. It was a lovely word if you wanted your baby – but it must be frightening if you didn't. She wouldn't in fact have chosen to become pregnant after only being married for four months. Still, in a couple of weeks she would know for sure. Until then she would keep it to herself, and listen to the song of the blackbird, the sound of the birch trees whispering in the breeze, smell the scent of the newly cut grass . . .

It was just after two, Andrew and Olivia having just finished lunch, when they heard the sound of the Daimler on the gravel drive.

'Here they are,' Olivia said, getting up to greet them.

Her father got out of the car, a small stocky man in a tweed suit, his squirrel-like brown eyes twinkling at the sight of his beloved daughter. He nodded to his son. He kissed Olivia then helped his wife out of the car.

'You're early,' Olivia said. 'We didn't expect you until four or so.'

'We lunched on the way back,' her father explained. 'Mother wasn't feeling all that well, it was very warm, and I had some work to do and some phone calls to make before tomorrow.'

Olivia hugged her mother. 'Are you all right? Are you sure?'

'Yes, my dear. Just a little tired. I wanted to get home. Where is everyone?'

'Gerald and Peggy came for a drink at lunchtime and a game of tennis. They didn't stay for lunch, had an appointment somewhere. There was just the two of us.'

She took her mother's arm and led her towards the house.

'Come in, darling, I expect you're tired. It's a long journey.'

'Yes, and it seems to get longer,' her mother said.

They walked up the stairs slowly together and into the main bedroom.

'I'll close the curtains and you can lie down and have a nap. Would you like the window open? The air is lovely and cool . . . Now, are you sure you're all right?'

'Yes, darling, I'm sure, and I would like a nap, I have to admit.' She took off her jacket and shoes. 'You know,' she confided, 'your father is fretting over this war business. I

27

don't know – he's got it firmly fixed in his head that there is going to be one, and I don't know if he knows more than he says but he is totally preoccupied with it. I can tell you, it's a little frustrating.'

'Of course it is,' Olivia murmured as Mrs Neville, still in her pretty silk-embroidered slip, lay under the satin bedcovers.

'Lie down and rest,' Olivia said. 'Everything is going to be all right.' And she went out quietly, closing the door behind her.

She walked out on to the wide landing and stood looking over the gardens, down towards the river, her thoughts elsewhere. Sometimes she wished she had been a man. Sometimes. Then, if there was a war, she could have joined the navy. How she would have loved that. Her father always said she had more of her forefathers in her than either of his sons. The famous Admiral Neville, his prowess, his battles . . . she knew them by heart. In her was a fierce patriotism. Her heart swelled with pride every time she thought of her illustrious family past.

Now she went downstairs and knew that the first thing her father would want would be a good strong cup of tea. It never failed to soothe him.

'Are you really worried about the situation in the mills?' she asked him as she sat on the sofa opposite his favourite chair.

'You're too young to worry about things like that,' he said.

'I am twenty-three,' she said, 'and I do have a good job at the Foreign Office.'

He looked at her gently. His daughter, the apple of his eye. If he had his way she would be married and at home, looking after a baby or two.

'You haven't seen Douglas this weekend?' He looked at her shrewdly, her glance downturned to the floor. Something was not altogether right, he thought. It's not only that she doesn't want that young man, but she's preoccupied over something else. Someone else? He wondered who it could be. Someone at the office? Well, she would tell them, all in good time. Pity about young Douglas though. Suitable in every way . . .

He held out his cup to her, with a twinkle in his eye.

'Just pour a little whisky in there to liven it, will you?' he said, nodding towards the cut glass decanters on a side table.

She got up swiftly and smiled.

'Of course, Daddy.'

Later that night she lay in bed, a slim figure in a pale silk nightgown, watching the moon ride swiftly, it seemed through white snowy clouds against a dark sky. It was a heavenly night – just the sort of night she should have spent with Richard. Then she recalled Peggy's questions. How had she managed to give herself away? Did anyone else suspect? How furious Richard would be if he had the slightest inkling that their affair was known to anyone else but the two of them. When had Peggy first begun to suspect? Part of Olivia's job was to give nothing away by her expression, it was all part of the training. Was she really wearing her heart on her sleeve?

From now on she must be careful. Perhaps invite Douglas around more. It seemed a little unfair. Still . . . what did they say? All was fair in love and war.

Chapter Five

Sarah knew there was something important going on today as soon as she opened her eyes. Today was the day her mother was going to see Miss Wood!

She leapt out of bed, excitement gripping her. Who knew what would happen? Perhaps Miss Wood would make her mother see sense. Convince her that a career on the stage awaited her eldest daughter.

Well, she knew she wasn't like the other girls in the school, but she didn't quite know why. She could remember standing in the garden by the chicken shed wearing the new pink silk dress her mother had knitted for her and thinking that God must surely see her as the prettiest little girl in the world, and she had only been five then. She was brought up with a healthy respect for God.

'God will know if you are naughty,' Eva Lowman always said, so Sarah lived out her days with the knowledge that God was looking over her shoulder. Once, when she was little, her mother had said that the fairies had brought her, and she used to wonder why they had left her with such poor parents when they could see she obviously belonged elsewhere. She knew better now, of course, and often wondered about her background, but Eva was never keen to talk about her life when she was young.

Well, it was up to her to aspire to greater heights, and she intended to put this right as soon as the opportunity occurred. Once she left school . . . She hummed a little, she was so excited, and made her way to the kitchen where

Valerie was having her breakfast and her mother waiting for her.

'Come along, Sarah.'

'Mum, what was Granpa's name?'

So sudden was the question that even Valerie looked up.

'Granpa who?'

'Your Granpa. Your father, I mean.'

'George. George Harris. And his father, that's your grandfather, was called Moses. Moses Harris.'

'Moses!'

'Yes – why?'

She was Jewish. That was what made her different. Whoever heard of anyone called Moses nowadays? Except her grandfather. And think of her uncles and aunts. Her mother was one of eight, six girls and two boys. Uncle John was fair and blue-eyed, like her mother, while Uncle Harry was dark and had curly hair and a rosy face. His eyes were like black boot buttons and shone like stars when he laughed, which he did often. Then there was Aunt Esther. Now she was Jewish if you like, with that glossy black hair and those strange green eyes. Oh, Sarah was sure now. That's what made her different, she was Jewish. She felt faint stirrings of excitement. Her eyes took on a look of deep intensity as though remembering tragic events and past suffering.

'Do you think we are Jewish – your family, I mean?'

Eva looked at her. Now what was she getting at? she wondered, but kept a straight face. Really, Sarah was such a strange child.

'I shouldn't think so. Here, eat your breakfast.'

Sarah sat down.

'Well, where did they come from?' she persisted.

'Kent,' Eva said shortly. 'Your great-grandfather was head gardener on Lord Bess's estate at Faversham in Kent, and his father before him, I think. So was your grandfather until they came to live in London.'

'Oh.'

Sarah's face fell. It didn't sound quite right, a Jewish gardener . . . But they might have come from the Russian

31

steppes, somewhere like that, and landed in Kent, having owned acres and acres of land . . .

'What about your grandmother? Where did she come from?'

Eva's eyes looked distantly out towards the fence but she saw nothing except a little old lady in a black dress with a lace collar.

'My real grandmother died young and my grandfather married again – a Frenchwoman.'

Sarah's eyes widened.

'I didn't know you had a French grandmother.'

'Well, I didn't – it was my grandfather's second wife.'

But Sarah was gulping down her tea and eating her toast. That was it. She was French – she had a French grandmother. When I apply for a job on the stage, I shall tell them, she thought, pushing in her chair. 'I had a French grandmother, so of course I am partly French.'

'Oh, do hurry, Sarah! Valerie's waiting for you. And you know I have to get up to the school.'

The day of Eva Lowman's visit to see Miss Wood dawned sunny only to cloud over later and pour with rain by the time the children left for school. Eva's heart sank as she saw the council workmen down the street busy erecting small temporary shelters to house their forks and spades. Well, she knew they would get to her end of Calydon Road sooner or later. Installing Anderson shelters indeed. Why, there was hardly room in the small yard for anything else, what with Tom's chicken run, and he did like to grow a few vegetables and flowers. Such ugly things they were, too. Corrugated iron which would soon rust, bound to. They didn't take long to instal, but that wasn't the point. One gang came along and dug an enormous pit, and the next day another gang arrived to instal the shelter. The terrifying thing was that there might be the need to use them. Her heart began to pound at the very thought. Imagine German bombers overhead and her precious girls in danger. Plans were already underway to evacuate them in the event of war, and she could only pray that such a wicked thing would not come to pass. It didn't bear thinking of. As for herself, catch her going down in one of those shelters! She'd rather stay in her own home any day.

One of the workmen passed her. 'Be with you sometime this week, missus,' he said.

She nodded and hurried inside. Her appointment with Miss Wood was not until two o'clock but she must see that she had everything ready. She wanted to look as nice as possible. It was quite exciting when you thought about it. A lady wore kid or leather gloves, never cotton. Cotton was a sign of poverty and ill-breeding, and no one who considered herself a lady was ever seen without gloves. She wore diamond patterned woollen stockings, and her Henry Heath hat such as she had seen ladies of quality wearing while strolling about the village. Second hand they may have been, but better that than new and cheap.

Miss Wood was slightly surprised by the appearance of Sarah's mother, quickly realising that she knew now where Sarah 'got it from'. She explained that both she and the rest of the staff were very impressed with Sarah's acting ability.

'She really has great talent, and it would be wonderful if she were able to go to a drama school. Would that be possible, Mrs Lowman? We would all back her up to the hilt – perhaps she could try for a scholarship.'

Eva was shocked.

'Oh, dear! Thank you, Miss Wood. We couldn't think of it. Not at all. Her father and I would not even consider such a thing.'

Miss Wood clicked her tongue and frowned.

'Oh, what a pity.' She felt genuinely sorry for Sarah. 'She has such a talent. I don't need to tell you, her speaking voice is good and her grammar is excellent. It is nice to hear her speaking so well, for I need hardly tell you, the King's English is seldom heard in this school.'

She saw Eva Lowman start in defence of herself and hurried on, 'Of course, it is fairly obvious that Sarah comes from a nice home.'

Eva looked down, pleased.

'May I ask if you have any plans for her?'

'We want her to go into an office,' Eva explained. The interview was not going at all the way she'd thought it

33

would. 'I know lots of girls go into factories around here, but I want something better for her than that. That's where I worked,' she said a little defiantly, 'in a factory.'

'And very good work it is too,' Miss Wood said staunchly. 'Still, I do see what you mean. Sarah is an unusual girl and she obviously has other talents – it would be a pity to waste them. I am sorry you don't feel you can support her in her acting career. It really isn't as fraught with danger as you might think. A lot depends on the girl's temperament and the way she is brought up. I am sure Sarah could take care of herself. Still . . .'

Eva bit her lip.

'It's not a very secure kind of job, and we would like her to have something that she could always fall back on, like typing and shorthand.'

'Is Sarah keen on this as a future?'

'Well, no,' Eva said. 'But then, they don't always know what is good for them at this age, do they?' She looked at Miss Wood for confirmation.

'No.' The teacher smiled.

'Well, Mrs Lowman, if there is any way in which we can help, do come and see us. We will be most pleased to give you any assistance you need.'

'That's ever so good of you,' Eva said, pulling on her gloves and taking her leave. 'Good afternoon, Miss Wood.'

'Good afternoon, Mrs Lowman.'

Oh, well, Miss Wood thought. I tried. Every so often a girl stands out and rises above the others and you just know that, given a chance, or luck, or whatever it was that decided these things, she might be destined for better things. She sighed. She could see Sarah would get no help from her mother, nice little woman though she was.

The nice little woman, meantime, walked down the side street home, a frown on her face. Oh, what a worry it was. She didn't want Sarah to be unhappy with what they wanted for her, but did a girl know best at that age? Sarah was full of dreams and nonsense. Look at the way Joannie Wilson's mother had gone out of her way to tell her that Sarah had told all the girls at school she was adopted. Now where had she got that from? It seemed as though she just wanted to be different. If only they could find her a respectable job – in an office, say – a ladylike job. Acting, indeed!

Still, she must count her blessings. She might have had a daughter like Julie Garrett with her flighty ways. Not that she knew anything against her – it was just the way she looked. Julie liked the boys, and dressed a little . . . well, not exactly common, for her mother dressed her in formal clothes, many of which she made herself, but you felt given half a chance she would wear real grown-ups' dresses with low necks, that sort of thing. Quite worrying.

She was lucky to have Valerie, a sweet natural child. Even at eight years old, Eva knew that she would be no worry to her. Sarah was different. In which case, who did she take after? Not Tom who was a contented worker of a man and asked no more than his home and his work and his mates and the occasional glass of beer. More like his sisters, four of them, all fair beauties who had married well and as a consequence were snooty and kept their visits to their old home down to a minimum.

As for herself, she had had a few high and mighty ideas when she was young, but had soon had those knocked out of her by the sheer pressure of day to day living and trying to make ends meet.

She must remember to call at the grocers for some Galloway's cough syrup. Little Valerie had started another cough. Eva did hope she was not going to be a chesty child. One thing about Sarah – she was as strong as a horse, despite being thin.

Besides, Miss Wood didn't know everything. Eva remembered the tall gaunt woman in the high-necked blouse and long skirt who had taught her as a child and whom she had thought must be at least ninety years old. She was probably about forty then, she thought wryly. Miss Dobson her name was. She had asked them to come back and see her sometimes, but none of them ever did. Life was so exciting when you left school, and you were glad to see the back of it. There was so much to do, it was a different world. You weren't to know then that you were going to follow in your mother's footsteps and do exactly as she did after all – get married and have a baby. Not that she didn't love Tom, he was a good man working out his days in Siemens' machine shop, but if only he had been like Albert Barton next-door, a proper foreman, things might have been different.

She pulled the string and let herself in with the key.

When Sarah came in an hour later, she ran through the passage like a whirlwind.

'What did Miss Wood say?' Breathlessly, she awaited Eva's answer.

She took a deep breath.

'Well, she said you are a very good little actress . . .'

'Did she? Oh, Mum!' Sarah's eyes were shining.

'Now don't get excited. Nothing has happened. She just suggested that you might like to go to acting school – if we could afford it, which we can't. That's one thing. The other is, even if we could, we wouldn't allow you to go. You already know what your father and I feel about that kind of thing.'

'What kind of thing?' Sarah's lip trembled.

'Well, the stage and that. Acting.'

Sarah was near to tears.

'I was really shocked, Sarah. I thought she was going to be helpful, give us some guidance. That she'd know – '

'She does,' Sarah said bitterly. 'She did. She told you what I should do.'

'She doesn't understand,' Eva said. 'She only sees you at school – what does she know of family life? What we feel like as your parents? She's had no children herself. What would she know about it?'

'She was trying to help me,' Sarah said. She felt empty, drained. All day she had been looking forward to coming home – and now this. She would be stuck in this awful hole, forced to do a job she didn't want to do. But she wouldn't! She would run away rather than that.

She looked so woebegone that Eva felt like putting her arms about her, but she was too big for that. Besides it would do no good. She had to learn you couldn't always get what you wanted. Why couldn't she be like other girls?

'Anyway,' she went on, in what she hoped was a reasonable tone, 'you're a clever girl – you deserve something better than acting. It's not a very ladylike thing to do.'

36

'What?' Sarah shrieked, at the end of her tether. 'That's all you care about – being ladylike. What's wrong with acting? It's a job like anything else. But not for you – oh, no. I suppose you see me striding around the stage with nothing on!'

'Sarah! That's enough!'

Sarah knew she had gone too far by the look in her mother's eyes, and flung out of the kitchen into the bedroom where she flung herself down on the bed and wept angry tears of mortification.

'Sarah! Come back here this minute.'

But Sarah made no move. She'd never forgive them.

Chapter Six

'You have got lovely nails, Julie,' Sarah said enviously, looking at the white tapering fingers and almond-shaped nails Julie was polishing with a buffer.

It was intensely hot on the asphalt in the school playground and the little group of girls sat under the corrugated iron roof of the shelter. Sarah had been holding forth as usual, keeping them enthralled with her stories. Now that they no longer chased about like the younger girls there was nothing they enjoyed more.

Julie spread her fingers, looking at them.

'Not bad,' she said, though Sarah knew she was proud of them.

'Is that part of the manicure set you got from Mrs Neville?'

'Yes, it belonged to the daughter, Olivia.'

'I know,' Sarah said impatiently, not only because she did not possess one but because of Julie's contact with the Neville family. Suddenly a feeling of excitement overtook her. 'I can't believe it – this is our very last day!'

'Do you know what you're going to do, Sarah?' one of the girls asked.

'Go on the stage,' she said.

'You're not,' Julie said equably, examining her cuticles. She had heard it all before.

Sarah sighed. 'I shall probably go and stay with my aunt for a time until I get a job. She really has the most beautiful house – set in a sort of parkland. It has fifteen rooms and I don't know how many bathrooms, and they have horses – that sort of thing.'

From her commanding position at the top of the school steps, Miss Wood stood beside the railings overlooking the playground. The sun burned her back and she wished now that she had not worn a jumper. Goodness, it was most unseasonal. Even the noise in the playground was subdued as the girls played desultory ball games or huddled in the shade provided by the three storey school building. In one such corner she saw Juliet Garrett and Sarah Lowman, both girls leaving today. An unlikely twosome but that was often the way, the attraction of opposites.

She would be sorry to see them go. They were an interesting pair, particularly Sarah, and she was more than sorry that the girl would probably end up in a mediocre job quite unsuitable for someone of her temperament. She had no such fears for Julie. The boys would flock after her, and she would be married in no time, like most of the others.

She glanced at the watch hanging on its gold chain at her bosom. What a heavenly day. One hoped it would last but it was probably a flash in the pan. This time tomorrow she would be on her way to join her friend who had already retired to the little cottage in Mayfield in Sussex. One day, next year, God willing, she would join her.

She took a deep breath and blew the whistle.

The girls got up and walked to their lines.

'You're the most awful liar,' Julie hissed pleasantly. No talking was allowed until they reached the inside of the building.

Sarah flushed to the roots of her fair hair, as they walked up the steps.

'You haven't got an aunt with a house like that,' Julie said.

Sarah shrugged. 'My Aunt Jane has a large house on Streatham Common,' she said. 'I've been there – once.' She tucked an arm through Julie's comfortably. 'I don't know what it is, Julie, but I add as I go along – I kind of get carried away.'

'I've noticed!' Julie laughed, as they took their seats for their very last afternoon at day school.

Not much work was done on that final afternoon, a large cake was cut during the afternoon break, and when they finished early, they all said their goodbyes and there were promises to keep in touch and lots of crocodile tears as they parted at the school gate.

Sarah and Julie walked home together, arm in arm. 'I wonder where we will be this time next year?' Sarah said.

'Working in a hairdressing salon, I hope. We might even be married.'

'Oh, no!' Sarah wailed.

'What's wrong with that?' Julie asked. 'We'd be gone sixteen – you'd be almost seventeen. My mother was married at seventeen.'

Seeing Sarah's woebegone face, she laughed. 'I'm joking, silly, don't be so serious.'

'They're still on about me going into an office,' Sarah said gloomily. 'Can you imagine – *me* – in an office?'

'Or me,' Julie said, and they fell about laughing. Presently they sobered up.

'I hate shorthand,' Sarah said.

'So do I. I never wanted to do it in the first place.'

'We didn't have much choice,' Sarah said. 'If I could go to London on the train every day to drama school, or work in a theatre, or with flowers,' she said, her eyes shining at the thought.

'Fat chance,' Julie said. 'Your mother would never agree to that.'

'It's only sevenpence a day workmen's fare before seven-thirty.'

'That's got nothing to do with it – it's travelling away from home. You know what they're like. Anyway, I don't mind working locally as long as it's not in an office.'

'Can you come out after tea?' Sarah asked.

'I expect so. Call for me when you're ready,' Julie said as Sarah pushed open the small iron gate. 'See you later.'

Sarah could not resist bending down to look at the spring bulbs – the daffodils in bud, the crocus in bloom, bright purple and yellow, dozens of them in the border under the window.

She let herself in and went down the long narrow passage with the dark varnished paper above the deep wooden dado.

In the kitchen there was the familiar smell of the fire scorching the plush tablecloth and the cool dark scent of floor polish vied with the acrid scent of hot blacklead. On the table was a vase of daffodil spears waiting to open.

Although it was warm, the range was lit for there was no other means of cooking, but the front door of the range was kept shut in the daytime when the oven was wanted for baking, being let down again when not needed. Then the fiery coals sent an orange glow over the room and the shadows danced on the walls.

No matter how much you pushed the table against the wall, there was almost always the slight smell of scorching cloth for the room was so small. One day her mother hoped to have a gas cooker. It was the thing she wanted most in life.

Sarah found her mother where she knew she would be, just inside the front room, where she stood with her hand to her face and a worried frown as she contemplated the latest move around.

It didn't take Sarah long to realise that the sofa was where the piano had been, the table was no longer in the bay window but by the folding doors, and the armchairs had been switched over. The tall potted plant stand stood in the bay.

Eva turned her head this way and that.

'What do you think, Sarah? Does it make the room look bigger?'

'Mmmm.'

It was better to agree. Her mother changed the room around every week, it was something the family was used to. Sometimes, when she had a headache, she changed it every other day.

'Dad said you weren't to move the piano,' Sarah said reprovingly, eyeing her mother's small plump figure. 'You might get a rupture or something.'

'I know my own strength,' Eva said. 'I push with my knees. I know exactly how to do it without using my stomach muscles.'

41

It wouldn't make any difference what you said, Sarah thought. Her mother would go on pushing furniture around until her dying day.

Well, she didn't intend to live like that. She had plans. She peered at herself in the mirror on the wall of the bedroom she shared with Valerie. Her hair was fair, thick and long, and blue eyes beneath dark lashes and straight brows stared back at her. She kicked off her heavy leather shoes and pulled up her long black stockings. She wished she was pretty like Julie. No, that wasn't right. Her sister Valerie was pretty – Julie was beautiful. Julie had lustrous dark hair with auburn lights in it and great violet eyes with golden flecks which sort of glowed. Sarah took a deep breath, straining against her liberty bodice. She wished she could have a brassiere like Julie, but Julie needed it, her mother said darkly. These days she always had a disapproving look when you talked about Julie. Her breasts pushed out her gym slip and all the boys were after her.

Sarah took off her gym slip and put on a dress. It was what she called a little girl dress. She wished her mother would buy her a grown up dress instead of making these little girl dresses with puffed sleeves and embroidery. Her mother embroidered everything. She was the only girl in her class who had embroidered petticoats. One day she would have a corselet with a wasp waist like the one in Brandon's window in the village.

In the kitchen she laid the table with a lacy tablecloth and real china cups and saucers. Eva would never drink out of thick cups. She had picked up the bone china tea service cheap at a street market because the transfer printing on the cups was smudged. She made the tea without being asked, and poured the milk into the cups, then sliced the bread and buttered it, all in the hope that her mother would be sufficiently impressed to allow her to go to the library.

Eva, coming back into the kitchen, noticed Sarah's satchel on the cane chair in the corner and was about to tell her to put it away when she remembered.

She was genuinely contrite. 'Oh, Sarah. Do you know I honestly forgot you left today!'

Sarah stood, hands on hips, staring out through the window.

'Well, that's that then,' she said.

'You'll look back and remember it,' Eva said. 'It's the end of an era.'

'Good riddance,' said Sarah.

Eva took a deep breath, and began to make the tea.

'Get Easter over and we'll see about getting you a job,' she said. 'There's no hurry.'

When tea was over Sarah cleared the table and put the things away, even going as far as to ask Valerie how she had got on at school that day, and was there anything else she could do?

The almost permanent frown which creased Eva's forehead these days had eased considerably when Sarah made her request. Holding her books, her face washed and her hair combed, she waited.

'Can I go to the library?'

She didn't look Eva straight in the eye. After all, there was no need to tell her that she was going to call for Julie.

'What, again?'

'I've read all the books.'

'Oh, all right, and don't be late. Back here by half-past six, remember.'

Carrying her books, Sarah left the house and walked along Calydon Road, passing the churchyard where old Mr Ransome bent over the gravestones with his shears, his flat cap pulled down over his eyes. He was a funny old man who scared her though everyone seemed to like him. 'Poor old Ransome,' they said, and it was an established fact that you never mentioned Mrs Ransome. Her mother's face would darken if you did and she would say with that funny cold voice: 'We don't speak to that woman, she's not very nice.'

Sarah often wondered what that meant because little Mrs Ransome looked nice enough. She always smiled at you, and wore jaunty clothes and berets on the side of her head, and her cheeks were so rosy that you just knew it was rouge.

When she reached Julie's road, Sarah looked around her with distaste. Fancy being poor and living here. There was always a mess in the road, and children played noisily, shrieking at each other as they played hopscotch or marbles and football across the road. The big boys always called out after her. Now she walked on, head held high. She was terrified of some of the bigger boys. Sometimes they pulled her hair until it made her eyes smart. She hurried towards Julie's house, knowing her mother would disapprove of her being in this street at all. Yet Julie's mother's steps were snowy white, even whiter than her mother's, while the coal hole gleamed like silver.

She rapped on the door and Julie opened it.

'Can you come out?'

Julie winked at her. 'Yes, I think so. Just a minute, I'll ask Mam.'

Sarah looked around her as she waited. Although it repelled her, there was a certain fascination about this area. All sorts of funny goings on here, according to her mother. A mix of people – foreigners, strange women who would jeer out loud if you stared too hard.

Sarah kept her eyes down and presently Julie reappeared.

'I mustn't be late,' she said, taking Sarah's arm.

'Nor me. I've got to be back at half-past six.'

'Where shall we go? Library?'

Sarah nodded. There was nothing she liked more. Inside the lovely old house which had been taken over by the council it was warm and smelled of old books. She loved it all: the polished floors, the high stacks of books, the silence all round. When she was quite grown up she was going to write books. She would be a novelist – that's if she wasn't a famous actress first. Miss Wood had said she could act, and that if she kept up her writing she might make a writer, but that it was very hard work and you had to keep at it. She didn't find it so. Sometimes the words simply flew along the page and she couldn't get them down fast enough.

Julie, however, had her eye open for the boys. It was the one place where they sometimes congregated in small gangs, there being lots of sports and other activities outside. Having met someone to talk to she stayed outside while Sarah chose her books.

On the way home they took their time, walking through the park. They passed a young nursemaid wheeling her charge home hurriedly, the baby sitting up in the shiny London pram and taking notice of everything going on around him.

'She can't be much older than us,' Sarah observed, eyeing the nursemaid.

'I wouldn't like that job,' Julie said scornfully. 'Looking after children? Catch me!'

'Nor me,' Sarah said. 'I wish my parents weren't so strict, especially my father.'

'I haven't got that problem,' Julie laughed, 'but I know what you mean.'

Reaching a seat, they both sat down.

'Won't you be glad when we can buy our own clothes?' Julie said. 'I can't wait.'

'How do you think I feel?' Sarah said mutinously. 'At least you don't have to wear these embroidered things.'

Julie shrieked with laughter.

'No! Honestly, I do feel sorry for you. I mean, they're pretty – for young Valerie, I mean – but at our age! You wonder sometimes if mothers were ever young, like sixteen, and wanting things. You would have felt sorry for me if you had seen the costume Mam brought home for me from the Nevilles'. Honestly! Tweed it was – sensible skirt, sensible jacket, you know the sort of thing. It had been expensive, Mam said, and I thought, I bet! But what did that have to do with anything? Anyway,' and her lower lip stuck out, 'I'm not going to wear it, and that's that. I can't stand second hand clothes someone else has worn – ugh!'

'I don't mind,' Sarah said. 'I've often worn second hand clothes – it doesn't worry me as long as I like them.'

'Did you ask your Mum again about cutting your hair?'

Julie eyed Sarah's thick plait. She often thought if she'd been made to wear a plait she would have cut it off, just like that.

'No hope there,' Sarah said gloomily. 'But I won't give up. She'll have to give in when I go for an interview.'

'That's true,' Julie said, her mind by now on something else. 'I saw Dick Harrold on the way to school this morning. You should have seen him – he looks about twenty one instead of seventeen. He's got a job in the city somewhere.'

'It's almost six,' Sarah said, glancing at her watch. Let's go.'

They walked home until they reached Sarah's gate, watched by an anxious Eva from behind lace curtains.

'I wish Sarah would find another friend,' she fretted.

Chapter Seven

It was Maundy Thursday, the day before Good Friday, when Ada Garrett prepared to take Mrs Neville's dress up to Arkley Lodge. It hung on its hanger, the silver grey skirt cut on the bias, forty-six tiny covered buttons from neck to hem, the sleeves narrow, the shoulders wide and pleated into the bodice. Ada was very pleased with what she had done. Mrs Neville had a delicate pastel silk scarf which she had bought in Paris with a background of exactly the same silver grey as the dress; had bought the material, in fact to match. Ada knew she was going to approve.

Julie having gone round to Sarah's house, Ada made her way to Arkley Lodge. She found Mrs Jenkins, the housekeeper, in the kitchen, ironing.

'Good morning, Mrs Garrett. You finished it, then?'

'Yes, just in time – and I think she'll be pleased.'

'They're going to a reception in London on Easter Sunday, I expect she wants it to wear then.'

'Shall I go on up?' Ada asked.

'Yes, she's expecting you,' Mrs Jenkins said. 'And stop for a cup of tea before you leave. I've got something to say to you.'

Having left a very satisfied client, Ada made her way downstairs with a further order for two blouses.

She and Mrs Jenkins sat at the deal table in the enormous kitchen. Ada stirred her tea.

'I just thought I'd mention,' Mrs Jenkins said, 'the job that is going at Neville and Sons in the City.'

47

'What would that be, Mrs Jenkins?' Ada could hardly see how it would concern her.

'Didn't you say your Julie just left school?'

'Yes.'

'Well, there's a job going in Mr Neville's office – he mentioned it to me for Our Grill.' Our Grill figured a lot in Mrs Jenkins conversations, being Mrs Jenkins' niece, the daughter of her sister. Having no children of her own, she was more than interested in Our Grill's welfare.

Ada had no idea if that was the girl's real name, who must be about eighteen by now. It was Our Grill who was too large for Olivia Neville's clothes.

'Seems it's for a telephone operator – something like that – a young girl, leaving school. But as I said,' and Mrs Jenkins' nostrils flared with pride, 'Our Grill starts work at the local council offices in September.'

Ada's face fell. A telephone operator – Julie wouldn't know anything about that. Besides, there was no way she could persuade her to apply for such a job.

'It's a pity, Mrs Jenkins, a nice opportunity for someone, but Julie can't bear the thought of office work. Although as you know she has learned shorthand typing at school. But up to now – '

'She'll be lucky to get a job at all,' Mrs Jenkins sniffed. 'They don't grow on trees.'

'You're right about that,' Ada said, wishing more than ever that Julie might be interested. 'But she's only just left school, she knows nothing about a telephone switch-board – that's what it means, doesn't it?'

'I expect so,' said Mrs Jenkins who had no idea. 'They'd train her, that's the point, and it's all good experience.'

'What would we have to do?' Ada asked, ever hopeful.

'Write in,' Mrs Jenkins said. She went over to the dresser and picked up a slip of paper. 'Here.'

'Neville and Sons, Eastcheap, City,' Ada read.

'Write to Miss Boxall – that's Mr Neville's secretary. Tell her I told you about it. You can but try.'

Ada folded the cutting and placed it in her handbag.

'Thanks very much, Mrs Jenkins. I'll let you know how I get on.'

Walking home, she rehearsed the best way to tell Julie what she had in mind. Whatever she said it would make no difference. Julie would be adamant.

Julie was about to leave Sarah's house for home. Her friend saw her to the door.

'Shall we go up to the fair on Bank Holiday Monday?' Julie said.

'Yes, let's. Unless my mum and dad decide to go somewhere.'

'Oh, we'll see then.'

'I'll tell you something' Sarah said, her voice low, 'I'm going to get Mum to agree to let me cut my hair. I'd feel ridiculous with this long plait going out to work – I'd feel silly.'

'Good for you,' Julie said. 'Good luck,' she laughed, seeing her mother coming down the street. Swiftly she ran towards her and put an arm through hers. 'How did you get on? Did she like it?'

'Yes, she looked lovely in it,' Ada said. 'And I got an order for two blouses.'

'Whee!' Julie cried. 'That's great, Mam, it really is.'

'So we'll put the kettle on and have a cup of tea,' Ada said, already slightly excited about what she had to say.

She made a business of making tea and getting out the cake, humming a little, talking a little. She was just putting the tea cosy over the teapot when she seemed to remember something.

'Oh, I knew there was something!' she said, but she didn't fool Julie, who looked up suspiciously.

'Mrs Jenkins said there is a job going at Neville's in the city – for a girl leaving school.'

'Oh, yes?' Julie said, eyebrows raised. 'What's the matter with Our Grill?'

'Well, she already has a job, and this is for a telephone operator . . .'

'Then that let's me out,' Julie said with finality. 'That,' she stated clearly, 'is just about the last thing on earth I would ever do.'

'Well, I was thinking, if you got a foot in the door, perhaps you could use your shorthand and typing . . .'

'No.'

'It seemed a good opportunity to me,' Ada said. 'It's useful to have contacts – and I know Mr Neville. He's such a nice man – '

'I daresay,' Julie said, 'but *you're* not being asked to spend your life working in an office in the middle of the City.'

'I thought you liked the idea of travelling up to town each day,' Ada said, knowing she was on a losing wicket.

'I do – but not for that,' Julie said, and they finished their tea in silence.

Sarah, having closed the door on Julie, decided to strike while the iron was hot.

Eva looked up from her sewing. 'Ah, there you are.' She saw by Sarah's face that trouble was on its way. She broke off the thread with her teeth. 'Get Easter over and then we'll discuss what you're going to do.' She anticipated stormy scenes ahead. 'There's no hurry.'

She re-threaded her needle. 'I've made a nice cake for your tea, so go and get changed and I'll lay the table.'

Sarah went over to the dresser drawer and took out a pair of large scissors.

'Mum,' she said, speaking more confidently than she felt, 'now that I've left, what about cutting my hair?'

Eva stared back at her, open-mouthed. Even Valerie looked up from playing with her dolls.

'Sarah! What are you doing with those scissors? Put them away at once – at once, do you hear?'

Sarah looked at her sulkily. 'Why not? Now that I've left school.'

Eva studied her, trying to calm herself down. Well, it was bound to come. The child was right. She couldn't go after a job with a plait hanging down her back. And she was honest with herself. Wasn't it because she and Tom didn't like the idea of their daughter really growing up that they had kept her hair long? But that lovely thick hair chopped off – she couldn't bear to think of it. She bit her lip.

'Please, Mum,' Sarah said. 'All the girls . . .'

'Yes, I know, but they haven't all got hair like yours.'

'You used to cut my hair.'

'When you were small I used to trim it,' Eva agreed. But to cut it short – what would your father say?'

'He'd soon get used to it. It's my hair.'

She was right. 'I'll think about it,' Eva said finally.

'Yes, I know, and that means it won't get done.'

She looks so miserable, so woebegone, Eva thought. She has had so much disappointment about doing what she wants to do. For heavens sake, it will grow again, and it will give her pleasure.

'All right,' she said suddenly, giving in. 'Come over here. If that's what you want – give me the scissors.'

Sarah gave a shriek of delight.

'You will? Really?'

'Come and sit over here.'

Eva undid Sarah's plait slowly, allowing the thick hair to fall in ripples down her back. She bit her lip, almost in tears.

'Oh, I don't think I can.'

'Oh, go on,' Sarah egged her on. 'After all, I can't go to work with a pigtail.' She was laughing now that she had her own way.

'Find me a comb, Valerie, there's a good girl.'

She got up from her playing and went over to the dresser. She watched curiously as Eva combed the thick tresses.

'She will look funny, won't she?' she asked doubtfully.

'Not half as funny as you do,' Sarah retorted.

Then Eva began to snip, and Sarah wriggled. 'I don't want it around my shoulders – I want it short.'

'Sit still, I shall cut you.'

'Just below my ears, please, Mum.'

'You'll look like a boy,' Eva grumbled, agonising as the luxuriant hair fell to the floor.

Sarah was growing more and more excited. She couldn't wait to see how she looked.

'There,' Eva brushed her shoulders. 'Stand up. I can see better how to level it off.'

She could't believe her eyes when she saw the change.

Sarah looked so different, so grown up – and so pretty. But this girl didn't look like Sarah.

Sarah hurried to the back door where her father's shaving mirror hung. She was obviously delighted.

'Oh, Mum, I look quite different! Grown up,' she said proudly, and was amazed to see tears in her mother's eyes.

Eva dabbed at them with her apron. 'Don't take any notice of me – get the dustpan and brush.'

Sarah felt embarrassed. She had not known that her mother could feel like that.

'I don't know what your father will say,' Eva said, sweeping up the golden hair from the floor. 'Well, we'll have to see how it goes – it will take a time to settle down, and you'll have to decide what to do with the front.'

Sarah scanned the magazines. Constance Bennett had her hair smooth and shining like a cap, Ginger Rogers in a halo of curls, while Garbo wore it smooth and long in a page boy, but that was all right for her with her classical features . . .

Tom Lowman exploded when he saw what they had done. It was like a physical shock. His favourite daughter stood before him shorn of her wonderful hair, and he knew it would be a long time before he could forgive Eva for doing it.

She tried to placate him. 'Tom, she's going out to work soon. She couldn't have had long hair for work, now could she?'

'She could have put it on top of her head or something,' he grumbled. 'In earpads, whatever they call them . . .'

Eva and Sarah shrieked with laughter.

'Oh, not earphones, Dad!' Partners in crime, they stood helpless with laughter at the thought of it, but Tom took a long time to come round and could hardly bear to look at her.

When Sarah opened the door on Easter Saturday morning, Julie was dumbstruck and stood there with her mouth open. 'Golly, I didn't recognise you for a minute. It's smashing. You don't half look glamorous – about eighteen. I'd never have known you if you'd passed me in the street.'

Sarah was content. She had Julie's approval.

'I thought we'd go down to old Sparkes for some magazines.'

'OK,' Julie said, 'but I'll have to call in to the Neville's first though. Mam has forgotten a pattern. It's not far out of our way – '

'That's all right,' Sarah said, anxious to walk about almost anywhere to show off her new hair do.

The two girls walked towards the village, and at the corner of the little road turned in at the entrance to the Lodge.

'I'll wait here,' Sarah offered.

'I won't be a minute,' Julie said, opening the gate and hurrying down the drive. She was halfway down when she saw the young man cycling towards her. Seeing her, he dismounted and smiled, causing her heart to beat faster. He was so good-looking about twenty or so, tall and fair.

'Hello. Want some help?'

Andrew Neville saw a young girl with deep violet eyes and a cascade of chestnut curls. He thought she was the prettiest girl he had ever seen.

Julie felt her legs go quite wobbly as the very blue eyes looked into hers. 'Er, no thanks. I'm just collecting something from Mrs Jenkins.'

'Ah.' Again that wonderful smile. 'You'll find her in the kitchen, I expect.' And mounting his bike, he rode on.

'Thank you,' Julie said, her heart beating fast. Golly, wasn't he handsome? She wondered who he was . . .

Visiting Sparkes was one of their favourite outings. Sparkes was a general dealer who kept a scruffy store at the bottom of Church Lane. Outside the shop was a stall of used movie magazines that came mostly from America. They cost a penny or twopence, and the two girls spent most of their pocket money on them. To each mother's questions as to where they got them, they usually said: 'Julie gave them to me' or 'Sarah gave them to me.'

They lay on Julie's bed poring over them with 'oohs' and 'aahs'.

'You don't half look different,' Julie said admiringly. 'Quite the young lady.'

'Really?' Sarah purred.

'What about Louise Brookes?' Julie suggested, thumbing a page. 'Smooth hair parted in the middle with a fringe.'

'All right if you've got that kind of face,' Sarah said.

Julie looked at the picture then back at Sarah. 'Ye-es, I see what you mean.'

Sarah laughed and flung a pillow at her.

'Why don't you have yours cut?' She eyed the unruly mane of Julie's chestnut curls.

'Oh, I don't think so.' Julie looked a little embarrassed. It was the last thing she would do. She was not unaware that her hair was her crowning glory. 'Look, if you parted yours on the side and let it fall almost over one eye. You know what I mean.' She squinted. 'A bit like Veronica Lake. If you ask me I think it could do with being just an inch shorter.'

'Oh no!' Sarah wailed. 'My mother would go mad. It was as much as she could do to let me have my plait off.' And they giggled helplessly.

'Tell you what,' Julie said, 'I'll do it for you, just half an inch. It would make all the difference.'

'Would you? You are a sport, Jule,'

'No time like the present. Here, sit here while I get the scissors and a towel.'

She draped the towel around Sarah's shoulders, 'Ready?'

'You won't cut it too short, will you?'

'Trust me,' Julie grinned, and snipped off the first half inch. 'See what I mean?'

'Yes,' Sarah breathed. 'It does make a difference – but no more, mind.'

Her mother looked up sharply when she came in, and Sarah paled.

'Oh dear,' Eva sighed. 'I'll be a long time getting used to that short hair.' And Sarah breathed again.

When her friend had gone, Julie went back into the kitchen where she found Ada cutting out the material for Mrs Neville's blouses.

'Was Mrs Jenkins there?' Ada asked. 'When you called for the pattern? I hope you apologised for me.'

54

'Yes, I did,' Julie said, and set about getting the tea.

'As I walked up the drive,' she said casually, 'a young man came down on his bicycle and asked if he could help me. He was about twenty.'

Ada was busy pinning the pattern to the material.

'I expect that was Andrew – the Neville's younger son.' she said. 'I've seen him once or twice – he was up at Oxford until this year. I think he'll follow his brother into the business from what Mrs Jenkins said.'

'Oh,' Julie said, and that was that.

On Easter Sunday morning, Sarah got ready for church, while Eva saw to Valerie. They wore their reefer coats and navy velour hats. Most of the other girls wore felt hats but the Lowman girls' were velour. It was worth paying four and eleven for velour instead of two and eleven for felt, Eva decided. She brushed Sarah's coat down with a clothes brush. 'Have you got your collection money?'

'Sarah nodded, her face set and cross.

'Now what?' Eva asked patiently.

'This hat doesn't fit properly now that I've got my hair cut.'

'Well, you're certainly not going to church without one,' Eva said reasonably, and led them to the front door, watching them walk up the road. She was so proud of her girls.

Once round the corner they were to meet Julie, but before they met Sarah took her hat off and carried it in her hand. 'You're not to tell Mum,' she said to Valerie, but her sister just walked on. The thought had not occurred to her.

Julie was waiting outside her house and Sarah noticed enviously that she wore a small felt hat on top of her curls, one she suspected she had concocted herself, probably out of one of her mother's old ones. Julie was clever like that. There was something about the way she dressed, the way she wore her clothes, the belts she wore, the angle of her hat. Sarah wouldn't have worn them herself, but she had to admit that on Julie everything looked smart. Now there was a secret smile playing around her mouth, and looking ahead Sarah saw that Jimmy Paynter was in front of them with

55

that awful Charlie Winter. Julie had had a crush on Jimmy for a long time and Sarah couldn't see why. She thought he was horrible. He leered and made jokes that she couldn't always understand, although Julie seemed to. Julie thought he was the cat's whiskers.

There was a new curate in the church, he looked so young and was so nervous that Sarah felt quite sorry for him, but Julie kept nudging her to make her giggle and it was as much as she could do to keep a straight face. Jimmy Paynter kept looking along the pew at them and she knew he was trying to pass Julie a note, but Julie kept her eyes straight ahead although Sarah knew she was quite well aware of what was going on.

Having put their pennies in the collection box they dawdled home, much to Valerie's annoyance. 'Come on, Sarah, you know Mum doesn't like us to be late.'

'Presently, as they neared the corner, a small boy ran up and thrust a note into Julie's hand. She took no notice but walked on, head high. Sarah knew that once round the corner she would open it, which she did.

'Cheeky devil,' she said.

But the prospect of a meeting with Jimmy Paynter had suddenly lost all it's savour. All she could see was a pair of intensely blue eyes, eyes that looked at her with open admiration . . .

That evening, as Ada sat sewing and they listened to the radio, Julie gave a loud sigh.

Ada looked up. 'What's that for?'

'Well, you know, Mam, I've been thinking . . .'

Ada waited.

'Perhaps I should take advantage of that offer of a job from Mrs Jenkins? After all, it can't be bad, can it? Our shorthand teacher said if you are asked at an interview if you can do anything, say you can, even if you can't. You can always learn afterwards.'

Ada couldn't believe her ears. She couldn't think what to say.

'If they answer my letter and ask for an interview, it will be good experience even if I don't get it.'

Ada got up and went to the dresser drawer, taking out a pad of notepaper and some envelopes.

'There is nothing like striking while the iron is hot,' she said. 'Now here's the address – and I'm sure you know better than I do what to say.'

Julie, tongue held firmly between her teeth, took up the pen.

Chapter Eight

On Easter Monday the girls walked towards Blackheath for the fair. As they walked, Sarah shook her head, a habit she had recently acquired. It was lovely to feel the freedom of short hair, and she ran her hand through it form time to time.

'Did I tell you,' Julie began, 'that's there was a vacancy for a telephone operator at Neville's in the City.'

'No. So who's going after it?'

'I am,' Julie said, feeling like a traitor.

Sarah stopped short and looked accusingly at her.

'You're not!'

'I am,' Julie said defiantly. 'I wrote to them at the weekend.'

Sarah began to walk on. 'I can't believe it – after all you said!'

'I know I did,' Julie admitted, but it did seem like a good opportunity. And, after all, I might not get it.'

'You will,' Sarah said. She never connected failure with Julie. 'Why did you change your mind?'

She couldn't tell even Sarah that. It sounded so ridiculous.

'Well, I thought about it and I suppose the idea of going up to town every day.'

'You said you didn't care about that.'

'Well, I changed my mind. I don't know, it just sounded interesting. After all, a telephone operator – it's not like doing shorthand and typing, is it?'

'No, and it won't pay as much,' Sarah said scornfully. 'I'm really surprised at you, Julie Garrett.'

But you couldn't keep Julie down for long.

Head held high, she walked on briskly, slightly ahead of Sarah who had to rush to keep up with her until she reached the heath. Sarah looked at the back of Julie's head, the riotous curls which tumbled over her shoulder, the lovely legs and curvy figure. Several boys stared at her or whistled, there was no doubt about her attractiveness.

She looked down at her own slim legs and the coat which Eva made her wear. It was good quality, but so old-fashioned. Wait until she bought her own clothes. She wouldn't be wearing stuff like this.

Julie had no money for clothes either, yet she could look smart in virtually any old thing. She had flair, Sarah decided. And now Julie was going to London to work – she couldn't feel more miserable. Especially as her father talked of nothing except the plans to evacuate the firm in the event of war. To Leicestershire of all places. She'd rather die than go there. Anyway, there was no point in worrying about it now – it might never happen.

'If you have to go for an interview, what will you wear?' she asked presently. 'Your best navy?'

'I'm not sure,' Julie said. Already she was getting used to the idea, and it didn't seem half bad. 'If it's warm enough, I'll wear my green dress. I like that.'

'Yes, I do, it suits you. My father says there are vacancies at Siemens' and Johnson's for office staff. But honestly, Julie, I couldn't.'

'You could do worse,' she said. 'Seems at the end of the day we're not going to get what we want.'

'That's true,' Sarah said morosely. 'Still,' and she cheered up, 'we're going to the cinema next Saturday, aren't we?'

'Yes – "Rebecca",' Julie said, glancing at Sarah and anxious to cheer her up.

'You know,' she said, 'you look a bit like Joan Fontaine.'

'Really?' Sarah said, delighted. Julie had made her day.

In Joseph Neville's office in the city it was warm, luxuriously appointed and as quiet as the grave. Miss Boxall, seated at her large mahogany desk at the far end of the room, looked up as her employer came in, dressed this morning in his

59

tweed suit of plus fours. So he was going to play golf which meant that he would be off early and that would be that for the weekend.

'Morning, Constance,' he said in that low deep voice of his, small brown eyes twinkling at her.

'Morning, Joe,' she said. As the oldest serving employee only she was entitled to use his first name.

'Anything special?'

'Clarke says the consignment from Sweden has at last turned up, and Bowater's are on the warpath about the German deliveries. Otherwise nothing much.'

'Is Gerald in?'

'Yes, I saw him earlier.'

He sifted through the opened post on his desk. 'I'll see him before I go.' He frowned. 'By the way, what are we doing about a new telephone operator for that switchboard out there?' He had to come through the reception area which held the switchboard on his way to his own office.

'I've someone coming for an interview this morning,' Miss Boxall said.

'Good. I don't want to put this one out of a job. See if Cartwright can find her something else to do, filing, something like that. It's important that people get a good impression when they come in.

'Yes, Joe.' And Miss Boxall made a note.

'Well, I'll be off then. Have a good weekend.'

'Thank you, Joe. And you.'

She watched him go, a short stocky little figure in his thick Braemar woollen socks with green tabs at the side, the highly polished brown brogues. Strange to think that all those years ago – thirty-five to be exact, for she was sixty now – they had had a passionate love affair.

She had been with the firm for about five years before she became his personal secretary – he had asked for her particularly and she had been only too willing to comply.

She had adored him, her first and only love. He had been strong and handsome, if a bit on the short side, with those twinkling brown eyes that could burn into hers over the desk, the way he looked at her . . . She was ripe for plucking, a young, eager, pretty little thing from Ilford,

60

travelling up to town every day on the train. Serious-minded, a churchgoer, she had been easy prey. It had started with a private dinner after working late, then some spark in both of them ignited and she was lost.

Now she could only recall it with wonder. An illicit affair – she, Constance Boxall, with a married man, her boss. It was as if it had happened to someone else. His wife, Sylvia, had borne him a son and a daughter, and Constance had thought about them only briefly then tossed her bonnet over the windmill.

How wonderful it had been though while it lasted – the intrigue, the secrecy, seeing him every day, the way his eyes held a passionate promise, the thrill when his hand touched hers. Had they managed to keep it a secret? She would never know now.

She sighed, coming back to earth. It wasn't often she thought about those far off days, a time in her life that was as dead as the dodo, dry as ashes in the mouth. When the affair had burned itself out as it was bound to do, there had been no question of her leaving. She was indispensable to him, and had settled down to what she had become, an elderly spinster with no time for anything but her job. Her life, in fact, she thought now, given to one man. A man whose wife had borne him another son after the affair, a man whose only interests were his business, his children, his golf, and the boat that he kept down in Hampshire where he had a weekend cottage.

She often told herself that she could have left and made another life for herself, she was free, but she had elected to stay. Now her whole life was the business, holding grimly on while the threat of war hung over them – they were more concerned than most seeing the business was the import of paper and board from Scandinavia and Europe. Suppose Gerald and Andrew had to go and fight? It would break her heart for she thought of them as the children she had never had, had watched them grow from school days to adulthood, and now Gerald was married with a life of his own, and Andrew was due to join the firm in September. If war broke out he would most certainly join the Royal Air Force.

61

She picked up the telephone. 'Put me through to Mr Cartwright, will you?'

'Yes, Miss Boxall.'

'Could you come and see me when you have a moment, Bill?'

'Certainly, Miss Boxall. Right away.'

A pity about the child out there. Still, Joe always knew best. He was probably right, She wasn't the best telephone operator in the world.

Cartwright was down from the second floor in no time, an anxious-faced elderly man who had been with the firm almost as long as herself.

'Close the door, Bill,' she said in answer to his knock, 'and sit down.'

He sat down and waited. He had the greatest respect for Miss Boxall.

'Mr Neville thinks that the little girl on the switchboard – what's her name?'

'Taylor, Miss Boxall Miss Taylor.'

'Mr Neville thinks she is not suitable after all. How long has she been with us?'

'Five or six weeks, Miss Boxall.'

'I see. Well, if you can find her something else to do. Filing, perhaps, export department.'

His face brightened. He never liked sacking anyone.

'Certainly, Miss Boxall. She's a nice girl, and a willing worker.'

'That's good. I am interviewing someone today for the post of telephone operator, so we shall have to see.'

'Miss Templeton could do with some help.'

'Then fix it up,' Miss Boxall said patiently, riffling through her papers in order to speed him on his way. He had the knack of staying on after an interview in order to have a little moan. 'That will be all, Bill.'

'He shuffled to his feet.

'Thank you, Miss Boxall.'

When he had left, she went over to Joe's desk and tidied it, putting everthing away, clearing for the coming weekend, then picked up some papers and bills of lading and made

62

her way to Gerald's office, placing some post on the post clerk's desk.

'See those get off safely, will you, Miss Marsh?' Miss Marsh looked up at her, her gooseberry eyes wet and shiny, her rather pretty auburn hair smooth as silk. She almost simpered.

'Yes, Miss Boxall.'

She went on her way. There was something she didn't quite like about Miss Marsh, never had. She had heard her quite often being rude to the telephone girl, for they shared the same office and on occasion Miss Marsh took over the switchboard.

She went on her way, a short dumpy figure in her blue woollen dress, with her thick pebble glasses, lisle stockings and low, sensible shoes. The staff liked Miss Boxall but they went in awe of her.

She gave a perfunctory good morning to Gerald's secretary in the outer office. 'Is he alone?'

'Yes, Miss Boxall.'

She tapped on the door and went in.

'Good morning, Gerald.'

'Good morning, Constance. How are you this morning?'

'I'm well, thank you. I brought you these.'

She put the papers down on his desk.

'Any messages?'

'No. Did your father come in to see you before he left?'

'Yes, he went off to golf.'

'Well, it's a lovely day. I don't blame him for taking advantage of it.'

He looked up from scanning his papers. 'These are all right, then, Constance.' He handed them to her.

'How is the new house?' She smiled.

'Coming along nicely – lots to do, but it keeps me busy.'

'Well, I'll leave you then.'

He watched her go. What would the firm do without her, the mainstay of the business? No one knew as much about the paper and board trade as she did, except his father. Hard to think she was a mere girl when she started – what had she been like then? As a schoolboy he remembered her as a nondescript little woman in sensible skirts and jumpers,

63

a pleasant face, and behind the thick glasses rather nice eyes. Well, there was no doubt about it . . . his mother would have had no fears on Miss Boxall's account.

Constance Boxall made her way back to the post room which housed the switchboard. She stopped and looked down at the girl who sat there and who had plugged in taking an outside call.

'Neville and Sons.'

She wore lots of make up, perhaps that was what Joe hadn't liked, and her hair certainly wasn't that bright red colour naturally. Still . . .

The girl turned and smiled brightly at her.

'Hello, my dear. How are you getting along?' Miss Boxall asked kindly.

'All right,' the girl said in her Cockney voice, but Miss Boxall was used to that. They were all Cockneys here.

'You know, my dear, I think perhaps you could do something a little more interesting than this. Do you type?'

The girl looked surprised. 'A bit.'

'I always think the switchboard must be so boring,' Miss Boxall confided, 'and they are short of staff in export – would you like that?'

The girl looked suddenly embarrassed.

'You think I'm not suitable for this? I mean . . .'

'Of course not.' Miss Boxall sounded quite shocked. 'But I think you would enjoy doing something more interesting. You look like an intelligent girl.'

Her face brightened. 'Thank you, Miss Boxall.'

'Well, we will have to see what we can do,' she said, stealing a glance at the post girl who was busy sorting post for she had the air of one who was listening and Miss Boxall hoped that she hadn't overheard. She had the nasty feeling that Miss Marsh could be unpleasant if she had a mind.

She pushed open the door of her inner sanctum and her feet sank into the deep pile carpet. Oh, she was glad she wasn't young any more.

She typed her letters, and glancing at her watch saw that it was almost eleven. Time for the interview.

She sat with Julie's well-written letter in front of her, and when the girl was shown in was pleasantly surprised.

Julie had never been in such a well-furnished room in her life. Beneath her feet the carpet was thick and pale grey while the furniture gleamed and there was a bowl of roses on Miss Boxall's desk. She had not imagined it would be anything like this.

'Sit down, Miss Garrett,' Miss Boxall said, and indicated a chair on the other side of her desk. The girl was naturally graceful, she thought, and such beauty – what a waste to coop it up in an office.

'I understand you heard about the vacancy from Mrs Jenkins, Mr Neville's housekeeper? You are not Mrs Jenkins' niece, are you?'

Julie smiled. 'No. My mother is a dressmaker, and it was while she was on a visit to Mrs Neville that Mrs Jenkins mentioned it.'

No side to her, thought Miss Boxall, and was pleasantly surprised at the girl's voice. It was low and clear. She spoke well, and with confidence.

'You have just left school, I believe, and know some shorthand and typing?'

'Yes.' And Julie looked doubtful. 'I really came for the post of telephone operator and office junior.'

'Do you know how to work a switchboard?' Julie's nerve deserted her. 'No', she said honestly, 'but I could learn.'

'Your duties would consist of other things too, of course, helping with the post, filing, and generally making yourself useful. All this when you are not busy on the switchboard, which must be your first priority. The importance of a good telephone manner cannot be underestimated. We demand courtesy from our employees. Politeness at all times, even if the caller becomes difficult. It is your job to smooth things over and make for a pleasant connection. Do you understand?'

'Yes, Miss Boxall.'

'I expect you realise that since you have no experience your starting wage would be quite low? Twenty-five shillings a week, and after six months a rise of ten shillings. I see here – ' and she referred to the letter ' – that you did shorthand typing at school. You would be very wise to keep that up in the future for you could earn a good salary as a shorthand typist or even a secretary.' She gave Julie a wide smile, but there was no show of enthusiasm on the girl's face.

'Also,' she went on, 'you will have your fares to find out of that. How would you travel? By train?'

Julie nodded. 'Yes, Miss Boxall.'

'I expect it would be worth your while to come up by workmen's train – it makes a great deal of difference to the fare, and simply means that you arrive in the city early. But so many young people do it, they usually enjoy the extra hour. The hours are from nine until five-thirty. Saturdays, nine until twelve-thirty.'

She smiled at Julie reassuringly.

'Well, I think I have made that clear.' She handed Julie a typewritten memo. 'Would you read out the first paragraph, Miss Garrett?'

Julie took it and began to read, and over Miss Boxall's face came a look of satisfaction. Unless she was mistaken, this girl would do very well.

Julie was feeling quite elated. She was almost certain now that she had got the job. The more Miss Boxall talked, the more confident she felt. With a smile, she handed back the memo.

'Well, Miss Garrett, when could you start?'

Julie gave her a brilliant smile. 'You mean I've got the job?'

'Well, shall we say you are on three months trial, but I am certain that once you have got used to the switchboard we shall have no trouble.'

'Thank you, Miss Boxall. I could start next week.'

'Good. Report to the post room at nine o'clock on Monday then, and I hope you will be very happy working with us.'

'Thank you, Miss Boxall.' Julie got up and walked to the door on air. Once in the corridor she almost ran, not waiting for the lift, hurrying down the stairs of the narrow tall building, out into Eastcheap, and thence towards Cannon Street Station where Ada sat in the waiting room, anxious to hear how she had got on.

Pleased with her morning's achievement, Miss Boxall

typed her letters until lunchtime when she took a short walk. She usually did this every day to keep herself in trim, going as far as St Paul's churchyard, and sometimes Fleet Street. She usually shopped in Nicholson's on a Friday for she preferred that to shopping at home in Colchester nowadays, and apart from her walks in the forest at weekends, and the occasional visit to her sister at Saffron Walden, walking during her lunch hour was the only exercise she got. She still lived in her parents' old home, and it was nice to be on your own, to be free to put your feet up and listen to the wireless, the plays, a concert, or read a good book. But she did worry about a war, and there was all this talk. She realised she would be in a very vulnerable position living in Essex if war came, and if it was true that bombs would fall on innocent people before soldiers had a chance to fight, then she would be in the front line. No wonder Joe had said that in the event of war they would get out of the City.

She shuddered and threw off her morbid thoughts, reminding herself not to meet trouble halfway.

As she strolled back she thought of the newest member of staff. She would certainly add interest to the lives of some of the young men who worked for Neville and Sons. Pretty little thing, Miss Boxall thought fondly, the same age as she had been when she started. Then smiled wryly as the thought struck her. There was not much chance of Miss Garrett ending up an old maid.

Chapter Nine

On Monday morning Julie was up early, dressed and raring to go. Ada looked her over approvingly, not without a little heart searching and hoping that she was doing the right thing. She watched her out of sight until she turned the corner, then went in and closed the door.

She had plenty of orders to keep her busy. Funny how they came in patches. She would have more than enough to do sometimes; at others the work was scarce. Right now she had six orders to complete and there was no time to waste. She must get on with things.

Julie was satisfied with her appearance. She had brushed her curls until they shone, her navy dress looked just right, she had polished her shoes under Ada's watchful eye until she could see her face in them. She caught the last workmen's train which arrived in the City at eight o'clock, seeing several boys and girls that she knew on the journey and strap hanging for dear life since there were fourteen people standing in that one carriage. She thought the journey was hilarious, as they joked and laughed, and enjoyed every moment of it. When they spilled out of the carriage some went one way and some another. Julie, finding herself with time to spare, walked slowly towards Eastcheap, taking in everything: the impressive buildings, the few shops and alleyways. Strange to think that the City, so-called, covered just one square mile. And all these people! Like ants, she thought, all going purposefully about their business, little time for dawdling. She felt proud to be one of them. She saw the Bank of England and the Royal Exchange and the

Mansion House, and decided that being early would make a good start.

The brass plates outside the Neville's building were polished so that you could use them as a mirror, and with a glance at her own reflection she entered the cool marble corridor and walked towards the lift. The peak-capped attendant smiled at her.

'Which floor, Miss?'

'Second, please,' Julie said, stepping in, and he closed the iron gates with a clang.

'Neville's,' he said. 'Are you the new telephone operator, Miss?' There was not much he didn't know about the office workers in his building. He and his wife lived in a flat right at the top as caretakers.

'Yes.' And Julie smiled proudly as they came to a halt and he opened the gates. 'Good luck,' he called after her as, smiling, she opened the door to the post room.

There was no one there and she looked around her – the room looked so different empty. Not half as forbidding. In the corner stood the dreaded switchboard, but she hastily averted her eyes and looked at the rest of the room. On the large table were several baskets with foreign place names on them, while on the long counter stood envelopes and a pair of scales and what she thought must be a franking machines. Alongside one wall were metal filing cabinets, and there were two chairs at the table and one at the switchboard. There was a clothes stand in one corner and she took off her coat and hung it up, just as the door opened and a girl with rather nice silky auburn hair came in, glancing quickly at Julie and away again. But it was as if she saw everything she needed to see in that one glance.

'Ah, I see you've made yourself at home' she said, taking off her coat. 'I am Miss Marsh, in charge of this department, so you will be responsible to me.' Her tone suggested that Julie should make no mistake about that. 'What's your name?'

'Garrett,' Julie said. 'Miss Garrett.'

'Well, Miss Garrett,' Miss Marsh said, her green glaucous eyes looking everywhere but at Julie, 'sit yourself down at the switchboard, study it, and try and make sense of it. Have you ever worked a switchboard before?'

'No,' Julie said, and Miss Marsh gave a deep sigh, her meaning only to clear. Not another brainless idiot.

The door opened and two women came in together.

'Morning, Miss Marsh.'

'Morning, Miss Winfield, Miss Sinclair – this is Miss Garrett, our new telephone operator.' And she rolled her eyes skywards, but the two women smiled brightly at Julie. 'Welcome to Neville's,' they said together, and going through one of the doors, closed it behind them.

'Shipping clerks,' Miss Marsh said. 'That's the Shipping Office.' Julie was impressed. It was all much larger than she had imagined.

She sat herself down at the switchboard, more than a little nervous at the prospect of working it, but Miss Marsh's attitude, had she but known it, only strengthened Julie's resolve to master it.

Miss Marsh dragged up a chair beside her.

'These four little silver caps are outside lines – our numbers are City 3456, 7, 8 and 9. Now when it rings, the cap falls down, and you take one of these plugs, there are two, and plug it into the line which is ringing. The second one you plug in where it says HOLD – that ensures that you don't get cut off. Now – above the four outside lines you have twenty extensions, each with a number, and each being the telephone in someone's office. Right?'

She talked so expertly Julie could only imagine how many times she had done it before. But she refused to panic, telling herself that if this girl could do it, so could she.

'Now,' Miss Marsh went on, 'pinned on the side here you have the names and the extension numbers, twenty of them. In your spare time you must learn these by heart. So – if the phone rings and someone wants Mr Roberts who is Extension 14, you plug in here, put the HOLD jack in, then with this little handle ring Extension 14. When he answers tell him you have a call for him and who it is. Only when he accepts the call do you take the HOLD jack out of HOLD and plug it into the requisite number, in this case, Extension 14. Got it? It's really quite simple, any fool can do it.'

70

Julie reminded herself that Ada had said she should act like a lady at all times, so smiled sweetly and made a vow that she would learn it if it killed her.

'The most important thing,' Miss Marsh went on, 'is your telephone manner. You must always be polite. With an incoming call say: "Neville and Sons" and wait. Then: "Will you hold the line, please?" and "I'm putting you through now" – that sort of thing. In other words you make it as pleasant as you can – and never any rudeness.'

At that moment the telephone rang and the silver cap fell down. Julie watched her. 'Neville and Sons,' she sang. 'Mr Seymour? Yes, of course.' And she rang Extension 9 and in the same affected voice said: 'Mr Seymour? Spaicer's for you', then switched the plug to Extension 9. When she had finished, all trace of the polite baby voice had gone. 'When they have finished, the extension cap will fall down and you pull out both plugs. Got it?'

Julie was to learn that filing was Miss Marsh's passion. She was almost fanatical about it. All morning people came through and spoke to her – with post, with queries, with telephone enquiries – and all, without exception, made Julie welcome. The uniformed commissionaire came through several times on errands and winked at her, his white curled moustache and smart peaked cap cutting a very dashing figure.

As she struggled throughout the morning she noticed that Miss Marsh's attitude towards men was very different from that towards women. When, for instance, Mr Gerald came by, she almost simpered: 'Yes, Mr Gerald' to his instruction to see that a letter was sent off at once.

When he had gone, she smirked, 'Oh, did you hear that? He is a card, Mr Gerald.' And when the office manager came by, she almost curtsied. 'Did you have a nice weekend, Mr Cartwright?' While when Mr Seymour gave her a parcel to despatch, she looked up at him, her strange green eyes gleaming, her lips wet where she had licked them. 'Is it urgent, Mr Seymour?'

'Yes, it is somewhat,' he answered, giving her rather a conspiratorial smile.

71

'He's a devil, Mr Seymour,' she said, giving Julie a secret smile.

Julie decided she was quite enjoying herself, and that office work was a sight more interesting than she had supposed.

As the week wore on she became more and more used to the switchboard. It took her three days to learn the rudiments to it, and she began to concentrate on the extensions and to fit each telephone to its user. She was sent up to the export department on errands, finding Mr Seymour in his own office while outside in an adjoining office sat four ladies of indeterminate age. 'Seymour's Harem, we call it,' Miss Marsh said, with one of her strange secretive smiles. Then there was the office boy, Harrison, who gave her sidelong glances and blushed to the roots of his hair whenever she spoke to him.

Three or four young men seemed to find plenty of occasions to wander through the post department, and at the end of the day Miss Boxall came to see her, carrying a sheaf of papers.

'For filing, my dear,' she said kindly. 'How are you getting along?'

Julie liked the little woman with the warm friendly eyes behind the thick lenses. 'Very well, I hope.'

'We've had no complaints so far,' Miss Boxall said, hoping that Joe would approve. He had been in Sweden for the past few days.

By the end of the week, Julie felt she had been at Neville's for much longer than that. She knew most of the staff by sight, particularly a young man from the shipping department who, she knew, travelled up on the same train. He was already on the train when she embarked and she had got into the habit of looking for him, glancing casually around for a sight of that dark smooth head of hair. One day he came through the post room and Miss Marsh looked up.

'Oh, John, would you give this to Miss Winfield?' She pleaded, her lashes fluttering up at him, eyes wide, holding him with her look.

'Yes, sure,' he said, and went on his way.

72

John, thought Julie, so that's his name.

On Friday, making her way home in a crowded carriage, she decided that it had all been worthwhile, that she had enjoyed it, and what's more had been paid for it. She had her pay packet in her handbag, the first money she had ever earned. She couldn't wait to tell Sarah all about it. She would see if she could persuade her to try for a job in the City; that way they could both travel up together.

Julie's exuberance was curbed when she saw her friend's face. 'What's the matter with you?'

'Come in,' Sarah said grumpily, leading the way to her room. 'Everyone's out. How did you get on?'

Julie sat down on the bed, 'Oh, it was fantastic! I really enjoyed it – I've learned about the switchboard, and the other girl, she's about twenty-one – she's a scream. You should just see – ' But she realised that Sarah wasn't listening. she was staring into the mirror absorbed in her own thoughts.

'Come on,' Julie taunted. 'What's wrong? You've got a face as long as a wet week.'

'So would you have,' Sarah said. 'It's all right for you, you're nicely fixed up.'

'Oh, stop moaning,' Julie said, losing patience. 'What's happened?'

'My Aunt Dorrie came to tea on Sunday – she's the one who has a very good job in Regent Street. My father's sister. Done ever so well she has, young Doris, made her way in the world – you'd never think she was born and bred in this house. Not that she often comes to see us, twice a year or so, when she feels like condescending . . .' And she was away, Julie realised, acting again. She took on the mantle of the people she was talking about, accents and all, so that you felt they were right there in front of you. There was nothing Sarah liked more than telling a story.

'Well, she started on about being apprenticed to Swan and Edgar where she had done her training. "I started at fourteen, Sarah, not like the young people today leaving school at fifteen and sixteen, my dear, and a finer training you couldn't have." Look where it has got her, she said. Manageress in a Regent Street store . . . just think, the

73

possibilities were endless. And she went on and on, and there's me standing there like a lemon and no one is asking me what *I* want to do . . .'

Julie felt really sorry for her. It must be awful to have a family who interfered. It was bad enough when parents insisted on their own way.

'So what happened? What did your dad say?'

'Well, he thought it was a grand idea – though Mum wasn't so keen. She can't stand Aunt Dorrie with her snobby ways. "A recommendation from me", Aunt Dorrie said.'

'Is she the one with the big house at Streatham?' Julie laughed.

'No, silly, she's not married – that's Aunt Jane. Aunt Doris lives in Putney.'

'Well, don't keep me in suspense. What are you going to do?'

'I've got an appointment at Swan and Edgar on Monday morning.'

'Oh, Sarah, you haven't!'

'I have, worse luck – and there's nothing I can do about it. The only thing in its favour – and it's not much – is that I shall be working in town instead of locally. That's if I get the job.'

'We could travel up to together as far as London Bridge,' Julie said excitedly, 'then I'd go on to Cannon Street and you to Charing Cross.'

Sarah's expression lifted a little. 'Yes, well . . .'

'But a shop!' Sarah wailed. 'I'd give anything to work in the theatre – or on a newspaper.'

'Look,' Julie said, jumping off the bed, 'get yourself up there and who knows what might crop up?'

'A war, if we are to believe my father. I'm so sick of hearing about this Leicester thing.'

'Oh, they want something to talk about,' Julie said, using an expression she had often heard. 'Anyway, are you coming out? I thought we'd go for a walk through the village.'

'If you like.'

'Come on, then, and I'll tell you about my job. I mustn't be late. Mam's going to wash my hair.'

* * *

74

Ada sat by the fire drying her own hair. A strand or two of grey she had noticed. Well, it was not to be wondered at, she would be forty next year, but that was the least of her worries.

She was more than pleased at Julie's acceptance of the switchboard job. What's more, she seemed to have enjoyed it, and the little bit of extra money would come in useful. It was funny though that Julie had changed her mind so suddenly after all her arguments. Youth, she thought.

On Monday, she decided, I'll spend the money I've saved in Randall's for a new bedspread for Julie. And a warm glow spread through her. It wasn't worth making it, she had so little time with so many orders – thank goodness. She brushed her hair with long strokes while the budgie talked to her in his strange little voice.

'Get away with you,' she laughed. 'You're cheeky, that's what you are.' But she pursed her lips at the cage and he came over to kiss her.

'Good boy,' he said. 'Good boy.'

She combed her hair in front of the mirror, sweeping it back off her forehead and into a bun at the back of her head. There, nice and tidy. No good Julie keeping on at her to have it cut – although sometimes she was tempted. 'Old-fashioned' Julie said. But not everyone had short hair. Think of Olivia Neville with that wonderful chignon she wore, like a gold serpent at the nape of her neck.

'Cut off your hair, cut off your character' her old mother used to say. Dead and gone these last twenty years but she had had lots of sayings ike that, old saws and superstitions that stayed with you long after other things had been forgotten.

Chapter Ten

Olivia Neville came down on this lovely spring morning dressed for the office, and joined her father at the breakfast table.

'Morning, Daddy.' She undid her napkin from its ring and gave him a brilliant smile.

'Good morning, Olivia.' He looked over the top of his newspaper at her, enchanted with her appearance as he always was. She looked positively radiant, as she did quite often these days. Either that or she disappeared into a silent shell. She was either one way or another, quite unlike her usual equable self. He suspected that there was a man behind it all, and he was damn sure it wasn't Douglas Avery.

'You were late home last night,' he said. 'I didn't hear you come in.'

'I know – I caught the last train. We worked until half-past ten.'

'Things are hotting up, aren't they?' He shot her a shrewd glance.

'Mmm.' Her voice was non-committal.

'I've got another late night tonight, so I think I'll stay with Margaret. I'm not too keen on these late journeys.'

'I can't say I blame you. It's nice for us that she can put you up. Your mother and I worry about you travelling home alone.'

'Oh, you mustn't worry about me, Daddy. I'm safe enough – it's just that it saves coming home late two nights running.' She dabbed her mouth with her napkin, got up and went round to the table end, kissing him briefly on his head.

Sitting in the train, she looked out of the window at the rows of grey-roofed houses, this part of London where the journey was so dreary, but saw nothing except the prospect of the coming evening. If she felt guilty, and she did, it was natural. She didn't like lying to her parents but what was she to do? What would their reaction be if they knew she was seeing a married man? The man for whom she worked, a senior Foreign Office official? Her heart turned over with the excitement of it all. The secrecy with which the affair was surrounded, the hole and corner meetings, all added to the spice of it, if it hadn't been so traumatic, sometimes so heart-wrenching and intense that she could hardly bear it. She hadn't wanted it to happen, it had been the last thing in her mind, but over two years the depth of her feelings for Richard had grown more intense, passionate, so that it was a revelation when she knew that he felt the same way.

It was not, she told herself, as if it was an ordinary affair between a married man and his secretary. This one was fraught with serious implications – the fact that he was a Government official of some high rank, for instance. So far it was incredible that they had managed to be alone for even an instant, and the lengths they had gone to to meet, even briefly, had engendered the most complicated of precautions.

Poor Daddy, her mother too, how shocked they would be if they knew.

On arrival at the office, she made her way to the inner sanctum, aware that Richard would not be in until lunch time. Then he had a meeting to attend, so that it would be late afternoon before she saw him again. In the meantime, when she had sifted through the post on his desk, she would have a word with Margaret.

Margaret Dayton, at fifty-four, was almost due for retirement, having been at the Foreign Office since leaving university. Bosses for her had come and gone, but this one, Richard Bannister, was different inasmuch as he was what the junior members of the department called a heart throb. He was, she had to admit, staggeringly good-looking and simply oozed charm – one of the reasons he had arrived where he was today. He dealt with people of all kinds and nationalities with the same smooth, urbane and easy manner. What a good thing, she thought, that he had a simply beautiful wife and family to match, a fact which possibly kept him out of the clutches of designing women for there were plenty of those about. She thanked the good taste and sensibility of Olivia for that. Having two feet firmly planted on the ground, she was not the sort of person to be carried away by someone like Richard Bannister.

It was she who had trained Olivia into this position since the girl had become her personal assistant three years before. Now Olivia had it all at her fingertips – knew how to deal with him, knew the job backwards. She would be a worthy successor to Margaret Dayton, M.B.E.

She placed her reading glasses on her nose as Olivia came in. She never failed to experience a moment of pleasure on seeing the girl, with her clear forehead, wide intelligent eyes, and that wonderful head of red-gold hair. It seemed to light up the room.

'Good morning, Margaret.' Olivia walked over to her desk and put some papers down.

'Good morning, my dear. What's on the agenda today for you?' Margaret asked.

Olivia glanced at her watch.

'I have a meeting at ten, which I suppose will last a couple of hours, Richard is also at a meeting until lunch time, then this afternoon I shall get on with the Foreign Affairs committee – that should take care of my day, I think.'

She smiled at Margaret.

'I'm going to a concert this evening – at the Wigmore Hall.' Margaret said, and Olivia's heart missed a beat. How awful if her parents needed to get in touch with her and found she was not there . . . She made a decision to cease using Margaret as an alibi. She must think of something else.

'Oh, that should be nice,' she said. 'See you at lunch time.' And she left the room to go into Richard's inner sanctum.

She seated herself at her desk, then drawn against her will

glanced across at the photograph on his desk of his wife Rosanna and their two children. At first she had felt guilty whenever she had looked at it; now she had grown to hate this other woman who shared his life, surprising herself with the strength of her emotions.

They didn't get on, Richard said. Never had. It had been a marriage of convenience, Rosanne came from a wealthy family and Richard had had nothing. He was born into a penniless if aristocratic family, inheriting only his personal charm and good looks together with his brain which was razor sharp. Olivia not only admired him, she loved him with all the feeling of which she was capable.

There was a time when she would never have believed any man who told her his wife didn't understand him but Richard was different. How could that wealthy, empty-headed socialite possibly have anything in common with the brilliant Richard Bannister? The two children were all that bound them together – and of course his position, for the slightest breath of scandal would finish his career.

At the end of the day, together they went over the developments of the previous meetings, discussing, arranging – no one looking in on them would have guessed, so circumspect were they both in their behaviour. If Olivia's heartbeat increased somewhat every time she felt herself close to him, an outsider would not have known it. If her pulse rate quickened when she sensed that familiar slightly tangy, manly scent that emanated from him, no one would have guessed. Slightly more difficult had he met her eyes and read the promise in them, but he was careful not to do that. When he closed the door at leaving, with a 'Goodnight, Olivia, Goodnight Margaret', no one would have been any the wiser.

'Who are you seeing this evening?' she asked Margaret, stowing files carefully into their boxes and locking them securely.

'Myra Hess – I can't resist an evening of hers,' Margaret said. 'Why not come with me sometime.'

'I'd love to,' Olivia said, thinking how adept she had become at the throwaway answer. 'Well, I'd better pack up.'

An hour or so later, she was entering the impressive block of flats where Richard had his bachelor apartment. He had had this base since before his marriage ten years earlier, and retained it for when he was kept late at the office and had no wish to return home to Surrey. When his wife stayed in town, she usually stayed at her father's quite palatial home in Brook Street. Rosanna hardly, if ever, visited the establishment, which suited Richard down to the ground.

Now, Olivia let herself in with her own key, and once inside, all doubts and worries and sense of guilt disappeared. Halfway across the room he came to meet her, arms outstretched, engulfing her tightly, then as she raised her lips, bent to meet them. The passion between them shook both to the depths, and wordlessly, as if by mutual consent, he took off her jacket and hat and smoothed the lovely hair, gazing at her as though he couldn't see enough of her.

'My beautiful Olivia,' he murmured against her ear.

She felt as though her body was on fire, but knew the procedure. Richard would not be hurried. He liked to prolong the lovemaking, make the most of every moment, and now, taking her cue from him she sank down into the enormous sofa while he went to get her a drink.

She looked around her at this very male sanctuary with its dark book-lined walls, heavy curtains and large comfortable chairs. There was nothing in the least bit feminine about this room, not a flower, not an ornament in sight, and yet it was impressive, and had a certain charm.

She had been here only once before but knew the rules, waiting until he brought her a perfectly iced martini which he set carefully on the side table before sitting beside her and with a slowly moving finger began to trace the outline of her cheek, her mouth, before moving down to the neckline of her blouse. She accepted the fact that he was an accomplished lover and had had a great deal of experience, unlike herself – she had been a virgin when she first slept with him. This was the fifth occasion she had met him in this clandestine fashion, and each time her anticipation mounted as she recalled the previous occasions they had made love.

She wished it could go on forever like this. Away from

everyone they knew, shielded from outside, together in a world of their own. It was heaven.

Later, in the bedroom, as she undressed before him, he watched her with eyes that were full of love, even adoration. She could not doubt his feelings for her. Every line of his face was dear to her: the shape of his mouth, his nose, the grey eyes, the distinctive black hair which rippled away from his forehead, the eyebrows with their particular set.

His eyes were smouldering now with desire as she lowered herself on to the bed beside him, her long red-gold hair like a cape about her shoulders as he folded her to him.

Later, much later, they lay side by side, exhausted with their lovemaking, delightfully replete, blissfully happy.

Despite making a vow to herself that she would not mention his wife's name, despite trying to bite back the words, nevertheless she was unable to keep silent. It was as if she had to say something, to establish the situation between them. Commonsense told her that silence was golden, she had been trained to keep a still tongue in a wise head, yet she heard herself say. 'Does Rosanna know you are here?' and felt the slight imperceptible stiffening of his body.

He lay, not looking at her, his eyes on the ceiling, but his voice was gentle.

'I thought we agreed never to talk about her – don't spoil things, Olivia.'

She was immediately contrite. 'I know, I know – and I'm sorry.' She kissed his hand. 'I don't know why I said that – she can't make any difference to us. I suppose I just want us to be like this for always.'

'We will, darling,' he said, turning to kiss her, his face looking down into hers.

'I love you so, Richard,' she said.

'And I love you too, darling Olivia,' he said. 'We must make the most of whatever time we have together, knowing as we do . . .'

'Don't!' She pulled him down to her.

One whole blissful night of love, no one to interrupt them, she had him to herself for one whole night. She must be the luckiest girl in the world.

She was up first the next morning, bathed and changed ready to leave for the office. He raised a tousled head and looked at her.

'What time is it?'

'Half-past eight,' she said. 'Time I left.'

She bent down and he dragged her to him.

'Richard! Mind my hair – it takes ages to do up.' But she kissed him fondly. 'Don't fall asleep again, will you?'

Olivia closed the door softly after her. She had a quick breakfast at the hotel on the corner, then hailed a taxi for the office.

It was as if she was taking part in a dream, but the reality was that so much was at stake. Mainly for Richard. Not a breath of scandal must reach the outside world. She had seen her father throw her doubtful looks, sly glances as though he knew she was up to something. Did she look different? Had she changed? She felt different. She would never be the same girl again.

For Richard's sake, she must be seen to be fond of Douglas Avery – ask him for Sunday lunch or the weekend. They were old friends – no more than that on her part. Her parents expected her to marry Douglas, but she never could do that, especially now. And Margaret . . . she must cease using Margaret's apartment as an excuse. What she would like more than anything would be a small flat of her own, where she could be free, where Richard could come and visit her whenever he wished. She would work towards that. Her parents, particularly her father, would be shocked. He liked to have her near him, his beloved only daughter. How could she explain to a doting father that she had grown up? That she had become a woman? A woman in love.

Richard was right. Knowing what they knew – war being a strong possibility – time was precious. Who knew what the future might bring? They must make the most of it.

Chapter Eleven

The rumblings grew more insistent as the summer wore on, although there were not many who thought war was inevitable. There must be another way, they told themselves, and felt that the powers that be would avoid it at all costs, for war would be madness.

'Sandbags everywhere!' Julie reported. 'Outside all the buildings, six deep in some places, and they're putting up large signs saying 'SHELTER', and at the office people came in to measure for black out blinds!' There was a measure of excitement in it for her.

Everywhere there were signs of activity for the war effort. Funny, Ada thought, that she had never really noticed before how many shelters were being dug everywhere. It looked so ominous. All those sandbags . . . Children were being evacuated to the country, whole schools found homes with foster parents – young Valeria Lowman had already gone to Devon, and many a tear was shed at the mainline stations as armies of small children with their gas masks and luggage were urged by their parents to be good and to write. Gas masks were issued to adults and call up began, taking the fit and able bodied men first – and there were many young men who did not wait for that but enlisted as soon as they could.

Every available person was put on war work, there was talk of women being called up for munitions and the services. People made sure their air raid shelters were comfortable inside in the event of a raid, and the larder well stocked in case of seige. There were those who said wild horses wouldn't move them from their house; they would rather die in their beds.

Sarah had secured a job on the haberdashery counter at Swan and Edgar which was turning out to be more interesting than she had thought, her main pleasure being able to travel up to town and back again with Julie. The work, she said, was dead boring, but she thought it better then being at school and a step in the right direction. Also the pocket money was much appreciated.

None of this mattered in the light of present events which took over the entire Lowman household for Tom had come home with the news that they definitely were to move to Leicester.

'I've told you, Eva,' he said patiently, 'we have to go. They'll provide us with a home.'

'In Leicester?' She said bitterly, and Sarah's heart sank. Leicester! Oh, surely not!

There was a silence between them, then they seemed to realise Sarah was there.

'I'll be in the garden,' Tom said, and went out to feed the chickens.

Sarah's mother looked the picture of misery.

'What is it?'

'Well, you heard what your father said. The firm is being evacuated because of the war to Leicester where they think it will be safer. Huh! Your father says we'll have to go. They're taking over a disused factory and building prefabricated homes for the employees with everything provided. All we have to do is to move up there lock stock and barrel for the duration – and the Lord knows how long that will be! I just can't believe it. It's wicked, that's what it is.'

'But we wouldn't all have to go, would we? Valerie? Me?'

'Of course you would, silly. We'd all have to go. How could we stay here with your father up there, with the bombs and everything – besides, what would we live on? They've got you where they want you. They move the breadwinner, and the women have to follow. It's always been the same.'

'And would we lose this house? Gran's old house?'

'It's not ours,' Eva said. 'Its rented. And if we're not here

84

to pay the rent, well, of course, that's that. What are things coming to, I'd like to know?'

Sarah stared out of the window at the Bartons next-door.

'Will they have to go, too? Everyone?'

'Everyone employed by the firm – they think we'll be in the firing line, that's obvious, near the river.' And she shivered.

'Oh, Mum, don't worry.' Sarah had a swift realisation of what her mother must be feeling. 'Perhaps it won't happen.'

'Now isn't that just like you?' Eva said crossly. 'Instead of facing facts, you with your airy fairy ideas!'

One Monday morning in August, and Julie thought the memory would be stamped on her heart forever, Miss Boxall came through the post room with the young man whose wonderful blue eyes Julie had never forgotten. Her heart leapt as he smiled down at her, sitting at the switchboard.

'And this,' Miss Boxall said pleasantly, 'is Miss Garrett, our telephone operator.'

'How do you do?'

'This is Mr Andrew,' Miss Boxall said, 'Mr Neville's younger son. He is joining us and will work in Mr Gerald's room for the time being. We will have another extension put in, but for now you can put calls through to Mr Gerald.'

'Yes, Miss Boxall.' Andrew's eyes met hers, causing a tingle to run through Julie. They moved away and she gave a swift glance across the room to where Miss Marsh sat almost swooning. Her shiny lipstick was wet and she looked up at the newcomer with undisguised admiration, her head on one side like a bird.

'Welcome, Mr Andrew,' she simpered, and Julie turned back to the switchboard impatiently. Silly thing, she thought. Yet he was terribly handsome. Fascinating, she would have said.

It seemed to her, later, that Andrew Neville filled her mind and her thoughts and her dreams. More than once when he came through the post room, he stopped for a word with her, causing her heart to flutter and her cheeks to flush at his near proximity, and whenever she had to ring his extension, his face appeared in front of her as though they were having an intimate conversation.

When she reached home that evening, she found Sarah's mother in the kitchen. The large fruit cake had been sliced and they had obviously enjoyed a cup of tea together.

Eva jumped up. 'Oh, is that the time! I must fly Sarah will be wanting her tea.' She smiled at Julie. 'Your mother and I have just been having a little moan over the war scare, and the children going away. It's a terrible thing when children are sent away from their parents – I don't know what things are coming to.'

She took her coat off the back of the chair. 'I've just been telling your mum about the new places we're going to in Leicester. Built specially for us, so they say, like small prefabs, I expect. But they each have a bathroom, and a modern kitchen. It sounds nice but it's all very well, we're a long way from home. I've never been farther north than Aylesbury, and that was when I was little.' She put on her coat. 'Oh, well, I must fly. I expect Sarah has been complaining about going, hasn't she?'

Julie laughed. 'You know Sarah. But you can't blame her, Mrs Lowman. I shall miss her, too.'

'Of course you will, duck. Well, I must be off. See you before we go, I expect.'

Ada saw her to the door. 'It's a shame,' she said. 'It's not easy to uproot yourself, especially at our age.'

A few nights later on Cannon Street station, Julie awaited her train. At the far end of the platform she could see John Halliday from the Shipping Department, his nose in the evening paper. This morning he had come into the post room to ask her to get a Continental number to Sweden, and he was so shy when he spoke to her that she couldn't help smiling.

'Now then,' Davis the commissionaire had said, his blue eyes twinkling at them, and John Halliday, his ears burning with embarrassment, hurried back to his room.

Davis leaned over Julie's shoulder and whispered, 'I think you've made a conquest there, my dear.'

Now, as she waited, she smiled to herself. They were all very nice at Neville's, even Mr Neville senior, who bobbed his head when he came through the post room, and looked at her as though he couldn't quite make out what she was doing there.

As the days progressed, the news became more ominous, and it was if the world waited, holding its breath. On September the first Hitler marched into Poland, and now there was not much doubt in anyone's mind.

On Sunday, Julie and Sarah were sitting in Julie's bedroom talking about new hair styles. 'Curls are definitely in,' Julie said. 'Everyone is wearing curls.'

Sarah's face brightened. 'Look, I'll show you,' Julie said.

Sarah sat down at the dressing table and Julie began to brush her hair. 'It shouldn lie flat on top and have rows and rows of curls at the back, like Ginger Rogers'. I can't do mine because it's too curly to lie flat, but you're lucky, you could do it. You'd have to put curlers in at night. See, flat on top. Perhaps you could have a perm for the curls. Your hair is lovely and thick, but as straight as a die at the back.

Sarah half closed her eyes and stared back at the reflection in Julie's mirror. she wasn't the Ginger Rogers type for a start. She couldn't sing, but she could act. By golly, she could. And another thing . . . she could write. 'Best-selling authoress.'

'Sarah!' Julie jerked her head to one side. 'Dreaming again, are we?' She put down the brush. 'Listen, why don't we go to the park?'

'Because I am supposed to be going to church, but my mother thought we should listen to what the Prime Minister has to say,'

'When's that?'

'Eleven o'clock.' And Julie made a face.

'I'd better be going,' Sarah said. 'I said I'd be back by quarter to.'

'I'll see you afterwards then.'

Every family sat listening to the wireless as Big Ben chimed eleven o'clock, and when the last peal died away Mr Chamberlain began to speak. Faces were grim, there was no doubt about the gravity of the situation, but when he announced that from midnight a state of war existed between England and Germany, there was a shocked silence. Those who recalled the first world war and the fever of enthusiasm and mounting patriotism, the urge to go and fight, sensed the difference between then and now. this would be a different war, a war that affected civilians and soldiers alike, and the prospect was horrendous. Women and children . . . it was unthinkable. Ada, knowing she must be strong, faced the news squarely.

'Well,' she said, 'that's that. I must say I never thought it would come. . .' Her face was pale and her hand was at her throat.

At that moment, the air raid siren started up, its uncanny wail alerting everyone to danger.

'Under the stairs,' she said. 'Quickly.' Her heart was racing like a mad thing. They bundled under the stairs, the two of them, hunched up, arms about their knees, waiting.

They could hear the roar of planes overhead and instinctively ducked, but after a few moments the 'All Clear' sounded, and never was there a more welcome sound. They got up and went outside where everyone was talking to everyone else, then ducked as a further flight of planes shrieked low over their heads.

'They were ours,' someone said. 'On reconnaisance over the Channel.'

'Oh!' A gasp of relief all round. But would the next ones be ours too?

Life had a sense of unreality about it for the next few days, but on Sunday morning a tearful Sarah arrived at Julie's front door.

'Oh, Sarah.' Julie began to cry too. 'We're off tomorrow,' Sarah said. 'I can't bear it.'

'Oh, it's not the end of the world,' Julie said staunchly, although it seemed like that to her. 'I'll come up and see you.'

'You will?' Sarah brightened. 'Really?'

'Promise,' Julie said, 'Come in and say goodbye to Mam.'

Arms round each other, Julie and Sarah, walked back to the Lowmans' house.

The next day Ada looked up as a large van went by and recognised the removers. She sighed. That would be for the Lowmans. So they were really off. She would suggest tonight that she and Julie went to the cinema. So far everything was open as usual – they would certainly close if and when the air raids started.

Life would never be quite the same again, she thought.

Chapter Twelve

Towards the end of the year the strange sense of unreality persisted, although cinemas and theatres had closed their doors and then reopened them and people flocked in droves to the shows. Anything to escape the outside world. Football and spectator sports were resumed with a limited crowd capacity in order to facilitate speedy exit should the occasion demand. Schools were reopened and many evacuees returned.

Yet behind it all, the wheels were turning, and no more so than in the case of Joseph Neville whose whole business was at stake. With his largest supplier, the German paper and board mills denied to him, he was left with two Scandinavian mills – and who knew how long that would last? He could only be thankful that he had been wise enough to stock pile in the past.

He was under no illusions that a waiting game was being played and laid his plans accordingly. When he was quite certain he was doing the right thing, he arrived at the office on a morning in December.

'Morning, Constance,' he said to Miss Boxall, closing the door behind him and hanging up his coat and hat. 'Tell that pretty little thing out there that we don't wish to be disturbed – I want to talk to you.'

'Yes, Joe,' she said. She could see it was something serious, and picked up the telephone.

'Now,' he said, sitting at his desk, 'I would like your individed attention.'

She waited.

'When this war takes off – and it will, make no mistake about that – we shall be in an extremely vulnerable position. At the moment it's being played like a game of chess . . .' And no one would know more about that than he, Miss Boxall thought, for he played chess every lunch hour at the Gambit in Budge Row with his cronies.

'We are packed like sardines in the City and you can bet Hitler will try to destroy the financial centre as well as bombing military targets and factories. So,' he stressed, 'I plan to get out. Evacuate – it's the only sensible thing to do, no one wants to be a sitting target. Everyone is moving – the big corporations, the banks – they'll leave only handful of staff in the City. Losing the German mills is a blow, but we still have certain obligations to our customers. So what I propose doing is this . . .'

Constance had been wondering for some time what his plans were, but she need not have worried. You could always rely on Joe to do the right thing.

'I have taken the lease on a house in Andover – near the town centre. I propose to move us down there. It's not too far from our home in Hurstbourne – I went to see it this weekend – and it seems most suitable for our purposes. Up to now it has been used by a firm of accountants who moved out when the lease lapsed. I've taken it over and I intend to transfer the business down there – lock, stock and barrel.'

'You had a busy weekend, Joe,' she said mildly.

He was not slow to catch the tonation. 'You'd come with me, Constance?'

She had a momentary glimpse of retirement slowly fading away and thought. What the devil would I do with myself in Essex – wait to be bombed out of my own home? It would be a lonely life in wartime.

'Of course, Joe,' she said.

'Good.' He had never doubted it.

'I plan to move in the new year,' he said, 'and the idea is this. I'd like you to talk to the staff about it and ask which of them is prepared to make the move. Of course it will be a depleted staff, of necessity. Young Andrew is going into the R.A.F. and I am fairly certain Gerald will go into the Fleet Air Arm. That leaves young Halliday who is due to be

91

called up quite soon and four of the other young men who may not think it worth their while to move down there. See what they say. I'd like the two shipping ladies to come – we can't do without them – and of course, any of the export department who may wish to join us. I am not sacking anyone, Constance. It is entirely up to them. Sound 'em out. I know it's a big upheaval, but the circumstances are such that they have no choice. Now, as regards accommodation – there is a self-contained flat at the top of the building, second floor, which you could have except that there are stairs to climb, Constance, and we are not getting any younger.'

She shrugged. 'I'd have to see it.' Somewhere, deep down, there was a slight glimmer of excitement at the prospect.

'There are plenty of cottages, mainly in the districts around, rooms to let, accommodation, bed and breakfast in the area – that would be something to go into. It would need quite a lot of organizing. And, of course, there would be a subsistence allowance.'

She raised her eyebrows.

'Isn't that going to be a bit costly, Joe.'

'Can't do anything else,' he said shortly. 'I've got to keep the business going – it's a family concern – and rather the staff that I know than people I don't.'

'What does Sylvia say?'

'She's pleased, of course. Delighted to be getting out of London. As you know, she's not all that well and the prospect of air raids terrifies her – not unnaturally. We shall be closing the house for the duration of the war. I've spoken to Mrs Jenkins, and this gives her the chance to go and live with her sister somewhere in the country, I believe. We have good help in Hurstbourne, anyway.'

'What will Olivia do?' She saw him frown.

'Stay in London,' he said. 'I suppose her job at the Foreign Office warrants that, although I have a shrewd suspicion that there might be a man at the back of it.'

'What about the juniors?'

'It's up to them. I shall find jobs for all of them if they wish to join us, but no pressure, Constance. it is their choice. I'd have liked Miss Prescott to come with us – she has been with us for so long, and she's a wizard with figures. Oh, and Nightingale – he's a good man. I expect old Davis will retire, and Carwright – hopefully.' They both laughed.

'Why don't you take a weekend down there – this weekend, constance? Stay at The Angel, it's warm and comfortable. Have a look around. You might be pleasantly surprised.'

She might at that, she thought, and her ageing heart began to lift ever so slightly at the prospect.

'You have until Christmas to think about it,' she told them as they stood before her in her private sanctum. Seventeen of them, and she wondered just how many would be prepared to go down to Hampshire.

Julie's heart sank. Just as she had found herself a nice job this blessed war had to come along, but she supposed Mr Neville was right. From what Miss Boxall said the Nevilles would be leaving their home for the duration which meant that Mam would lose a good client, but there was no way she could join them in Hampshire even if she wanted to.

John Halliday caught her up as she was walking to the station.

'Miss Garrett?'

She turned and smiled at him and his heart missed a beat. He felt braver now that they had something to talk about.

'What about that?' he said. 'Were you surprised?'

'Yes, I was,' she said, 'although you can understand Mr Neville's reasons.'

'Will you go?' He strode along beside her, his long legs making light of the distance.

She shook her head. 'No. I couldn't leave my mother. What about you?'

'A lot depends on my call up,' he said. 'If I thought I had enough time, I'd go. Anything for a change. I get bored with the journey every day, don't you?'

'I haven't been doing it long enough,' she said. 'It's still a novelty to me.'

'I've been doing it for five years, ever since I left college.'

'Oh,' said Julie. So he must be twenty-two or -three – just the right age for call up.

'There we are,' he said as they reached the platform and found the train waiting for them. He got in and sat beside her. 'Do you mind?'

'Of course not,' she laughed, removing her gloves and he noticed her beautiful hands with long tapering fingers and glossy nails. He couldn't believe he was sitting next to her.

'Don't you usually go farther down the platform?' Julie asked, as the train rattled on its way.

'Yes, it's more convenient when it stops – but it really doesn't matter. I can walk along.'

They were silent for a time as the train rumbled over the points.

'Is this your first job since you left school?'

Julie nodded.

'And do you like it?'

'Very much, or I did until I realised that it wasn't going to last that long.' And she gave a rueful laugh.

'It may not happen.'

'It will,' she said.

'Look,' he was gaining courage by the minute, 'I know we are both employees, but do you think you could call me John?'

She gave him a ravishing smile. 'John,' she said. 'My name is Julie – well, Juliet, really.'

'I know,' he said honestly. 'I found that out. It's a beautiful name.' And then the train screeched to a halt.

'My stop,' Julie said, gathering up her handbag and gloves. ''Bye, John.'

He watched her go, more than a little in love with her.

Walking home, she thought about him. He was so nice, and so easy to talk to. He had frank honest eyes, she decided, eyes that looked straight at you. Not like someone she knew whose blue eyes laughed wickedly into hers, suggesting all sorts of things . . .'

She hurried. She had lots to tell Mam when she got home.'

*   *   *

94

'Well I never!' Ada said. 'So that's what it's all about. I heard a rumour in the village that they were going.'

Julie looked quite down cast, and Ada became thoughtful. It was strange how she had settled down so well.

'Would you have liked to go?' she said. 'You could, you know – I'd not stand in your way.'

'Mam! As if I would. I couldn't leave you up here with me miles away. Who would look after you?'

Ada laughed. She always loved Julie's sense of humour.

'They've got until Christmas to decide,' Julie said.

'Well, anything can happen before then,' Ada replied. 'I heard today that the schools will be reopening after Christmas.'

'Funny old war, isn't it? All that parting and upset families. Now they're coming home while we are on the point of leaving . . . What a waste of time!'

'Let's hope it stays that way.' Ada said.

Julie went into her bedroom and sat down in front of the mirror. Today at the cut price chemist in Ludgate Hill she had bought a new lipstick called Fire of Flame for six pence. Pouting her lips, she applied the lipstick and licked her lips. It was a rich scarlet – Mam wouldn't approve. She would have to be careful to apply it lightly and add to it when she arrived at the station platform.

Strange how she had seen so little of Andrew Neville since that day, although someone had said he had already joined the Royal Air Force. He attracted her, and she knew the feeling was mutual. Take, for instance, John Halliday – good-looking, tall, nice, but she didn't feel her knees go wobbly when she talked to him. Yet the very mention of Andrew's name was enough to send her heart racing. And much good it will do you, Julie Garrett, she told herself, making a face. Come to think of it, it was time she wrote to Sarah.

In the weeks up to Christmas almost the sole topic of conversation in the office was the removal of the firm to Hampshire. For the duration, they told each other, as if saying the word brought the end of the war nearer. There were some who knew immediately they would not be going. Miss Marsh, for instance.

'Not for me, she said firmly. 'I couldn't move out of London. Besides, I'm getting married.'

There was surprise all round.

'Are you? We didn't know you were engaged.'

'Just because I don't wear a ring,' she retorted.

'Anyone we know?' The shipping ladies were madly curious.

'No, as a matter of fact,' she said archly. 'He's a lawyer, and terribly rich.'

They were very impressed, except afterwards Miss Pettigrew from export sniffed loudly. 'I don't believe a word of it,' she said. 'That girl is a little liar.'

'Gertrude!' they cried, but greatly admired her daring.

Miss Taylor, whose position Julie had taken, left that week. She had found herself a job on the *Daily Sketch* so she had no interest in going to Andover.

Two weeks before Christmas, the firm was surprised by a visit from Andrew Neville, who came to wish them good luck and farewell. He was dressed in his uniform as a Pilot Officer.

Miss Marsh surveyed him, and on the point of leaving the company, said the first thing that came into her head.

'My word, we do look smart!'

Unperturbed, Andrew grinned. 'I'm glad you approve.'

'Very dashing. You'll have all the girls after you, Mr Andrew.'

'I hope so,' he said, while Julie kept her eyes on the switchboard. Show off, she thought. Still, he did look handsome, nevertheless.

He moved towards the switchboard and looked down at her.

'Well, Miss Garrett?' He smiled. Those eyes . . . he had never seen such eyes. Glorious violet eyes – he couldn't tell what she was thinking.

'Are you going to wish me well? I don't suppose we shall be seeing each other after today. You're not going down to Hampshire, are you?'

Julie shook her head.

'No, I don't think so.'

'Pity,' he said.

'Good luck, anyway,' she said, giving him a dazzling smile.

'Thanks' And he walked through into his father's office.

Julie looked after his retreating back, those broad shoulders in Air Force blue – he was quite a hero in her eyes. she rested her chin on her hands. Wouldn't it be wonderful if . . .'

'Day dreaming won't get you anywhere,' the cold clear voice of Miss Marsh broke into her thoughts. 'He's not for you, my dear.'

'Be with you in a moment,' Joseph Neville said to his son as he finished signing his letters. Andrew stood by the window looking out at the dome of St Paul's, thinking hard. My word, but she was an attractive little thing, little Miss Julie Garrett, and he wondered about the possibility of asking her out. It was his last night, after all, and he had thought of giving Ursula Lambert a ring – but although the heartiest of girls and a jolly good sort, a chap wanted a little more than that, a bit of romance. By golly . . . He made up his mind.

'Now, Andrew,' his father's voice broke into his thoughts.

I'll do it, he thought. I'll ask her. She looks as though she might be game for a bit of fun.

Ten minutes later he stood by Julie as she made a switchboard connection, very much aware of the young man at her side and pleased that Miss Marsh had disappeared upstairs to the export department.

She swivelled round in her chair, looking up at him. One look from those eyes quite disarmed him.

'Look,' he began, 'what are you doing this evening?'

Julie's heart leapt although she tried to keep cool. she raised her eyebrows.

'I mean – are you doing anything special?'

Surely he wasn't asking her out? Julie thought. But what else could he mean?

'Well . . .'

'Would you come out with me?' he pleaded, his blue eyes looking earnestly down into hers.

Would she!

'It's my last night,' he said. 'Please.'

How could she resist him? His last night – of course she would. There was nothing she would like better.

She broke into a smile, her cheeks dimpling, eyes smiling up into his as he waited.

'I would love to,' she said.

'You would?' He looked as pleased as punch.

I can't think what Mam will say, thought Julie, but I'll worry about that later.

'That's great,' Andrew said, and meant it. 'We'll go out to dinner. I know a wonderful little place.'

He glanced at his watch. 'Can I pick you up this evening? Where do you live?'

Julie swallowed. She wouldn't have him come and pick her up for anything. Not for him to see she lived at the wrong end of the street – it wouldn't be so bad if it were Sarah's end.

'No, there's no need for you to do that. I'll meet you near the park.'

'Where do you suggest?'

'At the main gate?'

His mind was racing as he found himself already looking forward to it.

'Great. Would seven suit you?'

Julie's eyes were positively shining. She nodded.

'See you at seven then. Don't be late.'

'I won't!' She sat back in the swivel chair. She still couldn't believe it – but what would Mam say? He didn't even say where they were going.

Ada was scandalised.

'Julie! What are you thinking of?'

'What's wrong with going out with him?' Julie's lower lip stuck out, her eyes were mutinous. She knew she was going, come what may.

'It's just not right – that's what's wrong with it,' Ada said, unaware that she had made a joke. 'The employer's son. We all know about that sort of thing.'

'what sort of thing? You know Mr Andrew – you said yourself he was a nice young man.'

'I'm not saying he isn't,' Ada said firmly. 'It's just such a pity that you haven't met someone of your own class – an old school friend perhaps.'

Julie decided to change her tactics, putting on her most appealing expression, adopting a more reasonable attitude.

'Mam, it is his last night before he goes – that's why he's asked me out. Is there anything wrong with that? I think it's a kind of compliment. After all, who knows what might happen? He may never come back.'

She was horrified after she had said it for she hadn't thought of it before in those terms. Now she could see the doubt in Ada's eyes.

She pressed on, taking advantage of Ada's hesitation to press home her point.

'After all, you do know him – it's not as if he was a stranger, is it?'

'Well . . .' Ada was obviously in two minds. 'Where's he taking you?'

'I don't know. Out to dinner, he said.'

'Oh, Julie!' Ada sighed. Already she was wondering what her daughter could wear.

'Julie's eyes began to sparkle. 'Oh, come on, Mam! Don't spoil it. You can trust me.'

'It's not you I'm thinking about,' Ada said grimly. 'And in any case, it's not that I was worrying about.' She looked across at Julie. 'I wouldn't want you to get fond of him and get hurt.'

'Mam, I've only just met him and he's asked me out for the first time – now what's so awful about that?'

'Yes, you're right,' Ada said at length. 'You're a sensible girl and I don't want to spoil your fun – after all, you're only young once.'

Julie ran over and hugged her. 'Thanks, Mam. I'll go up and get ready.'

Ada watched her – she was such an affectionate girl – then smiled as Julie came hurtling back down the stairs.

'What shall I wear?'

After much debating it was decided that she would wear the navy crêpe dress with the leg-of-mutton sleeves which were all the rage. In Princess style, the long narrow cuffs to

99

the elbow edged with tiny buttons, the skirt flared in eight godets, dozens of tiny buttons from neck to hem, the important full sleeves topped by a cut out applique on the shoulders – Ada had seen the dress in a French magazine and copied it. It fitted Julie like a glove, showing off her tiny waist and almost hour glass figure. Over it she wore a matching long fitted coat of navy bouclé with a large fur collar. Once ready, her lovely face emerged from the fur with eyes dancing. Ada bit her lip.

How lovely she was, she had to admit it, the prettiest girl in the neighbourhood.

'Now mind how you go,' she warned, 'and Julie – don't be late. You know I shall worry.'

Julie kissed her. ''Bye, Mam.' She almost ran up the path, a small youthful figure in the blackout, the gleam from her small torch showing her the way. Ada sighed.

It was difficult to see anything in the blackout until one's eyes got used to it, and the high park gates were silhouetted against the night sky as Julie reached them. Parked by the gates was a small sports car, its sidelights just showing with a blue glimmer. The tall dark figure of a man stood waiting there beside it – she just knew it was Andrew.

He smiled into the darkness and took her hand. 'Julie?'

'Hallo,' she said. 'It's me.'

He took her round the other side and opened the door of the small car.

She wouldn't have told him for the worlds but it was the first time she had been in a car – and she knew that if Ada had seen she would have been horrified.

He tucked a rug over her knees, and got in to the drivers seat.

'You're were right on time,' he said, putting the car into gear. 'Right, off we go.'

How on earth did he find the way in the blackout? Julie wondered, as the small car weaved its way in and out of the traffic, not as heavy as going into London at this time of night. He drove expertly. She glanced at the gloved hand on the wheel and a shiver went through her. She wished it would go on for ever. Sitting beside her hero, a pilot officer in the Royal Air Force, it wouldn't be natural if she wasn't overcome with it all. And he was so good-looking – a man, not like the boys she had been to school with.

What, wondered Andrew, was she really like? What sort of girl was she? There was something exciting about taking out a girl you really didn't know. Apart from the fact that she had just started with the firm, and her mother made dresses for his mother, he didn't know her at all. But what did it matter who she was in wartime? she was the prettiest girl he had ever seen, and she looked like a lot of fun.

'Are you warm enough?' he asked suddenly. 'I'm afraid the car is a bit draughty. Still, you're nicely wrapped up.'

'Warm as toast,' Julie said. She had kept quiet, wondering if it was better not to talk to him while he was driving. Down the Old Kent Road and over Westminster Bridge she could see the Thames shining blackly, the lights all dimmed, here and there a red or dark blue glimmer. He drove past the Houses of Parliament and up the Haymarket until, in Regent Street, he turned into a side street and parked.

Locking the car, he took her arm and walked her towards a shuttered restaurant where a subdued lamp shone in the doorway. A hanging sign bore the name 'Le Petit Montmartre'. Inside it was warm and inviting with the delicious smell of French food.

A waiter showed them to a corner booth, the seats hidden by dark red curtains on a brass rail, the seats warmly padded with crimson velvet. Seated across from him at the intimate table for two, with its snow white cloth and gleaming silver, the tiny red lamps showed just enough light for them to see each other.

Julie took a deep breath – it was like something out of a Hollywood film. She met his blue eyes across the table.

'You look simply lovely,' he said. 'And I love your dress.'

'Thank you,' she said. She could hardly bear to look at him. If only he knew how much she had thought about him, dreamt about him. She hoped her eyes didn't give her away.

'Do you realise we know nothing about each other?' Andrew said. 'I don't even know how old you are.'

'I'm almost seventeen,' she said, hoping he wouldn't think she was too young. 'I shall be seventeen in January.'

He smiled as he took the menu from the waiter who appeared by the table. 'Shall I choose for us both?'

'Oh, please,' Julie said fervently, which didn't escape him.

'Is there anything you don't like?'

She shook her head.

'Right, then I think perhaps a small hors de'oeuvre to start, followed by veal – or lamb?' He looked at her.

'Veal, please,' she said, and he handed the menu back to the waiter. She was game to try something different.

'You said this was your last night,' Julie began. 'Where are you going tomorrow?'

He smiled back at her. 'Can't tell you that, I'm afraid, but I am off to do my training – somewhere in England, as they say, although there is a distinct possibility that I may be sent abroad. Canada perhaps.

Julie's heart sank.

Oh, it would be too cruel if he were to be sent far away now, but she smiled brilliantly at him across the table.

'How long have you been in the Royal Air Force?'

'I joined up as soon as war was declared. I had been a member of the Oxford University Flying Club while I was at Oxford so I wasn't new to it all. There was no difficulty in getting into the Force so now I'm about to begin my training. to learn to fly Spitfires if I can manage it.'

Starry-eyed, Julie took it all in. It sounded wonderful and so romantic – except that when the war really started he would be in danger. Her mind's eye saw it all, Andrew in his Spitfire, roaring up into the clouds, engaged in combat . . . She swallowed hard and put all such thoughts to the back of her mind.

'Could be jolly dangerous,' she grinned at him, and he smiled.

'No.' He laughed. 'You'd do the same if you were me, wouldn't you?'

'Of course I would,' she said staunchly.

'Have you ever flown?' he asked her.

What a joke, Julie thought. He might as well have asked if she had been to the moon.

She shook her head, as the waiter arrived with a dish of hors d'oeugvres.

'Help yourself,' Andrew said, and she did so, taking very little, but it was so delicious she went back for more.

'Tell me,' he said, between mouthfuls, 'about you. Your family. I know your mother, I've seen her once or twice – but your father?'

'I haven't a father – he died when I was three,' Julie said, dabbing at her mouth, and he saw the lovely white hands with their oval polished nails. They were beautifully kept.

'I'm sorry,' he said. 'That can't have been easy for your mother – being a widow with a child to bring up.'

'No, but she's wonderful,' Julie said enthusiastically. 'My best friend.'

'That's nice.' He laughed. 'And useful.'

The evening wore on. They laughed a lot, and talked incessantly, and by the time they were ready to leave, felt they had known each other for years.

When they had finished coffee, he glanced at his watch.

'Good Lord, it's almost ten and I expect you don't want to be awfully late.'

Julie, who had wished that the evening would never end, nodded regretfully.

'I promised I wouldn't be late.'

Andrew settled the bill. She wasn't, he thought, quite what he had expected. She was a nice girl – not ready as some of them were for a spree on the town. If he had wanted that he should have asked someone else. She probably had no idea, he thought, how attractive she was to men. Those eyes, that figure . . . they were enough to bowl a man over, and he was conscious of the admiring eyes of the two waiters.

'Come on then.' And taking her hand, he led her out of the restaurant and back to the waiting car.

Oh, it had gone so quickly! Now that it was over, or almost, Julie could have wept. Would she ever see him again? It had been the most wonderful evening of her life.

She glanced sideways at him – his profile, the way his hair grew on his forehead – and, turning, he smiled at her.

'Did you enjoy it?'

'It was lovely,' she said.

As they reached Blackheath Hill and drove along the top road he slowed down.

'Now tell me where you live and I'll drive you home.'

'If you would drop me at the top of Church Lane,' she said.

'Is that where you live?'

'No, at the bottom, but I can walk.'

'You'll do no such thing,' he said, and turned the car down the lane. At the bottom, she put a restraining hand on his arm.

'Here – please,' she said, and coming to a stop, he applied the brakes.

They had not spoken on the journey, each with their own thoughts, but now he turned and kissed her. Her mouth was soft and warm, like the petals of a flower, and he thought with wonder. She is not used to being kissed.

Julie was seized with such a powerful emotion that she could do nothing but break away before she lost her head completely. Oh, this was nothing like the swift snatched kisses on the way home from church . . . Nothing like it at all! She wished he would do it again, and he did, taking his time now. Slowly her arms crept around his neck. He buried his face in the fur of her collar, lost in the wonder of this girl who moved him so strongly. His hand went inside her coat and in a flash she broke away, her face flushed, her eyes dark and mysterious.

'I have to go now,' she said, huddling herself into her collar. 'I've had a most wonderful evening.'

He looked down into her eyes, feeling himself almost lost, then kissed her briefly on her cheek and getting out of the car, came round to let her out.

'Are you sure you won't let me drive you?'

'No, I live just down there,' she lied, pointing across the road.

He put his arms round her. 'Goodnight, Julie – and thank you for this evening.'

'I loved it – every minute,' she said, and on tiptoe, kissed him, a butterfly kiss that lingered long after he saw her disappear into the blackout. 'Good luck, Andrew,' she whispered, and was gone.

She danced rather than walked home, the moon lighting her way, until she reached her front door. Letting herself in, she saw that Ada was busying herself preparatory to going to bed. She put the cloth over the canaries' cage, before turning to look at Julie who she could see was still starry-eyed.

'Nice evening?' she said. 'Where did you go?'

'Oh, Mam – it was simply wonderful.' Julie took off her coat and twirled round, flopping into the big cane chair by the fire.

'Well, you can tell me about it tomorrow,' Ada said. 'Bed now – you've to get up in the morning.'

Julie got out of her chair.

'No good telling you you shouldn't have waited up,' she said.

'Wild horses wouldn't have sent me to bed,' Ada said, seeing her daughter's lovely tousled hair, those remarkable eyes so like her father's.

'Goodnight, Mam,' Julie said, kissing her.

Ada watched her go before putting up the front of the fire and damping it down. It's no good, she told herself, you can't hold on to her forever – you have to let her go sometime.

Chapter Thirteen

No one was more surprised than Julie when the Christmas card arrived from Andrew. A glitter card, with silver words and a church in the snow and a robin – Julie held it to her heart as if it was the most precious thing she possessed, which indeed it was.

'Well?' Ada, said, although she guessed what it was.

'It's from Andrew,' Julie said tremulously. She read again the message inside. 'Hope you enjoyed the other evening as much as I did. Andrew.'

She hadn't stopped thinking about it ever since. She knew now that she was in love with him, head over heels in love with him. It was like nothing she had ever experienced before, but it was hard to realise that in their circumstances probably nothing would come of it. They were from two different worlds, there was a war on, and who knew when he would be back again?

Ada kept a still tongue in a wise head, hoping that in time Julie would meet someone else to take her mind off the boy, but it wasn't easy, with all the young men being called up. Christmas came and went, a quiet Christmas which they spent at home listening to the radio. There was a dance on New Year's Eve at the Assembly Rooms to which Julie went dressed in her first long dress, made by Ada in green taffeta. It had slim shoulder straps and a low backline – she was the belle of the party, but she came home alone.

'It wasn't exactly a hilarious evening then,' Ada said, looking at her.

'It would have been all right if Sarah had been there,' she said. 'I do miss her, Mam.'

'I'm sure you do,' Ada said. 'Is there any chance of her coming down to see us? I've never heard from Mrs Lowman since that first card she sent.'

'I don't even know what Sarah's doing,' Julie grumbled. 'Fine friend she turned out to be, and I've written her ever so many letters.'

'Never mind,' Ada said. 'It's your birthday soon, and we must think up something really special. Seventeen, goodness! I can hardly believe it.'

Julie sat down, chin on hand, staring at the fence that separated them from their next-door neighbour. I'd like Andrew for my birthday, please, Mam, she thought. Just to see him again.

And then it was back to work, her birthday came and went, and Ada bought her a pretty fur hat to match her fur collar.

The office was in a state of turmoil, with everything being packed up or put into store ready for the move to Andover.

'Well,' Miss Boxall said one day as she passed through the post department, 'who is going to look after our post and filing, I wonder?' and looked at Julie from behind her pebble glasses with a twinkle in her eye. Julie felt as though she was deserting a sinking ship.

A few days later the city was filled with rumours of threatened air raids, that German planes were being massed on the other side of the Channel, that they would drop bombs full of poison gas over the big cities and industrial areas. Even the newspapers seemed intent on spreading alarm and despondency. Julie made her way home thoughtfully.

'Mam,' she said, almost as soon as she had taken her coat and hat off, 'I've been thinking. I suppose it's not possible that we could go to Andover, both of us.'

Ada stared at her open-mouthed.

'Whatever do you mean?'

'Well, there's been a lot of talk at the office about air raids – when they come, I mean, and I thought, if and when they do come, we're not going to like living here, are we? Just by the river, in the heart of London, it stands to reason.'

107

Ada still stared at her. Was young Andrew at the root of all this? But with a glimmer of what Julie was getting at was slowing dawning in her mind.

'I mean, we don't have to live here, do we? Aren't we free to live where we like? You could get a job down there – it's country and green. You'd like that.' She could see that the idea was not totally rejected and pressed on. 'I could still work at Neville's – I know they've no one to take over my department.'

Ada was worried. She did hope it wouldn't be seen as Julie following Andrew around – if anyone knew about it, that was. That would be shameful.

'Well, duck, it's not as if you've a good job there. You've only been there a little while.'

'I know, Mam, but I like it, and it's only for the duration.'

Ada looked doubtful. 'Oh, I don't know, Julie – it's such a big step.'

'But it would be something to look forward to – anything to get us out of this place. You don't want to stay here forever, do you?'

Ada sighed. 'Of course not. I thought in a few years, when you're married. . .'

'Oh, Mam, who knows when that will be! Miss Boxall said there are lots of cottages and rooms to let.'

'I wouldn't like to go into furnished accommodation,' Ada said. 'I've got my own home.'

'Yes, I know, Mam, but I could go down first, p'raps, and look about and see what it's like. They did ask me to go. After all, I may not like it.

Ada stood still, biting her lip.

The result of this was that on the following Sunday, she and Julie had a day excursion to Andover. They left Victoria in a Blue Line coach and travelled through the outskirts of London and down into the countryside. Alighting at Andover they were pleasantly surprised at the small country town. There was a cafe open at the top of the High Street where they had lunch. Afterwards they breathed in the fresh country air and Ada's cheeks got rosier and rosier, and soon her eyes were sparkling.

'It's a long time since I went out for the day, it's a real

treat – and it's a bustling little place,' she said as they walked towards the end of the High Street and out on to the main road. There were several large houses given over to offices which filled the description of Neville's new premises, and Julie began to feel the first stirrings of excitement.

'I wonder which one it is? It could be any one of these.'

Then they wandered round the side streets to look at the small terraced houses, and down to the end of one street to find themselves on the edge of the countryside, where a cold azure sky stretched into the distance with nothing but green fields as far as the eye could see.

'Ah,' Ada said. 'It's beautiful – really beautiful.'

Then they looked on the boards in shop windows and saw advertisements for rooms to let and situations vacant.

'There certainly seems to be no shortage of jobs,' Ada said, noticing also that there were scores of young men in uniform strolling about the town. This would be better for Julie – there was more life down here. She glanced at her and saw that her eyes were alive with enthusiasm, at the thrill of doing something different. Well, she thought, South London is not the best place in the world to live, especially in wartime, and we could always go back . . .

Later they had a cup of tea and a home made scone with jam while waiting for the coach to take them back to London.

'Do you really think you would like living down here?' Ada asked Julie. 'It's not like London.'

'I'm game if you are,' she said.

'We'll see,' Ada replied, wondering if she wanted her head examining. They might feel quite differently when they got home.

It was more or less settled when Miss Boxall asked Julie into her office.

'Sit down, my dear, she said. 'I was wondering if you had come to any decision about going down to Hampshire with us?'

'My mother and I went down there on Sunday – just to see what it was like.'

'And what did you think?' Miss Boxall found herself

109

wishing that the girl would go with them. There was something about her that she liked.

'We liked Andover – of course there is the question of accommodation. My Mam would want an unfurnished place – I couldn't ask her to give up her home.'

'Of course not, my dear,' Miss Boxall said. 'I wanted to talk to you for another reason. I think you told me that you know shorthand and typing?' She saw Julie's slight frown.

Ignoring it, she went on, 'You see, I am going to need some help down there, and I was thinking more on the lines of a personal assistant.' Now she knew that she had captured Julie's attention. 'There will not be a switchboard as we have here, just a couple of lines, and the post room will be somewhat depleted, but I thought if you were in charge and gave me a hand when I needed it . . .'

'Yes, Miss Boxall.'

'Does that appeal to you?'

'Oh, yes, Miss Boxall.'

'Well, we had better see what your shorthand is like. Take this.' And she handed Julie her own shorthand pad and pencil.

She dictated a letter, which Julie managed to get down, if not every fast, quite competently. She handed the pad back to Miss Boxall who examined it. 'Can you read it back?'

Julie did so.

'Well, my dear,' Miss Boxall said, 'If you want the job, it is yours. And of course there will be more money in it for you. I suggest you go home to make up your mind and let me know as soon as possible. If you decide to come with us, we will talk about accommodation at some later date. I have to go down next week to sort out a few things, so let me know by then.'

Julie walked home on air, all her feelings of revulsion at doing secretarial work behind her as she made her way home to Ada.

At the end of the week they had finally decided to take a chance on it. Julie would go first with the rest of the firm and get digs in the town with Miss Boxall's help. After that, she would look around for somewhere for Ada to live, although Miss Boxall said she thought unfurnished accommodation was scarce. The firm would be moving at the end of January so there was little time left.

On a bitterly cold February morning, Julie sat in the office of the Citizens' Advice Bureau.

Oh, it was nice and warm in here! She undid her fur collar and took off her fur hat and gloves. The room in the large old Georgian house which had been taken over by the Citizens' Advice Bureau as a temporary measure, was packed with people awaiting attention, while three assistants were run off their feet. This town must be wondering what hit it, Julie thought, what with being crammed full of troops and evacuees and many who had just wanted to get out of London.

The staff from Neville's who had voluntered to come down to Hampshire had been given a few nights' stay in a guest house so that they could look around for digs. Miss Boxall had suggested that Julie go along to the bureau for there they kept a list of addresses of people who were willing to take in boarders.

Mrs Eastman, who ran the bureau, looked up in despair, All these people not yet seen – still, with a bit of luck she would get around to them sometime, and hopefully they would be found accommodation before the end of the day.

Julie wondered how Miss Boxall was getting on.

At that moment she was sitting on the back of the green Hillman motor car which surprisingly had Miss Winfield as the driver. Both Miss Winfield and Miss Sinclair had agreed to be evacuated for the duration – indeed, it was difficult to imagine them doing anything else, for they had worked together at Neville's for almost twenty years.

They had decided to pool their resources and were to see a furnished cottage out at Amport, a pretty village near Andover. Miss Winfield had offered to drive them there, for it seemed she and her brother Edwin jointly owned the Hillman Minx, but now that he had joined up and would probably be sent abroad, his sister had full use of the car.

I hope they get on all right, Julie thought. She had become quite fond of them.

Mrs Eastman looked up at the pretty face of the girl in front of her. She thought she knew exactly where this one

111

would go – she would do very nicely. She took a certain pride in trying to match the applicants to the vacancies.

'Name?' she asked, busily filling in a form.

'Juliet Garrett.'

'Age? Address?' Th questions went on.

Mrs Eastman sat back and sighed. 'So you are staying in temporary accommodation at the Green Door Guest House?' she said, and withdrew a card from a long box and studied it.

'I have a Mrs Newman who lives in Allendale Road out on the Weyhill Road whose daughter has just got married and moved away, leaving her with a spare room. Now I know that Mrs Newman would prefer someone on a fairly permanent basis – she is not all that keen on changing tenants.'

Julie bit her lip.

'I am afraid it would be temporary. My mother is due to move down in a few weeks – well, as soon as she can – and then there would be two of us.'

'I see. What sort of accommodation would you require then? Presumably unfurnished? You would not require meals, would you? You are out all day, I take it?'

'Yes.'

'And would your mother be working?'

'She would have to find a job,' Julie said. 'She is a dressmaker, really, but I expect she would do anything, war work – whatever she could find. She is a widow.'

'I see – and you don't want to be separated,' Mrs Eastman said sympathetically.

Julie smiled. 'Not if we can help it.'

Mrs Eastman seemed suddenly to have an idea. 'Look, leave that side of it with me – I have just had a thought. In the meantime, if you'd like to take this card – ' she scribbled a note ' – and go round and see Mrs Newman and tell her we sent you, and that it will be for a short time until your mother arrives – I am sure she will accommodate you on a temporary basis.'

Julie took the introductory card.

'Go along the main road for about half a mile, and you will find this address on the right. Number eight.' Julie stood up. 'Come back tomorrow and tell me how you got on and I may have some further news for you.'

She put on her fur hat and pulled the fur collar of her coat around her – there was a strong east wind blowing outside. Thanking Mrs Eastman she left the warmth of the office and made her way through the town.

The bitter wind stung her cheeks, it seemed much colder than in London, but she walked briskly until she came to the turning, a row of Edwardian brick villas, each with a tiny front garden. Number eight also had a sleeping dog in the porch, a spaniel who made no effort to bark at her but simply raised his head and nuzzled her hand.

'Well you're a silly old thing,' Julie laughed, patting him. 'I could be about to rob your house.'

But his great brown eyes looked up at her, full of trust, and she stepped over him and rang the bell.

The door was opened by a small dark woman in her early forties, who wore a kerchief around her head and a welcoming smile on her face.

'Good afternoon,' Julie said. 'I've come about the spare room – from the Citizens'.'

'Oh, come in, come in,' the woman said. 'I'm Mrs Newman.'

'And I'm Julie Garrett.'

'How do you do, Miss Garrett?'

The woman shook her hand warmly and invited her into the house.

'Now get down, Tiddles,' she said, pushing a cat off a chair. 'I hope you don't mind, I have three cats and a dog, Noble – he's the one outside.'

Before julie could speak, another cat made its way into the room, sliding itself against Mrs Newman's skirt. She picked him up and hugged him to her and held him against her face. Julie realised that they looked alike – Mrs Newman had the same heart-shaped face, the feline eyes. Where had she heard that cat owners grew to look like their pets?

Mrs Newman put the animal down. 'Now run along, you naughty boy.'

Just as long, Julie thought, as he doesn't climb up on to my bed. She had never lived with cats before.

113

'From London, are you?' Mrs Newman asked, her strange green eyes watching Julie.

'Yes.'

'Well, I'll show you the room. My daughter got married two weeks ago – such a lovely girl – you'd have to go a long way to find someone as beautiful. And lovely with it, you know what I mean? Lovely nature. He's a lucky young man, I can tell you. In the army, so they've moved away. I can't tell you where – everything's secret nowadays, isn't it? My husband's in the army – a Captain – based in . . . but there, walls have ears. Be like Dad, keep Mum.'

By now they had reached the top of the stairs and Julie was shown into a room with pink walls, pink bedspread, and a pink rug on green lino.

Mrs Newman banged the bed.

'It's very comfortable,' she said. 'Here, sit down, you'll see.'

Julie did as she was told, and nodded. 'Yes, it is.'

'When would you want to move in?' Mrs Newman asked.

'At the end of the week – but I have to tell you, Mrs Eastman said, that it would be temporary. My mother is coming down soon, and we should want to be together.'

Mrs Newman looked worried. 'Well, you can't both sleep in that bed,' she said, looking at it.

'No, of course not, but if I could stay until we get something fixed up, I would be very grateful.'

This seemed to mollify Mrs Newman. 'Didn't she have anyone who wanted a longer stay?'

'I really don't know.

Mrs Newman sighed. 'Oh, well, we'll have to settle for that then. Now, about terms . . .'

They went downstairs, and into the kitchen where Mrs Newman put the kettle on. 'I daresay you'd be glad of a cup,' she said. 'It's freezing outside – my washing near froze on the line – but you look warm enough in that fur.'

She disappeared and returned with a photograph album.

'Here, you be looking at that while I make the tea. You'll see what I mean – isn't she lovely, my Barbara? I've a son, but he's only fifteen. I work at the hospital three days a week, so I've not a lot of time – would you require meals?

Julie remembered Ada's admonitions to get somewhere where they would cook for her in the evening, and looking down at all the empty cat saucers and dishes, wished there was some way of getting out of it.

When she didn't answer immediately, Mrs Newman busied herself getting the cups and saucers.

'We'll just muck along somehow,' she said. 'It'll be a bit of give and take, I expect. Oh, lovely, where did you come from?'

Her voice had sunk to a low-pitched croon, a sort of lullaby, as she picked up a tortoiseshell cat who eyed Julie triumphantly. 'Whose Muzzer's baby then?' she crooned, her strange eyes full of love and warmth. Julie buried herself in the album – no wonder Barbara got married, she thought, seeing a pretty girl with a soft, petulant mouth standing beside a good-looking young man.

They sat and drank tea while Mrs Newman told her Barbara's life story until Julie said it really was time that she went. Having discussed terms, they parted on a friendly basis and Julie walked back to the guest house where over the evening meal they had a good laugh over their various activities and successes.

The next day she went along again to the Citizens' Advice Bureau where she waited her turn to see Mrs Eastman.

'Now, my dear, I think I mentioned to you yesterday that I might have something in mind for you and your mother? I am not going to say without seeing her that this would suit, but I will tell you the circumstances. An elderly lady who is confined to a wheelchair has a large house not far from the town centre. It is a beautiful Georgian house with lots of rooms, and as I expect you know, people with spare rooms have to take evacuees. It really is not suitable for children, for Miss Farquarson, that's her name, is a spinster, and neither does she want to take men boarders . . . I can see you have some doubts, but bear with me.'

She smiled at Julie. 'She has a resident nurse/housekeeper who looks after her, and a daily woman who leaves around four every afternoon. I understand there are two rooms which she could let, and I wondered if you and your mother would be interested? Of course, she would have to see you both and it may not be what your mother is looking for, furnished accommodation, that sort of thing.'

Julie was becoming more interested as Mrs Eastman went on.

'Now – there are snags, as there always are. Miss Farquarson has a nephew who lives with her normally but at the present time he is in the navy and so almost always away. The other thing is that she is difficult – she is crippled with arthritis which makes her somewhat irritable as you may imagine, but she is also keen to do her bit for the war effort. It seems to me between us we might work something out, although I have to say I have sent two people along already and she has refused both of them.'

'Oh,' Julie said. Nothing was as easy as it appeared to be. 'It doesn't sound very hopeful, does it?'

'No – but you never know. You would have a lovely home there if things worked out, and you can but try. What do you think?'

'I can't speak for my mother, and she might not like the idea, but I will let you know.'

'If you would, dear. I am anxious to get Miss Farquarson settled. I have known her since I was a small girl and her bark is often worse than her bite. Another thing, there would be two of you, and I would have to prepare her for that, but if you think your mother might be interested let me know, and I will arrange for an interview.'

Ada came down on Friday morning at the start of her weekend while Julie was at the office. Reporting to the bureau, she was interviewed by Mrs Eastman and given instructions how to get to Flag Walk. As she walked through the churchyard she couldn't help wishing that everything would go well. She had missed Julie, and couldn't wait to get down her to be with her. The more she saw of Andover town, the more she liked it. It had begun to feel like home. Flag Walk was an enclave on its own, with Georgian houses and a paved sidewalk. Opposite was a small park behind iron railings, probably part of someone's estate, and when she reached number four, with its beautiful front door and polished brass knocker, she took a deep brath and pressed the brass bell.

A woman answered the door and ushered her through a cool hall to a reception room where she knocked on the door and went in.

'Mrs Garrett, Madam.'

'Show her in.'

The voice was deep and mannish, and Ada found herself confronted by a woman in a wheelchair who was eyeing her fretfully, a decided frown upon her face.

'Good morning,' Ada said and faced the woman coolly. No one ever intimidated Ada.

'You are very young,' Mrs Farquarson said.

'I am thirty-nine next birthday,' she said. 'A widow – and I have a daughter, Juliet, who works in Andover.'

'I thought they said you came from London?'

'We do, but my daughter has been evacuated down here with the firm she works for, and I would like to be with her.'

'So I suppose you would want to bring her too?'

'Of course,' Ada said. 'I am not interested in the accommodation otherwise, Miss Farquarson.'

'Are you not, Mrs Garrett?' And Ada caught a slight Scottish accent.

'How do you earn your living?' Miss Farquarson asked.

'I am a dressmaker by trade, and I should need to carry on with that.' And Ada felt a sudden compassion for the woman who lived in this beautiful house and yet was tied to a wheelchair.

Through the window she could see a delightful garden with a river flowing through and on the bank a cluster of ducks. Her heart surged. Oh, how wonderful it would be if only it would work out.

'Please sit down,' Miss Farquarson said, and Ada felt she had not been entirely rejected.

Miss Farquarson examined the report she had been given and looked up. 'You realise that the accommodation is furnished? How would you feel about that? I suppose you have your own home in London.'

'Yes,' Ada said. 'If I – we – came here I would close it up – for the time being. It would depend how long I could afford to do that.' How long the war lasts, she wanted to add.

'Your daughter – how old is she and what does she do?'

Ada explained, and thought how removed this woman seemed to be from all that was going on in the outside world, yet she had a feeling that whatever was going through Miss Farquarson's mind, when the interview came to an end, she was going to agree to the idea.

'You would have to share the kitchen with my housekeeper,' she was saying now as Ada dragged her eyes away from the garden where the mother duck was leading her five little ones down to the water's edge.

'Yes, of course, I understand.'

Miss Farquarson looked up sharply.

'Do you like gardens?' she asked, her troubled eyes on Ada's serene face.

'Yes. I do. Although I've never seen one as lovely as this,' Ada replied truthfully.

'No, well, you wouldn't in London,' Miss Farquarson said, thus dismissing London and all that it stood for.

At the end of half an hour, Ada stood up, the interview over. A rent had been agreed upon, rules made – not to be broken, mind, said the lady of the house. No young woman coming in late and waking the whole household, and no men visitors. And she would like to meet Miss Garrett without further delay.

Ada walked back to the town, her head in a whirl. There would be difficulties, of course there would, she was used to her own home. But what an opportunity. She hoped Julie would like it half as much as she did.

Miss Farquarson seemed to see in Julie all the things she would like to have been. Far from being envious of the young girl, her youth and beauty, she seemed to regard her as the daughter she had never had.

'Now you and your mother must make yourselves at home,' she said. 'I suggest you take the single bed from one room and put it alongside the bed in the large room and make the smaller room into a sitting room. It overlooks the garden – I have a feeling your mother would like that. Now, child, you must come and see me sometimes – I like someone to talk to from time to time and I like to hear what

118

is going on in the outside world, however miserable it appears to be.'

'Thank you, Miss Farquarson,' Julie said, delighted with the turn of events. She felt she could put up with almost anything herself, but she did want Ada to be happy. It was quite a wrench at her age to move away from her roots.

'Well, Constance,' Joe Neville said, coming into the office a week later, 'how is it going?'

'Remarkably well,' she said. 'We have all got fixed up – some of us in the most unlikely places, but I am sure with a bit of luck it will work out.'

'I noticed how nice the reception area looked when I came in. She's a pretty little thing, Miss Whatsername – is she settling down?'

'Indeed she is, and she works well – and listens which is more to the point.'

'I like the touch of the flowers – a vase of daffodils in the entrance hall.'

'Yes, it was her idea. Apparently the garden where she lives is full of them and her landlady suggested she take some to the office. Wasn't that nice?'

He smiled at her. 'Yes, Constance.' He rubbed his hands together. 'I think I've done the right thing, coming down here.'

'I'm sure you have,' she said. He very seldom made a bad move. 'How is Olivia settling down in her new apartment?'

'Tickled pink,' he said. 'Of course, it's only a one-room flatlet. Still, it's all she needs – although I have to admit, Constance, at the first sign of raids, I hope she'll come down here. I don't like the idea of her being up there on her own. So that's the three of them – Andrew in the Air Force, Olivia at the Foreign Office and Gerald about to go into the Fleet Air Arm. I wish I was young enough to go myself . . . still, I did my bit in the last war. The war to end wars, Constance, if you remember.'

'I do indeed,' she said grimly.

'Well,' he said, 'let's get on – I'll have some letters presently. I'll just pop upstairs and see everything is in order. By the way, a cup of coffee might be a good idea.'

'Yes, Joe,' Constance said. It really seemed much more domesticated down here than it had in London.

'Good morning, Miss Garrett,' he said as he passed through Julie's office. 'Everything all right?'

'Yes, thank you, Mr Neville.'

Goodness, he had remembered her name . . .

Chapter Fourteen

Eva Lowman stood surveying the living room of the new bungalow. Together with many others identical in size and shape, the house was in a development provided for families evacuated from London who had worked in Tom's factory. Essential work for the war effort necessitated such drastic steps, it was important that production could go on, unhampered by air raids. They weren't pre-fabs, Eva decided, more like small one-storey dwellings, but brand new which was something in their favour.

Hardly anyone who had come up from London had lived in a new house, and these were brand spanking new – basic but new. There was a kitchen with a gas stove and a free standing boiler that used gas to heat the water, which was one improvement to say the least. The floors were concrete and tended to be cold but by now almost all the new occupants had bought linoleum to cover them. There were two bedrooms, one at the front and one at the back, and joy of joys, a bathroom. This alone made the move from London worthwhile. A rather lethal-looking geyser sat on one wall, but once you were used to it, it was fine. Eva never tired of cleaning the bath and the sink, seeing her reflection in the bowl as she polished the taps.

The sitting-room furniture was another matter. Sarah wondered if if they would ever find the room in the same order as the day before. You might be sitting by the window one day and by the door the next, but at least the move had enabled her mother to play at moving around to her heart's content.

Another advantage was that the new residents had formed a club and the women took turns to help out at the local Red Cross. There were knitting bees, women providing teas and cakes at the local canteens. All in all, life had taken on a new momentum.

For Eva, the greatest comfort was having Valerie back home. She had joined the local school and had settled in, delighted to be home again after a sojourn as an evacuee in Devon. Another advantage the Lowmans had discovered was that after living in London, social life was very different up here. Whereas Tom might go for a pint of bitter in his local pub at home, up here it was more a social event for the wives went too. The pubs were enormous and friendly, bearing little resemblance to the dark, small interiors of some of the old London pubs. On a Saturday he and Eva would stroll down to their nearest public house, and spend a pleasant evening with their friends who had been moved up with them. Secretly, Eva wondered whether she would ever want to return to the old life.

Sarah took advantage of her parents' preoccupation with the move to concentrate on her future. After they settled in, Eva suggested that she went into the city to sign on at the local Labour Exchange, so Sarah found herself free to wander about and take in all the local colour.

She loved this new freedom. With Valerie home again, the spotlight was removed from herself, and on a venture into the city, she answered an advertisement for a junior in a local newspaper, deciding if she got it she would worry about the rows at home later.

She was a little disappointed at the interview for she was seen only by the assistant editor who ogled her. Since her only experience of newspapers was from Hollywood films, she'd imagined the office would be one long bustle of men wearing green eyeshades and the offices hung with low green lampshades.

It looked almost casual though the assistant editor eyed her with more than a fatherly interest. Sarah decided she could cope with that.

'Why do you want to work on a newspaper?' the man asked.

'I want to write,' she said.

'You mean be a reporter?'

'Yes,' Sarah said, although she meant no such thing. But to get a foot in the door.

'Well,' he said, 'we all have to start somewhere. Here you would be a general dogsbody, fetching and carrying, at everyone's beck and call basically. Do you think you could do that? Is that what you want?'

Poor little bugger, he thought. Her head full of big ideas, just up from London, she was in for a few disappointments.

'I can do shorthand and typing,' Sarah said, loathing herself for admitting it but needs must.

'I don't suppose you'll get much chance to use that,' he said, 'but if you're willing to start at the bottom and learn, you'll do all right.'

'You mean I can have the job?' Sarah asked. She couldn't believe it. It had all been easier than she imagined. Wait until she got home and told her parents – but that might be another story.

Eva stood, horrified. 'Just wait until your father gets home!' she said at length, running out of words. What did you say to a girl of almost seventeen who stood there, her blue eyes firmly meeting yours, adamant, resolute? Oh, who would have daughters!

Sarah came out of her bedroom to face her father who had been primed by Eva. He took a deep breath, knowing that he couldn't please them both.

'What's all this then?' he asked, facing his beloved daughter and trying to look as stern as a father should. He secretly admired her for daring to go against her mother.

'It's just a job, Dad,' she said. 'A job on the local newspaper – *The Leicester*.'

'Doing what?'

'You may as well ask,' Eva said grimly, standing with her arms folded, her mouth in a straight line.

'Just office work, Dad. Fifty shillings a week – it's not bad.'

'It's not the sort of place a daughter of ours should be working in,' Eva said. 'A newspaper office.' And she clicked her tongue.

'Why not?' Sarah said coolly.

'It's just not suitable,' Eva said, for in truth she really didn't know why. It just didn't sound right. You could imagine all sorts of funny goings on working in a newspaper office.

'It's what I want to do, Dad,' Sarah said, and he looked at her helplessly. He had no reason to prevent her, if that's what she wanted to do.

'Look, Eva.' He turned to his wife, and saw how unhappy she was, and then to Sarah who looked so determined. Sarah won.

'I don't see the harm in it,' he said, and Sarah's eyes began to sparkle. 'If that's what she wants, let her give it a trial – she might not like it.' But Eva had turned on her heel.

'It's always the same. You spoil her,' she said. 'Giving in to her.' And she left them both staring at each other as she slammed the door after her.

'Thanks, Dad,' Sarah said, but he had gone, hurrying after Eva in an effort to make the peace.

Well, her mother had been right in one way. It wasn't much of a job, and working in a newspaper office was certainly not the glamorous life she had imagined. From taking the tea round to running errands, a bit of proof reading, helping out the crossword man, checking the facts, cutting out the pictures, endless filing in an office full of cigarette smoke. One day she wrote an article on what it was like to leave London and be evacuated to the provinces, and submitted it to the assistant editor.

The next day he handed it back to her. 'Very good, dear,' he said. 'Shows promise. I'm afraid we can't print it, we don't have room for that sort of thing. Still, keep trying.' And Sarah, hating his silly leering face, stormed back to her room.

Things began to look up when she saw a poster advertising an amateur dramatics production at the local hall. 'The Importance of being Ernest', Thursday, Friday and Saturday. When her parents went on their Saturday evening jaunt, she bought a ticket for the show.

She was carried away, totally. I could do that standing on

my head, she thought. Reading the programme, she saw that 'NEW MEMBERS ARE WELCOME'. Wasting no time, she went backstage to see the Stage Manager after the show had ended. She found a party going on, and hung about until someone found Charlie Dawson, for it seemed he was the person she wished to see.

'Can't talk now, dear,' he said. 'Come and see me on Monday – that's the next meeting – and we'll give you a run through then. Eight o'clock at Hostler's Barn – that's where we rehearse. You'll find us round the back. Come through the kitchen.'

Well! Eyes like stars, Sarah walked home. This was more like it.

On Monday evening she arrived at Hostler's Barn at ten minutes to eight, and found a group of people in the kitchen drinking coffee.

'Oh, you're Sarah – Charlie said you'd be coming. Here, have some coffee, he won't be long.'

She was called into the large hall which was used for rehearsals some ten minutes later, and found Charlie Dawson waiting for her.

He was a little man with a balding head, sharp eyes behind rimless glasses, but a good voice, clear and strong with no trace of an accent.

'Sit down, dear,' he said, 'and don't be nervous. I'm not going to eat you.'

Sarah took a deep breath. He handed her a book, open at a speech. 'Read that, will you?'

Sarah did so. He said nothing but handed her a script. 'How are you on regional dialects?'

She shrugged and smiled at him, and he asked her to read from the page he had indicated. It was a North Country comedy and she read it with an accent. He looked at her approvingly.

'You have just received a letter from your mother to say that your brother has been killed on the battle front. I'd like you to read this, and show me your natural reactions.'

This was just the sort of thing Sarah loved, she had done so much of it at school, and now she put her heart and soul into it.

'Well done!' he said at the end of it, and was not surprised to see real tears in Sarah's eyes.

'I'll put your name before the committee for their approval, which I am sure we will get, then welcome you to the Hostler's Dramatic Society. Mrs Turner will tell you about the subscription and the date of the next meeting, which should be next Monday at eight, when we shall be reading Barrie's "Twelve Pound Look" – we are doing a festival of one act plays. We meet on Mondays, and Thursdays are rehearsal nights, concluding with the Friday and Saturday before the show goes on.' He held out his hand. 'Welcome to the best dramatic society in the county.'

Sarah almost ran home, she was so excited. Wait until she told them what she had been up to! Nothing could stop now, she was on her way.

Eva listened to all this with mixed feelings, a strong sense of disapproval of anything to do with the stage, and pride at what Sarah had achieved. For heaven's sake, if that would satisfy her, then no harm would be done.

It was no surprise to anyone on casting night when Sarah got the part of Sir Harry's wife in 'The Twelve Pound Look'. Small part though it was, she registered, and although there were one or two sulky faces, no one minded too much for she had only a few lines to say.

'Well!' Eva said, speechless, while Tom couldn't wait to get to work the next day and tell them all about it.

Sarah attended every rehearsal assiduously, was word perfect, and when the final rehearsal took place in the hired clothes from the theatrical costumiers, the producer knew he had made the right choice.

In her lovely satin Edwardian gown, with the narrow elbow-length sleeves edged with deep lace, the low-cut neckline showing off her fair skin, her hair smooth as silk, everyone in the audience was riveted. It helped that Sir Harry himself was a fine character actor who had had experience on the London stage, and Tom and Eva in the audience couldn't take their eyes off her.

There was enormous applause as the curtain came down.

After the next two plays by other societies the adjucators made their choice, and it was no surprise that the Leicester

Players won with 'The Twelve Pound Look.' Sarah's picture was published in two Leicester papers.

'No end to your talents,' the assistant editor said with a sneer. He found it difficult to forgive her for the way she brushed off his attentions, but she was past caring now for she had other plans. The small success in the amateur dramatic world had only served to ignite the fuse that was already there.

She cut out her press notices and cuttings and photographs, and stuck them in a new large exercise book. That'll do for a start, she told herself.

She became friendly with Ruth, a girl in her early twenties who was a leading light in the dramatic society. It was Ruth who advised her on make up, had indeed made her up for the festival play, and gave her a gift at Christmas of some Leichner stage make up. With large sticks of five and nine, as she called them, she taught Sarah how to age and where to put the shading and the lines.

Sarah was fascinated, and more determined than ever to start a theatrical career, but how was she to do that? Giving it a great deal of thought she came up with a plan. If she could join a repertory theatre, in any capacity, she would have made the transition from office girl to the stage.

But first there was the Easter production to be dealt with.

'There is no reason,' Charlie Dawson told them, 'why we shouldn't carry on and plan for an April production. If we lose members of the cast, then we shall replace them – it will take more than a war to close us down. Are we agreed?'

Much clapping and cheering from the members, together with some stamping of feet. Sarah was delighted. She would hate to give it up now.

'So, with that in mind, the committee has decided to put on Bernard Shaw's "Pygmalion".' There were gasps all round.

Sarah was delighted. She could see herself now as Eliza Doolittle. She caught the eye of a girl who was furious at not getting the part of Sir Harry's wife in 'Twelve Pound Look.' She almost knew what the girl was thinking. The Cockney character of Eliza Doolittle – who was going to get that then? It was fairly obvious Charlie would give it to

127

Sarah Lowman, as obvious as it was that she was his favourite. Even though his taste didn't run to girls . . .

Sarah walked home on air. It was all decided, fate had come down in her favour. She was quite certain that she would land the part of Eliza – she daren't think otherwise – and after her success in that, her parents, or at least her mother, could not possibly deny that she had a stage career in front of her.

Anyway, they had done it at school, and she had done Eliza then so she almost knew it backwards. Yes, the Leicester theatrical fraternity was in for a treat. She would give it all she had – and that was considerable. Who, she wondered, would get the part of Professor Higgins?

They would see. In the meantime she pushed open the front door to find them all sitting round the fire, listening to the radio. They looked up, seeing her rosy face and shining eyes.

Living up here certainly agreed with her, Eva thought, and it had been a good thing to get away from South London – they said it was terrible down there now. Nothing but sandbags and barrage balloons and shortages and closed entertainment halls.

No, it had certainly been a good move to come up here.

Sarah took off her hat and shook her hair.

'We're doing a production of "Pygmalion" for Easter,' she said.

Eva looked up from her sewing. 'Is that good?' she asked.

'Oh, Mum!' Sometimes she was appalled at Eva's ignorance. 'It's only one of the most famous plays in the world,' she said patiently.

'Oh,' Eva said in a subdued voice. 'Will you get a part in it?'

'I certainly hope so,' Sarah laughed. 'Goodness, I should hope so.' And humming one of the latest songs, she went off into her bedroom she shared with Valerie.

Tom Lowman looked up from his seed catalogue.

'What did Sarah say?'

'She expects to get a part in the next production of something or other.'

'Of course she will,' he said confidently. 'Of course she will.'

Chapter Fifteen

'So you are quite happy with your little pied-à-terre?' Joe Neville said to his daughter Olivia as they sat by the fire in the drawing room of the cottage in Hampshire.

'It couldn't be more convenient,' Olivia said, feeling guilty in the knowledge that now she had a place of her own she and Richard could do as they pleased.

'I think,' she said carefully, 'from now on things will begin to hot up in the air war – or so I understand from the pep talk we had before I left on Friday.'

Joe Neville looked serious. He knew, although she was his daughter, Olivia would never betray any confidential confirmation that might be passed on, even accidentally.

'There is no sign that you might be sent away, is there? I would have thought your branch – '

'Some of them have gone but my department is to stay put, at least for the moment,' Olivia said.

'Well, you be careful,' he growled.

'Oh, Daddy!' Olivia laughed, and glancing at her, seeing the shining eyes, the way she looked these days, he was more than ever sure that she was in love. No one could look as radiant as she did unless there was a lover in the background somewhere. What worried him was why she had never told them about him. What was so secret about this love affair? She never mentioned Douglas these days, never said if she had heard from him, for Douglas had been one of the first to go, and was probably even now somewhere in France.

He was just about to ask her, casually, if there was a

special friend she would like to bring down the next time she came, but something stopped him. She was staring into the fire, a secret smile on her face, absorbed in her own thoughts – he wouldn't interrupt her. You couldn't help worrying about a daughter, they were so much more vulnerable than sons. He thought about Peggy, Gerald's wife, pregnant with his first grandchild, who had gone down to Devon to be with her parents. He didn't blame her. With Gerald away in the Fleet Air Arm, there was nothing to keep her in Kent, a very vulnerable area.

And now here was Olivia, his pride and joy, driving herself back to London to live in that minuscule flat – what did she do with herself in the evenings and most weekends?

She kissed them both warmly.

'Don't overdo it, Mummy – and don't worry!' She smiled. 'I'm perfectly all right, really.'

'Bye. Take care,' they called from the cottage door.

Olivia sat back, easing her fox furs for the short ride. There, that was that. Another duty visit accomplished. How boring life must be for them when you compared it with hers. Already her heart was beating in anticipation. Would Richard be there to meet her at the flat? He had a key. She never knew when he would turn up. She could only hope . . .

She turned the key in the front door and knew in an instant that he wasn't there, fighting down a keen sense of disappointment.

She pulled the curtains and turned on the gas fire – really it was a homely little place, and her very own, for the time being at any rate, for she had rented it on a yearly basis.

Going into the bathroom, she undressed and got ready for her bath. It was lovely to be free to do as one liked, to take leisurely baths, to eat when one liked. No pressures, she was as free as a bird, except that Richard held her heart captive. It she had been told that she could feel like this about any man, she would not have believed it – until now. Richard was her life. Without him . . . well, she couldn't imagine life without him.

It was nine-thirty and she sat in her silk dressing-gown on the sofa by the fire reading, then glanced towards the door as her heart made the familiar jump at hearing the sound of a key in the door.

Richard! She got up at once and went towards him as he came in; his familiar face, his lovely smile, the manly scent that seemed to emanate from closeness to him. 'Oh, Richard!' She flung her arms around his neck as he caught her to him, kissing her deep and long, feeling the soft, silky stuff of her dressing gown beneath his fingers.

He drew away from her, looking at the red-gold hair around her shoulders which seemed to have a life of its own. He buried his face in it. 'Olivia, you can't know how good it is to see you.'

She lifted her face to his and drew his head down. 'Don't talk, just love me.'

Presently he took off his overcoat and threw it over a chair, loosening his tie. Looking up at him, she undid his shirt buttons and removed his jacket while he watched her, his expression enigmatic. 'You're insatiable,' he said at length.

'Am I?' Her gold-coloured eyes looked deep into his. She slipped the dressing gown from her shoulders and stood before him in all her glory, never taking her eyes from his face.

He looked at her from top to toe, then caught her to him as they sank down into the cushions, their passion for each other overwhelming them. She never ceased to marvel at his power over her – like this, he could do anything. Pleasing him was all she wanted, and in doing so experienced physical pleasure she had never dreamed possible.

Much later, when they emerged from their idyll and Richard was in the shower, she prepared supper in the tiny kitchen. Two-thirty and she was deliciously tired. Like this, it was as if they were married. It was a game she played often, more and more as time went by.

He came in, standing behind her and putting his arms around her waist.

'I love you, Olivia,' he said, kissing the lobe of her ear.

What wonderful words, she thought. She had no doubt in her mind that he meant them and could even feel it in her heart to feel sorry for his wife. How much she was missing, not to have the love of such a man.

He waited until they were getting ready for bed before he told her the news which he knew would please her.

'Rosanna is taking the children to the States.'

Her eyes widened with delight.

'Richard! Why didn't you tell me before?'

She came round to his side of the bed and kissed him. 'Oh, darling, how wonderful. For how long? I mean, is she staying?'

'No, I'm afraid not. She's taking the children to California, some relative of her father's – for the duration. I'm pleased they are going, I shall feel safer in my mind when they are there, but of course after a brief holiday she will be back. About two to three weeks, I expect.'

'But even so – that's wonderful.'

She lay beside him as he slept peacefully. She wished Rosanna would never come back. Never. Richard belonged to her. Rosanna was a wife in name only – didn't she realise that?

But for the moment he was hers. She turned over towards him, and put her arm across him as though to bind him to her. He stirred in his sleep, and she soothed him. Better to make the most of it while they could. Who knew what would happen in this ghastly war?

In the cottage down in Hampshire, Joe Neville couldn't sleep. He had tossed and turned in the single bed next to his wife's since coming to bed – it surely must be daybreak. These days with thick black out curtains it was difficult to see what time of day it was. He glanced at the luminous dial of the bedside clock. Three-thirty – still time to get some sleep.

'Can't sleep, Joe?'

It was the voice of his wife, Sylvia. She always slept badly so it was no surprise.

'No, and you are still awake.'

'Well, you know me, Joe.'

'Perhaps I'll go into the spare room – I don't want to disturb you.'

'You're not disturbing me, Joe. What's worrying you?'

132

'Nothing, really, except perhaps Olivia.'

'I thought that was it. Me, too. I've got a feeling she is keeping something from us – and then I tell myself she has every right to. She's twenty-three and well able to look after herself. I just wish she'd find herself a nice young man.'

'You don't think that boss of hers, that Bannister chap –'

'Joe! He's a married man!' She sat up and switched on the bedside lamp. 'What are you saying?'

'Well, he's a ladies man, isn't he? Hasn't he got a bit of a reputation where women are concerned?'

'I really wouldn't know.' Sylvia's voice was cool at the very idea of her beloved daughter behaving in such a way. 'You should be ashamed of yourself, Joe.' She sounded aggrieved.

'Well, you thought she was hiding something.'

'Ye-es. I thought perhaps she had met someone – someone she wishes to keep quiet about at the moment.'

'Why would she want to keep quiet about him?' When she didn't answer, 'Eh, Sylvia?'

She switched off the lamp. 'Oh, go to sleep, Joe, and stop worrying. Olivia is a very sensible girl.'

He wished he could believe that. 'Goodnight, Sylvia.'

He woke early, as he always did, even after a bad night, and made his way to the office. Constance Boxall was waiting for him with a message.

'Andrew is driving down today – for a twenty-four hour leave. He says to expect him sometime this afternoon.' She didn't add that he had asked her for Julie's address in Andover, wisely deciding that he didn't want everyone to know. She had thought about it, surprised, since she didn't know that they had met outside the office.

Well, good for him, she thought. She's a nice little thing but Joe was already looking better – seeing Andrew would be as good as a tonic.

Joe heard the roar of the M.G. soon after he and Sylvia had finished lunch, knowing that Andrew would have had a pub lunch on the way down.

The little car came to a halt in the courtyard and out stepped Andrew, a sight for sore eyes in his uniform, pilot officer's wings on his chest, his fair hair ruffled, blue eyes shining with pleasure.

'Hello, Dad.'

'Good to see you, son. Did you have a good journey?'

'Only from Northolt – via Tangmere – but I'm on my way north tomorrow.'

'How far north? Scotland?'

'Yep.'

'I thought that might be it. Come inside, your mother can't wait to see you.'

Later, he wandered round to the garage where Andrew was polishing the M.G. preparatory to putting it away for the duration. He would use the little Austin Swallow for transport to and from his new air base, it was more economical on petrol.

Joe was proud of both his sons, eyeing Andrew now, his fair hair glinting in the sun, his face streaked with oil, looking up at his father with a devilish glint in his eye.

'I think I'll have to take her for one more spin before I put her to bed,' he said, standing back to admire the polish he had just given her.

'As long as you don't ask me to come with you,' Joe said. He thought sports cars were lethal.

Later, Andrew started her up and roared down the narrow lane towards the village, which seemed to be asleep on this late afternoon. There was only one thing he liked more than speeding along quiet country lanes in his M.G. and that was being up there among the clouds in his Spitfire. He would make for Andover and Julie's address, hoping he would find her home. They finished at the office at five in the winter months, his father told him, since many of them had quite a journey to make. He couldn't wait to see her again.

He was going at a reasonable speed on the other side of the town when he saw her at the bus stop. A solitary figure, he would know her anywhere. Wrapped up as she was in a coat with a fur collar, a fur hat atop her luxuriant curls, her eyes anxiously scanning the road for a bus – there was no mistaking her. As he slowed to a stop he saw her turn away, head in air, careful to avoid looking at whoever it might be who was trying to pick her up. He leaned through the window. 'Julie?'

Startled, she turned and faced him. One look from those violet eyes and he knew just why he hadn't been able to forget her in the past few weeks.

'Andrew!' she gasped, her pleasure at seeing him unmistakable.

'Hop in,' he said. 'Where are you going?'

'Home – to Flag Walk, the other side of the town,' Julie told him.

'Hold on.' He got out of the car and went round to the other side and opened the door.

'At your service,' he grinned, and a smiling Julie climbed in.

But once beside her, he threw all caution to the winds and took her in his arms, kissing her long and hard. 'Oh, Julie, I've missed you.'

'I've missed you too.' Her heart was beating like a sledge hammer.

He moved away and looked at her. 'I was going to drive to your address – Flag Walk, isn't it? I asked Constance – Miss Boxall.'

'Andrew, you didn't!'

'Why not? You're not ashamed of me, are you?'

She smiled at him, a tremulous smile which touched his heart. He shouldn't tease her. It wasn't fair.

'Look,' he said, turning off the engine, 'I'm being posted tomorrow.'

Her eyes clouded over, becoming dark. 'Does that mean –'

'Yep, quite a way, so I thought perhaps we could go out again this evening? There's a nice little pub at Amport. The Mucky Duck. We could have a meal there – yes?'

There was no doubt at all in Julie's mind but she would have to go home and tell her mother – and however much Ada disapproved, she knew she would go.

'I'd love to,' she said swiftly, and he squeezed her hand.

'Good, then I'll drive you home now and pick you up around seven – will that do?'

She nodded, eyes shining.

'Now tell me which way to go.'

'It's not far. Turn at the corner and along here.' As she gave him directions, she stole a look at his profile, watched his gloved hands on the wheel. Could a girl ask for more? A straight nose, well-shaped mouth, a pair of blue eyes that hinted at fun and laughter – how dashing he looked in his uniform – and saw his wings.

A thrill of pride went through her. Her hero. And she was going out to dinner with him this evening.

'Second house on the left,' she said, and he applied the brakes.

'What a delightful spot. I'm glad you got fixed up all right. This is where you live?'

'Yes, with my mother.' She saw the query in his eyes. 'She came down from London with me – to look after me, I suppose she would say, but really it's because we're quite close. She is a widow, and I am all she has.'

The blue eyes were serious now as he turned to look at her. Their eyes met and seemed to last for ages, until Julie looked away, afraid that he might read in them the depth of her feeling. It really wouldn't do to wear her heart on her sleeve.

'Well,' she said, 'I'd better be going.' And he brushed her hair with his lips then got out and opened her door for her. 'See you at seven,' he said, and the little car roared away.

Unlocking the front door, Julie made her way upstairs.

Her mother was sitting sewing as usual. The curtains were drawn and there was a fire burning in the grate.

She looked up, perhaps sensing the air of excitement that clung around her daughter, and saw her shining eyes. Julie whipped off her hat and coat.

'You'll never guess who brought me home!'

Ada bit off a thread. 'No – who?'

'Andrew – Andrew Neville.' And she saw the frown on Ada's face. 'Oh, Mam, don't look like that. I'm going out to dinner with him this evening.'

'Well, if you've made up your mind,' Ada said coolly, 'there's nothing much I can say, is there?'

'I don't understand why you disapprove of him.'

'It's not that I disapprove of him,' Ada said. 'You get me

136

wrong. He looks a nice lad, but he is not for you. Young chaps like him, they're out for a good time – stands to reason with the job they do. I can't say as I blame them, but I don't want to see you getting hurt. You like him, I know you do –'

'I wouldn't go out with him if I didn't,' Julie said. This wasn't the time to tell Ada she was in love with him, head over heels in love. There was nothing anyone could do about that now. No matter what the end of it all, that's how it was.

'Mam, trust me. I know what I'm doing. He's going away – perhaps for a long time.'

'You said that before, and that's what it will be like all the time. You'll get all upset.'

'I'll have to put up with it,' Julie said, and went upstairs to change.

She came down in the same navy dress she had worn before, her hair brushed until it shone, wearing perfume she had had for her birthday from the other girls in the office, her seams straight, wearing her best high-heeled shoes.

'You look smashing,' Ada said ruefully, meaning it, and Julie smiled such a smile of relief that they both ended up laughing.

'It'll be all right, Mam,' she said. 'And I won't be late, honest.'

'See you're not,' Ada said. 'Well, have a good time.'

'Thanks, Mam,' Julie said, and hurried to the door as they heard the short sharp sound of a car's horn.

'That's it,' Ada said. 'You'd best be off.'

Julie flew down the stairs, seeing Miss Farquarson in her wheelchair in the open doorway of the drawing room.

'Oh, hello, Miss Farquarson. Excuse me, I'm just going out.'

'So I see,' Miss Farquarson said grimly, wondering where the girl was going and with whom. Oh, to be young!

They drove through darkened lanes until they reached the pretty village of Amport, and there, in the car park, Andrew parked the car and turned to Julie, taking her in his arms and holding her tight.

'Oh, I've missed you!' he said. 'I've thought about you every moment.'

'Not while you are flying, I hope,' Julie laughed, but she was delighted to hear his words just the same. Me, too, she could have said. I think about you all the time.

He bent his head and kissed her slowly, finding her tongue, while shivers of ecstasy flowed through Julie as his kisses became more passionate. Much as she wanted to surrender, to give herself, to return the kiss totally, a tiny warning insisted on pushing itself forward. His hand found her breast beneath the coat and she broke away, flushed and in a turmoil, so passionate were her feelings towards him. So this, she thought, this is it – this is what it's like to be in love, to want someone more than anything else in the world.

'Andrew – '

He looked at her perfect mouth, soft and crushed where he had recently kissed her, and made to move forward again. She was irresistable. He had never met a girl like this before, never felt like this before, and he had known some attractive girls. But this one was different.

He kissed her lightly on the nose. 'I got carried away,' he said without a trace of regret. 'I'm afraid it's all your fault.'

She smiled up at him, seeing the blue eyes meeting hers and knowing exactly what he meant. That was just how she felt too.

'Come on,' he said. 'Let's go and eat.'

It was more normal facing each other across the tiny table in the corner of the small dining room. Dim, because of the blackout, with a restricted menu. Food, however, was the last thing they had in mind. Andrew held her hand and sipped from her glass of wine, giving it to her, and she pressed her lips against the glass where his had been. Not only was he the most handsome man she had ever seen, but she loved him – loved everything about him. Their eyes looked into each other's until the waiter had to disturb them in order to serve, and hated to do so. He had had many young lovers in this restaurant, particularly lately, but this couple . . . He sighed.

Andrew looked across at her, unable to take his eyes off

that luxuriant hair which tumbled over her shoulders, those wonderful eyes, the smooth skin like silk, her exquisite colouring. That soft, full mouth, just aching to be kissed. It had tasted like nectar – and, he guessed, had never really been kissed before.

They saw nothing about them, only each other, drank their coffee in a haze, and hand in hand stumbled out into the car park where once in the car he began to make love to her, slowly, gently – but insistently, until almost beside herself with these newly discovered sensations, Julie took a grip on herself and sat up straight, her mother's past teachings forcing themselves uppermost. What had she said? 'You can't blame the man – it's his nature – but it's up to the girl to keep him straight. If he loves her, he will respect her. A good girl will save herself for marriage.'

Oh, Julie moaned within herself, it's awfully difficult. How wonderful it would be to let go . . .

'Let's go home, Andrew, please.'

'Right ho,' he said, as though she had asked nothing untoward, and starting up the car, kept silent for a long time. Whether he was annoyed or hurt, she had no way of knowing.

She sat still, not speaking, a small fur-wrapped bundle beside him, and presently, as they neared Flag Walk, he looked at her.

Now, having cooled down, he could think straight. Disappointed – of course he was. And yet – in a strange sort of way, pleased that she had not given in so easily. Nevertheless, he could not hide his real feelings from himself. He wanted her, it was almost too much to bear.

When they stopped, she looked at him with anguished eyes. Didn't he realise that she wanted him too? Wanted him to ravish her, to make love to her until she cried out – but she couldn't. He must think her so naive after all the girls he had known. Girls who thought nothing in wartime of surrendering their innocence, of tossing their bonnets over the windmill – but she couldn't. Not even for Andrew. Yet her body was hot as if it were on fire. If he kissed her like that again . . .

'Well,' he sighed, putting on the brake. 'Here we are,'

Never was there such an anticlimax.

Julie managed to pull herself together, to think of ordinary things.

'Do you know, in all this evening you haven't told me yet where you are going. Is it far away?'

'Yes, it is rather – a long way north.'

Her heart sank. He probably meant Scotland – lots of airmen were stationed up there. So far away. She might never seen him again. Her mouth trembled and she bit her lip.

He took her chin in his hand.

'Pretty little Julie,' he said. 'I am going to miss you. You will write to me?'

'Of course,' she cried. 'Of course I will.'

'Here, you can reach me at this address.'

And he pencilled a cryptic forces address on a slip of paper and gave it to her. Would he forget her once he had gone? she wondered.

She took it and put it into her handbag, then he bent forward and kissed her gently. Slowly she put her arms around his neck, holding him to her, returning his kiss. She might never see him again . . .

The kiss lasted for ages until she drew away and hurriedly picked up her fur hat. She opened the door.

'Don't get out,' she said, 'I can manage. Thank you for a lovely evening.'

And closing the door, she left him sitting there as she ran up the steps to the front door of the house in Flag Walk.

Once inside the hall, she felt like bursting into tears, so emotional had the evening been, but she braced herself, and walked upstairs to their sitting room.

Ada looked up, surprised, glancing at the clock.

'You're early,' she said. 'Did Andrew have to get back?'

'Yes, he goes off tomorrow,' Julie said, swallowing hard.

Her lovely eyes were misty, and she turned away.

'Shall I make a cup of tea?' she said brightly.

'Lovely,' Ada said, although she had just had two. Please don't let her get hurt, she prayed. I remember how it was to be young – although it was a long time ago. Falling in love could be agonising.

Chapter Sixteen

Life had changed for Eva Lowman since coming to Leicester. She sometimes thought it was the best thing that had ever happened to them, for her home, although small, was modern and easily run, she had a part-time job in the local school, and her days were more than full. She knitted for the forces comforts fund and had made many new friends among the workforce evacuated with them – people she never would have met if they had not left London. There was a camaraderie, a warm and natural friendship between people in wartime that seemed to be sadly lacking in peacetime England.

Eva enjoyed her Saturday evening jaunts with Tom to the local pub where visiting artists entertained them, and where they sang songs like 'Roll out the Barrel' and 'We're going to Hang Out the Washing on the Siegfried Line' to the accompaniment of whoever it was on the piano, and where she sang as loudly as the rest. She would never have gone to a pub in London.

Then there was young Valerie, who was doing so well at school that she had won her Junior Supplementary Scholarship to the local grammar school. She and Tom were so proud of her – she was a little brain box, really. Sometimes she sighed, thinking of Sarah and the promise the girl had shown. She had always thought Sarah clever, if a little odd. If only she had ploughed her brains into something really worthwhile instead of working in that awful newspaper office and spending all her spare time in amateur dramatics.

The funny thing was, up here they thought differently.

They thought it a matter of pride that she should have a daughter who was such a good little actress, and they always bought tickets for the show.

Take last week – it was a sell out as they called it. Sarah and Eliza Doolittle was a sensation, no less. You should just read what they said about her in the local papers. As a matter of fact, she had cut the articles out with the photograph and put them away in a drawer. It didn't do for Sarah to be getting big ideas – she had enough of those already. Eva hadn't liked it much when it started – Sarah with that awful Cockney voice – but when that Professor Higgins came along and taught her how to speak properly . . . not that Sarah needed that, she always spoke well, but in that high falutin' way, very posh, well, Eva couldn't but feel proud of her and had glanced around at the audience, seeing them engrossed. It had given her quite a thrill. As for Tom – well, he always was dippy about Sarah. Still, to make your living at it. The things that went on – kissing and that.

Well, as long as it was just a hobby.

She glanced up at the clock. Tom would be in soon. There was always a nice atmosphere about Fridays – pay day. Tom would come in a quarter of an hour earlier, although this week he had been on overtime – more money but such a lot of extra work. 'Something big,' Tom had said, and she didn't know if he knew what it was or wouldn't tell her. Things were hotting up, that was for sure. There had even been a few raids, and it looked as if the 'phoney war' was coming to an end.

She guessed that Sarah would go shopping around the city when she left the office, it being Friday night. There was nothing she liked more, buying make up and stockings and scented soap which they threatened would soon be in short supply. The more factories being given over to war production, the less there would be for civilians to buy.

She heard Tom's key in the lock and put the kettle back on, he always liked a cup of tea when he came in early, but one look at his face showed her that all was not well. He looked strained, and she could tell by his eyes that something was wrong.

He took off his cap and hung it on the hatstand, went

straight out to the kitchen to wash his hands as she watched him.

'What is it, Tom? What's up?'

He pulled down the roller towel and turned to face her.

'I don't know how to tell you this, Eva.' And her heart lurched. She put a hand to her chest. 'It's not Sarah?'

Valerie was in the bedroom doing her homework, so she knew it wasn't her, and Tom was here.

'What is it?'

'You're not going to like this, Eva, but we're being moved up to Scotland – six of us.'

She sat down abruptly.

'Oh no, Tom!' She stared at him. It couldn't be true. Just as they had got settled.

'Well, that's the way of it,' he said. 'And there's nothing I can do about it. I can't even leave and take another job, you know how it is.'

She did. 'Oh, I can't believe it. Who are the others?'

And he told her. All men she knew.

'But why?'

'Something special. Hush hush, you know the sort of thing. I've an idea what it is, but I dursn't say. Lots more will follow on, apparently. They've taken a factory over, way up north. Pretty desolate, for what I can make out but we will be near a town.'

'We?' she asked. 'You mean all of us – the wives as well?'

'Seems so. If you want to – and you wouldn't want to stay here without me, now would you? They'll allow you to stay here if you want to – I'd come back whenever I could – but I can imagine how much free time I'd get what with travelling and that.'

He sat down. Poor Tom, she thought. He wasn't a young man to be sent all over the country. 'I'll make the tea,' she said.

As an instrument maker, she knew he did valuable work, especially in wartime, and there was no way he could get out of it. But Scotland! It was like the other side of the world.

'When do we have to go?'

'In about a month or so. They say we'll have to go first

143

and you follow on. I'll look around for digs or somewhere for us to live – it won't be like this, Eva.'

She had a sudden thought. 'Sarah!' she said. 'She won't want to come.'

'I can't worry about that now,' he said. 'If she wants to stay down here then she'll have to.'

'Tom! What are you saying? Leave her down here on her own? Never! That's just what she'd like, that is! No, she'll come with us.' And her mouth set in a determined line. 'Where is it near?' she asked. 'Is it very isolated?'

'The factory is,' Tom said, 'but we'd be driven in each day from the town – Inverness, I think they said.'

Glasgow, Edinburgh, Inverness – it was all the same to Eva.

She poured out Tom's tea and began to put the sausages in the tin. She pricked them and poured the batter over, then put it into the hot oven which she had ready. Just as she had got used to this new cooker and all the mod cons of this place, who knew what awaited them up there? She thought, but only briefly, about staying put – but it was gone in an instant. Your duty lay with your husband, to be with him no matter what.

Sitting in the bus taking her from the city on the short ride home, Sarah looked out but saw nothing. Her thoughts centred chiefly on Jon Dangerfield, the young male lead with the dramatic society. The very sight of him was enough to make her heart beat faster. He was so handsome, so charming, and such a good actor. All the girls were a little in love with him, but he had eyes only for Sally Bateman, a little ingenue who looked up at him from large round eyes, the way she looked at all the men. They all had a soft spot for her, and really Sarah couldn't see why. She was pretty enough, small and dark-haired, petite, and she usually managed to secure the part of the French maid or the youngest daughter who had fallen foul of some man or other. She had joined the dramatic society when she left shcool, and now she was twenty.

Well, she didn't covet the parts Sally tried for, she was much more interested in character parts where she had to make up to look old, or quaint, or hideous even. It was a challenge to her acting ability. Just to be the pretty lead was not Sarah's idea of acting.

Ruth, who had become a close friend of Sarah's, agreed with her. 'She's a silly little thing,' she said.

Sarah took out the new lipstick she had bought, Raspberry Pink, so shiny she couldn't wait to get home and try it. She slipped it back in her handbag. Back to Jon Dangerfield. How could she make him more aware of her?

Ten to one he would get his call up soon, which would put paid to his dreams of becoming an actor – but now the bus had stopped, and the conductor took her arm in order to help her alight. It was not often that he had such a pretty passenger. He watched her walk away as the bus moved off. Cut above most of them, he thought.

Sarah inserted the key in the lock and went in. The bright light from the kitchen dazzled her after the darkened streets and the small dark hallway. They were sitting there, in the kitchen, Valerie as well, and all looked up as she came in.

'Hello,' she said, taking off her hat.

'Didn't you go shopping?' Valerie asked.

'No, I only bought a lipstick,' Sarah said, taking off her jacket.

She suddenly became aware of the silence. It was as if they had suddenly stopped talking when she came into the room.

'We're going to – ' her sister began.

'Valerie!' Her mother's unusually sharp reprimand quite shocked the girl.

'What is it?' Sarah asked. 'What's wrong?'

'You may well ask,' Eva said grimly.

Sarah waited.

'I'm being sent to Scotland,' Tom said.

Sarah stood, mouth open. 'What?' she asked. 'Scotland? Whatever for?'

'To work. Special orders. There's nothing I can do about it. I've got to go. There's a war on,' he said, almost with despair.

'But they've only just sent you up here,' Sarah said, but knew by her mother's face she had already accepted it. There was nothing she could do.

She turned, her face set. 'Well,' she said, 'I'm not going and that's that.' And going out of the room she closed the door firmly. Eva went to follow her, but Tom put out a restraining hand.

'Leave it, Eva,' he said wearily. 'Leave it for now.'

She felt a sudden compunction. Poor Tom, it wasn't his fault. He no more wanted to go than she did.

There followed a weekend in which rows were uppermost. Shouting and scenes when Tom in desperation went out to see the bulbs coming through the newly dug virgin soil, spears peeping through. He liked this time almost better than when the flowers appeared. At least out here he was at peace, anything rather than listening to the two of them going on. And Eva was fighting a losing battle, he knew. There was no way the girl would go with them. He knew his own daughter by now. Asked for his opinion he would have said he didn't blame her, but it was almost more than he could bear to face a life up there without her.

Valerie sat in the bedroom she shared with Sarah, hands over her ears most of the time. She hated rows more than anything, hated what it did to her mother.

'If you think we are going to leave you down here to fend for yourself at your age –'

Sarah's blue eyes were stormy, her mouth set in a determined line.

'You can't make me go.'

'Oh, can't we, young lady!' Eva was not too sure of her ground here, but she was determined to win the battle.

'You are so selfish! You think of no one but yourself! You don't realise how much you are upsetting your father.'

And this really did sink in. Biting her lip, Sarah stormed out of the front door, only to return a few minutes later when she made her way through the kitchen to the small garden. Seeing her father stooped over his flowers, she had a sudden lump in her throat. He didn't look up, didn't acknowledge that she was there. They can all go and jump in the lake, except him, she thought. She stood there silently for a few seconds before she spoke.

'Dad?'

'Yes?' He spoke softly, still not getting up.

'I don't want to upset you, Dad.'

He stood up, straightening his back. 'And I don't want you upsetting your mother,' he said. 'Life is hard enough without you making problems.'

She wanted to weep now. She had thought he would understand – be on her side.

'I can't go up there, Dad,' she said, and he looked at her, seeing the misery on her face, her blue eyes unhappy, she was only a kid after all.

'I know,' he said. 'Your mother – we – only want what's best for you. Why can't you understand that?'

She doesn't, Sarah thought. She only wants to hold on to me forever, never letting me do what I want. I shall be an old maid if she has her way. But she said none of this.

'I would be all right, Dad, honestly. I know I would. I can look after myself, and I would come up to see you – perhaps at weekends.'

And how long would that last? he wondered. They stood to lose her if she stayed down here on her own – but they stood a greater chance of losing her altogether if they thwarted her at every turn. He reminded himself that one of his sisters had married before she was eighteen.

'War does terrible things to families,' he said. Suddenly Sarah's eyes filled with tears and she ran indoors.

She couldn't wait for tomorrow and Monday night at the amateur dramatic society where she belonged more than anywhere. She would tell Ruth – Ruth would understand. She had already left home when she was twenty-one because her parents hadn't liked the idea of her marrying Phil, to whom she was unofficially engaged. She had come from a country village in Rutland and had a bed sitting room in the city. She was now twenty-four and her engagement to Phil had long since been broken off but she managed to keep herself as a single girl, working somewhere in the city.

Oh, if only Julie were here – she would understand. She missed her, missed her terribly. Self-pity taking over, she subsided into floods of tears.

In silence, they got through breakfast after Tom had gone. While Eva cleared away the dishes, a look on her face which hardly encouraged conversation, Sarah left for the office, her mind on what she would do when they went to Scotland, for as sure as eggs were eggs, she wasn't going with them.

At last the day ended and it was time for the dramatic society. Although there were no rehearsals in progress, they were reading all sorts of plays, taking turns to read the parts which Sarah enjoyed enormously. They gathered in little groups around the room, Sarah making a bee line for Ruth who sat in the corner, reading.

'Oh, I've been dying to see you!' she cried, and Ruth looked up, patting the chair beside her.

'What's up?' she asked, and Sarah told her, embellishing the tale as she went along. 'You can't imagine,' she ended.

'Oh, I can!' Ruth said. 'I've been through it all. There's nothing you can tell me about parents. Still, what will you do?'

'Stay here,' Sarah said.

'It's more expensive than living at home,' Ruth said. 'I mean, do you earn enough to keep yourself?'

Sarah hadn't given much thought to that side of things.

'Well, I shall have the money I usually pay at home.'

'Hmm,' Ruth said, as the secretary clapped her hands and announced that the play readings would begin.

At the tea break, Ruth sought out Sarah and took her arm.

'Let's sit over here – I've had an idea.'

Sarah was all attention.

'Look, if I can help out, I will. I've been thinking it over – you could share my room with me if you'd like. Temporarily, mind.'

Sarah's blue eyes shone.

'Oh, Ruth, could I?'

'Well, it's large enough, in an old Victorian house, and the rent's not bad. It's a front room, use of bathroom and kitchen downstairs, although I don't use that much. I've a gas ring which I use most of the time. My bed is a large single, but there is a bed chair and for the time being you could manage on that . . .'

Sarah wanted to throw her arms around Ruth, she was so excited.

'Oh, if only I could! Do you mean – you really would?'

'Temporarily,' Ruth said firmly. 'We'd have to come to some arrangements about what you paid, sharing the gas and cooking and that sort of thing. Also I'd have to ask my landlady but she's a friendly soul, and if she knew you were in a tight spot and it was a temporary arrangement, I am sure she would agree.'

But Sarah's thoughts were racing ahead. Her mother would never agree to that, not unless she met Ruth and approved. If she could get Ruth to come and meet her mother it might be different.

She spoke on impulse. 'Look, would you come and have tea with us on Sunday?'

'Tea? Oh, well, I don't really want to get involved, Sarah.'

'You won't be, honestly. I'd like you to come anyway, if you're not doing anything.'

'We-ll, I was going to . . .'

'Oh, please, Ruth! Please come. Once my mother meets you, she'll know it's all right.'

It was hard to refuse, Ruth thought, seeing the blue eyes beseeching her so earnestly.

'Oh, all right, then,' she said. 'Give me the address. What time shall I come?'

'About half-past three,' Sarah said, taking a chance, not even sure what her parents were doing. She'd have to worry about that later.

There was no one more surprised than Eva when Sarah walked in from her dramatics with a pleasant smile on her face. Things must have gone well, Eva thought, pleased nevertheless that Sarah had come round.

'How did you get on?' Tom asked.

'All right, Dad. We're only reading at the moment, not rehearsing.'

'Oh,' he said, and went back to his paper.

'I was wondering,' Sarah began, 'whether Ruth could come to tea on Sunday? Ruth Paynter.'

'Ruth? Do I know Ruth?'

'Yes, you met her when you came to see "Pygmalion" She was at the party afterwards.'

'Oh, yes, I remember now,' Ada said. 'She's a lot older than you, isn't she?'

'Oh, yes,' Sarah said fervently. That would hold Ruth in good stead. 'She's twenty-four.'

'Yes, of course she can,' Eva said, but long after she had gone to bed was wondering what Sarah was up to.

Sarah had all the week to wonder quite how she would put her case to Eva, for Eva had to know of Ruth's proposition by Sunday. By Wednesday, she had met Ruth outside her office and gone with her to the somewhat rundown area where she had a room, quite near to the city centre. It was pleasant enough, very large, and certainly roomy enough for two. It was shabby and not very well kept, and Sarah knew her mother would totally disapprove, but she had to keep her wits about her and stick to her guns.

Her father helped her by coming home on Friday evening with the news that he had to leave by the end of the month. Eva would follow on.

She stood worrying, hand to her mouth, the frown line between her brows. Now what? Another battle – but Sarah was at her friendliest.

'I was talking to Ruth at lunchtime,' she announced. 'We had lunch together at the corner cafe – and guess what? She said I could stay with her until I get fixed up.'

'Sarah!'

Eva knew she had been hoodwinked, but it was too late now to go back over it all again.

'You're coming with us, let's get that quite straight,' she said.

All Sarah's acting talent came to the fore. She shook her head sadly, lovingly almost. 'No, Mum, I'm not, and you know I'm not. If I can stay with Ruth I shall be all right – I can keep my job until something better turns up. After all, it's better than joining one of the forces – you wouldn't like that, would you?'

Ingenuous blue eyes looked into Eva's brown ones. Eva was beaten, and she knew it.

'We'll see what your father says,' she said.

She had won. A feeling of exaltation filled Sarah's heart, so much so that she almost went over and kissed her but it would be such an unusual gesture that her mother might change her mind.

Just wait until she wrote and told Julie – living on her own in digs. Well, almost. Then, she thought, once I've broken away – it's back to London for me. If they think I'm going to stay in this part of the world, they're mistaken. There's a whole new life waiting out there.

In the event, Tom went up to Scotland long before the end of the month, being whisked up there with his co-workers in less than two weeks, leaving Eva behind to cope with the contingencies. Her only thought was to join him as soon as possible; even the problem of Sarah took second place.

His first letter home assured that it wasn't as bad as he had thought it would be. They were working overtime on an important project, but were being given a day off to find accommodation for wives and families. He would let her know when he came up with something. He and two others had found digs with a Mrs Macpherson in one of the oldest parts of the city of Inverness which was different, he stressed, but not too bad. He had a comfortable bed and the food was all right, but he couldn't wait for her to come up and join him.

In less than a month he had found an unfurnished flat for them in a quiet street near the city centre and had been told of a grammar school where Valerie would be accepted. He suggested that Eva come up for the weekend to sort things out, and if she was agreeable they would arrange to move their home up north.

'It's only for the duration,' he consoled her.

Eva received this news with mixed feelings, but knew that she was one of the lucky ones, that not every wife was able to join her husband when he was transferred. She came back from the trip not too displeased. It had been great to see Tom again, she had missed him so much. Now, with Sarah about to go to live with Ruth, who seemed such a nice girl, she had accepted the fait accompli. Ruth was sensible, she would keep an eye on Sarah.

Goodness knows, she thought, clicking her tongue, some-one has to do it.

Chapter Seventeen

By the end of March, Andrew Neville, based at Drem in Scotland, had been on almost continual duty over the North Sea: flying cover for the large convoys seen threatened off Montrose, intercepting enemy marauders, following intelligence information that German navigational beacons were more than usually active.

The weather was very cold, and flying on dawn and dusk patrols over the Firth of Forth, the gales and heavy rain did nothing to alleviate the bitter winds that greeted them on their return, the landing flares roaring a welcome in the strong winds as the men made their way back to the dispersal hut.

Then came a change of plans which necessitated Andrew's squadron moving to Dyce where an unexpected pleasure awaited him when he met up with an old friend from flying school days, Bunny Burroughs.

Dyce was positively lacking in many of the amenities to be found at Drem and they were told that the new Operations Centre was in an advanced stage of planning which caused many a laugh in the mess. The airfield was grass, soft and muddy after the winter of heavy rains and snow, which made landing and take off difficult.

Several Norwegians arrived, having escaped in some way or another from under the Germans' noses, and told them that the only British fighters still flying were being operated from a frozen lake.

British bombers returning from night operations were landing anywhere they could on the coast to save flying back to their bases further inland, so that the coast guards were kept on their toes day and night.

In April the first British civilian was killed in a German air raid on the Orkneys, and this alerted everyone to the probabilities of the future. There would be no stopping the German Luftwaffe now. People were dissatisfied with Neville Chamberlain's government and a period of unease and unrest could be felt throughout the country, resulting in the resignation of the government to be replaced by a National Coalition led by Winston Churchill.

The German land forces wasted no time. In April they invaded Denmark and Norway, the Netherlands and Luxembourg, so that by May, when they invaded France, the message was clear. Great Britain would be next. Could the great German military machine be halted?

The Germans began operating from captured airfields in Norway and there was an increasing number of enemy planes in the area, particularly active against the navy at Scapa Flow. Many of them were mine layers, and again and again Andrew's squadron flew out from base, the severe stormy weather making flying difficult, while British bombers joined them on the airfield to step up support to Norway.

The snow had arrived, making conditions at the base difficult, but operations were hotting up and a new incursion of personnel including some WAAFS greatly helped to cheer the men who were fed up with ghastly weather conditions as well as the news from France and Norway, and frustrated that they couldn't do more.

Then came the news that the Germans had made enormous headway in France and had captured Arras and Amiens, forcing the British troops to retreat towards the channel ports, thus placing a heavy burden on Fighter Command. Talk was of serious losses sustained by the British, and a possible move south for Andrew's squadron, and when orders finally came, the move, as they had suspected, was to Hornchurch, in Essex, from which they would fly out over the channel to protect the French channel ports.

Andrew's first reaction was that he would be nearer to Julie, for sometimes he had wondered if he would ever see her again. Vivid memories of that last night he had spent with her stayed with him, and he wrote to her telling her he was safe and was being moved.

When the letter arrived Julie was overjoyed. She had no idea where he might be – just as long as he was safe, for the news was ominous and rumours abounded: that the Germans had already penetrated the barbed wire entanglements on the sea front at Bognor, that German parachutists had landed in Kent, that Germans disguised as nuns had been found in a convent in Kent, and so on. The real fear and horror of war finally made itself felt. Would the British be able to stop them?

The phoney war was over. The time had come to face up to it – whatever it was – and once again the people were united. Germans in Britain? Never!

A round up of aliens began, quite ruthless in its intensity. Men were herded into camps preparatory to being sent to the Dominions, there were attacks on aliens in the press, and when Italy joined Germany and declared war on England and France, many Italian shops and restaurants were attacked.

And then began the battle for Dunkirk, a desperate battle when little ships and big sailed across the channel to rescue the marooned armies of soldiers. The Hurricanes and Spitfires took off from Kentish and Essex airfields to do battle in the skies against Heinkel bombers or Messerschmitts. Patrol after patrol took off, the skies buzzing with the sound of machine gun fire and the zooming of the diving planes. Weary from exhaustion, pilots returned to base only to be sent up again and again after brief respites. Then, their faces pale and strained, haggard from lack of sleep, eyes red-rimmed, they were off again, boots pulled on and jackets fastened as they hurried across the tarmac.

On the fourth day Andrew came out of the briefing room with Bunny Burroughs and soon they were climbing up off the English coast, could see Calais and Boulogne below them, when seven MellO's came towards them, the leader with a shark's jaw painted on his nose. Andrew took aim and watched as the Messerschmitt turned over and went straight down into the sea. It was his first direct hit – but he had no time to realise it for suddenly the air was full of tracer bullets and smoke trails and he could see Bunny quite near giving him the thumbs up salute, a grin on his face, as they engaged in a furious battle, twisting and turning, climbing then diving.

At one point he knew his tail had been hit, then caught sight of Bunny again, four MellO's following him, and turned sharply to join in the attack – firing at another MellO, seeing the pilot's grim face behind his goggles, feeling inside himself a fury he hadn't known he possessed as he let go with all eight guns, crouching down in the cockpit to make himself a smaller target. His guns blazing, he knew after a few seconds he would have to return to base to re-fuel and re-arm, and diving lower he levelled out and made for the landing strip, once again thanking his lucky stars that he had made home safely.

Sinking into an armchair for half an hour's doze before taking off again, he stretched out his legs. Every moment of relaxation was vital to being fit for the task. He woke suddenly to a hum of low voices, and saw three or four men looking his way.

He sat up, yawning, doing up his jacket buttons.

'Not bad, eh?'

'Great. Well done.' Two of them exchanged glances and he had a sudden premonition. 'What's up?'

'Burroughs bought it.'

'I thought he was behind me.'

'So did we.'

Andrew swallowed hard. Bunny . . . he was a good chap. They'd been at school together. He might be all right but the chances up there were slim. The luck of the draw . . .

'See you, chaps,' was all he said.

They flew another patrol early that evening and ran into a flight of twenty Messerschmitts. At the end of the dog fight they had lost three more men but claimed they had shot down twelve.

Then exhaustion took its toll. After three days of this, Andrew was flying not far from the coast when he saw a Stuka making directly for him, guns blazing. His eight guns firing, he twisted and turned, then saw another formation of three coming out of the clouds towards him. He used all the ammunition he had left before he knew that he had been hit by a Bofors gun in the wings and petrol tank. The cockpit filled with petrol and the machine caught fire. He heard the shouts from behind him, knowing he must bale out – not an easy thing to do in a Spitfire, since the perfect way was to turn the plane upside down, but there was no time for manoeuvres.

He heard shouts from a couple of friendly Hurricanes who had taken up the chase and baled out, seeing a Heinkel diving towards the earth black smoke pouring from it as it went down.

His parachute opened and he floated down, landing on marshy ground somewhere in Essex. Extricating himself from his parachute, bruised and sore, he got to his feet, his right ankle was painful but he was otherwise unhurt. Two farm workers were hurrying his way, and limping towards them, he put an arm around each man's shoulder and hobbled to the nearby farmhouse where representatives from his air base were sent for to prove that he was really who he appeared to be.

'You never know, mate,' the farmer said. 'We've 'ad one or two scares with parachutists.'

Relieved to be back on English soil, and with his ankle tightly bandaged, Andrew flopped out on his bunk bed. Exhausted as he was, he was unable to sleep. His mind was full of Bunny and his dive to death, of the plane he had shot down, of the face of the pilot in the goggles in the MellO – and of Julie, when he finally slept.

Next day, he was posted to Biggin Hill and given twenty-four hours' leave.

His first thought was to telephone home. He got through to his mother who was delighted to hear from him. He assured her he was fine and would be calling in for an hour or so in the afternoon. Then he asked the operator for his father's office number in Andover.

'Julie?'

Her heart turned over. She would know that voice anywhere.

'Andrew! Where are you?'

'On my way home.' He grinned. It was wonderful to hear her again. 'I've got the shortest leave – twenty-four hours. Could you meet me this evening?'

'Of course I can. Where?'

'I'll be outside the office – say six-thirty – or why don't I pick you up at home?'

'No, I'll see you outside the office at six-thirty. Oh, Andrew, I can't believe it's really you.'

'Same here. Now can you put me through to my father – is he in?'

'Yes, hold on.'

She pressed a button. 'Miss Boxall? It's a call for Mr Neville – his son.'

'Oh, put him through, my dear.'

Having made the connection, Julie sat back in her chair. Miss Boxall hadn't asked if it was Andrew or Gerald. Oh, this was the happiest day of her life! Andrew was safe. Andrew was home, even for the shortest time. It would be wonderful to see him again.

She hurried home, dancing on air, and Ada could see by her face when she came in that something had happened.

'You'll never guess!' Julie said, flinging her coat on to a chair.

Oh, yes, I can, Ada thought. It's that young man again. She sighed deeply. Well, what had to be, had to be, she supposed.

'No – what?' she asked, busy laying the table.

'Oh, Mam, I don't think I shall want supper – Andrew's home!'

Ada looked up. How could she put a dampener on such radiance.

'Oh, is he? Well, you're happy then.'

Delighted that Ada was not making trouble over it, Julie ran over to her and kissed her.

'Oh, Mam! I've waited such a long time for this!' And she ran into the bedroom where Ada could hear her opening and shutting the wardrobe doors, humming to herself.

She tried first this dress then that. She was never short of clothes, Ada taking the greatest pleasure in making them for her whenever she had the time, for by now she had managed to get quite a few jobs doing alterations and re-styling clothes.

She finally decided on a cream shantung dress, in a tailored style, material that Ada had picked up in the market at Salisbury. With its scarlet belt and buttons, and her red shoes and handbag, she had been saving it for just an occasion at this. When she had bathed in the enormous cold bathroom which everyone shared, she emerged as flushed as a rosy peach, her riotous curls damp, her eyes sparkling. She looked so young and lovely, Ada swallowed hard.

But as the time drew near, Julie's excitement died down and she became more reflective. Would he find her the same – as attractive as he had before. Had he met lots of lovely young women – sophisticated young women of the world who had left home and were finding freedom for the first time . . .

Well, it was her, Julie Garrett, he had telephoned. She had her answer there.

She twirled around for Ada's benefit. Her mother bent and picked off a piece of cotton from the hem.

'Very nice,' she said. 'I'm glad we made it up in that style.'

Julie picked up her handbag. 'Well, I'm off. I don't know where we're going.'

'Don't be late, Julie,' her mother said.

Julie turned and faced her. 'I don't know what time I'll be in, Mam,' she said, and there was something about her expression that caught at Ada's heart.

'Oh – well, then, have a nice time,' she said, and from the window watched her as she walked down the street towards the town.

Julie walked on air, swinging along, her high heels clacking on the pavement. Many a pair of eyes followed after her, and presently she had crossed the High Street and was making for the old white-painted house on the main road out of town. And there he was! In a little Austin Swallow, maroon-coloured, the top open. It was as much as she could do not to run towards him.

He had opened the door and slammed it shut, then hurried down the street to meet her, limping slightly, taking her in his arms, oblivious of the stares of passersby. 'Oh, Julie, Julie!'

'Andrew – you're limping!'

'It's nothing – just a sprain. I had to bale out.'

'Andrew!'

He looked tired, she thought. Not the bright-faced boy with the laughing blue eyes she had seen several weeks before. Here was a man. His shoulders seemed broader, there was a tighter look around his mouth that hadn't been there before, and his eyes were strained – but it was the same wonderful man she had fallen in love with then and was still in love with now.

His kiss seemed to last for hours, and when she broke away they stared at each other for what seemed like minutes. Then, releasing each other, Andrew took her hand and they walked back to the car. 'Hop in,' he said, opening the door for her and getting in the driver's seat. He started up the little car and drove fast out of Andover and on to the Weyhill Road.

'Good thing it's your left foot,' Julie said, but he simply grinned at her. 'You look – wonderful,' he said, every now and again taking his eyes off the road to look at her.

Julie smiled. 'So do you.'

'I'm being moved again,' he said, 'not too far away. But I'm going to be busy. Have you had many raids?'

'Lots of false alarms,' she said. 'It's mostly when a German plane manages to get through the coastal guns that the warning goes – and then the barrage is quite fierce. It's more noisy than anything.'

'Julie,' he said, suddenly concerned, 'when it hots up – and it will – you will take shelter, won't you? Those public shelters are better than nothing.'

'Of course.' She smiled. 'Where are we going?' She wanted to take his mind off the war and all its evil implications.

'To a nice little pub in the prettiest village you have ever seen.'

Now that the road and streets signs had been removed in order to confuse any enemy parachutist, Julie had no idea where she was but soon they found their village and a picturesque little pub, creeper and ivy-covered, with a hanging sign splendidly painted of a pheasant and a lurking fox. On a lovely May evening such as this, you couldn't have found a better spot.

She smiled. 'Isn't it pretty?'

'I knew you'd like it. Come on – let's see what they have to eat.'

They went inside into the narrow passage and then into a low-ceilinged room with dark oak tables and chairs and a heavily beamed ceiling, the walls blackened with years of smoke fires which burned continually.

'Let's go through to the garden,' Andrew suggested. 'Now,' he said, looking at her. 'Tell me what you've been doing while I've been away?'

She looked into his eyes, and what she read in them sent a shiver of excitement down her spine; while he, looking deeply into those wonderful violet-coloured eyes, saw the long lashes curling on her cheeks and felt he wanted to take her in his arms and hold her forever.

He took her hand instead and held it tightly, and she made no effort to take it away. The feeling was wonderful, like an electric current between them. Only when the bartender appeared did Andrew release it.

'What can you offer us to eat?' he asked.

'We have some nice game pie, and a fine piece of Stilton.'

Andrew looked at Julie. 'What do you think?'

'Anything,' she said. She really didn't care.

'And I'll have a pint. Julie?'

'Tomato juice.'

They smiled at each other.

'Tell me what you did to your ankle – is it painful?'

'Not really, it's much better now. I had to bale out when my plane got shot up. It's only bruised – I was lucky not to break it.'

Julie was horrified. 'Andrew! You mean . . .'

'Yes, in my parachute, which fortunately opened. I landed somewhere in Essex with nothing worse than a bruised ankle.'

'I've thought about you so often – up there, protecting us

160

all. I can't imagine what it must be like, flying around in a tiny plane and being shot at.'

'Oh, it's not that bad,' Andrew said, the understatement of the year. 'You get a certain kick out of it, you know.'

They talked further over the game pie and the salad, then Stilton and port for Andrew, and as they talked his face darkened as memories came back.

'Tell me about Scotland,' Julie said. 'I've never been there.'

'It's beautiful, under certain circumstances. But on war-time aerodromes – it can be a bit hostile.'

He sipped his coffee, watching her, seeing her face light up, her eyes sparkle or dim, according to what he was telling her.

'It's a wonderful feeling, being with the other chaps, knowing you're all in it together. They're a terrific bunch. We'll get those blighters, Julie – they won't get away with it.'

He stubbed out his cigarette.

'I lost a friend. He came down in the drink. I was at school with him, and at flying school.'

'When did that happen?' she asked quietly.

'Three days ago. No, two.'

She wanted to take him in her arms and console him. He was like a small boy, she thought. Sometimes she felt older than he. She wished that everything would be perfect for him, always. That he would always be happy and young and brave. But life wasn't like that. The reality was that soon he would be gone – perhaps out of her life – and she couldn't bear it.

'Tell me,' he said suddenly. 'Tell me about you, Julie. What do you want out of life? What are you going to do with yourself if this war goes on?'

'I suppose I've been taking it one day at a time,' she said, 'but you're right, of course. I shall be wanting to do more than I am doing at present. Not,' she added hastily, 'that I am not happy working at Neville's.'

He regarded her seriously. 'You're an awfully nice girl, Julie Garrett,' he said. 'I mean – apart from your obvious charms.'

He stood up suddenly and Julie realised that he was pretty much on edge, not relaxed. Well, who could blame him, living the sort of life he was leading?

He took her hand. 'Come on, let's go for a walk. It's a lovely evening.'

Outside the cottages were tubs of tulips and wallflowers and the scent as they passed them was almost overpowering. Some of the houses had window boxes from which spilled mauve aubrieta and yellow alyssum. Julie just stood and stared.

'To think what people miss, living in London?' she exclaimed.

'You don't miss city life?'

She shook her head. 'No – surprisingly, I don't. I could live here forever.'

'Like here?' he asked as they reached the end of the village where a small Georgian house stood, covered in ivy, its garden unkempt, curtains sagging at the windows, a FOR SALE board by the front gate.

'Oh, what a shame! Julie cried. 'It looks so sad.'

'Owner off to war,' Andrew said.

To the side of the house was a narrow lane, fringed by elms. They sauntered down it then stood beneath some chestnuts with their pale green sticky buds and late-budding birch trees which looked as though they wore black lace.

At the end of the lane was a small copse. They walked hand in hand until they came to a sheltered spot where without saying a word they sat down on the grass and turned to each other.

Above them a blackbird sang, and Julie thought that for the rest of her life she would remember that lovely sound. She had no doubts or fears as Andrew began to make love to her, arousing sensations so powerful that she almost forgot where and who she was, her only thought being that she was here, with Andrew, her beloved, and that she might never see him again.

As his kisses became more sensual, more urgent, she was filled with a desire that demanded to be satisfied. She gave no heed to the warnings that flashed through her brain, to the sensible advice she had been given, and she put her

162

arms around him and held him to her, returning his kisses until neither of them were capable of any coherent thought.

Then he broke away and looked down at her.

'Julie?'

In the half light he could see her eyes shining, misty with love, and he gave a small groan.

'Julie . . .'

Her lovely mouth was still warm and damp from his kisses, and he brushed it gently with his lips.

'Julie – would you? Would you really?'

She had no doubts whatever, only a desire to please him.

'Julie, you've never . . .'

She put a finger over his lips and smiled up at him.

There was no turning back. She didn't want to, and she gave herself up to him with all the joy it was possible to experience. She cried out with the initial pain, but then the exquisite rapture which followed was almost unbearable in its intensity. She clung to him as if she would never let him go, and he buried his face in her hair.

'Julie, I love you so.' And her heart soared at his words. He looked down at her, her lovely pale skin exposed, and kissed her gently – her face, her breast, her shoulders.

'Do you love me, Julie?'

She nodded. 'More than anything in the world.' And he kissed her and made love to her again.

They stayed there until it was quite dark, until they heard an owl hooting in the darkness, then Andrew drew her gently to her feet and held her tightly.

'I'd better drive you home,' he said, looking at her regretfully. She smiled.

No matter what happened, she would never, never forget this night. But it wouldn't end here, she knew. He loved her, she was sure, and now, after this, nothing could come between them – so long as he stays safe.

On the way home it dawned on her that she would have to face Ada. Would her mother see any difference? Would she know? Mothers were very perceptive about those things. But suddenly she didn't care. It was Andrew who mattered, his happiness.

163

When he stopped the car, she turned to him and kissed him lightly on the lips.

'No regrets?' he asked anxiously.

'None,' she answered. 'I love you, Andrew.'

'And I love you, little Julie,' he said, caressing her hair and face. He took her hand, turning it over, and kissed her palm.

'I didn't really mean for it to happen – but I'm glad it did,' he said. 'Julie, you were wonderful – but you will be all right? You will let me know how you are?'

'Of course I will – I shall write to you. But you must promise me to take care. Please, take care of yourself.'

'You too.' But she had gone, just as she had before, running up the steps, the key inserted in the door, and he sat for quite some time looking after her.

Now what had he done?

Chapter Eighteen

Joe Neville came down late to breakfast after a bad night and drove himself to the office.

'Good morning, Constance.' His tone was brusque and he said no more, leaving her to wonder what was wrong. When he had finished going through his post, she looked across at him. 'Everything all right, Joe?'

'I slept badly last night, and if there is one thing I must have it's a good night's sleep,' he said grumpily.

She took a deep breath. Oh, was that all it was?

'I'm concerned about Olivia – she's not been down for a couple of weeks and she knows how her mother worries.'

Constance smiled reassuringly. 'I expect the truth of the matter is that she has a young man, Joe. A pretty girl like Olivia . . .'

'I don't doubt it,' he said tersely. 'It's who the young man is that worries me – or "man", he amended. 'If I thought for a moment it was that chap she works for . . .' And his dark brows knitted.

The thought had more than once occurred to Constance but she refused to let herself dwell on it. Surely Olivia would not be so foolish as to have an affair with a married man?

'And then there's Andrew,' he said. 'Came home on a twenty-four hour pass – and what does he do? Rushes in and out again – and that's all we saw of him. Said he was taking Miss Garrett out.' And he nodded over his shoulder. 'Is there something going on I should know about?' But his eyes were twinkling and that took the edge off his words.

Constance had no wish to become involved, and shook her head.

'Joe,' she said gently, 'they're both young – you can't blame them if they want to make the most of life while they can. Imagine being a Spitfire pilot. He's not going to want to spend any free time with his parents, now is he?'

What would Constance know about having children? he thought. It was different for her. Nevertheless, some of the worry lines had gone from his brow.

'As for Gerald – since he joined the Fleet Air Arm we've hardly had any news of him. It's pretty hard on Peggy, expecting her first. I'm glad she's gone down to Devon to be with her parents.'

'When is the baby due?'

His faced brightened. 'This week, as far as I know,' he said. 'My word, but I'm looking forward to it. A grandchild.' And his brown eyes shone.

It was three days later that the call came through. Gerald Neville's wife Peggy had given birth to a son at her parent's home in Devon. Mother and baby were both well, and the boy was to be called Joseph, after his grandfather.

Joe Neville blew his nose loudly. 'This calls for champagne, Constance,' he said. 'See if you can find a bottle somewhere in the town – we'll drink a toast to the lad when we finish today.'

She sent out Framlingham, who had come down with them from London and who lived in the top flat with his wife. She herself had never shopped for alcoholic liquor in her life.

'So we had champagne to drink the baby's health,' Julie told Ada, her eyes still shining from the fizzy drink which had made her feel quite woozy.

'Well I never!' she exclaimed. What were things coming to when they drank champagne in an office? She was still puzzled over Julie's friendship with Andrew Neville, but she seemed to be the only one who was. Julie had had a card only this morning, and she certainly wrote to him enough. There was no holding her when the postman arrived.

'Oh, Mam! There's a war on – live for today. It's old hat now all that class thing. Out of date.'

166

Is it though? Ada asked herself grimly. What would the family's reaction be if the lad wanted to marry Julie? She would bet it would be a different story then. Still, they were young and enjoying themselves. There was no question of Julie getting married yet awhile – thank goodness.

A few days later, a long awaited letter arrived from Sarah. Julie opened it eagerly and read it with surprise.

'Well! Who would have believed it! Scotland!'

'Come on,' Ada said. 'Put me out of my misery.'

It was a long letter, and when Julie had finished, she went back to the beginning again.

'Sarah's parents have been moved to Scotland and she has stayed behind in Leicester – can you believe it?'

'Scotland! Oh, my goodness.' Ada was quite shocked.

'Yes, Mr Lowman had to go apparently – had no choice, and Sarah doesn't say how her mother likes it. She refused to go with them, she says, and is living in digs with a friend, a girl called Ruth.'

Ada clicked her tongue. 'I can't imagine Mrs Lowman liking that situation. Is Sarah still working for a newspaper?'

'Yes, but she's looking around. It seems she has joined a dramatic society and is quite the leading light. Well, Sarah would be, we know what a good actress she is – but she seems to think she could get a job on the stage, and I expect that's what she will try to do, now that she's broken away from home.'

How a war changes lives, Ada thought. If it hadn't been for the war, both Sarah and Julie would still be living near each other, and be courting, perhaps, nice young men. Poor Mrs Lowman, she felt sorry for her. She would take a bet that going up there was not her wish, nor leaving her precious daughter behind.

'Here, you read it,' Julie said, tossing the letter over to her. 'It's all about her dramatic society. Oh, but I would like to see her again, Mam.'

'Of course you would,' Ada said. 'Well, you never know.'

'I wouldn't mind going up there,' Julie said, 'just for the day.'

'You won't, my girl,' Ada said grimly. 'Not with these air raids starting.'

That weekend, the air raid sirens sounded three times, and each time the sound of a plane could be heard, the crack crack of anti-aircraft guns, and it was clear that the odd German raider had broken through the coastal defences.

During a lull Julie hurried out to the shops, and on the way back saw Miss Farquarson saying farewell to a handsome young man in naval uniform at the front gate.

He was tall and dark with brown eyes which looked into Julie's with admiration as she smiled at Miss Farquarson.

'You are just in time to meet my nephew,' Miss Farquarson said proudly. 'Jamie, this is Miss Garrett – Miss Julie Garrett – who is staying with us for the duration.'

'How do you do?' They shook hands, and Julie found herself smiling up at him as though sharing a secret.

'Jamie is my sister's son – my only relative,' Miss Farquarson said. 'He managed to call in to see me on his way to . . .' But he flashed her a warning look.

'I forget sometimes there's a war on,' she said irritably. 'I live such a sheltered life, you know. Still, I mustn't grumble. When I think of what some people are going through . . . Well, you'd best get on,' she said to him, and he bent and kissed her cheek. 'Goodbye Aunt.'

'Dear boy,' she said.

He put his hand out again and took Julie's. 'Nice to have met you,' he said. 'I hope I shall see you again sometime.'

She smiled. 'Good luck,' she said, and went on indoors.

'I just met Miss Farquarson's nephew, Jamie,' she said to Ada, putting her basket on the kitchen table.

'You know, I thought I saw a young man with her in the garden earlier,' her mother replied. 'You can't help admiring her – she never bothers to go indoors when the siren goes. Says she would rather die in the garden that have a pile of bricks fall on her. She's right, I suppose. What's he like – the nephew?'

'Dishy,' Julie said, smiling to herself. 'Good-looking, obviously fond of his aunt, very smart in his naval officer's uniform.'

Ada put the things away in the cupboard. Now wouldn't that have been nice? she thought.

Julie handed her a bag of sugar. 'Now don't start getting any ideas,' she said. 'He's not my type.' And, laughing, went off into the bathroom to wash her hair.

When in June the Germans occupied Paris it was almost like a death knell. People could not believe it. It was almost as if Hitler had invaded London. Anglo-French resistance had virtually ceased, and faces were grim as France surrendered on the fourteenth of June. The German air force occupied airfields along the northern French and Baltic coasts as well as Norway, thus coming nearer and nearer to the coast.

The battle for Britain had begun.

There followed the greatest fight for freedom the nation had ever experienced. It began in July on the Kent coast and as the German Luftwaffe flew farther inland, people were forced to take to the shelters as the ominous whine of planes overhead came nearer. The sound of the anti aircraft guns boomed incessantly by daylight and on moonlit nights. A clear sky and a full moon spelt disaster for many.

'Thank God we didn't stay in London,' Ada said fervently. 'I heard that Greenwich had been razed to the ground, but of course it could be rumours. It makes you wonder how all the people we knew are getting on. And what a good thing it was that the kiddies were evacuated.'

Julie thought only of Andrew – up there in the skies in that tiny plane – and prayed. Heaven knew what his parents must be going through. Every day she searched Mr Neville's face when he came in, reading there anxiety, worry and stress, and was powerless to share her concern, not knowing if they had any idea that she had been seeing their son.

There were stories of pilots having so little sleep that they went up again almost immediately after arriving back from pitched battle in the skies – those who were lucky enough to return. There were so few of them doing such a magnificent job that people thrilled at their bravery, although no news was given except to announce at the end of each day how many German planes had been shot down, and there were doubts about that. The number were probably exaggerated as a morale booster.

I'm glad, Julie told herself, over and over again, I'm glad

169

that we had that lovely evening together – even if I'd started a baby, I wouldn't be sorry. I would have something to remember him by if anything happened to him. And she shivered. Please God, keep him safe. Andrew's letters, brief though they were, said the same thing – that he would never forget her, but thought of her constantly.

These were the really dark days. Everyone was on full alert. British fighter planes, heavily undermanned, went up over and over again. There were some spectacular dogfights overhead and the sight of a plane screaming towards the earth, black smoke pouring from it, was not unusual.

Sixty-two people were killed in scattered attacks in Surrey and although some German planes were being shot down, there were never enough British fighters to stop them getting through.

German bombers attacked the whole of the south coast, from Dover to Cornwall, while spasmodic attacks were launched at towns all over Britain, so that no one could afford to feel safe.

Joe Neville sat back helplessly, having watched his business recede farther and farther into enemy hands. His offices in the city had been bombed, a right old mess if the janitor could be believed, to say nothing of watching Sylvia fret about Andrew and himself worrying about Olivia working in London. They were bombing the city by day as well as night, and it was no good her telling them she went down to the shelters beneath the War Office – when she wasn't on fire guard – why on earth didn't they get them out of London?

It seemed his prayers were about to be answered when she telephoned one evening.

'Thank God,' Sylvia heard him say. 'About time too. Have a word with your mother – here she is.'

'It's all right,' he said to Sylvia, a hand over the receiver. 'It's Olivia, phoning to tell us she is all right.'

When Sylvia returned, she was looking relieved.

'Well, Joe, she hasn't been down to see us because their office has been transferred from London to – where she isn't allowed to tell us. Sufficient to say it is well out of London, she has good accommodation in a large house with the rest of the staff, and they only come up to London when it's absolutely necessary – and then they work in the basement or the vaults. So it seems as if she is safe and well and not in immediate danger from the raids.'

'Did you ask her when she's coming to see us?'

'Now you know she would if she could, Joe. It may be some time before she can get away. She's on very important work, as you well know, and I told her we quite understood. We know she will come as soon as she is able . . .'

'Yes, well,' he growled. He was too old for wars, he told himself. Had he been younger, able to fight with the best of them as he had in nineteen-fourteen . . .

She picked up her knitting. 'Did I tell you, Peggy's mother phoned to say Peggy is taking the baby to Plymouth for the weekend – just long enough for Gerald to see baby Joe before he sails off again.'

'Poor devil,' Joe said. 'I don't know if I agree with her taking the little chap with her. You never know . . .'

'Oh, Joe!' Sylvia said. He was such a worrier –

It was Constance Boxall who brought the news. The telegram arrived from Peggy's parents early on Monday morning. All three had been killed in a raid on Plymouth on the Saturday night – Gerald, Peggy, and Joe's baby grandson. Joe had to break the news to Sylvia.

Driving himself home, his teeth clenched, hands rigid on the wheel, he was a broken man, all the life knocked out of him. His son and his grandson – the baby had had no chance to live at all – and young Peggy, his daughter-in-law, God only knew how he was going to tell his wife.

It was a house of mourning that welcomed Olivia when she arrived home on compassionate leave. Her parents were inconsolable in their grief, and her own problems were forgotten in trying to comfort them.

'Shouldn't we let Andrew know?' she asked.

He had just returned to base from a particularly nasty encounter on a day when his squadron had lost three Spitfires with no loss to the enemy. It was a different story now on the 'drome. Pilots gave little heed to regulations, often going up and flying in shirt sleeves rather than getting

171

dressed up in Irvin suits and gloves; flying with their cockpit canopies open, making it easier to bale out in an emergency.

Below him in the channel it was not unusual to see fighters of both sides nosediving towards the sea, the pilot having baled out since if he stayed in the plane it would plummet to the bottom like a stone. Sometimes a passing trawler or lifeboat putting out from the shore would pick up a survivor. They were the lucky ones for British fighter pilots had no dinghies at this stage of the war, and often no strength to blow up their 'Mae West's' in their exhausted condition. Ditching was a bleak prospect, particularly when he had come to realise that the British fighters were no match when faced with German tactical skills.

He knew he had been lucky so far – had escaped a hundred times – and prayed that his luck would hold. He knew it played a great part, however brilliant the pilot, and meanwhile he gained in experience every day the war went on. Last night he had gone to the mess for a small party held to celebrate a fellow pilot's wedding to a W.A.A.F. officer on the base. She had asked for a transfer to Northolt in order to be with him, and was in the operations room.

He had watched them both, in love as they were, and thought, if only it were me and Julie . . . Julie, whom he loved with all his heart. Julie would be strong; she would be there to comfort him, to love him when he returned home – and at this rate how long did a man have? Was he to be denied the pleasure and thrill of having a wife to come home to just because there was a war on? And Julie – would she marry him? He knew in his heart what the answer was. Of course she would, he was sure of it. Julie loved him. What sense was there in his being here and Julie somewhere else?

He made up his mind. If he got through the next big one, he would ask her to marry him on his next leave.

It came sooner than he expected.

He had just returned from a heavy air battle after news that morning of a big raid building up off Cherbourg. Twenty odd fighters were sent up, and as over a hundred German bombers escorted by Messerschmitts reached mid-channel, eight further squadrons were sent up. There was heavy dogfighting between the fighters, while the bombers went on to attack Weymouth and Portland almost unscathed. The scene below him in the channel was indescribable as each side sought to rescue their pilots from the sea.

He limped home with a damaged tail, and with a great sense of relief touched down at Northolt by the light of the setting sun.

He had hardly cleaned himself up when he was sent for by his commanding officer who broke the news to him of Gerald's death. He had been through so much that day that the news hardly sank in until much later.

Group Captain Mears eyed the young man before him – his red-rimmed eyes, the lines of exhaustion on his face.

'Sorry about this, Neville,' he said. 'I think you're due for a spot of leave. No need to return here until – Monday, shall we say?'

'Thank you, sir.'

Andrew found his way down the corridor and into his room where he flopped on to his bunk, sleep overtaking him almost at once.

When he woke it was just before midnight and the awful realisation dawned on him. He raced to the shower and got himself dressed in ten minutes flat. All he could think of now were his parents. It was Thursday – no, Friday morning, he amended. Poor Peggy – and the baby – and Gerald. He swallowed hard. He was going to have to put a brave face on this terrible situation for his parents' sake.

A raid was in progress as he drove through the darkened streets towards London. The sky was alight with searchlights and he could see the tiny silver planes up there caught in their beams. The sound of ack-ack guns could be heard booming above the noise of the car's engine, and once or twice, having crossed London, he had to make a detour to avoid the debris caused by bombs on the road towards the south.

It was three o'clock when he drove up quietly to his parents' cottage. There was a light upstairs in Olivia's room and he thanked God that she was there to give them moral support. He let himself in and almost immediately his sister came down the stairs, her eyes red from crying, and fell into his arms.

'Oh, Andrew, I's so glad you're here.'

He kissed her. 'I came as soon as I could – where are they? Are they all right?'

'They left this morning for Peggy's parents' home, Mother said it was the least they could do, to be with them at a time like this. She wanted me to stay here and hold the fort in case you came down – after all, as she said, there is nothing we can do now.' And she burst into fresh tears.

'What a bloody awful thing to happen! Peggy and the baby . . . Gerald – all of them.' And he turned away to hide his emotion.

He took a deep breath. 'Well, what can we do? Shall I drive down there – follow them?'

'It wouldn't do any good, Andrew. I think they'll be just as pleased to see you when they get back. They won't stay long down there.'

Then the telephone rang and it was Andrew who answered it. It was his father.

Olivia walked quietly into the kitchen to put the kettle on.

'They'll be back some time tomorrow,' Andrew said, returning from the hall. 'Is that for tea? Good.'

It was some time later, when he and Olivia had talked, that he went upstairs to his room and lay thinking. He had not changed his mind – not in the slightest. He might have got the timing wrong as far as his parents were concerned but he was determined and did not intend to waste another precious day.

When Julie came out of the office at the end of the day, Andrew was sitting in the car waiting for her. He got out and came towards her, seeing her lovely face wreathed in smiles, eyes shining at the sight of him, and knew he was about to do the right thing.

'Andrew,' she said softly, and raised herself on tiptoe for his kiss. He took her arm.

'I was so sorry to hear about your brother. I suppose they gave you compassionate leave?'

'Yes,' he said, putting his arm around her. 'I have until Monday morning. But I have a lot to say to you. May we walk – you're not in a hurry, are you?'

174

She shook her head and fell into step beside him. How tired he looked, his handsome face taut with strain, his blue eyes bloodshot. How much had he seen in his theatre of war. Her heart ached for him.

He was silent until they had gone halfway along the High Street, when he stopped, turned, and looked at her.

'Were you on your way home?'

She smiled. 'Yes.'

'Could I come, too?'

Puzzled, she looked up at him. 'With me? Why?'

'I want to marry you – and I think we should have a word with your mother.'

'Andrew!' Her face paled. The idea was ridiculous! What had come over him? She thought swiftly. He was probably still in a state of shock. She turned. 'Let's go back to the car,' she said.

They turned and walked slowly back, holding hands, then he unlocked the car door and they got in.

'Now,' she said, but she smiled warmly at him, 'did I hear you aright? A girl doesn't get proposed to every day.'

It would be better, she decided, to humour him.

He ignored her question. 'How old are you, Julie?' he asked softly.

'Eighteen next April,' she said. 'But – '

'That's what I mean. I will have to ask your mother for her permission.'

'She wouldn't hear of it!' Julie said. 'She's never even met you.'

'That's easily remedied,' he said, with a trace of the old grin.

She stared at him. 'You're serious, aren't you?' she asked in disbelief.

'Of course I am! What did you think? That I was playing some kind of game?' He took her in his arms and kissed her, holding her as if he would never let her go. When he finally released her, he looked at her triumphantly.

'Are you going to tell me you don't want to marry me?'

'How can I tell you that when I love you so much?' And her lip quivered.

175

'Well, then,' he said, and kissed her again, almost hurting her in his urgency. She broke away.

'Andrew, if it weren't for the war – you wouldn't . . .'

He looked at her, honesty in his blue eyes, and she felt such love for him that she could have wept.

'Just listen to me. I love you, and I want to marry you – be with you. I need you.'

She put her arms around him then and held him, his head on her breast, and made her decision.

'Let's go home,' she said. 'You know the way.'

His eyes lit up. 'Righto,' he said, and turned the ignition key.

When they both got out of the car, they looked at each other, the light of battle in their eyes.

'Come on,' Julie said, taking his hand.

She unlocked the door and led him into the spacious hall.

'Shall I wait here? Perhaps you had better prepare her.'

'Certainly not.' Julie smiled. 'We're in this together, aren't we?'

He followed her up the wide staircase, then she turned and gave him one of her wonderful smiles before opening the door into the sunny living room.

Ada sat by the open window where a breeze lifted the lace curtain. She had been sewing and put it down when Julie came in. Looking up, she saw her with a young man in Air Force uniform, and recognised the schoolboy she had seen a long time ago.

'Mam,' Julie said, 'this is Andrew.'

Ada took a deep breath. She knew, just as if she had already been told, what they had come for. She held out her hand.

'Hallo, Andrew,' she said.

Chapter Nineteen

Ada regarded Andrew and Julie across the living room where they sat side by side on the sofa. It was easy to see why Julie had fallen in love with the boy – he was handsome and charming, in fact seemed to be everything a woman could want in a future son-in-law – but Julie was so young. She simply could not agree to this outrageous suggestion. Why, the girl hardly knew him. But she must be careful and deal with the suggestion gently and fairly. No sense in putting their backs up.

'You see, Andrew, Julie is only seventeen – and, goodness, she hardly knows you.'

He looked at Julie who looked back at him. No doubt about her feelings, they were there for all to see.

She had never, Ada thought, had another real boy friend.

'Another thing – have you spoken to your parents about this?'

'No, Mrs Garrett.'

Ada was triumphant. She had nothing to worry about – of course his parents would not agree. The whole idea would be a waste of time.

'Well,' she said confidently, as though that was an end to the matter, 'I really don't enjoy disappointing you, but I am sure you will see later on that I was right.'

Andrew stood his ground. 'I don't think you realise how serious I am about this, Mrs Garrett.' He faced her squarely.

No, there was no doubt about his intentions, Ada thought.

Julie spoke almost for the first time since the suggestion

had been put to Ada. 'I want to marry Andrew, Mam. I know what I'm doing. We want to be together, and I love him – very much.'

'Oh, it's easy to say that with the war at it's height – so many people marry just to be together, young people who would never have considered marrying in peacetime.'

'That's just the point, Mam. How do we know what will happen? We want to be happy now.'

'And face up to the fact that you may be an eighteen-year-old widow!' She stopped herself. 'Oh, I shouldn't have said that. I'm sorry.' But Andrew laughed out loud.

'You are quite right, Mrs Garrett – I sincerely hope it won't happen, but at least we will have been together.'

They were all three silent for a time.

'You know,' Ada said at length, 'I think you are rushing into this and I suspect it is due to the shock. Losing your brother is a terrible thing – you've hardly had time to get used to it.'

'I had made up my mind to ask Julie to marry me on my next leave, but you're right, the news of Gerald's death only confirmed my feelings – that we should grab life with both hands and enjoy it while we can. Anyway, I want to take Julie home to meet my parents – they get back tomorrow.'

'Andrew,' Julie said, later that evening, 'are you quite sure this is the best time to tell them? They'll still be in a state of shock – they can do without any more worries.'

'Why should it be a worry to them?' he asked. 'They'll be pleased that at least I am still here.'

'Oh, Andrew! Wouldn't it be wonderful if we could just run away together?'

Olivia was waiting for her parents when they arrived back from Devon, anxious to be back in her own world, while Joe and Sylvia Neville, looking white and strained, were pleased to be back in their own home.

She kissed them both, and seeing the expression in their eyes, blinked and swallowed hard.

'You poor dears, I can't imagine what it must have been like.'

She thought, Daddy will never get over it. Mother is

178

stronger – she's a woman. 'I'll put the kettle on,' she said. 'Doris left you a light lunch in the pantry.'

'Not just now,' they both said, and she knew they wanted to talk. She would have to listen. It was better that they got it off their chests – no good bottling it up.

At the end of two hours she was exhausted – two hours of concentrating on the horrific details of the tragedy which had befallen Gerald and Peggy and little Joe. Several times she came near to weeping.

Once her mother looked across at her. 'You mustn't fret, dear,' she said. 'You look so pale – it might have been better if you had come with us.'

'Oh, no,' Olivia put in swiftly. 'I had to wait for a telephone call which came earlier. I hate to rush off but I have to be back – something has come up.'

'I don't like the idea of your going back,' Joe said tersely, tapping his knee.

'If it wasn't this job, it would be something else.' Olivia smiled. 'We all have to do something in this war.' And she felt ashamed of her glib answer. 'Anyway, Andrew is home for a few days.'

Sylvia brightened. 'Yes, that's good – where is he?'

'Do you know, I've hardly seen him since he got back.'

'Well, you get on your way, my dear,' Joe said gruffly, and knowing she just wanted to get back to Richard, and feeling guilty, she gave him an unexpected hug.

'Are you sure you will be all right?' she asked them.

'Of course, my dear,' Sylvia said, and Olivia thought how strange it was that although her mother always seemed delicate, and the weaker of the two, when it came to times of trouble, she was always strong.

'Say goodbye to Andrew for me.' She kissed them both.

'Ring us when you arrive,' Joe said. 'We like to know you've got back safely.'

When Andrew walked in, they didn't know whether to laugh or cry. Hugging him as if she would never let him go, Sylvia had a little weep but quickly dried her eyes.

'Now tell me all about it,' Andrew said.

They were only too glad to go through it all again. It was as if it were a sort of therapy. Andrew clenched his teeth

179

and bore all the details, gruesome though some of them were.

He made them all a stiff drink towards six-thirty, by which time they had had a rest upstairs and come down refreshed.

'You don't have to go back for a while, do you?' Sylvia asked.

'No, I've got until Monday.'

'Oh, that's lovely!' his mother said.

'But – ' as she raised her eyebrows, 'I do have rather a lot to do.'

'Oh?' his father said.

'I want to get married,' Andrew said, and now that he had actually said it, felt a great sense of relief.

'Married!' Sylvia said. 'When? Who . . .?'

His father hadn't taken his eyes off him. 'Well?'

'To Julie – Julie Garrett.'

Joe was dumbstruck. 'Julie Garrett . . . Our Julie? In the office?'

'The same.' Andrew grinned.

'I didn't know you knew her that well,' Joe said.

'Yes, Dad. I've known her for some time, and I would like to bring her home to meet Mother.'

Sylvia and Joe looked at each other.

'All right, Andrew. Whatever you say.'

It had been a little hard on them, Andrew reflected, to spring it on them at a time like this, but in a way, it had worked out for the best for they might not have accepted the situation quite so easily had the circumstances been normal.

'I think I should tell you that we want to get married this leave,' Andrew said. 'I shall take her back with me – we can find digs near the base.'

Sylvia gave Joe a warning glance as he went to say something.

'Well, dear, when would you like to bring her to see us?'

'Thanks, Mother. This evening, after dinner – we won't stay long. I expect you could both do with an early night.'

Andrew held Julie's hand tightly as they walked up to the front door of the cottage. 'They won't eat you,' he said.

'Hello, my dear,' Sylvia greeted her, seeing the pretty girl in front of her and smiling. 'We're not strangers, I think. Don't I know your mother?'

'Yes,' Julie said, and dimpled as Mr Neville took her hand.

'Well, Julie Garrett,' he said. 'I must admit this is a surprise – a pleasant surprise.' And the ice was broken.

Later that night, in bed, and exhausted with the day's events, Joe put out the light above his bed.

'Are you happy about this?' he asked Sylvia. 'After all, it's not exactly what – '

But she stopped him. 'Joe, we have him with us, he is our son, and if this is what he wants – what does it matter? She's a nice girl, and if she can make him happy, I for one will not argue with it.'

He lay thinking for a moment or two. At length he said, 'You're right, of course. What does an old dodderer like me know about it? I've had my life.'

'Not yet, Joe, I hope,' Sylvia said fervently.

'So you see, Mam,' Julie said reasonably, her arm through Andrew's as they stood before her mother, 'Mr and Mrs Neville are quite happy about our marriage.'

'Where will you live?' Ada asked fearfully, and Julie knew she was halfway there.

'We shall find somewhere near the base,' Andrew said. 'Lots of the air crews have their wives with them – there are plenty of digs near the 'drome.' He looked down at Julie's smiling face.

'Seems a strange way to start married life,' Ada said, and Julie knew that the battle was over.

'Oh, Mam.' She broke away from Andrew and hugged her. 'It will be all right, really it will.' Her eyes were brimming with tears of happiness.

They were married by special licence in Winchester, with Ada Garrett and the Nevilles in attendance. Afterwards Joe took them to an hotel for a celebration, and if Ada thought that her own little world had come tumbling down about her ears, she behaved with perfect grace and dignity. Julie looked so lovely, and so young – her beautiful eyes so like her father's, her riotous hair tumbling about her shoulders. She wore a small hat at an angle, an elegant suit, and carried a small bouquet of flowers which complemented its colours. Never, Ada thought, had her daughter looked more beautiful, while Andrew stood beside her in uniform, tall and straight. Please God, she prayed, let them be happy and keep them safe.

The young couple drove down to Bournemouth where Andrew had booked into an hotel, and almost with a sense of unreality, it had all happened so quickly, Julie found herself standing by his side as he signed the register: Mr and Mrs Andrew Neville. She saw the receptionist's smile as he saw the spray of tiny rosebuds pinned to her jacket – they needed no stray confetti to betray the fact that they were newly married.

Andrew had booked the best available room which overlooked the sea. Once inside, he took her in his arms and held her close.

'Happy?'

'I didn't know I could be this happy. I do love you, Andrew.'

'You know, I think I knew right from the first time I saw you that this is how it would be,' he said. 'My pretty little Julie.'

Later, those lustrous eyes looking up into his, completely trusting him, he thought how lucky he was to have this beautiful girl as his wife. She was everything a man could want. They made love throughout the night, savouring every moment, rejoicing at being together, falling asleep from sheer weariness just before dawn.

Julie woke first, almost unable to believe what she saw – Andrew's fair head on the pillow beside her. She kissed him gently, and putting on a wrap, went over to the window and looked out at the sea in the distance, at the barbed wire barricades preventing people from going down on the beach, at the installations along the front, the war like deterrents. At the same moment, the warning went and she went back to bed as Andrew woke and opened his eyes, immediately putting out his arms and gathering her to him.

182

'Let's forget the war,' he said. 'Let's pretend it doesn't exist.'

But Julie felt suddenly sad. It was almost worse to have had this idyllic happiness and to know it would be taken from her in a very little while. Still, for Andrew's sake, she must always be bright. No moping, no outward signs of worry. That much she owed him.

She bent over him and kissed him, her soft white hands caressing his face, his eyes, her lips touching his hair, his body, until he could bear it no longer – and his arms went round her and held her to him. Slowly he made love to her, taking his time, which was almost more than she could bear. Only the enormous crump of a nearby bomb and the sound of anti-aircraft guns brought them back to reality.

Afterwards, when the all clear sounded, they went down to breakfast and then strolled along the sea front toward Canford Cliffs where they sat, hand in hand, looking out to -sea for a few minutes before retracing their steps.

They had so much to talk about, knew so little about each other, that the time flew by. They returned to the hotel and Andrew made plans.

'We'll call in at Andover on our way back – you could telephone Miss Farquarson to let your mother know. Perhaps you'd like to pack a bag with some things and I'll book a room for us near the base? There's a nice little hotel at Denham which is no distance from Northolt. I'll book us in there for a few days, then you could look around for some digs – I'll ask around at the camp, there are bound to be quite a few in the area.'

'I shall always remember this room – in this hotel,' Julie said dreamily, and looked down at the slim gold band on her finger.

Andrew took her hand then gave a start. 'God, Julie, I'd forgotten.' And he dived into his top pocket, bringing out a small box.'

He handed it to her. Open-mouthed with surprise, she opened it to disclose an antique gold ring set with a yellow stone. 'Andrew! It's beautiful – where did you get it? When?'

'I didn't.' He looked sheepish. 'Mother gave it to me just

as we were leaving – it belonged to her grandmother. I've never seen it before, but she thought you would like to have it, just until I can buy you one.'

Her eyes filled with tears. 'Oh, it's beautiful. How kind of her to give it to me.'

He slipped it on her slim finger, where it sat as if it belonged there, above her wedding ring. She held out her hand. 'Thank you.' And drawing his head down to hers, she kissed him lingeringly.

'I really don't want to leave,' she said, smiling through her tears.

He took her hand without answering and led her through the door and down the stairs to the waiting car.

By evening, they were on their way down the Western Avenue out of London towards Northolt.

'There it is.' Andrew nodded. 'That's where my base is – but we're going on for a bit. The farther out of London, the safer you are – or that's the way it's supposed to be. You'll like Denham, it's one of the prettiest villages in this part of the world.'

The sun was setting as they drove into the small village with its idyllic cottages and wistaria clad hotel. Inside the hotel it was snug and warm, and there were one or two men in Air Force uniform at the bar. The landlord showed them to their room under the eaves.

'Well, this wil be home for a while,' Andrew said. 'What do you think?'

'I can't think of anything nicer,' Julie said, looking through the small latticed panes of the old hostelry, the chintz curtains and bedspread.

'Monday tomorrow – and I have to report back to base. Still, I know you are near me, and you will be busy. One of the first things I must do is to teach you to drive. You'll find it necessary to get about – I don't suppose there's much of a bus service in these parts.'

But the next day, with Andrew driving himself off to Northolt, she began to wander around, going by bus to various places nearby and searching the area. By the end of the week she was getting used to it all, and had met several of the young wives of Andrew's colleagues. They were full of helpful advice: where to look for accommodation, where to shop, the transport problem, and most of all how to cope with young husbands who flew daily from the air base into the skies in order to do battle.

After ten days at the hotel she had found accommodation in a bungalow on the outskirts of Denham golf course. It was somewhat isolated, and transport might be difficult, but sometimes Andrew would give her a lift, and the owner's wife also went into town occasionally. It was so delightful that she agreed to take it.

Pam Gardiner, the wife of a friend of Andrew's, had told her about it. 'I know Mrs Anderson hasn't anyone at the moment and she usually takes single men only – doesn't like another woman in her kitchen and you can't blame her. But, still, it's worth a try.'

Grateful for any suggestions, for obtaining digs was proving much more difficult than they had expected, Julie made her way up the hill on a sunny afternoon where at the end of a long drive she found the bungalow, sitting in its own grounds, surrounded by the most beautiful gardens. The view from up here was quite spectacular, and as she reached the house she saw a woman in the garden, wearing a long dark red velvet housecoat, carrying a trug of cut flowers, her long black hair falling down her back. Almost mesmerised, Julie stood still and stared. It was an idyllic scene, like something out of a film. The woman, sensing perhaps that someone was there, came towards her. Her face was heavily made up, Julie saw as she approached, and she must have been around forty.

'Can I help you?'

Julie began to explain, as she had on many other occasions, that she needed to find a home, a room of their own for her husband and herself – her husband was based on an aerodrome.

The woman seemed very undecided about this. 'Well . . . I don't know.' Julie was quite certain that she had had a wasted journey when the woman turned towards the house. 'Come and meet my husband – we'll see what he says. We usually take one person – a man, usually, because then he can share a meal with us. I quite like cooking, and we do

185

feel that we must make our contribution towards the war effort.'

Julie followed her, captivated by the woman's appearance and her surroundings. She tried to imagine the husband: handsome, wearing tweeds, smoking a pipe, forty-fiveish. The woman reached the front door.

'William,' she called. 'William – there is someone to see you.'

She held out her hand. 'I am Mrs Anderson.'

'Mrs Neville,' Julie said, still getting a slight shock and a thrill of pride whenever she said it.

The hall was large and square, with warm carpets and wood panelling and flowers everywhere. They overflowed from bowls and jardinieres, from the fireplace and from dark corners – and the scent was almost overpowering. On the stairs stood a giant vase of white arum lilies.

Then the tall, bent figure of an old man came in through the French windows at the back of the hall, his white hair sparse, a drooping white moustache beneath a strong, hooked nose on which perched rimless glasses. Afterwards, Julie hoped she hadn't stood there with her mouth open. Leaning heavily on his stick, he came towards her.

'William, this is Mrs Neville – she and her husband are looking for accommodation. He is up at – well, I expect we know where he is stationed. Anyway, what do you think?'

He held out his free hand and took Julie's.

'How do ye do?' he said, and turned to his wife. 'I thought you said you didn't want a woman in the kitchen?'

She frowned. 'I don't really, darling – but, well, it's very hard on these young people. Are you out at work, my dear?'

'No – not yet, but I expect to get a job soon,' Julie explained. 'We've just moved here – we only got married recently, you see.'

'I thought so.' Mrs Anderson smiled. 'Well, I expect we shall manage somehow, just as long as you don't want to take over my kitchen.'

Julie laughed. 'I don't imagine so. I haven't had much experience as yet.'

'That's it then, is it, Ive?' the old man said.

'Oh, I wish he wouldn't call me Ive!' the woman said crossly, leading the way up the stairs. 'I like to be called by my second name which is Pandora – you may call me that, if you like.'

'Thank you. I'm Julie.'

'There's only one room upstairs, and a small bathroom. We had the loft fitted out at the beginning of the war for visitors,' Pandora explained. 'So you'd be quite alone up here – and private.'

It was delightful, dark mahogany furniture and yellow chintz, in a room with a wonderful view.

'What do you think?'

'It's lovely!' Julie said, her eyes shining.

'Now I'll show you downstairs.'

She led the way down, showing Julie the pink bathroom outside which stood a small summerhouse filled with flowers, one of which Julie had never seen before – with vivid blue flowers which were trailing in through the window, tangling up with pink geraniums.

'Oh!' she gasped. 'What is it?'

'The blue? It's called plumbago.'

'Not a very nice name for a lovely flower!'

'And this is the kitchen.'

It was small, and neatly kept, with a gas cooker and shelves for saucepans and a small table at which to eat.

'Well, what do you think?'

'I think it's simply lovely. Would you really let us come and live here?'

'You had better ask your husband to come and see it, hadn't you?'

Julie smiled. 'If I like it, I am sure he will approve. Er – what about the rent? How much would it . . .'

'Let's go and find William. I expect he's listening to the news – he has it on all day.'

'William, this young lady approves of us and would like to come and stay. She wants to know how much rent we should ask.'

He looked at her over his spectacles, and knocked out his pipe in the ashtray before replacing it in his mouth.

'Well, then.' And he puffed away. 'What do you say to

thirty shillings a week each to include light and heat and cooking?'

'I'm sure that is all right,' Julie said. She still couldn't believe her luck.

'Then that's settled,' he said, striking another match. 'You'd better bring your young man along to see us.'

'Oh, I will – perhaps this evening if he is free. I could telephone you.'

'We'll leave it like that then,' Pandora said, and walked Julie back to the end of the drive.

Julie couldn't wait to see Andrew and to tell him the news. It was nine o'clock before he could drive them up, as amazed as Julie at the pleasant house and its surroundings.

When they were all seated in the low drawing room with its beamed ceiling and low lamps, William looked at Andrew and then at Julie.

'So this is your new husband, is it?' he asked, his faded blue eyes twinkling, while Pandora stood behind his chair smoothing his partly bald head.

Julie smiled. 'Yes.'

'You've got a lovely young lady there,' he said. 'Mind you take care of her.'

'Yes, sir,' Andrew said.

'Well, we'll take it as settled, shall we?' he said, and Pandora bent down and kissed the top of his head.

'I'll make us some coffee,' she said.

'Can you believe our luck?' Julie cried as they drove down the long drive. 'And aren't they an extraordinary couple, Andrew?'

'I think I'll send you on all the family errands,' he said.

She leaned over and kissed him. 'I'm so happy, Andrew, I just can't believe it's really happening.

Once back at the hotel, she sat down to write some letters. One to her mother, then to Andrew's parents, and finally to Sarah.

Sarah . . . from whom she had had no news for a long time. What was she doing now? What would she have to say when she knew her school friend was married already, and to Andrew Neville of all people! She looked across at him, seated by the open window of the hotel bedroom. A new life was starting for them – please God keep him safe.

She took up her pen and began to write. 'Dear Sarah . . .'

Chapter Twenty

Sarah felt life had really begun when her parents left for Scotland. With them out of the way, she felt she was free to do just as she liked – although in her heart of hearts, just at first, she missed them.

Travelling the short distance from Ruth's flat to the office took no time at all, and once she had been installed with her few things, the bed chair made up as a bed, she found it no hardship at all. She and Ruth spent many happy hours discussing the theatre, and what their future might be.

Another uplifting thing had been her promotion on the newspaper – not a very good one, but a step in the right direction, although the increase in salary was not enough to get excited about. It entailed helping out the crossword man, Harry Adams, and giving help to the department which dealt with competitions and raising money for the war effort.

'You reckon you're good at English – ' the assistant editor said to her 'see how you get on there.' One of these days, Sarah thought, I'll throw something at him!

At first she had been delighted, but as the days wore on and her work for Harry became more and more boring, what with the crowd of girls taken on to deal with competitions and war savings, office work became more like being back at school, and each day she vowed that her stay with the newspaper would not be for much longer.

But at the moment it was her hobby that mattered. Rehearsals for the new play took up a lot of the time, and

Ruth was full of advice to Sarah as to how to get on in the theatrical world.

'Do you know what I'd do if I were you? I'd join a repertory company – even as assistant stage manager – for the experience. Although God knows the pay is bad. You'd have to be a fool to want to do it, but then actors are – fools, I mean. It's different for me – I know my limitations. I'm just not good enough to make a career of acting. Besides . . .'

'Besides what?'

'Nothing, really,' Ruth said. 'It's just that I can see you're cut out for something better than what you're doing right now.' And Sarah dwelt on this advice most of the time – that is, when she was not thinking about Jon Dangerfield.

He was still with them, although he expected his call up any day, but as spring wore on into summer, they were reading for the last play of the season. After that, she was going up to Scotland for a long weekend as part of her annual holiday. She had promised them for ages.

Fortunately for her, air raids dictated everyone's travelling. It was easy enough to say that trains had been delayed, that a bomb on the line had disrupted services, that the long coach journeys had been cancelled. So far she had got away without going up to Scotland at all, but soon she would have to take the plunge. It was only fair.

Now, the excuse would have to be rehearsals for the next production for which they had already had the readings which she always enjoyed. It was so interesting to see the way in which each person read. It was a foregone conclusion on her part that she would get the role of Sybil in J. M. Barrie's 'What Every Woman Knows'; it was inconceivable that Sally would get it, for heaven's sake. You had to have a sense of humour for that part which Sally certainly didn't possess.

Jon would almost certainly play the lead, he was a natural for it, which was why she particularly wanted to play opposite him. He seems to be so taken with Sally, Sarah grumbled to herself, and she's such a silly thing. Even Ruth says so.

So it was a complete shock as the parts were read out at

191

the final audition when she found herself playing understudy to Sally, in prompt corner, and second assistant stage manager.

Her first instinct was to walk out, but head high she smiled sweetly at everyone and congratulated Sally, who simpered her thanks. 'Thanks awfully, Sarah.'

There followed two weeks of rehearsals at which Sally repeatedly apologised for forgetting her lines – it seemed that her father was ill at home in Dorset, and she was having difficulty concentrating on her speeches for worrying about him.

On the third Monday evening, Sarah sat in the wings with the prompt copy of the script, seeing Sally's anguished eyes turn in her direction over and over again.

' "It is so cruel",' Sarah prompted for the third time, and Sally responded gratefully.

A few minutes later it happened again. Even Jon was getting impatient.

Sarah sighed. Well, Sally Bateman might be a better actress but she was blooming awful on her words.

'I'm sorry, Sarah,' Sally apologised when she came off. 'I don't know what's the matter with me – I can't seem to remember a thing.' She turned anxious eyes to Sarah. 'My father is ill, and I suppose half my mind is on him.'

'Oh, I am sorry,' Sarah said. Perhaps there was just the teeniest chance that Sally might have to return home to Dorset?

In the event, that was just what happened. Relinquishing her part, Sally made a hasty exit to Dorset and Sarah fell into the part.

It was a totally renewed Sarah who took over, determined to do her best. It helped, of course, that her leading man was Jon Dangerfield, and she threw into the part all the passion of which she was capable. It came all the more easily because of her feelings for him. Surely, she thought, he can see how I feel about him?

Whatever the reason, Sally's absence or Sarah's fervent performance, Jon asked her out to dinner.

Sarah was in her element. They dined at a good restaurant, Jon choosing masterfully from the menu. When he took her home, he kissed her expertly. It was her first real kiss, and not to be compared with anything they did on the stage. She ran upstairs, her lips quivering, her face burning, her body restless with a longing she had not known she possessed.

Ruth sat up and put on the light. Sarah blinked and hid her face.

'Nice time?' Ruth asked.

'Yes – lovely, thanks.' And Sarah hurried into the bathroom.

After that, she saw Jon after every rehearsal, then on Sunday he told her he was hiring a car and driving out into the country. 'Like to come?' he asked her, his blue eyes raking her from top to toe, fair hair glinting in the sun.

Sarah nodded. She couldn't think of anything nicer.

They drove through countless villages, and sat outside a small pub where they had a bread and cheese lunch. They parked and walked through leafy woods, where they sat down on a grassy knoll and Jon kissed her until she could bear it no longer and sat up, beseeching him to stop, afraid of her own need for him.

He looked down at her – the thick fair tousled hair, the vivid blue eyes beneath the straight dark brows looking up at him with unrestrained ardour.

'Have you never been with a man, Sarah?'

She blushed to the roots of her hair. 'What do you mean?'

'Come now. How old are you – nineteen?'

She nodded. 'No.' She was scared, yet she wanted him to go on – against her will, even.

He got up and helped her to her feet. She brushed down her skirt, afraid to look at him, so much did she want him.

'Come on,' he said. 'Back to the car.' And she didn't know whether to feel relieved or miserable.

It was dark when they reached the city outskirts, and he parked beneath a large tree and turned off the darkened sidelights.

He took her in his arms and she went willingly. Presently, when she stirred and resisted a little, he said: 'Don't fight me, Sarah. I won't hurt you – trust me.'

What followed she couldn't have stopped if she'd wanted

193

to. After the initial agonising thrust, she relaxed and gave herself up to him, knowing that this was what the loss of her virginity meant. That now it had happened, she was really free. What's more, it was fantastic – no wonder people raved about it, fought wars for it, killed for it.

Afterwards she sat up, her eyes shining in the darkness.

He took her face in his hands. 'I didn't hurt you, did I?'

'Yes, you did, but don't apologise. It was as much my fault as yours.'

He kissed her and her arms went around his neck as a tap came on the window. Jon lowered the window to see a policeman with a torch. 'Come on you two, move on.'

'Right, officer.' Jon grinned and started up the car.

Did she look different? Sarah peered at herself in the cracked bathroom mirror. She looked softer, more vulnerable, but her eyes continued to shine. She wasn't sorry – not a bit.

Sally returned two days later, relieved that her father was on the mend. 'I'm so glad I went,' she confided. 'He was so pleased to see me.'

'Oh, good,' Sarah murmured. Now what would Jon do? Already she felt that he was hers, but they kept away from each other for a time.

She hadn't long to wait. As the week's performances came to an end and they held the usual after show party, Sally was wearing a tiny emerald engagement ring which she flashed to all and sundry.

'Congratulate us, folks,' she said. 'Jon and I are engaged.'

There they stood, the handsome young couple, Sally looking up at him adoringly, Jon looking down into Sally's eyes, and when he did look up to smile at the well wishers, it was to look at everyone in the room except Sarah.

It was a salutary lesson and one that bit deep. After sobbing herself to sleep for two whole nights, she emerged feeling drained and a fool but determined never to allow herself to be used so lightly again – if she could help it, she thought wryly, and found it in herself to smile. Poor Sally . . .

Now, she told herself, is the time to get on with my life. To do what *I* want to do. With advice from Ruth she wrote off to the Midlands Repertory Company telling them she was free to join them if a vacancy could be found for her, and sat back to await the result.

Her appointment was in Birmingham at two-thirty in the afternoon, with a Mr Arthur Lewin. When she arrived at the station, she went straight to the ladies' waiting room to check her appearance. A dab of powder on her nose, a touch of lipstick, then she moistened her lips and smoothed her thin brows and checked her stocking seams with a damp finger.

She set her beret dead straight on her fair hair, pulling it slightly at the front until she got it right. She was more than pleased with the effect. The image she wished to present was just right – she looked about nineteen.

'Ah, Miss Sarah Lowman,' Arthur Lewin said. He was a short man with a mass of iron grey hair which curled down into his sideburns, and very shrewd dark eyes which took in every asset of Sarah's appearance from top to toe. He opened a silver cigarette case and offered her one.

She shook her head. 'Thank you, I don't smoke.'

He picked up her letter and scanned it.

'So you don't sing and you don't dance – what *do* you do?'

'I am an actress,' Sarah said, playing a part and loving it.

'Your letter is postmarked Leicester yet you say you are from London?'

Sarah sighed deeply. 'Yes, my home is in London, but my people have a place in Leicester – a country home – although at the moment they have had to go to Scotland. My father is on work of national importance and Mummy is terribly unhappy up there – but there is nothing she can do about it.'

He coughed gently. 'What experience have you had, my dear?'

Sarah crossed one elegantly clad leg over the other.

'Quite a bit. I was in the last show at the Adelphi before it closed down for the war, then previously I was at the Haymarket in the 'Doctor's Dilemma'. She sighed, and frowned, as though there were too many to remember. 'Then . . .'

'What part did you play in that?' He looked down and made a few notes.

'I worked backstage, actually, it was my first job.'

'I see. And you are – nineteen, you say?'

'Yes, well, almost,' Sarah said. Really, it all came too easily. It was just as it had been at school when she got carried away.

She smiled pleasantly across at him, a man with something of her father about him and none of the coy nonsense that the assistant editor had.

He returned her smile. He hadn't believed a word of it. She wasn't a day more than seventeen, and he doubted if she had any real experience, but you couldn't stop these stagestruck kids. They'd stop at nothing to get their way.

'Well, Miss Lowman – is that your real name, by the way, or a stage name?'

'My real name – Sarah Lowman,' she said. How well it sounded! Sarah Lowman in 'Pride and Prejudice' with Laurence Olivier . . .

'Well, Sarah,' he said. 'You would have to start right at the bottom here, and work your way up to parts. Stage managing, props, scenery – that sort of thing. You will be given an audition, that's part of the rules, but I am sure there will be no difficulty there. The money is poor, but of course you know that. And in any case – ' he looked at her under his lashes ' – you would seem to be a fortunate young lady as far as family is concerned.'

She smiled demurely.

'We have a couple of committee members here at the moment, so if you would like to step into the next room?'

It was all over in half an hour, and Sarah emerged, cheeks glowing, after learning that she could start on the lowest rung of the ladder with the Midlands Repertory Company. Not only that, but they had been able to suggest theatrical digs for her – true, she would have to share a room with three other girls, but what did that matter?

She walked home on air, wondering as she did if indeed Eva and Tom Lowman were her real parents. After all, it was not inconceivable – many an actress had had to abandon her baby in order to carry on working. It just seemed slightly ludicrous that her parents should be so ordinary.

Ten days later found her in Birmingham, in a shabby but

genteel house on the outskirts, sharing a room with Marcia and Barbara and Olive, who was a middle-aged actress who had once appeared with Geilgud. Sarah was as excited as she could possibly be, and had taken her leave of Leicester, her job and Ruth without a backward glance.

'Good luck, kid,' Ruth said. She was given to Americanisms, and saw herself as the English Joan Blondell.

Having parked her scanty belongings in the room to establish possession, Sarah caught the bus for the station where she was to embark for her first journey to Scotland. She had written to her parents to tell them what she had done, wishing to avoid a confession when she arrived. With a Birmingham address, they would wonder what she was up to.

Eva Lowman stood and surveyed the room in the tall, dark house in which they rented accommodation in Inverness. With its high ceilings and large rooms, sometimes they worried that they would ever get warm again. But she had made a home of it although she hated the idea of living with other people's furniture and hardly had time to change the room around these days, much less want to. With its dark sofa and big old chairs filled with horsehair, its antimacassars and old-fashioned lace curtains – still, she had done the best she could, and at least she was with Tom and had Valerie with her. She also had a part-time job, for all the Scotswomen seemed to work, and truth to tell she enjoyed it and the money was welcome.

And now Sarah was coming up to see them! She couldn't wait to see her daughter again – it had been such a long time. She just hoped there wouldn't be any raids while Sarah was on the journey. Eva had got used to being away from her – as Tom said, they could never have stopped her – and now see what she had done! Joined a theatrical company – she never would have done that if she'd been living at home! Eva would give her a piece of her mind, see if she didn't – but now, all she could think of was seeing her again.

It was late morning when the taxi cab arrived outside number fourteen, and Eva flushed with pleasure. The neigh-

197

bours would see Sarah arriving in a taxi – little minx, her mother thought. How on earth could she afford a taxi? but that was typical of Sarah. If she could show off, she would.

She watched her walk down the tiny path. How smart she looked! Her long slim silk-clad legs – and those high heels! How on earth did she walk in them? She'd ruin her feet. And that tight-fitting dark suit worn with a white blouse – and the perky hat pushed forward on a mass of curls – she looked like a film star, Eva decided, but she wouldn't tell her so. Sarah was vain enough as it was.

And yet when she opened the door, she was near to tears at seeing her, this beautiful elegant elder daughter.

'Oh, it's lovely to see you!' she cried. 'Come in. Dad's in the garden – he's working nights this week.'

Sarah leaned forward and kissed her mother. 'Hello, Ma.' even her voice, Eva thought, was quite posh these days.

Sarah smelled the old familiar scent of furniture polish and Wright's Coal Tar Soap, but above that was the inviting smell of roast beef and Yorkshire pudding.

She slid off her kid gloves and threw them down with her handbag on to a chair – real leather, Eva thought – but those shoes . . .

'Sit down. I'll tell Dad you're here.'

Sarah looked around. God, what a gloomy place! Fancy having to come up here – she might have been on the other side of the world. Yet somehow it was home. Strangely, after living in digs it was nice to come home – just occasionally.

Eva walked through the kitchen and into the garden. Ma, indeed! Where had she got that from? So common! Still, she had blossomed, was quite beautiful in fact, and very smartly dressed.

Tom regarded his daughter as though she was someone from Mars – with a mixture of pride and disbelief. One of these days he felt sure she would be famous. Took after his sister Dolly, although he would never have said as much to Eva. Besides, Sarah knocked Dolly into a cocked hat.

Over lunch they told her how well Valerie was doing, and she was genuinely pleased. 'At least you have one clever daughter, Ma,' she laughed. 'One out of two – not bad.'

198

'You're both clever,' Tom said, 'in different ways.' He was not going to have his elder daughter denigrated.

Eva was cutting the apple tart before she mentioned Sarah's move into the theatrical world. 'So how did that happen, then?'

'Well . . .' And Sarah told them, adding or subtracting here and there, making a point of how disgusting the assistant editor had been. 'There, what did I tell you?' Eva said, appealing to Tom. And so after everyone, simply everyone, at the amateur dramatics had told her she was a born actress, that she must, simply must *try*, she stressed, for it was the most difficult thing in the world to get accepted into, she had managed it! By this time Eva had found herself praying that they would accept her, which was just what Sarah had intended. Her mother even gave a sigh of relief when the story came to an end.

'I should think so!' Tom said, pouring custard over his apple tart, and Sarah relaxed with the confidence of a story well told – a job well done.

'They get a lot of raids in Birmingham,' Valerie said.

'Oh, dear.' Eva's spoon was halfway to her mouth.

'Don't exaggerate, Val,' Sarah said kindly. 'No more than anywhere else. Leicester, Bath – that sort of thing.'

'What do you do when you are in the middle of a performance and the warning goes?' Valerie persisted. Sarah had not told them she was general dogsbody.

'Well, the show stops for a moment, then the manager comes out and says, "Will those of you who have to leave, or wish to leave, please do so?" And then we carry on.'

'Golly,' Valerie said, impressed. It was what had happened one night when Sarah was at the theatre in Leicester. 'Besides,' she went on, 'there is an excellent shelter beneath the theatre itself, and a public shelter immediately opposite.' Catch me going down it, she thought.

'Oh, dear,' Eva said. 'I can't bear to think of it.'

'Now then, Eva,' Tom said. 'You can't be sure you're safe anywhere these days.'

So the weekend passed pleasantly in complete acceptance of Sarah's new life in Birmingham. She wouldn't have believed it would go so easily and even shed a tear on leaving, much to her own surprise.

Sitting in the train going home, it was with the satisfaction of a job well done. She couldn't wait to get back to her new life. In the boarding house, the three women were waiting to welcome her.

'How did you get on, dear?' Olive asked. She was the eldest of the three. 'Did you find your parents all right?'

'Yes, thank you,' Sarah said. 'Mummy is being terribly brave about it.'

'Poor soul,' Olive said, commiserating. 'It's awful to have to uproot yourself like that. Still, I'm sure she must be pleased that you've found yourself nice digs. We'll look after you.'

'You're very kind.'

Then on Monday morning a letter arrived from Julie – forwarded on by Ruth from Leicester. Sarah opened it eagerly and read it, then flopped into a chair, speechless.

Julie – married! It wasn't possible . . . Married already – and only seventeen! And to that handsome young Neville chap. My word, she hadn't wasted much time. Well, she wished she'd known that before she went to Scotland – imagine what her mother might have said. She would have been shocked beyond words. That would teach her to know when she was well off. She wouldn't find her daughter marrying as young as that – whoever he was. She had a future to think about, and no man was going to mess that up . . . Still, good old Julie. What wouldn't she give to see her. She might one of these days – where was she? She turned the letter over. Denham, in Buckinghamshire, wherever that was.

Well, it was her turn for the bathroom, and wrapping a towel turban round her hair, she wandered off and up the stairs to the next floor to cope with the erratic geyser, humming an Al Bowlly song as she did so. 'Let's fall in love, why shouldn't we fall in love – '

Yes, a whole new world lay waiting out there for her.

Chapter Twenty-one

As the summer of nineteen forty continued, so did the horrendous air battles which were fought over the mainland of Great Britain. Julie saw less and less of Andrew as the pressure from the German Luftwaffe grew in intensity, and settled herself in for a long wait at the home of Mr and Mrs Anderson. Every spare moment Andrew spent with her, teaching her to drive the little Austin Swallow, for he was sure she was going to find it indispensable in the months to come.

She soon became proficient enough to drive the car on her own, taking Andrew to the airfield and being free to drive herself around the area where she had decided to do war work before being called up, for everyone had to register on arriving at a new address.

While the air battles raged nearby, for they were on the fringe of London in Denham, she spent many sunny afternoons in the delightful garden with William Anderson while Pandora drove into town for shopping. The old man taught her the names of flowers, and how to propagate them, and she spent many happy hours with him in the greenhouse, potting up the baby plants.

'All this is for Ive,' he said once, spreading his arms to encompass the gardens. 'She was the prettiest little thing you ever saw when she came to work for me. Sixteen, that's all she was, and me a man with three grown-up sons. But she stole my heart away, and I left my wife and came south with her. "I'll surround you with flowers" I told her, and that's what I've done.'

'It's beautiful,' Julie said.

What a romantic story, she thought. Poor first wife – she wouldn't have stood a chance against someone like Pandora. That week she decided to help out at the forces canteen in Uxbridge, for to get anything more permanent was against Andrew's wishes.

'I may be moved off any day,' he said, 'so there would be no point in starting a regular job. Couldn't you spend your time here, helping William in the garden?'

'Andrew, I must be doing something for the war effort – when I think of what you are doing and hundreds like you.'

'You are doing your bit just being here with me. Julie, I love you so. I never cease to tell myself how lucky I am that we met when we did. Are you happy?'

'Blissfully.' Julie put her arms around him and closed her eyes.

He was exhausted, she thought. Being made to do more than they should – they were all in the same boat. The other pilots, all so young, all doing more than their fair share, being sent up time and time again after refuelling with never enough breaks in between. Oh, surely it must come to an end soon?

'The first chance I get we'll go down to Andover,' Andrew said one evening after arriving home for a three-hour break. 'You'd like that, wouldn't you? I expect you can't wait to see your mother again.'

Julie's eyes shone. 'Oh, Andrew, could we? It would be wonderful!'

There came a time in September when she thought he would never return. He was gone for long spells, and she knew that vital airfields near the coast were being strafed by enemy bombers. Dogfights took place overhead, and everywhere there was an atmosphere that it was now or never. It couldn't go on like this.

Once, in Uxbridge, shopping for the evening meal after her session at the canteen, she caught sight of Pandora with a handsome young Air Force officer. They were arm in arm, swinging along the pavement, laughing – when the air raid warning sounded. Some people went straight to the shelters, but Julie made for the station where the little car was parked, and drove herself home.

Poor old William – but there was an inevitability about it. There was a war on, and people were going to make hay while the sun shone.

Pandora arrived home long after Julie, and William was furious.

'Where've you been, Ive?' he asked crossly, but she went over to him and kissed him and smoothed his head.

'There was an air raid warning – didn't you hear it, darling? I went down the shelter. I knew you'd be cross with me if I didn't.'

'Yes, you must always take shelter, Ive,' he said.

That weekend Andrew was given a twenty-four hour pass and they drove down to Andover, through a heavy air raid, where the sky was dark with gunfire and smoke, and a pitched battle was taking place over their heads. They watched from the doorway of a concrete shelter as German planes zoomed towards the earth, black smoke pouring from their tails, while to the east the sky was ablaze with an orange glow from what must have been enormous fires below.

'Looks like one of the worst yet,' Andrew said grimly, as taking a chance, they got back into the car and drove south.

They stayed with the Nevilles, and went to see Ada who had taken over the departed housekeeper's duties and was looking after Miss Farquarson.

'Mrs Edison left – she wanted to do war work in a local factory – so I stepped in.' Ada seemed quite pleased at the idea.

'It's not too much for you?' Julie asked anxiously. Being at the beck and call of someone as difficult as Miss Farquarson could be quite hard work.

'No, I enjoy it. She's not a bad old thing when you get to know her – and at least now I have the kitchen to myself. And what about you? I must say, you look wonderful. Although poor Andrew – he does look tired.'

'He is.' Julie agreed. 'This is the longest break he has had since we got married.'

'Well – I'm not going to pretend that I don't miss you,'

Ada said, 'But I think you did the right thing at the end of the day.'

Julie spent a happy couple of hours telling Ada all her news, about the lovely home she and Andrew were staying in and the odd couple – enough to keep her mother engrossed for a long time after she had gone.

'Well, I never!' Ada said, again and again.

On Sunday morning, the Nevilles were delighted by a surprise visit from Olivia who had come in response to her father's telephone call.

'I simply had to meet the bride. You got married so quickly there was hardly time.'

She was rather lovely, Julie thought. Tall and slim and elegant . . . and there was something else about her, a light in her eyes that was not there because of seeing her brother again. She's in love, Julie decided. She has that look about her, a special radiance which makes her eyes sparkle and her skin glow like fine porcelain.

It seemed to be a case of mutual admiration for Olivia more than approved her brother's choice.

'She is so pretty, and quite a little lady, Mother,' she said. 'Mrs Garrett's daughter, isn't she?'

'She is,' Sylvia Neville said, 'and you couldn't find anyone more genteel than that. Anyway, she makes Andrew happy, that's the main thing.' She bit her lip.

'Now, mother,' Olivia chided. 'We've all got to be terribly brave and not think sad thoughts. We must concentrate on victory.'

Easier said than done, Sylvia thought.

Olivia drove herself home, conscious that she had pleased her parents enormously by her visit. Poor old sweeties, both she and Andrew away from home, and Gerald gone – but how could anything be more important to her than Richard? And how happy Andrew and his new young wife were. If only she and Richard could be married . . . but she might have to wait some time for that. Still, it would happen one day. And smiling to herself at her pleasant thoughts, she changed gear and began the climb uphill.

Things had gone very well for her since leaving London and moving down to Wiltshire. With Richard's promotion, and consequently hers, and Miss Dayton leaving at the end of the month, Olivia was on top of the world. She had slipped into a senior position with no trouble at all, to say nothing of her private life with Richard.

For his wife, Rosanna, had stayed on with the children in the States, on advice from Richard. There was no point, he told her, in coming back to an air bombardment. He would worry about her and feel much happier knowing she was over there.

It seemed a much more sensible arrangement all round, especially as the hours they now worked were long and arduous, sometimes all through the night with a few hours off during the day. It was a slightly unreal lifestyle for all high-ranking government officials and Richard, with his eye on a position in the cabinet of the future, worked harder than most.

They made a good team, Richard and Olivia, although now they worked so closely together it became increasingly difficult to play the charade of employer and secretary. Sometimes they went to Richard's apartment in the large mansion which had been commandeered for the war effort, sometimes spent the night in the air raid shelters provided for them or drove out during snatched moments to somewhere quiet and isolated. The intrigue added more romance to the situation than if they had still been in London.

At least. Olivia thought, I know where Richard is – which is more than can be said for little Julie. It must be simply awful not knowing each time if Andrew is coming back. And she shuddered. She must telephone home as soon as she arrived.

'Well, she got back all right,' Joe said, coming back into the drawing room from answering the telephone.

Sylvia was thoughtful. 'She looked well, didn't she, Joe? And happy.'

'Mmm,' he grunted. He wasn't going to say how worried he was that it might be because of the chap that she worked for. You couldn't control them once they had grown up.

Arriving back in Denham, Andrew put the little car away, taking out the rotor arm to make it immobile. The Andersons were already in bed, for it was quite late, and he followed Julie upstairs to the pretty bedroom.

She yawned. 'Is it four tomorrow morning?' she asked him.

Andrew grinned. 'Yep – but don't worry. I'll drive myself unless you need the car.'

'No, I'll take you,' she said. It was something she loved to do on early stints, driving down the lanes as the dawn was breaking, seeing the sun come up, flooding the earth with a pinky glow. With Andrew beside her she could have driven to the end of the world.

Julie worked most mornings in the forces canteen, and afterwards made her way home. One evening Pandora had been to the cinema in Uxbridge with a neighbour from down the lane. When the time grew late, William had worked himself up into a fine state. At the sound of a car, he turned to Julie.

'If I thought,' he said grimly, 'that young Ive . . .' But in came Pandora – no doubt in Julie's eyes as to where she had been and with whom – and crossing over to William, went into raptures about the film. 'You should have come with us, Julie,' she said. 'You'd have enjoyed it.'

Julie smiled. 'I'm sure I would. Well, I must go up.'

'I am making cocoa for William. Would you . . .'

'No, thank you,' Julie said. 'Goodnight.'

A sour note had been introduced into what had been a perfect haven, and Julie sighed. Well, it had been nice while it lasted. She prayed that Andrew might be safe.

On the fifteenth of September, a date which afterwards was thought to have been the climax of the Battle of Britain, huge formations of German bombers closed in on London, but now Fighter Command had sufficient strength to inflict decisive losses, and while the battles raged overhead and across the channel, London seemed to be on fire. The glow could be seen from the high point between Middlesex and Bucks, and the sky was dark with planes. Julie, who had gone with other pilots' wives to watch the distant scene, felt she could bear it no longer, and walked slowly back to the house.

Oh, it was too much. She couldn't bear to watch it any longer. Andrew, up there – what chance did he have?

Telling herself she must be strong, she busied herself in the garden, finding a sort of sweet therapy in weeding and tidying the flower beds, seeing the new growth on old bushes, inhaling the scent from the dark red roses that had been grown especially for Pandora.

The radio gave the news at six o'clock that twenty-seven fighter planes had been shot down, but fifty-six German aircraft had been destroyed.

'Wonderful! Well done!' William cried, almost tearful in his appreciation. He was the most patriotic Englishman Julie had ever met.

It was not until Monday morning that Julie received the official news. Andrew had not returned to base. His aircraft was missing, and there was a personal letter to her from his commandant.

She could hardly bear it. She had been in the kitchen when the news arrived, and now she fled upstairs and threw herself down on the bed, her eyes dry, her teeth clenched, her body taut with despair.

Much later she broke down and wept. It was William who came upstairs with a tray of hot tea and some biscuits.

'Here, lass, drink this.'

She took it from him wordlessly, looking at him, and he thought he had never seen such beautiful eyes in all his life.

'He's not dead,' she said. 'I know he isn't.'

He covered her hand with his. 'Good girl, that's the stuff.'

Later, when Pandora came up, her eyes red from weeping, she sat by the side of the bed.

'You're terribly brave,' she said. 'I'm such a coward.'

Julie managed a smile. 'So am I,' she said, 'but Andrew will come back – I know he will.'

Pandora swallowed. How wonderful to have such faith. But she was so young . . .

'Try to get some sleep,' she said, and kissed Julie's damp forehead.

The days which followed were empty days, barren days when nothing seemed to matter except news of Andrew, which never came. Each night when she went to bed, Julie wondered how she would face the next day. It was almost better to stay awake all night than sleep and face the shock when she woke that Andrew was missing all over again.

It was on one of these mornings that she woke up feeling queasy and realised for some time now her breasts had been heavy and tender. The realisation that she might be pregnant was almost too good to be true, but as the days wore on and she realised that it was indeed not only probable but almost certain, she could hardly contain her delight. She would say nothing to anyone for the time being.

Julie waited for two weeks until she felt she was ready to leave Denham behind. Armed with the knowledge that she was going to bear Andrew's child, she stood looking at the little maroon Austin Swallow motor car outside the garage. I shall have to get you home, she decided. She had never driven farther than a fifteen-mile radius but armed with Andrew's maps, for all signposts had disappeared by now, she knew she would make it. Taking her time, not rushing things, there was no hurry.

When the day came, she looked about her once more at the bedroom where she and Andrew had been so happy and went downstairs into the flower-strewn hall. The Andersons were waiting for her and kissed her fondly, telling her to write to them and come back and see them. When she got into the car, she found the back seat full of flowers of every kind: dark red roses, tiny pink ones, exotic dahlias, early chrysanthemums. As she drove away, the scent from them overwhelmed her and she started off with tears raining down her face.

Soon, concentration on the journey took her mind off her departure, and she found herself manoeuvring the small car in and out of traffic and convoys on the road with ever increasing dexterity. She stopped for lunch at a wayside cafe and studied the map for the way down to Hampshire.

It was four o'clock when she drove into the Nevilles' cottage, having decided to go there first before going home to Ada. They had known she was coming and were waiting for her with a warm welcome.

'Oh, my dear!' Sylvia cried, and taking Julie in her arms, looked at Joe above the girls head and bit back the tears.

Presently she released Julie, and Joe kissed her warmly. The news had aged them, Julie thought sadly, first one son and now another.

'Mrs Anderson gave me so many flowers – may I bring some in?'

'Of course, dear!' Sylvia said. 'Let me help you.' Thus the first few anxious moments were over, and soon Julie and the Nevilles were drinking tea and talking round everything except the fact that Andrew had not returned from his last mission.

'I must say, you did jolly well driving down – you've only just learned, haven't you?' Joe said admiringly.

'Yes, I'm feeling quite smug,' she said. 'I feel if I can cross London, I can drive anywhere. It's all due to Andrew's tuition, of course.' And at the mention of his name, you could have heard a pin drop.

The elderly couple looked at each other miserably.

'He's not dead,' Julie said calmly. 'I know it. I can feel it – here.' And she pressed her heart.

Joe Neville got up and walked slowly out of the room.

'Julie dear,' Sylvia began, 'don't you think you should . . .'

Julie smiled. 'I know what you are going to say . . . get used to the idea that he is not coming back. Well, I think he is. Lots of pilots are shot down and make their way from somewhere or other.'

What faith! Sylvia thought, then took a deep breath.

'You are a very brave girl,' she said. 'Now, I wasn't sure where you would be staying. I'm sure you know that you are so welcome here – we have the room and would simply love to have you. But I expect you will want to get home to your mother. We will quite understand, but you will always have a home here.'

'Thank you,' Julie said. 'I thought I'd stay with Mam for a time, it's only natural she would want me to, but after that perhaps I could come here? You have more room – for a baby.' She said shyly, her cheeks rosy.

It took a moment for it to sink in. 'Julie! You're pregnant! Oh, that's wonderful. Joe – Joe!'

'What is it? He came hurrying back, looking startled.

209

Sylvia put an arm around Julie's shoulder. 'The most wonderful news, Joe. Julie is going to have a baby.'

Slowly his dark squirrel-like eyes began to sparkle, then he coughed and blew his nose, obviously overjoyed at the news. A grandchild!

'I was going to offer you your old job back, but not now.'

'I should like that,' she said.

'You can sit at home and put your feet up and read all day as far as I'm concerned,' he said. You are going to take care of that baby, young woman.'

She smiled at both of them. 'I must get off home and see Mam. She'll be wondering what has happened to me. I can't wait to tell her my news – she'll be so thrilled.'

Upstairs, in Andrew's old room, she brushed away a tear as she laid out his silver-backed hairbrushes on the mahogany chest.

'Please come back, I miss you so much,' she whispered, then composed her face into a smile as she went downstairs to his parents.

Chapter Twenty-two

By November the German air attacks had increased in intensity. The whole of the centre of Coventry was devastated; four hundred planes dropped five hundred tons of bombs and thirty thousand incendiaries. Fifty thousand houses had been damaged and hundreds of people killed. This was followed by horrific raids on Birmingham, Liverpool, Manchester and Sheffield and many other cities.

In December, Olivia paid a fleeting visit to her parents, staying overnight. Richard was in the country, having received Christmas parcels from the children and Rosanna, and still the raids continued. Olivia could hardly wait to join him again, despite the journey back to Wiltshire, but it was wonderful to see Julie looking so well, so settled in the spare room at the cottage. The tiny room next door had been made into a nursery, and was full of baby things like a cot and basket, an Enna bath on a stand, and there were fresh new curtains up at the window.

On the night the raiders passed over the secret hideout of the Foreign Office on their way to devastate the City of London at the end of December, Richard and Olivia had driven out to a small restaurant in a tiny village nearby. In the distance they could see the flares in the sky and hear the ack-ack barrage some way off. Richard had said nothing on the journey, his eyes fixed on the narrow dark lane in front of him, Olivia at his side, a little apprehensive.

He drove into the darkened car park, then took her arm and led her into the dimly lit restaurant. They were shown to a corner table which was hidden and discreet.

He wasted no time telling her. 'Rosanna is coming back.'

Her eyes clouded. 'Oh, Richard – no!'

'Sshh,' he whispered, although there were few other diners. 'Look, my dear, it was to be expected. I never really imagined she would stay away this long.'

'When is she due back?'

'I have managed to get her a special flight on Tuesday next week.'

'It won't make any difference to us, will it?' Her eyes beseeched him.

'Of course it will – at first,' he said. 'You can't expect otherwise. It's been wonderful up to now, but it can't go on forever, you must see that.'

The full implication of what he was saying sank in, and her heart began to beat faster.

'Richard, you don't mean . . .'

'For a week or two – until she gets settled in. It's only right, Olivia, you must see that. I can hardly confront her with the news that I have – '

She put out a hand. 'Don't,' she whispered. Everything had changed. A few words, and her whole life lay around her in ruins. That woman – his wife – how dared she come back! On the day Margaret Dayton had left, she and Margaret had been in Richard's London office, and seeing again the photograph of Rosanna on Richard's desk, Olivia had done what she had vowed never to do. The words were out before she could stop them.

'What is she like – Richard's wife?'

Margaret had looked at the photograph and smiled.

'Rosanna? Oh, she's a poppet, awfully nice. He's a very lucky man.'

Only afterwards did Margaret wonder a little on the way home in the train. Funny Olivia should have asked that, after all this time. There had been occasions, once or twice – but she thrust the thought from her. Olivia wouldn't. She was much too sensible for that. Much too sensible to add to the long list of girls who worshipped at Richard's feet. No, not Olivia.

Now, Olivia recalled what Margaret had said. The words

were burned into her brain. A poppet – awfully nice – a lucky man.

She came back to reality to find the waiter hovering beside them. 'Olivia?' Richard said.

'I'm sorry.' She smiled playing her part. 'I was dreaming.'

When the waiter had gone, she looked up at Richard tremulously. 'I'm really not very hungry.'

'Darling, you must eat,' he said, looking at her across the table, her fair skin even more pale against the rich auburn of her hair. Her long slim fingers toyed with a spoon, her eyes were downcast.

'You knew it was bound to happen sometime,' he said gently. 'Rosanna was not going to stay away forever.'

'I know, I know,' she replied. 'I was living in a dream world, I suppose. It has been so long, and we have been so free – I imagined it would go on and on.'

He covered her hand with his. 'Life's never that easy,' he said, giving her one of his rueful smiles which never failed to move her.

'Oh, I am being so selfish!' she cried. 'I never gave a thought as to how you must feel. Poor darling.'

He looked almost dejected, she thought. Poor man – what an awful situation to be in. Now was not the time to moan, to let him down.

Her face brightened. 'Let's make the most of it,' she said. 'After all, we have a few days.'

Soon she was smiling, and they laughed over the meal, returning in the small hours, having made love in the car in a dark country lane, with giggles and passion and avowals, until utterly spent they made their separate ways into the grand house which served as their evacuation unit, not to meet again until the next day.

And so the days wore on until Sunday when they both left for town where they spent the night in Olivia's small flatlet with Richard leaving at four in the morning in the middle of an air raid. She knew no peace until the next day when she saw him at the important meeting. Now she would not see him again for ten days during which he would have met Rosanna at an RAF base to welcome her home. How would she be able to bear it?

The war news was grim with appalling loss of life when Bank underground station was bombed in January, killing one hundred and eleven people. All around them were scenes of devastation, and it was then decided that the department should move permanently to a safer place. London would see them no more until the end of the war.

Olivia went with mixed feelings – she had loved her tiny flat and the intimacies she had there shared – it was far more difficult for her and Richard to see each other alone in the new environment, but at the moment, she was not seeing him at all. Ever since Rosanna had arrived home, in fact. He kept strictly to the rules. It was much as it had been when she first started working for him. Short, crisp requests, staccato orders, refusal to meet her eye, until she could have wept with frustration.

It was during this period when she was missing him most, that she realised she could be pregnant. Consulting her diary, she sat at the dressing table in her room, the blackout curtains pulled across the windows, staring at herself in the mirror, the rosy pink lamp reflecting her eyes which had grown enormous. Her face was deathly pale in this light, and her hands began to tremble. She held on to the dressing table to steady herself – she had never felt more like fainting in her life. She could be wrong – and she held on to that fact tightly – but commonsense told her she was probably right. Oh, God! What would she do? Where could she turn? What would Richard say? She felt physically sick.

A doctor – that was the next step. After all, it happened to many women in wartime. But, please, not to her. Too much was at stake. She mustn't – she couldn't – be pregnant. God, what a mess.

Driving herself to Salisbury the next day, she found a medical practitioner who seemed not at all surprised at her fears, and said that it was much too early to tell, but if she was really anxious to know then a urine sample might help. At the end of a week she learned that undoubtedly she was almost two months pregnant.

Part of her was horrified – an unmarried mother! But it was Richard's child, the offspring of their love. Now they would have something tangible to share between them, and he would know that the time had come for him to leave Rosanna. How she would deal with the disgrace of having a baby out of wedlock she couldn't imagine, for even if Richard started divorce proceedings right away, these things took time and there would be no way he could marry swiftly. And her parents! It could not be more of a disaster. Richard must know immediately – she needed him, he would understand and comfort her. Then again, how would they face the department with this knowledge? It might be better if she went away until the baby was born, resigned, then Richard could come to her wherever they decided she should be.

She was due to see him on Friday evening, the first time since Rosanna's return. They would go to the same small restaurant where they had dined that evening. Rosanna was staying in a hotel in the village nearby before looking for a cottage to rent, and had gone to town to see her father who was still living in his London house. Olivia had caught sight of her briefly waiting in the car park for Richard. She had seen her many times at official functions but never actually met her. Now she could hardly bear to think that Rosanna was even staying nearby. London was so large it had seemed to absorb her, but down here . . .

She was due to meet Richard at the restaurant at seven for he was driving and she was to take the local taxi. She had put on the blue dress he loved for the occasion, and wore the perfume which he had given her on her birthday. Her heart thumping wildly, she walked across to his parked car. He smiled at her, opened the door, and she climbed in.

'Olivia, my dear.'

'Richard, it's been an age. I've missed you so.'

He bent and kissed her. Was it her imagination or was he different? Had the enforced parting changed him? Had something happened?

She took his hand. 'Richard, I have something to tell you.' She had rehearsed the moment but now that she was with him again, couldn't wait before blurting it out.

He released her, and made a move to get out of the car. 'Come on, let's go inside for a drink. We deserve that.'

'Wait.' She held him back. 'Listen. Richard –'

'Can't you tell me over a drink?' He was frowning slightly. He hated to be thwarted in any way.

'No, I'm afraid not. You can celebrate later if you like – but, Richard . . .' She tried to find the courage to say what she had to say. There was a long silence as he waited.

'Richard, I'm pregnant.'

He sat staring in front of him, then he said softly, 'Christ!'

'Oh, Richard, you're not angry. Please say you're not angry!'

'My dear Olivia, what do you expect me to be?'

She felt the first twinge of annoyance. 'It takes two, Richard.'

'I know that,' he said. 'It's as much my fault as yours. Are you absolutely sure?'

'Yes, I've been to see a doctor.'

'My God,' he said, looking at her as though seeing her for the first time, and her anger subsided. 'Richard, I didn't want it to happen – how do you think I feel?'

He turned then and kissed her swiftly. 'My poor little darling, of course you feel awful. I have to say it is the last thing I'd have wanted.'

She turned anguished eyes to his.

'At this time,' he said, 'with a war on.'

'But, Richard – it may be the best thing. After all, you are going to leave Rosanna.'

'But I can't do that right away, darling,' he said, as though speaking to a fractious child.

Olivia pressed on. 'I've thought about it, and come to the conclusion that if I left the office and went away somewhere, then you could visit me whenever you were able. I realise it is going to be difficult.'

'Difficult!' he exploded, then almost immediately calmed down and took her hand.

'Olivia, darling, much as I dislike the idea, you are going to have to get rid of it.'

'Richard!' She was horrified. It was the last thing she had expected him to say. 'How can you suggest such a thing?'

'It's the only way, my dear. You don't really want a baby, now do you?' He looked at her as if she were twelve years old. 'Think of all it means – the talk, the possible repercussions. I'm thinking of you, my dear, it's always the woman who pays in these situations. To go through all that, at this time, when I haven't got things sorted out with Rosanna.'

'Damn Rosanna!'

He sighed. 'I know how you feel but we must face this sensibly, Olivia. I can't rush things now – not when she has come back home. Let's think about it, and plan the future. I am sure we can find someone . . . Look, let's go in and have a drink. I could do with a stiff whisky, I don't know about you.'

They sat at the usual corner table, and now having regained his composure, he regarded her, seeing the dark smudges under her eyes, the transluscent skin.

'You're not thinking straight, darling,' he said firmly. 'You've been through quite a strain this last week, but I'm sure you will come to see that what I suggest is the only thing possible.'

Her expression was mutinous. 'What if I want this baby?'

'Shh, darling, do keep your voice down. Have you thought of the position we are both in – senior government servants? They expect us to be more cirumspect, and to arrange matters discreetly.'

'Well, we can.'

'Not if you intend to – '

'Have it?' And her eyes sparkled dangerously.

He decided on a different tactic. 'You are a little goose,' he said, and put his hand over hers. Her face cleared and her eyes shone.

'Oh, Richard, I knew you'd understand. It must have been a shock. It was to me.'

'Let's order,' he said, picking up the menu.

They talked of everything else except the most important thing until it was time for coffee. By this time they were both calmer.

'After all,' Olivia said reasonably, 'you always said we would get married one day when you left Rosanna.'

He ignored this and pressed home his point. 'Another thing, don't forget my – our – future is at stake. I can't afford to let the slightest hint of scandal interfere. We don't want anything to upset that, do we?'

'Of course not,' she said staunchly.

'That's why, my dear, we have to see this latest problem as something that has to be resolved right away – before it is too late. I am thinking of you, darling. I am afraid it is a little indulgence we cannot afford at the moment. Besides, what on earth would you say to your parents? They've just had two jolly rotten experiences – how on earth would they cope with this? You're not thinking of them, Olivia – in fact, I think you are being quite selfish.' He looked at her reproachfully and waited for this to sink in. 'Besides, didn't you tell me they have no idea about us?'

'No, they haven't,' she said hurriedly.

'Well, then,' he said reasonably, but her face still wore its obstinate expression, and there was a long silence.

'Aside from anything else,' she said at length, 'I don't like the idea of an abortion.' She lowered her voice. 'I can't bear to think of being messed about with.'

'Olivia.' He took her hand. 'We shall find the best man available, I promise you that. Just trust me and leave it to me.'

They drove home in silence, Richard dropping Olivia at the front door of the mansion where she hurried into her room.

He drove to the hotel where Rosanna was staying, and got out his papers to work through the night. She would be back sometime on Sunday morning, and after a couple of hours' sleep he was up and dressed and ready to welcome her back.

He heard the MG roar into the car park behind the hotel and pulled aside the lace curtains. Yes, it was Rosanna – petrol rationing never worried her, she seemed to have an endless source of things that were in short supply for other people.

When the key turned in the lock, he stood up to greet her.

'Rosanna, darling.' His arms went round her as she lifted her face for his kiss.

Then she took off her perky little hat and smoothed her hair. He studied her trim figure in a beautifully cut man-tailored suit of fine tweed, her silk blouse fastened at the neck with a gold brooch – a gift from her father.

'How was the old man?'

She smiled. 'Difficult, you know him, but he's all right. He intends to stay put – nothing, he says, will drive him away from London. Not Hitler, not bombs, etcetera, etcetera. You know how he is.' She turned to him. 'Well, did you tell her?'

They looked at each other for what seemed like ages, before he said, 'She's pregnant.'

'Oh, no, Richard! No!' All the colour drained away from her face.

'I'm afraid so,' he said.

'You are a swine, Richard,' Rosanna said slowly. 'That poor girl.'

She sat down opposite him. 'How do you know it's true?' She didn't put it past any girl to use any method she could to get him.

And he told her, almost word for word, and as he spoke, she knew she had heard it all before. Not the pregnancy part – that was new – but girls . . . would he never learn? They fell about for him, that was the trouble, she had done so herself, but apart from the fact that she understood him, what made him tick, understood his relentless ambition and his overpowering attraction for the opposite sex – they liked each other. And, she thought grimly, I have the most important thing – the money. Would he have stayed with her so long if she hadn't? That was something she would never know.

'So what's she going to do?'

'She wants to have it.'

She laughed. 'Oh, my God! How ridiculous! And I suppose you told her that you were going to leave me and marry her, just like you did poor Rosie Delaney?'

'Well . . .'

'Men like you are a menace, Richard, but we'll forget you for the moment and concentrate on Olivia.'

She had known about Olivia from the beginning. Nothing much escaped Rosanna, she knew all the signs and read them expertly. Knowing him, he always had to have someone in tow; in fact he rather enjoyed the intrigue of it all, and rather than disturb what was obviously a close relationship between them, she had settled for that. She knew he never could, nor would, be faithful to her, it was an impossibility, but she had long ago decided that no one would come between them. Better to suffer the indignities of paramours and extra-marital affairs than lose him. She loved him, and enjoyed being Mrs Richard Bannister.

'So you got nowhwere,' she said thoughtfully.

'How could I? She greeted me with the news as soon as I saw her.'

'You know one of these days, Richard, some husband or father is going to thrash you within an inch of your life. It's what you deserve.

She looked across at him. He was so good-looking and had such a way with him – presumably he would go on like this for the rest of his life. She recalled some of the other women in his life. She hadn't much time for any of them, they had all known he was married, but this one . . . from what she had seen of her, and what she knew, Rosanna felt rather sorry for. Of course, if girls would play around with married men they deserved all they got. But a baby! That was something else. She was quite certain it had not been intended. It didn't sound the sort of thing the girl would do deliberately in order to ensnare him – but now she must act quickly.

'You know, Richard, not a word of this must leak out. Imagine what would happen. The press . . .'

'I know,' he said grimly.

'Well, what do you intend to do about it? It's your mess, you should get yourself out of it.'

'I told her she must get rid of it but she was shocked – oh, you know how they are, these well brought up girls. Daddy's darlings.'

'All the more awful for her,' Rosanna said blandly. 'She's not far along, is she?'

'She said she had been to a doctor and had it verified.'

Rosanna got up and stood in front of him where he sat on the chintz-covered sofa, legs outstretched, a look of relief on his face knowing she would get him out of it.

He looked up at her, his blue eyes ingenuous, his expression one of trust and faith in her, yet withall with a look of desire and admiration, a promise.

Am I a fool – or clever? she wondered. He really is a monster, a menace to young women, especially the vulnerable ones like Olivia Neville.

'Richard,' she said at length, 'I sometimes wonder if you need me at all except to get you out of scrapes. It is hardly flattering to have one's husband continually chasing after other women.'

He jumped up in a moment, his arms about her. 'Need you? Of course I need you, Rosanna. You are the only woman I have ever loved!'

She looked up at him and smiled incredulously.

'After all,' he said, 'you weren't here. I missed you so badly –'

She broke away. 'Please, Richard, don't lie! I can bear anything but lies. It had started a long time before I left for the States.' She sat down on the sofa. 'The thing is, we have to work out the best thing to do. Are you prepared to tell her it is all over? That it's finished? And I do mean *finished*, Richard.'

He looked quite sulky, she decided, like a small boy who has been refused a toy, his cheeks flushed, his eyes downcast.

'Well?'

'You'd have to give me time,' he said. 'After all, in view of the circumstances, I can hardly . . .'

'That's just what we haven't got – time,' she said coldly. 'What are you going to do?'

'I need to think.'

It was soon after lunch the next day that she presented herself at the reception desk where the commissionaire in his army uniform waited to vet any visitors. She showed him her identity card and he waved her to the desk.

'I would like to see Miss Neville,' she said. 'I am Richard Bannister's wife. Is it possible to have a word with her?'

'Of course, Mrs Bannister. She's on the ground floor, number four, at the end of the corridor on your left. I don't know if she's in, though.'

'Never mind,' Rosanna said, 'I'll find her.'

She tapped lightly on the polished mahogany door of number four, and at first there was no reply. She knocked again and presently heard the door being unlocked. Then she was face to face with Olivia in the narrow hallway.

Rosanna gave her warmest smile. 'Miss Neville?'

The girl looked awful. She was pale enough to start with but when she saw her visitor almost swooned and held on to the door. Her beautiful red-gold hair hung about her shoulders and she was as white as a sheet. Her amber-coloured eyes looked at Rosanna through a mist of pain. She wore a dressing gown, pulled around her. She was obviously ill.

When she said nothing, Rosanna stepped inside and closed the door firmly behind her, locking it.

'Did you just get out of bed to answer my knock?' she asked.

Olivia nodded.

'Then you get right back again,' she said firmly, taking the girl's arm and leading her towards the bedroom. Olivia made no demur but allowed herself to be put back into bed and covered up warmly with the eiderdown.

Presently she spoke. 'Rosanna . . .'

'Yes,' she said, 'Richard's wife.' As though to establish the situation from the very beginning.

'Why have you come?' The girl spoke in a whisper.

'I think you know why,' Rosanna said gently, sitting down on a chair at the side of the bed.

Olivia lay back, her eyes closed, her face pale, almost transluscent, and Rosanna had a sudden thought.

'You don't look at all well,' she said slowly, choosing her words carefully, and Olivia turned her face away as a sob escaped her.

Rosanna put out a hand and touched Olivia's brow. It was feverish, although the girl was shivering, and she had a sudden compunction.

'I know all about it – Richard told me,' she said. 'And you're not to worry, everything is going to be all right.'

At this, large tears welled up in Olivia's eyes and spilled

222

down her cheeks. 'Oh, you mustn't cry!' Rosanna was horrified. Nothing was going at all as she had intended it.

Presently, Olivia stopped crying, sniffed, then blew her nose and seemed to take control of herself.

'You've nothing to worry about any more,' she said miserably, very much on her dignity. 'I've lost it – the baby, I mean.'

'Oh, my dear!' Rosanna said, the first great surge of relief swiftly followed by compassion for what the girl must have gone through. Her eyes searched Olivia's face.

'Yes, I'm sure,' she said, in answer to Rosanna's unspoken question.

'But how?' And she saw the shut down look come over Olivia's face.

'I'm sorry, it's none of my business,' Rosanna said, and could not escape the feeling that as the older woman she had some kind of duty towards the girl. 'You must excuse my asking, but did you have a doctor?'

'No.' Olivia turned away.

'Then you must see one,' Rosanna said. 'Just in case.' And Olivia turned startled eyes to her.

'I had a similar experience before I had my children, and I know that there is the need for attention.'

'Why?' Olivia asked fearfully.

'Just a minor sort of thing – after all, you want to be sure that you can have babies in the future. Think of it as a cosmetic operation – a beauty treatment, if you like.' She looked straight into Olivia's eyes. 'If you agree, I shall put you on to my own doctor. He's quite a wizard – I know a little about these things. My brother is a surgeon.'

She was fully aware of Olivia's doubts.

'Trust me,' Rosanna said.

'Why did you come?' Olivia asked. She twisted her hankie between her fingers and looked quite exhausted.

'I thought you would understand that,' Rosanna said. 'It was to ask you – to implore you – to reconsider your wish to go ahead and have the child.'

'In the event,' Olivia said bitterly, 'you've got your own way.'

223

'You will realise in time that it is the best thing,' Rosanna said. 'He isn't worth it, you know.'

'It's easy for you – you're his wife!'

'Between you and me, my dear, it has never been easy for me.' And Rosanna smiled ironically. 'It is not perhaps the best time to tell you but you are not the first, not by a long chalk. I have had a lot of experience dealing with young ladies who are in love, or think they are in love, with my husband.' And Olivia buried her face in the pillow.

'Did you know about us?' she asked at length.

'Yes, of course I did,' Rosanna said. 'You can't be married to someone like Richard without knowing – he almost wants you to know. It's all part of the game.'

'How awful.'

Rosanna got up. 'I'm going to make us a good strong cup of tea,' she said. 'We both need it.' And she disappeared into the kitchen. When she returned, Olivia was lying still with her eyes closed.

'Drink this,' she said, 'and swallow a couple of aspirins.' She eased the girl up on her pillows, saw her thin, pale hands take the proffered cup and saucer.

'I shall be back to see you in the morning,' she said. 'That is, unless you would rather I didn't?'

Olivia gave the vestige of a smile.

'If you are well enough, we shall drive up to London in my car and I shall take you to see my doctor.'

'Oh, but – '

'No buts,' Rosanna said firmly. 'You need some attention, that's all I am saying. And you're not to worry. Would you like me to come back this evening?'

'No – really, thank you.'

'Then I suggest,' Rosanna said carefully, 'that you take a long rest. I don't imagine you will want to return to the office for a while?'

'No,' Olivia said gratefully. She looked straight at her visitor, golden eyes wide. Rosanna could quite see how Richard had fallen for her. 'I didn't do anything,' Olivia said. 'It just. . .'

Rosanna smiled. 'Try to sleep. I'll see you in the morning.'

Back at the hotel, she found Richard waiting for her. He looked up anxiously.

'Did you see her?' he asked. 'How did she take it?'

She ignored him and taking her suitcase from the wardrobe, began to pack it.

'What are you doing?'

'Packing – ready for tomorrow, Richard,' she said. 'You can forget your worries – there's no baby, luckily for you – but Olivia does have 'flu rather badly. I have advised her to stay in bed for the time being so she won't be coming to the office.'

His face was a study.

'No baby. You mean she made it up?' He sounded incredulous.

'No, Richard, she lost it. But she is not at all well. She has 'flu, as I told you.'

He looked down at her suitcase, half full of clothes.

'I suggest you sleep in your room over the road tonight,' she said. 'I shall leave in the morning after breakfast. And you can forget about the cottage – I'm going back to town to stay with Father.'

'Rosanna! What are you saying? You can't leave now – now that –'

'Everything is all right? But I can, Richard, and I won't be coming back for a long time. At the moment I feel sick inside. I feel I never want to see you again.'

He went to take her in his arms. 'Rosanna.' But she backed away. 'No, Richard.'

His arms fell to his side. 'You've had a shock,' he began.

'Perhaps,' she said, 'it's been more like a rude awakening to me. Please go, Richard. There's no point in your trying to change my mind.'

When he had gone, she sat down abruptly at the dressing table, staring at herself in the mirror. She saw a pretty woman, still attractive at thirty-six – the mother of two lovely children. Was she doomed to spend the rest of her life clearing up after Richard's escapades?

No, she told herself grimly. There had to be another way.

Chapter Twenty-three

It was on the journey back and forth from Scotland for Christmas and the New Year that Sarah finally decided that she would leave Birmingham for good. With time to relax and think objectively, she had gone over in her mind the events of the past three months and knew that for her things were not moving fast enough – not by a long chalk. She was sick and tired of sitting in prompt corner, of watching other members of the cast acting parts she could have done standing on her head, of being props manager, seeing that the ashtray was on the table, and the chair in place. Of working backstage to see that the right costumes had been delivered from the theatrical costumiers who were under-staffed in war time and liable to send the wrong props, or checking the stage scenery, ordering the scripts. Most of all at the time she had to spend doing nothing and for very little money.

Looking on the bright side, she had gained a lot in experi-ence, an this was mostly due to the good advice of Arthur Lewin who had taken her in hand. 'You're a good little mimic, dear,' he said in the beginning, 'you can take off any-one, but acting is not just that – it has to come from in here.' And he thumped his fist against his chest. 'Also,' he went on 'your voice is a bit thin, a bit nasal – that's the Cockney in you. You'll want to get rid of that. Large, round vowels.'

Fuming inside, Sarah smiled sweetly and wistfully.

'If I might make a suggestion? Go and see Elvira Sim-monds. She does voice production. It will be money well spent. Once a week – you'll soon catch on.'

Well, she had, and had to admit that Mrs Simmonds had worked wonders. A large elderly woman, who could control an army let alone a single pupil, she had made Sarah practise over and over again until she was hoarse. 'From down here,' she bellowed. 'Your voice is coming from your mouth – not your abdomen. Breathe deep, deep . . .' It was amazing, after a few lessons Sarah had got the message, and when she was alone practised reading aloud, the words coming from somewhere deep down inside her as she breathed deeply.

On the down side, she was fed to the teeth with Edwin Braithwaite, who was becoming a nuisance. He watched her like a hawk, her comings and goings, spied on her, was intensely jealous of her, although he had no right to be. He even wrote poems to her, for God's sake. To think there was a time when she would have been so impressed with a famous old actor following her around that she might have done anything for him. Well, almost anything. He wasn't that old, fiftyish, and as handsome a man as you'd find with that wonderful head of hair. She always thought he imagined himself to be a descendant of Charles the Second. Add the profile – you couldn't fault it, the strong aquiline nose, the beautifully shaped mouth – and his voice! Oh, he was handsome all right, and charming with it.

She looked down at her lap. It was Edwin who had given her the handbag and gloves for Christmas, and she thought. Well, if he wants to spend his money on me, who am I to refuse? To say nothing of the flowers and the messages. It had been flattering at first, but now it would be easier to leave and start something else. He was an old man – old enough to be her father.

The bomb on Friday night had decided matters. Falling just short of the theatre, but doing enough damage to put it out of action for some time, it seemed to Sarah to be the decisive factor. Even though Arthur Lewin had begged them to try to stay together, with diminishing audiences and lack of male actors there was no doubt in her mind that this was not the best time to start an acting career.

Besides, she missed London. She was a Londoner born and bred, and at this a crocodile tear came to her eye and her pretty mouth quivered, so that it was all the gentleman in the seat opposite could do to prevent himself putting a fatherly hand on her knee to console her.

Yes, she would go back to London. No need to tell the parents. As far as they knew she was happy and content in Birmingham. Why worry them before she had to? Best to do as she had so far. Do it – and tell them afterwards.

They were delighted to see her, this actress daughter who was doing so well, having proved she could look after herself, who looked so smart and elegant. Like a film star, Tom Lowman thought. Only Valerie privately disapproved. Birdy, she thought, which was her word for something common. With those high heels and curls, plucked eyebrows and lipstick, Valerie just hoped none of her grammar school friends would see her sister. Especially up here – it was not like London where she might have passed unnoticed.

Eva Lowman had little time now for moving the furniture around for she worked in a food-packing factory which she enjoyed, seeing the other women and sharing their worries and fun. They were a jolly lot, and not in the least what she had expected. Tom worked hard, lots of overtime, and she worried sometimes that he was overdoing it, but it was lovely to be a family again, especially at Christmastime and Hogmanay.

Sarah returned to London with a real tartan skirt, a present from Eva, and bought herself a black velvet tam-o-shanter which suited her to a tee. She wore it on the train home, much to the enjoyment of troops making their way south.

Her first surprise – and shock – was a letter from Julie which had been forwarded on after much delay from Leicester. On reading it her face paled. Oh, it couldn't be true! Her fears had been realised, Andrew Neville was missing . . . She took a deep breath. So that was that. It was over so soon, Julie a young widow – for Andrew would never come back, how could he? Being shot down what chance did he have? And Julie pregnant . . . it didn't bear thinking of. Poor Julie. She stifled a sob, a real one, and going into the bedroom, lay down on the bed and cried a little, thinking of Julie and their young lives together, then brushing away her tears, got up suddenly, her mind made up. She would go down to Hampshire to see Julie, suddenly wanting to see her more than anything in the world. How could she have stayed away so long? But first she must put her house in order. Give in her notice to the repertory company, to the landlady, pack her things, scant though they were. A sense of excitement overtook her. She was on her way. Back to London. That's where it was all happening. She counted her money. Well, not a lot, but enough to get her there. Something would turn up, it always did.

Her blue eyes bright with excitement, in her tartan skirt and black beret, she stood on New Street station during an air raid alert. Above her she could hear planes whining and the sound of anti-aircraft guns, but by now everyone was so used to it that unless there was imminent danger, they carried on as if nothing was happening. Of course you could never tell if you were going to be unlucky, that was the gamble you made, but it took more than an air raid to frighten Sarah. She had nothing but contempt for German bombers.

The platform and the waiting rooms were full of people, soldiers and airmen, most other people in uniform of some kind or another. Sarah stood out in her civilian clothes. A man standing next to her took sidelong glances, his haversack at his feet, smiling at the sight of her youth and beauty – what a grand picture she made, this Scots girl – and then suddenly everyone dived for cover as a whistling sound rent the air. They knew what it was. It exploded quite near, in the goods yard farther down the line, and people picked themselves up, the dust now seeping everywhere, covering everything with a fine layer of ashes and soot. Now everyone was smiling again, even laughing. They were safe – that one had not been for them – brushing themselves down, finding porters to reassure them that the train would arrive, the scene a sea of activity and enthusiasm now that they knew they would survive.

Sarah took off her beret and shook it, ramming it down on her curls again, then brushed down her new skirt. No damage, she thought angrily looking up at the sky, seeing the tracer trails of fighters. Andrew would have been one of them, she thought. Poor Andrew, who would never see his baby . . .

'Are you all right?' the man beside her asked, and saw blue eyes that were full of anger – not fear. Sarah turned to see a good-looking man in civilian clothes.

'Thank you, I'm fine.'

'That was too close for comfort.' He smiled. 'Are you waiting for the London train?'

'Yes.'

They were interrupted by an announcement over the loudspeaker that the train had been delayed owing to a bomb on the line and would be anything up to an hour late.

There were groans from all the would-be passengers who began to move away from the platform, and in the ensuing melee Sarah made her way to the station buffet where she ordered a cup of tea. Taking it back to the table, she found the other occupant was the man who had stood beside her on the platform. She put down her cup and smiled at him.

'Hello again,' he said. He had a lovely speaking voice without any trace of an accent, something Sarah had become very conscious of since taking elocution lessons.

'You know,' he said, as she stirred her tea, 'I thought you were a Scots girl.'

'Oh, no.' She laughed. 'I'm from London.'

'Going home?'

She nodded. 'Yes, I've just been to see my people in Scotland – it's such a drag. Still, what can one do?'

Unconsciously she had assumed a role.

'They are up there for the war?' the man asked. 'By the way, I'm Giles Meredith.' And he held out his hand.

Sarah took it. A nice, firm grip. 'Sarah Lowman,' she said. 'And what are you doing up here?' she asked, her blue eyes meeting his candidly.

'I've been visiting my sister for the weekend,' he said. 'My sister and my new godson.'

His sister, she thought. Not his wife. He was very good-looking, about thirty or so, with a quiet air of authority about him. Pity he was so old . . . Why wasn't he in uniform? She was becoming a little bored and looked around. There were dozens of good-looking young men in the buffet – most of them with their eyes on her.

She looked down coyly, her darkened lashes on her cheeks like twin fans, then up at him. Let's see, she thought, what makes him tick. It looked as if she was stuck with him until the train came.

'I've been working in Birmingham,' she said. 'Ghastly place, isn't it? I'm sorry if you come from here, but really it is . . . I'm an actress, on my way to London for auditions.'

She smiled dazzlingly at him, but if she was hoping to impress or shock him, it hadn't worked.

'Really?' he said coolly. 'By a strange coincidence, I am a film cameraman.'

'Oh.' Her mind raced – cameraman, films, a starring role opposite Laurence Olivier, break up of Laurence and Vivienne, Laurence meets Sarah – and she had the grace to blush furiously.

'Goodness,' she said, for want of something better to say.

'Here, let me get you some more tea.' And he got up and took her cup and saucer. As he made his way to the counter, she noticed he limped slightly.

So that was it – he had probably been invalided out of the army. Poor man. But how lucky to meet someone like him he could be just what she needed.

'There you are.'

'Thank you,' she said, although she hadn't wanted a second cup.

'So what have you been doing in Birmingham?' he asked, taking out a silver cigarette case and offering it to her.

She shook her head. 'No, thank you, I don't. Well . . .' And she realised that he might have seen the latest production at the Royal Theatre and would know she was lying. 'I've been visiting a friend – we used to be in Birmingham Rep together.' He wouldn't know the difference, she thought, between that and the Midlands Repertory Company.

'So you've had excellent basic training?' he said, his eyes fixed admiringly on hers.

'I should say so!' she enthused. 'If you're in rep, you really know the meaning of hard work.'

231

At this point there was an announcement over the loud-speaker to the effect that an emergency train would be brought out of sidings and was due shortly, and everyone began to collect bags and baggage and make their way to the platform.

Sarah was quite happy to allow him to find her a seat next to his where he put her small suitcase on the overhead rack. She decided he might be very useful to her in the future, and put herself out to be as friendly as she could.

'Tell me,' she said 'about your work. It must be awfully interesting – being a cameraman.'

'It is,' he said. 'I worked in films before the war then got called up, was at Dunkirk – hence the foot.' He grinned, and Sarah looked down sympathetically. 'Anyway, I was invalided out, and now I'm working on a new project – making propaganda films for the government.'

Sarah's face dropped. Oh, was that all. How disappointing. Nothing very glamorous about that.

She was thoughtful. 'I'm actually going down to Hampshire to stay with an old schoolfriend of mine for a few days. Her husband was a Spitfire pilot and is missing.' Her blue eyes clouded over.

'I say, I am sorry,' Giles said. 'What rotten luck.'

They chatted for some time after this quite naturally and Sarah found she enjoyed talking to him. She heard that he had just returned from Canada and was now working on a film of Nöel Coward's about the navy.

At this her interest perked up again and she listened avidly. If only . . . But it wouldn't do, she must not be too eager and cheapen herself. The journey passed very quickly with Sarah learning a bit more about him, that he was not married and hoped they would meet again sometime. Where was she staying?

Sarah said that she wasn't sure yet. After she returned from Hampshire she would know how she stood.

'Look,' he said, delving into an inside pocket as they stood on Euston Station, the crowds milling round, 'here is my card – if ever you feel like getting in touch or if I can be of any help . . .'

Her eyes sparkled. 'Thank you,' she said.

'Good luck,' he said, and with a smile she watched him as he went to the taxi rank, with his broad shoulders and close-cropped hair standing out above the crowd.

She slipped the card inside her handbag. He was rather nice – pity he was old enough to be her father. Well, not quite. Still, now for the next leg of the journey. How good it was to be back again. London even smelled like London, with its piles of sandbags and protected buildings, the barrage balloons high above, the uniformed crowds in the streets. She took a deep breath. Oh, it was good to be back.

On the Southern Railway line, the train ambled along through Surrey and Hampshire, past fields of cabbages and rows of vegetables and little stations and small gardens given over almost completely to digging for victory. Sarah had never been so far south before and was pleasantly surprised when the train pulled to a stop. She came outside into the waiting room, and saw the little maroon Austin Swallow car parked outside before she realised that standing just beside it and searching the people off the train was Julie – looking as pretty as a picture, but as plump as a fine duck. A sob caught in her throat and she hurried forward. 'Julie!'

'Sarah!' And then their arms were about each other, hugging tightly, laughter and tears mingling together as they clung to each other. Then Julie stood away from her.

'You look simply wonderful!' she said admiringly, seeing the slender figure in the tartan skirt, the black beret on the blonde curls. 'You're so slim!' she wailed.

'That's more than I can say for you!' Sarah parried, glancing down at the fine round bundle Julie carried beneath her coat. 'That's a girl!' she cried. 'Carrying high – high for a girl.'

'Low for a boy!' Julie joined in. 'Oh, it is good to see you – I didn't realise how much I missed you. Come on.'

'Is this yours?' Sarah asked in astonishment looking at the little car.

'Of course,' Julie said. 'Get in.'

'Can you really drive?' Sarah looked doubtful.

''Course, silly.'

And so the meeting, which Sarah had almost dreaded, wondering if she would find a tearful and distraught Julie,

233

passed without trouble. But the expression in Julie's eyes, those lovely eyes, was almost enough to bring tears to Sarah's own.

'Where are you living?' she asked, looking about her. 'I say, it's quite a nice place, isn't it?'

'I'm living with Mam for the time being, but next month I'm going to stay with Andrew's parents – they've more room there for the baby.'

Soon she turned into a little backwater behind the church, and stopped outside a redbrick Georgian house, with high railings in front.

'Is this it?' Sarah sounded incredulous.

'Yes, here we are,' Julie said, applying the brakes.

And then there was Mrs Garrett waiting to greet her upstairs in the big sitting room where the table was laid for tea, and a window was open overlooking a beautiful garden at the bottom of which ran a river.

Sarah, ever impressed with beauty, was silent. 'Oh, it's lovely,' she said at length. 'I don't wonder you're happy down here.' She couldn't help thinking of the dour lodgings in Inverness where her parents were living, that cold northern clime, and shivered.

'Well, here I am,' she said, giving them her lovely smile.

'Oh, it is nice of you to come!' Ada cried. 'It was just the tonic that Julie needed.' She saw her daughters face now, lit up, as it had been as soon as she received Sarah's letter. 'Now you two sit and natter while I get busy in the kitchen, I expect you could do with a cup of tea, then we'll have something to eat.'

Well, Sarah looked a treat and no mistake, but then there were no flies on that young lady. How she had ever managed to get away from those doting parents Ada couldn't think. Poor Eva must have had her share of worries about her. Still, she would bet Sarah could look after herself. She wasn't likely to fall for some young man and marry him in a hurry . . . but then she wasn't a warm-hearted girl like Julie, and Ada wouldn't change Julie for all the tea in China.

She came in with the tray to find them both chatting away like magpies on the window seat. Just what Julie needed.

'I hope you can stay for a while now you're here,' Ada said with a smile.

'Please, Sarah,' Julie said, putting out a hand.

She gave them one of her special enigmatical smiles.

'I could stay for a few days,' she said. 'I don't have to be back in London just yet.'

'Oh, you must tell us all about it! I can't wait to hear what you've been doing.'

Ada, smiling to herself, went off to prepare the evening meal, knowing that Julie was happy and she didn't have to worry about her. Once the baby was born there would be no time to brood.

They spent five wonderful days together, Julie introducing Sarah to her in-laws and the office staff at Neville's, taking walks, and sitting in the lovely garden by the river.

'When is the baby due?' Sarah asked. 'I shall come down to see you whatever I am doing.'

'The beginning of April, but suppose you have the lead in the latest production at the Haymarket Theatre?' Julie teased.

'Then my understudy will have to take over,' Sarah answered loftily.

'You haven't changed a bit,' Julie said fondly. 'Still got your head in the clouds. Seriously, though, Sarah, what are you going to do?'

'Whatever turns up – I'm not worried,' she said. 'Something always does. As a matter of face, I'm thinking of going into films.'

'Films!' Julie's eyes sparkled. 'How? I mean – why didn't you say? You are a dark old horse, Sarah.'

'Well, I have had an offer, but I'm not in a position to say anything more at the moment . . . As soon as I hear anything, I'll let you know.'

'Oh, I do wish you luck, Sarah. You deserve it! It might be just the thing – and the money would be good, wouldn't it?'

'I'm not bothered about that,' she said. 'It's doing what I want that matters.'

'Of course,' Julie agreed.

'You will let us know how you get on, won't you?' she pleaded when they said goodbye.

Sarah thought about Julie and her mother all the way home. Blessed war, she thought. If it hadn't been for the war things might have gone on just as they were, she and Julie seeing each other, having boy friends, going to dances or the cinema.

The train pulled to a halt, and she got out and began to make her way to the address one of the Birmingham girls had given her. It was in a street just off the Charing Cross Road, a seamy area but she never bothered about things like that. They had a room, cheap but scarcely cheerful. She pulled down the blind and washed herself before climbing into the narrow bed which was as hard as iron. This would do for tonight. Tomorrow she would begin to look for work and she certainly wouldn't stay here again. She could just imagine her mother's face could she see her daughter now. Sarah grinned in the darkness. She would have a fit.

Yawning, she turned over, and thought about Julie and that beautiful house by the river.

She woke in the morning, full of energy, and leaving the boarding house, made her way to Charing Cross Road and Wardour Street where she had been given the names of several agents. Sitting in the bare waiting rooms with other young hopefuls, girls every bit as pretty as she was, girls who could dance and sing, being told that there wasn't a lot of demand at the moment, what about ENSA? she began to feel a little deflated but still defiant. Well, it was never going to be easy, she had never thought it would. Over a cup of coffee in Lyons Corner House on the corner of Tottenham Court Road, she opened her purse and took out the card given her by Giles Meredith.

It had an address in Chelsea, not an area she knew, but she would take a bus there and call on him. It was much more sensible to take the bull by the horns and appear on his doorstep. She found herself getting quite excited at the thought.

Half an hour later, she was walking down Waite Street towards the river, past the terraced houses, some with boarded up windows, a few occupied. Many occupants had fled the city during the raids. Three stories high with a basement they all looked the same and the familiar smell of a muddy old river came back to her. Number fifty-three was obviously flats, and as she mounted the five steps, she could see the plates at the side giving names and number. Top floor, Giles Meredith. She rang the bell and waited.

A woman came to the huge front door and opened it.

'I'm looking for Mr Meredith,' Sarah said with her most friendly smile.

'Top floor, dear, I should go on up,' the woman said. And her heart beating slightly faster than usual, Sarah began to climb the stairs to the top. She tapped on the door and rang the bell. Oh, please, let him be in . . .

To her surprise Giles opened the door, and seeing her, for a moment or two was non-plussed. Then he smiled at her. 'The girl on the train.'

'Sarah Lowman,' she said.

'Come in, come in,' he said. 'How nice to see you.'

It was more of a studio than a flat, with a huge room and bare boards, inadequately scattered with a few warm rugs, while photographs lined the walls and stood about on the floor. One wall was given over to books, dozens of them, reference books and files. It was a masculine room, not the sort of place Sarah had ever been in before.

'Sit down,' Giles said, indicating a chair. 'Would you like some tea?'

'Er – no, not really, thank you,' Sarah said, feeling somewhat out of her depth, but she was never that for long.

'You were on your way to see a friend, weren't you?' he asked.

'Yes, I stayed until this morning – had a wonderful time – but you gave me your card and said if I needed help . . .'

'I did indeed,' he said.

'Well, I think I need it,' she said. 'Not desperately, you understand,' she hastened to reassure him, and looking up into his handsome face and meeting those frank grey eyes which showed understanding and sympathy, felt for once in her life she wanted to be truthful.

'I need a job,' she said.

'Oh,' he said, and with some relief, it seemed to her,

walked away towards what she imagined to be the kitchen. 'I think I'll put the kettle on.'

He was probably giving himself time to think, Sarah decided. When he came back, he sat down opposite her.

'Now, young lady, how can I help? I think you said you were going for auditions?'

'Well, I was,' Sarah said vaguely. 'But as you know, there's not a lot going on at the moment, and I don't sing and I don't dance.'

'How old are you?' he asked her.

'Nine – well, eighteen, really,' she said, and he smiled.

'What did you do when you left school?'

'I worked on a newspaper.'

'Did you like it?'

'Not much, it was boring – and I was only a general dogsbody. I thought I was going to get the chance to write.'

'Do you like writing?'

'Oh, yes, but I'd never get a job at it, would I?'

'I'm not sure,' he said thoughtfully. 'But you'd rather act?'

'Yes, it's much more fun.'

'Excuse me.' He disappeared and returned with a tray of tea. 'Would you like to do the honours?'

'Yes, of course.' She had done it many times in stage productions.

'Well, now,' he said, taking the cup from her, 'I'm wondering whether we could find you something to do at the studios.'

'Oh!' The blue eyes shining with anticipation were like stars.

'Mind you, I'm not sure about this. You'd probably end up being general dogsbody as you call it all over again – but there are jobs for stand ins and script girls. I'm working on a new film at the moment – 'In Which We Serve' – which I have to say looks rather promising, but I have something in the pipeline myself. I've always rather fancied myself as a writer and recently I was given a script to work on – that is, making a script out of a story for presentation to the cameras – and, can you believe it, they liked it! So I have hopes for that in the future, and I'd like to do some more of that sort of thing. In the meantime, I'm still a cameraman at the studios and I'm sure they could find something for you there. Does that appeal?'

She looked quite beautiful, Giles thought, in her radiance, in the smile she gave him, the blue eyes which shone up at him – she was a very pretty girl. Was he building up her hopes too much?

'Tell you what, if you're free on shall we say Friday, how would you like to come to the studios with me?'

'Oh, I'd love to!'

'Right. Well, meet me at Sloane Square station at seven in the morning on Friday. Is that too early?'

'No, I'll be there.'

'Have you got somewhere to stay?' he asked suddenly, realising she probably hadn't.

'Oh, yes, I'm staying with my aunt,' she said easily.

'Good. Then I'll see you then.'

Sarah stood up. 'I'll see myself out,' she said. 'Thank you.'

She positively sang as she made her way back down the stairs. Who would have thought it? It just showed you – nothing ventured, nothing gained.

Chapter Twenty-four

Throughout the spring of nineteen forty-one the German air raids continued, some of them the heaviest raids of the war, on Liverpool and Clydeside, the Midlands and Humberside, but by now people were so used to them that they carried on as normally as possible. After the shock of initial attack the horror of adapting to the loss of friends and relatives, homes and treasured possessions, the fact that communications were broken, railway lines and trains affected, public transport working under the most difficult conditions, morale was not as low as it might have been. Worst of all was not knowing how long it would continue.

Unknown to the general public there were fears that an invasion was about to begin, and the country was in a state of alert. Leaflets were distributed as to what to do if the invader came, which although read with much laughter and joked about, hid a genuine fear. What did you do when faced with a German invader?

Constance Boxall called the staff to a general meeting following the government's guidelines, suggesting that the women carried pepper in their handbags in case of meeting a German parachutist disguised as a civilian. As they were near barracks at Salisbury Plain and air fields in Wiltshire, it was realised only too well that they were in a vulnerable position.

Joseph Neville came into the office only twice a week nowadays. How long his stockpiled reserves of paper and board would last was questionable. Salvage of waste paper was going on throughout the country, but it was a slow and costly business, and every scrap was destined for the war effort.

What kept him going, both he and Sylvia, was the imminent birth of Julie's baby. With her living with them, they could keep an eye on her, and were delighted that she was in such good spirits. It was months now since Andrew had gone missing and no longer did she talk much about him or refer to his coming back. It was as if she had resigned herself to his loss.

They were awaiting a visit from Olivia, whom they had not seen for some time. Pressure of work, they supposed. On that visit she had looked very much under the weather, having had flu rather badly. Sylvia's heart had caught in her throat as she'd eyed her daughter, she was so thin, and with that pale transparent skin the heavy weight of auburn hair accentuated her fragility.

'You should have told us, darling,' she said. 'We would have looked after you.'

'I was really too unwell to travel,' Olivia said easily. 'Besides I was in a warm room, with excellent care and attention.'

She had been glad when the visit had come to an end. Now, in a better frame of mind, her past unhappiness behind her, she walked down Wilton Street until she came to the number she was looking for. Carrying a huge bouquet of flowers, she knocked at the door which was opened by a little maid in black and white uniform who was highly pregnant.

'I've called to see Mrs Bannister,' Olivia said. 'Will you tell her it's Miss Neville?'

'Yes, miss.'

There but for the grace of God, Olivia thought, and smiled as Rosanna came towards her, hands outstretched.

'Olivia – how nice of you to call!'

'I'm on my way to see my parents, and to give them my news.'

'Are these for me? How kind of you. Well, come in. You look simply wonderful! How did you get on at the interview?'

241

'Extremely well,' Olivia said, following Rosanna into the house. 'They've accepted me.'

'Wonderful! You must be pleased. It will be just the thing for you. And in that uniform, my dear . . .'

'I feel I owe it all to you,' Olivia siad. 'If it hadn't been for you . . .'

'Nonsense, my dear,' Rosanna said. 'I was only doing what was necessary.'

She was obviously in her element, Olivia thought. Having gone straight to her father who owned the freehold of many London properties, and asking him for the next one which became vacant, she had promptly set to and put the empty house to good use by using it as a home for unmarried mothers.

'Make some coffee, please, Alice,' she said to one of the girls. 'We shall be in the drawing room.'

'Yes, Mrs Bannister.'

Two of the girls in the kitchen wore green aprons and were busy peeling vegetables. Another girl came in wearing a hessian apron and carrying a basket of polishes and dusters. They were all at some stage of pregnancy.

'They all have to work hard,' Rosanna said, 'and they have to take turns at each job. There must be no unfairness. So far it works very well. I'm thinking of opening one in the country so that we can grow vegetables and be quite self-supporting!'

'Where do you find them?' Olivia asked.

'They come or get sent to me – of course there are far more of them than you think. This is my way of helping – and I have to say, Olivia, you did me a good turn. I'm probably more content now that I am doing something useful than at any stage in my life. With the children safely in the States, I have plenty of time.'

'How long do they stay? I mean, where do they go after the baby is born?'

'They have the baby in hospital, and usually either have it adopted – my dear, there must be thousands of them – or find foster parents, not usual in these hard times. I'm afraid after that they're on their own. It is hard for people like us to realise that these girls are not accepted by their families,

242

they are thrown out to fend for themselves. Many of them have already left home to come south, and have nowhere to turn.'

When the girl came in and placed the tray down on the sofa table, Olivia glanced at her. She could have been no more than sixteen or so, a pretty little thing with long fair hair, her slim figure from the back making her look like a schoolgirl until she turned round and you saw the large protuberance of her stomach.

'It's awfully sad, isn't it,' Olivia said. 'When you think of the price the woman pays.'

Rosanna threw a swift look at her then poured the tea. 'There is one thing for certain, Olivia, one must never get emotionally involved. Never ask why or who. It is done, over with.'

'I couldn't,' Olivia said. 'I'd be wanting to know who, and the whys and wherefores.'

'No good,' Rosanna said. 'Absolutely fatal. You're better off in the WRENS.' And she laughed. 'Now, tell me all about it.'

Olivia stirred her tea. 'Well, I had the most thorough interview. Of course they wanted to know why I wanted to leave the good job that I had and so on – but to cut a long story short, I have to report on Saturday at Portsmouth. I can't wait to see Daddy's reaction when he knows what I've done!'

She spent a pleasant half hour with Rosanna, going over the tall narrow house and seeing the spartan bedrooms, each one of which took up to three girls, and which they kept as clean as a new pin. 'For most of them it is a first attempt at housewifery,' Rosanna said, 'and I do believe that the majority enjoy it. You can have no idea what sort of home some of them come from.'

Olivia admired Rosanna enormously. There were many rich women like her doing such good work, the nation owed them a debt of gratitude. What an irony it was that neither of them had mentioned Richard.

She hadn't told Rosanna that after a few days in the London nursing home, she had gone down to Blackheath, to Arkley Lodge, which looked as bleak inside as she herself

243

felt. But after she had removed the dust sheets from the drawing-room furniture, and put on the electric fire in her bedroom, she settled back for a few days' rest. She shopped for food in the village and tucked herself into the house, venturing out in the gardens from time to time to look at her favourite view across the river. The barrage balloons covered the river and the city as far as the eye could see, like silver sentinels, and when the sun caught them it was a magnificent sight. It was not so fine at night when the air raid warning went. The guns nearby deafened her with their barrage, and the awful drone of the bombers could be heard overhead. Sometimes she dived for cover beneath the table or in the cupboard under the stairs when an unusually loud crump hit something nearby – but generally she was content to savour being alone.

There was a distant bird's eye view of the river which she loved, winding as it did through Greenwich. As a child she had often sat for hours watching the boats tied up at the wharves, the ships making for the port of London. The river traffic never failed to fascinate her, and now, even in wartime with the barrage balloons aloft and the occasional air-raid siren, the sight was enough to set her pulses racing. It had been just what she needed – peace, relaxation, and a recognition that the last few months had been fraught with tension. Thank God for sanity. Now she knew what she wanted to do. A few minutes' studying the faces of her illustrious forbears in the full naval uniform of admirals in Their Majesties' Royal Navy, and she was sure.

After a few days she put everything back as she had found it, locked up, and closed the door of Arkley Lodge behind her, making her way to the station for her journey down to Hampshire.

Still on sick leave, she had gone back to her small bed-sitting room and had carefully made her plans.

She had applied for permission to join the WRENS, had her interviews, passed her medical, and emerged triumphant.

When the taxi pulled up outside the cottage and she got out, collecting her suitcase and small overnight case, the front door opened and Joe Neville came out to greet her.

'Olivia!' He came towards her, his face lighting up as it always did at the sight of this tall elegant daughter. 'My dear girl!'

She bent and kissed him, a stocky little man whom she topped by four inches or so, saw his small black eyes shining like pebbles and could see that he was visibly moved. And then there was her mother, so surprised she could hardly speak, then she held out her arms. 'Oh, what a lovely surprise!'

Olivia smiled, waving off the driver and picking up her luggage while her mother tucked her arm in hers.

'Well, just don't stand there, Joe – come on in.'

They all went inside and Olivia dumped her bags. 'How's Julie? Any sign yet?'

'No, not yet, and she's very well. Resting upstairs at the moment.'

Olivia took off her hat and made her way to the drawing room, standing in front of the big mirror. 'I have some news for you,' she said, casually patting her hair.

Sylvia's face fell. She's engaged, she thought – nothing else would explain that air of suppressed excitement.

Joe's heart sank. Please God, it won't be that chap she works for. Is she priming us for a shock.

Olivia gave them one of her beautiful smiles.

'I've left the Foreign Office and joined the WRENS.' She waited for the news to sink in.

They were silent, then her father's eyes filled with tears and he took out his handkerchief and blew his nose.

'Good for you, darling,' Sylvia said proudly.

When Joe looked up, his small eyes were twinkling merrily. 'Well, by Gad!' he said. 'When did you decide on that?'

'I thought I needed a change,' Olivia said, although Sylvia noticed that her eyelids flickered just for a moment. There was more behind this than met the eye, and she decided that she had no wish to know what it was.

'Did you have much difficulty in resigning?' Joe asked.

'Not when they knew what I wanted to do,' Olivia said. 'Although I had to pull a few strings and drop the names of a few ancestors – that seemed to do the trick. They hoped, they said, that I would carry on the old tradition,' And she saw her father's face cloud over as he thought of Gerald.

'I think this calls for a drink,' Joe said, going off into the dining room.

'When do you have to report? You can spend a few days with us, can't you?' Sylvia asked.

'Yes, I have until Saturday, when I have to report to Portsmouth.'

'Well, this is wonderful news,' her mother said. 'Julie will be so pleased to see you. The days are hanging rather heavily, you know. Poor girl.'

'How does she seem?'

'Well enough in herself, but I think she is fretting about Andrew – at first she was so optimistic but now it seems as if it has finally sunk in that he is not coming back.'

'There's still a chance.'

Sylvia shook her head. 'It won't do for her to think like that. Better get used to accepting it.' She bit her lip. 'It's seven months tomorrow since we got the news.'

'Oh, Mummy, don't upset yourself.' Olivia jumped up and put an arm around her shoulders. 'Think of the baby.'

'Your father and I think of nothing else,' Sylvia said.

When Julie came downstairs later, Olivia was surprised how well she was looking considering that she had grown to such a size.

'Julie, dear,' she said, going over to her and hugging her. 'You look simply wonderful!'

'I feel enormous.' She laughed. 'Well – I am enormous – and I shall be jolly glad when it's over. It seems to have been so long – '

'Not long now – another couple of weeks?'

'About the end of April, beginning of May,' Julie said.

'And Olivia has some news for you, Julie,' Sylvia said. 'Tell her, Olivia, while I make the tea.'

Julie could hardly believe it. She had always imagined Olivia safe and secure and happy in her job. There must have been a reason why she would give it all up, but that was something she might never tell them. Having no sister of her own, she had grown quite fond of Olivia who was not in the least like the girl she had always imagined but a warm

246

and friendly girl. Her faintly aristocratic air had been a bit off-putting until you really knew her.

'By the way,' Sylvia said, coming in with the tea, 'Julie would like to go over and see her mother tomorrow afternoon, and we thought, since we have a little petrol, that you might drive her – I don't like her driving at this stage. You never know.'

Julie laughed. 'I'd be all right.'

'Yes, dear, I know, but we don't want to take any chances.'

'I'll come with pleasure,' Olivia said. 'I'd like to see your mother again, and that delightful house. If it's nice perhaps we could sit by the river.'

On the short drive, with Olivia at the wheel of the little Austin Swallow, Julie stole a sidelong glance at her sister-in-law. She was so lovely, almost ethereal. It was difficult to imagine her in uniform, but she would be a knockout. Wonder why she'd done it? Unhappy love affair? Could be. But it was no one's business but her own, after all.

Olivia thought once again what a lovely house this was, situated as it was on the banks of a tributary of the River Avon. Gracious, yet with a warm atmosphere, and now that Julie's mother had the sole responsibility for it, it was immaculately kept. The pots and pans hanging in the large kitchen gleamed so that you could see your face in them, the china on the dresser shone, the large kitchen table was scrubbed until it looked like cream cheese.

Ada was busy cutting sandwiches.

'Nice to see you again, Olivia' she said. 'I'm just making tea. Doesn't Julie look well? Not long now.' She looked at her daughter fondly.

If anyone had aged, Olivia thought, it was Mrs Garrett. The anguish of her daughter's loss had aged her ten years.

'And Olivia has some news for us too, Mam,' Julie said, sitting herself in the big wicker chair.

'I've joined the WRENS,' Olivia said.

'Oh, my goodness!' Ada was not so much impressed as shocked. Not in her wildest dreams could she imagine anyone doing such a thing. Still, it wouldn't do for us all to be the same, she thought.

'Now, I'll just take Miss Farquarson's tea to her room, and we'll have ours in the garden, I always like to get out when it's nice – and it's a lovely day, although it's only April.'

'I'll help you,' Olivia said, putting the tea things on a tray.

'Thank you, dear. The chairs are out – we were sitting out there yesterday. Miss Farquarson's nephew stayed overnight on his way up north.'

'Oh, is he home again?' asked Julie. 'We've seen quite a bit of him lately.'

'That's because he's based locally. Soon, I understand, he'll be off again, and she does like to see him. It makes her day. He's about the only relative she has in the world.'

Sitting by the river in the sunshine, you could believe there was no such thing as a war, Olivia thought. Peaceful and still – that is, until the next air raid warning. A few eider ducks swam by and the reeds were still. There was no breeze. Glancing at Julie, she saw that her eyes were closed. What was she thinking about? Andrew? How wicked was a world that allowed wars like this.

Thinking of babies, she decided to tell Julie about Rosanna and her new project. It would take her mind off her own troubles knowing that there were girls in the same situation who had no one to care about them.

Julie's lovely eyes darkened as she heard about the young girls in Rosanna's home for unmarried mothers. 'Oh, Olivia, how sad. Imagine . . .' Until Olivia decided to change the subject and tell her about her WRENS interviews and what it involved.

Julie was such a good listener, particularly since she saw so few people and was glad of company.

'Are you happy living wiith my parents?' Olivia asked presently.

Julie flushed. 'Yes, of course I am, Olivia. They're so kind to me. I have to admit I would rather be with Mam at a time like this – you would yourself, wouldn't you? but it's not possible to inflict myself and the baby on Miss Farquarson. After all, it's not Mam's house, although she has complete freedom to run it as she likes. Besides Miss Farquarson can be quite – difficult, shall we say.' And they both laughed. 'Must be jolly rotten, being in a wheelchair all the time.'

Towards the end of the afternoon, Miss Farquarson appeared at the French windows being wheeled by a young man in naval uniform.

'That's Jamie – I expect he's just leaving,' Ada said, getting up and going forward to Miss Farquarson.

'Julie's sister-in-law has brought her over to see us,' Ada said, know her employer would be pleased.

'Ah, that's nice,' Miss Farquarson said, looking curiously at Olivia with whom she was very impressed.

'My nephew Jamie,' she said with pride, and watched him shake hands with Olivia. 'Miss Olivia Neville.'

'Not only that, Jamie, but she's going into the WRENS,' Julie said. 'She goes to Portsmouth on Saturday.'

'Well, congratulations,' he said. 'I expect you'll have a whale of a time.'

Olivia, who was tall, found herself shaking hands with a good-looking man in naval officer's uniform whose grey eyes met hers at eye level.

He's nice, she thought. 'How do you do?' But almost at once, she realised it was Julie who had his attention. But her eyes were on the garden – at the ducks swimming at the water's edge – at a distant spot no one knew anything about. Poor Jamie, thought Olivia.

'Did I tell you about my friend Sarah?' Julie asked on the way home.

Olivia shook her head.

'She's the one who acts – well, she *is* an actress. She has got a job at the film studios as a continuity girl.'

Olivia laughed. 'What's that?'

'I'm not sure, but I can't wait to hear all about it. It seems the last time she came down to see me she met this man on a train – he's a cameraman or something. Anyway, he introduced her to the film studios, and lo and behold, she has a job. It sounds just like Sarah.'

'I'd like to meet her,' Olivia said. 'She sounds quite a character.'

'Oh, she's that all right,' Julie laughed, then held her side. 'Oh!'

'What is it?' Olivia asked, glancing quickly to the girl at her side.

'It's nothing – I've had several false alarms. Don't worry, it's probably indigestion.'

'Oh, I hope so,' prayed Olivia, pressing down the accelerator just a little.

But all was well. It was not until the last day of April that Julie woke at four in the morning certain in the knowledge that her baby's arrival was imminent. She tiptoed along to Sylvia who was sleeping alone so as to be ready for any emergency.

'It's me, Julie – I think I've started.'

'I'm coming.'

In a flash, Sylvia was out of bed and had taken charge, making Julie a warm drink, asking questions and telephoning the doctor. Julie was due to have the baby in a private nursing home.

By seven o'clock Sylvia had telephoned Ada and the two women sat in the waiting room at the nursing home while Julie, agonising and breathing as she had been told to do, trying to relax, swore as every young mother does that she would never, never go through it all again. It was not until six o'clock in the evening that he was born, a handsome boy weighing seven pounds – and the sister gave him to Julie to hold, wrapped in a soft hand-knitted shawl.

'Ohhh . . .' Julie took the tiny bundle and saw a little red crumpled face. He was so much smaller than she had imagined. He wasn't like her or Andrew, and she couldn't see the colour of his eyes because they were closed. She looked to see if there were five fingers on each hand. Such tiny fingers. She put her own little finger in one hand and felt the tiny fingers close around hers.

'Is he all right?' she asked fearfully. 'I mean, is he all there?' She felt his legs, tiny little sticks beneath the shawl.

'Oh, he's all there,' the sister laughed. 'He's a beautiful baby.' And then the tears came, pouring down Julie's face, tears of joy and gratitude and sadness. 'Andrew – I want Andrew to see him.' The words came between the sobs.

'There, there,' the sister soothed her, taking the baby from her and nursing him. 'Look – isn't he a lovely boy?'

And she crooned to him as Julie cried as if her heart would break.

The sister waited, gently nursing the baby until Julie's grief had subsided, then she went over and placed the baby in his cot.

'You must rest now,' she said gently. 'You've tired yourself out, and we want to be strong, don't we, if we want to feed the baby?'

Julie sniffed and blew her nose and swallowed hard.

'I'll be all right now, sister. It was just – '

'I know, dear,' the sister said. 'I know.'

Julie's eyes were enormous, dark grey-violet, the long lashes wet with tears – it was all the nurse could do not to cry herself, but she was used to it by now or should be, she told herself firmly.

'He's lovely,' she said. 'What are you going to call him?'

'Andrew,' she said without hesitation. 'Andrew – after his father.'

The nurse bit her lip. 'Well, dear,' she said brightly, 'I have two very impatient ladies waiting outside – they've taken turns to wait all day. Shall we let them in – just for a moment?'

Julie brightened.

'Oh, please, sister.'

Chapter Twenty-five

It was all due to luck, Sarah decided, lying on the narrow bed and looking up at the ceiling. Luck and nothing else had led to her meeting with Giles Meredith, a visit to the studios, and now a job.

She had walked on air that day she left him and made her way to a hostel where she found a room which was cheap and cheerful and where she could leave her luggage until she found something fairly stable in the way of employment.

At six-thirty on Friday she had been up and ready to leave, her excitement knowing no bounds as she almost skipped her way to Sloane Square station. Giles was there, in the booking hall. She had half imagined that she had invented him, but there he was, reading his newspaper, navy blue duffel-coated, looking up to see her hurrying towards him. He folded his paper and greeted her.

'Good morning, Giles!'

'Hallo, Sarah. An early bird, I see. Good.'

She chatted all the way there, asking him questions, telling him about her visit to Scotland, and he found himself smiling at her sheer exuberance.

'By the way,' he said, when he could get a word in, 'you said you were staying with an aunt?' He felt somehow responsible for her.

'Oh, yes,' Sarah said breathlessly. 'She lives in Mayfair – Charles Street.' It was the first name that came into her head.

'Isn't that off Grosvenor Square?'

Sarah nodded. She had no idea.

'Sounds rather nice and very convenient,' he said.

'Oh, it is,' Sarah said fervently. 'Of course, she's awfully rich – my father's sister. It's an absolutely super flat. I can stay there any time I want.'

'That's nice,' he said. 'What number?' Taking out a pencil and diary from an inside pocket.

'Number?' she repeated. 'Oh – twenty-three.'

'Twenty-three,' he repeated, writing it down. 'You never know, I may need to get in touch with you. And your parents, they live in Scotland?'

'Yes,' Sarah said. 'On the family estate,' she began.

'So you are a Scots family then?'

'Oh, no – my father inherited the estate.'

'I see,' he said gravely. 'I recall that you said you needed a job. That was not quite the case then?'

'Oh, yes, I need a job – to preserve my independence,' she said on a sudden brainwave. 'You know how it is – they really would like me to do nothing at all but I feel I must. You understand?'

She looked anxiously at him and he searched her face, but she looked back at him with frank and honest eyes.

He slipped the diary back into his pocket, ruminating. She was an odd one and no mistake.

When they arrived at the studios he got out a card and held her arm as they came to the commissionaire's office.

'This lady is with me, George,' he said, showing his card. 'I'll be responsible for her.'

'Just the name, Mr Meredith,' George said, handing him a yellow slip.

Giles wrote down 'Miss Sarah Lowman' and signed it. Once inside, Sarah walked briskly by his side. There was an air raid alert on. Giles pointed to the red light. It seemed miles to walk to the actual studios, passing sound stages and outside sets that looked so real it was hard to believe she wasn't somewhere else, but once they arrived at Giles' studio, she recognised the atmosphere instantly.

She breathed deeply. Oh, it was wonderful – the arc lights, the huge studio, the equipment – it was nothing like she had imagined. There were so many people about. It was a place of work, almost like a factory. People stood huddled about in little groups, conversing seriously, and it was warm – almost hot – after the cold outside.

'Most of this film is in the cutting room now,' Giles confided. 'We've actually finished shooting. But there is another one in progress on another set. We'll go there presently. In the meantime, keep close to me so that you don't get in the way, and above all, don't make a sound – don't even breathe.'

Sarah hunched her shoulders and smiled. She felt like a conspirator, keeping close to Giles as a leech – which wasn't difficult, she thought, giving him a sly glance. He was obviously someone to contend with, very much respected by the men she imagined to be the crew, and obviously in authority. Here and there, going round the set, he introduced her. 'My new assistant,' he said with a smile, leaving them all to guess what that meant.

It was busy! Something was going on all the time. Once he took her to a set where shooting was in progress and she was mesmerized. When a red light went out, he squeezed her inside the door and they stood quietly. When the light came on again, she saw the director with the megaphone and the arc lights blazing so that she had to shield her eyes for a moment or two, watching the actors do a scene over and over and over again. How awful, she thought. Would I have the patience to do that? And it wasn't much of a scene. She was surprised how pernickety they were. She watched a girl with a board which she referred to all the time, a girl not much older than herself who seemed to be in charge of something or another and who dashed about from time to time, and a young man called a clapper boy – oh, there was so much to take in.

The studios seemed to cover acres of ground. Behind that simple façade so much was going on. Towards lunchtime Giles showed her where the canteen was.

'Go in and find yourself something to eat – I can't join you, I'm afraid, I have to be on another set. Here's Petronella, she'll take you.'

Petronella! Was that really her name? Here was the girl she had watched on the set. 'Pet – would you take Sarah to the canteen? Sarah Lowman – Petronella Casebow.'

'Sure. Come on, luv,' Petronella said. Her long black hair was tied back with a scarf, and she had large brown eyes behind tortoiseshell glasses.

'Lucky you,' she said, looking over her shoulder. 'Is he – er – a special friend?'

'Yes,' Sarah said coolly – for he was – leaving the girl to put whatever construction on her answer she liked.

She followed Petronella to the lunch counter and bought a frugal meal, going back with her to a table. Glancing around for famous names, she was disappointed to find none. Guessing, Petronella smiled at her. 'Wrong canteen, luv,' she said. 'Only the hoi-polloi in here.'

'What do you do?' Sarah asked. 'What's your job called?'

'I'm continuity girl,' Petronella said, 'which speaks for itself, I suppose. What do you do?'

'I'm an actress,' Sarah said. 'Theatre . . . stage' but the girl was not overly impressed.

'Not much work at the moment, I imagine?' she said, tackling her salad.

'No, I'm looking for a job,' Sarah said, deciding that with this girl, honesty was the best policy.

'As far as I'm concerned, you can have mine,' Petronella said, and Sarah's heart leapt.

'Really?'

'I'm going into the WAAF's,' she said. 'I'm bored with all this – I want to be where the action is. There's only another week's work on this one, and then I'm off.'

'Do you think I could do it?'

'Darling, I haven't a clue!' Petronella said. 'It's who you know in this business – not what you know.' Her mouth twisted. 'You've a nice line in introductions there, sweetie. He's quite something round here – the blue-eyed boy *and* the new director, so I'm told.' She looked curiously at Sarah. 'I thought you were an actress?'

'I am,' Sarah said confidently, 'but you have to start somewhere if you want to get into this business.'

They exchanged looks for a moment or two then Petronella laughed.

'See what you mean,' she said. 'Well, I wish you luck.'

And lucky she had been. Looking back over the last few

days, Sarah could hardly believe it. In her heart she knew that she still wanted to act, but if she was to do it this way, then she would. The job of continuity girl would be no problem to her – with her training, she would fit in in no time. And with Giles to help her . . . He really was so nice, she liked him quite a lot. It didn't seem to matter that he was so much older. Come to think about it, she really preferred older men. Young men were so – naive.

Everything seemed to be happening so quickly, she must put her house in order. She would stay on at the hostel for the time being; the room was adequate and convenient. From it she looked out on the rows and rows of slate roofs of neighbouring streets, some of them with gaping holes where bombs had fallen, shattered chimneys, broken windows – her mother would have had a fit. She had written home and told them where she was and what she was doing. It was a bit late now for them to object – she had moved too far away from them. Pity, though, that she had told Giles those lies – she had a moment's compunction at the thought. He was so nice. Still, if you wanted to succeed, you had to do what you had to do. And what harm was there in that? It didn't hurt anyone.

She had written to Julie to give her the address, and of course in the studio personel office they had to know where she lived: 12 Gaynor Street, WC1. There was no reason for Giles to know. Once she had arrived at the studios she could move on from there. Find out about casting, the best way to get in. Perhaps one of the stars would be ill or faint, and she would have to take over . . . Oh, it was all going to be wonderful. There was no doubt about it, she had been enormously lucky. Here she was, already working on a short Ministry of Information film, good way to gain experience.

That first week, when Petronella was still there to show her what to do, it had been easy. Then, on her own, Sarah had managed on a mixture of bravado and commonsense born of her previous stage experience. It was a little like prompt corner work, except that time was of the essence; there was nothing dilatory about film making. Every second counted. Not that you would have noticed it, she decided, the number of times they did a take. And oddly enough, she soon discovered that it was the cutting room that fascinated her.

Funny, too, how quickly she got used to seeing famous people in the flesh. They were hardly ever what you had imagined them to be, often visibly suffering from nerves in front of the camera, and a few of them quite glad to be called in to do work of any kind in order to help the war effort. There were lots of 'darlings' and 'sweeties' thrown around – the film world had a jargon all its own.

She saw very little of Giles once she started at the studios. He was kept working until all hours and often had a six o'clock call in the morning. Next week he was to be away on location and she knew she would miss him.

'I'm off tomorrow,' he said. 'Going down to Bath for a few days. Are you doing anything this evening?'

She shook her head. Since she had started work at the studios she had hardly gone anywhere. By the time she got home and bathed and washed her hair there was precious little time before the air raid warning went. Time simply flew by.

'I've written a new script – it's nothing to do with the studio – and I wondered if you'd like to come back with me and go through it? I'd be interested to know what you think.'

Sarah felt very complimented. 'Yes, I'd like to.'

'Why don't we pop into the corner Cafe and have something to eat first and go home afterwards? I don't like to think of you being out after dark.'

Sarah felt a warm glow – it was so long since anyone had bothered to worry about her.

'Oh, I'll be all right,' she assured him.

'Not a good idea to be on the streets during an alert.'

Sitting in the cafe, she felt comfortable with him. There was never any need to worry when you were with Giles. Except for the guilty feeling that she had told so many lies. Well, she wouldn't tell any more. From now on she would be truthful. With Giles, anyway.

Later, upstairs in Giles's studio flat, as the red sun set over the river, they read through his new script, and Sarah was fascinated. From her brief experience of the studio she could well see that Giles had scored a success with his first script. It had been written from the camera angle, with all the directions for panning and lighting, so that it made a producer's job easy. Now he was about to offer this, his second script. Occasionally she made a tentative suggestion. 'Oh, she wouldn't have said that' or 'Wouldn't he have been surprised when . . .' He studied her reactions with interest, noting her criticisms.

'It's based on your experience in the army, isn't it?' she said finally, looking up at him. 'Must have been awful, but it's a marvellous script.'

'Do you think so?' he said eagerly. 'I was interested to know what you thought of it from a young girl's angle.'

'I think it's great,' she said with feeling. 'Er – Giles, how do they go about casting for films like this? I mean, do they have someone in mind?'

'Like yourself, for instance?' He smiled. 'I suppose you see yourself in the part of Sister Wilson, the hard-nosed nurse with a heart of gold?'

'Something like that.' Sarah laughed. 'Seriously, though, Giles, how would I get a part in a film?'

'Shall I tell you what I think?' he said, studying her intently. Those vivid blue eyes, the heavy gold hair casually tied at the nape of her neck, the dark eyebrows so much a part of her attractiveness.

'Yes, please,' she said, her long legs curled beneath her like a child, lips parted, all attention.

He had a sudden desire to kiss her, but instead answered her seriously. 'All right. I know you can act – although film acting is totally different from the theatre. Still, in my opinion you'd do well to stick to the writing side of things. You said yourself you were good at it at school, and you like writing.'

'Oh, Giles!' she wailed. 'I'm far too young to make an impression in that direction! Why, I've never even had anything published.'

'You have to make a start somewhere, and you have a great imagination. Vivid, if I may say so.'

She was suddenly deflated. He was not going to help her at all, and he could have done so much.

'What would you say to co-writing a script with me?'

'What?' Her eyes were wide, incredulous.

'I mean it. There's no reason why we couldn't co-operate. Your ideas and my expertise.' He grinned. 'What about it?'

'Well . . .' It seemed to her a slow way of getting anywhere. How did he know it would be successful? Was that really the way to make a name for herself as an actress? She bit her lip.

The trouble was, Giles decided, he was falling in love with her. This child, so young, gauche and vulnerable, was beginning to take over his life. The whole thing was ridiculous. He knew nothing about her except that she would lie her way out of anything, and he had never had any time for actresses. You never knew where you were with them, they had the knack of confusing real life with romantic dreams.

'Just an idea,' he said lightly as Sarah wrestled with her thoughts. She was lucky, she supposed, to have someone like Giles, yet she had been hoping for something much more dramatic, especially now that she had actually got into the studios.

'Dear Giles,' she said, placing a hand gently on his arm, as she had done in the last play but one, 'you are so sweet.' And getting to her feet, she yawned delicately. 'I really must be going.'

And now, suddenly, he didn't want to lose her, could sense her disappointment. She was so young and he had no wish to hurt her – rather would have liked to protect her, to keep her under his watchful eye. That way he would know she was safe. Perhaps his feelings towards her were fatherly? But he knew they were not.

'Don't go,' he said. 'I'll make some coffee.' And he disappeared into the small kitchen and emerged with a tray, placing it down on the coffee table.

'I had lunch the other day with Sam Bloxburg. He's producing my film.'

Now she was all attention, her blue eyes smiling up at him with interest.

'What's he like?'

'Bloxburg?' He made a face. 'Like all producers – anxious to make money and to have a big success.'

259

He poured out the coffee and handed it to her. 'As a matter of fact, there's talk of letting me direct it.'

'Oh, Giles!' And now she was positively glowing with admiration. 'That's wonderful! Why didn't you say so before?'

He looked so pleased, so boyish, Sarah thought. He really was rather attractive, quite good-looking, so different from any of the men she had met up till now.

When they finished the coffee, Giles went to get his coat. 'I'll come with you – I can't have you walking home if the air raid warning goes.' But she stayed him, a flush coming to her cheeks.

'No – please, Giles. I'll be perfectly all right. It's still light.'

He could see she was adamant. 'I'll come downstairs with you then.'

When they came to the top of the steps, she turned and smiled at him. 'Thank you for a lovely evening.'

He put his arms round her and held her to him, feeling the slim shoulders and the fullness of her breasts, then on impulse brought his lips down to hers and at the touch of her warm mouth against his, felt desire rush through him with an intensity he had thought never to feel again. Sarah returned his kiss with a passion that had nothing to do with pretending. When he finally released her they stood for what seemed like an eternity looking into each other's eyes before Sarah eased herself from his arms and hoisted her handbag over her shoulder.

'Good night, Giles. Have a good trip to Bath.' And she was gone.

That was the trouble with an actress, Giles thought morosely, you never knew where you were. Had she felt as he did? That exultant feeling that at last he had found what he had been waiting for . . . He could have sworn she had felt something too. Surely she couldn't have returned his kiss like that otherwise?

He closed the front door, wishing now he had insisted on taking her home. He shouldn't have listened to her. She had no business to be on the streets alone at night. And he came

260

to the conclusion that despite being in a sophisticated profession, he knew less about women than most men.

The air raid warning blared out just as Sarah reached home, her mind in a whirl of thoughts. Who would have thought Giles could have kissed like that? Bringing to life feelings she hadn't experienced since that time when . . . but she wouldn't think about that. She had put all that behind her in order to get on in her profession of actress. Still – he was rather nice. She liked the way his hair grew on his forehead, and the way he smiled. And he was awfully kind. Just because you were ambitious to be someone, it didn't mean you couldn't enjoy – well, the physical side of things. Yes, you could say she had grown quite fond of him. Sort of platonic . . .

When she opened the front door, Miss Miller the house-keeper was in the hall.

'Coming down to the shelter, Sarah? The warning's gone.' She stood there in her man's thick dressing gown, the greying plait of hair down her back.

'No, I'm going to bed,' Sarah said, closing the door behind her. 'I have to be up early in the morning.'

She had been in bed some time, unable to sleep for the sound of anti-aircraft fire, and as the noise of the German bombers came nearer, once or twice almost decided to get up and go downstairs but decided against it. She had never thought she was in danger from air raids, and she didn't now. That wasn't the way she would meet her end. She had far too many things to do, a life to live. The noise however did keep her awake, and every so often the memory of Giles' lips on hers took her mind off other things, and his face intruded on her thoughts. A clear-cut face, with a straight nose and firm mouth, and his eyes were clear and sort of dark grey . . .

This wouldn't do. She must concentrate. How was she going to get a part in a film? She had every advantage of already working at the studio, for certainly nothing seemed to come up from the casting agent, and then she had a brainwave. Sam Bloxburg! He had an office at the end of the corridor in the admin block – and everyone knew Sam Bloxburg was a worker, often turning up at the studios an hour before everyone else. Tomorrow was Saturday and she was working to finalise the documentary they had just finished. Her eyes began to glow in the dark. Would Mr Sam Bloxburg be there tomorrow? If he was, then he was in for a pleasant surprise . . .

She was up at six, dressed and ready to leave. Once outside the familiar pall of dust that dried the mouth, the sulphurlike smell hung over everything after a night of bombing, and without a bus in sight she began to walk to the station, hoping against hope that the trains were running.

The studio manager greeted her effusively, blowing her a kiss. 'Hi, there, darling, so glad you're always early – not like some I could mention.'

By eight o'clock the arc lights were full on and the last day's shooting under way. Roddy Musgrave, in full make up, moved effortlessly into his part of naval officer. He was one of the lucky ones who once on the set forgot about everyone else, much to their disgust, and threw himself into the part. The scene was set in a wartime Southampton pub, and the film aimed to show how dangerous it could be to divulge secrets of any kind. Sarah watched him, idol of so many girlish hearts. If they only knew, she thought . . .

Roddy came off the set at the finish, cocksure and full of himself, preening his feathers like a peacock. Sarah had met lots like him in her travels.

'Was that O.K., sweetie?' he asked her, sure in the knowledge that he had turned in a good performance.

'Excellent, Mr Musgrave.'

In the mid-morning break, she hurried along to the office block and asked at the reception desk for Mr Bloxburg. She had been to see him once before with a message from Giles.

'Sorry, luv,' the clerk said. 'He's not in today. Any message?'

'No, thank you,' Sarah said, disappointed. Oh, well, there would be another day.

It was late afternoon when she arrived home and the first thing she saw was a letter from Julie. She tore it open without waiting to go upstairs to her room and sat down on the bottom stair, tears in her eyes. A son! Julie had a son!

They were both well, and now Sarah was crying from sheer emotion and relief. Oh, she must go down to see her as soon as possible – next weekend. She would stay over Saturday night until Sunday. How wonderful and how sad. If only his father could have seen him.

On Tuesday, there was another letter from Julie.

Dear Sarah,

I have a favour to ask of you. Will you be Andrew's godmother? I'll tell you why I am asking you now. I really have only one man to ask to be godfather – as a boy I know he should have two – and that is Jamie, Mrs Farquarson's nephew. Olivia, Andrew's sister, will be the other godmother. Oh, say you will, Sarah, it would please me so much.

There is one snag – Jamie can get home only once before he leaves – he's on submarines, and heaven knows how long he will be away for then – and that's this coming Saturday. We are hoping that Olivia will be able to manage it as well. Perhaps it is too much to ask for you all to be here at the same time! Miss Farquarson had a word with the vicar, and since she is very generous to the church, he has agreed to christen Andrew privately on Saturday instead of Sunday. Isn't that nice? So you see everyone is rallying round.

Please say you will, and try to come, Sarah. If you can't manage to get down, you could be godmother by proxy, which Olivia might have to be.

Please say you will, Sarah.

Lots of love,
Julie

Sarah put down the letter. Godmother to young Andrew! She would be delighted and proud. She sent off a telegram right away.

DELIGHTED! ARRIVING EARLY SATURDAY
LOVE SARAH

Chapter Twenty-six

The tenth of May was a perfect day. A high sky and few clouds as Sarah caught the morning train to Andover. She spent her last ten shillings in the jeweller's shop in the town buying Andrew a second hand silver egg cup. One day, when she had some money, she would have it engraved for him.

She walked through the town, feeling quite at home here now, and as she neared Flag Walk, saw that the little maroon Austin Swallow was outside and the front door open. She walked in to find Miss Farquarson in the hall in her wheelchair, at her side a handsome young man with dark hair and eyes. 'My newphew, Jamie, Sarah,' Miss Farquarson said proudly.

Then Julie came running in from the kitchen and hugged Sarah, and suddenly everyone was talking. Andrew's parents were there, and Ada Garrett, everyone looking especially nice.

'Where is he?' Sarah whispered.

'Outside in the parm. This way.'

They went through the side door to the garden where in a high pram – a gift from Miss Farquarson – lay the baby. Sarah caught her breath. He was so tiny but beautiful. To think – Julie's baby. A soft covering of hair, fairish, Julie's lovely mouth, but he was a real boy.

'So much for carrying high,' Sarah said. 'He doesn't even look like a girl!'

'He'd better not,' Julie laughed.

And then, after a light lunch, they all made their way to

the church, Julie carrying Andrew in a beautiful silk gown made by Ada, who had really gone to town. Old lace from Mrs Neville, and pieces of real silk, had all gone into the making, and the little retinue walked proudly to the church – all except Olivia, who had not yet arrived.

As they stood round the font, and the vicar carried out the service and wet the baby's head, she walked in, breathless from hurrying. Afterwards there was much jollification, Jamie holding the baby as to the manner born, then giving him to Sarah, who was terrified of dropping him.

Later, at her favourite occupation of watching everyone, Sarah looked from Jamie to Julie and then back again. He was obviously fond of her. Miss Farquarson, too, you could see what was in her mind, but in real life things didn't always work out as perfectly as that. Andrew's parents were obviously delighted with their grandson who had stayed quiet throughout the ceremony despite being urged by Ada to cry – just a little. But he was most agreeable.

Sarah thought she had never seen Julie look so lovely. Motherhood suited her. Her face was slightly thinner, quite classically beautiful, especially with those wonderful eyes. They had a faraway look, almost as if she was searching for something in the distance . . . She must have loved him very much, Sarah thought.

Once, seeing Sarah watching her, Julie smiled.

Then there were champagne toasts and lots of good things to eat and much talking to be done between old friends while young Andrew slept on, oblivious.

It was agreed that Sarah would stay with Ada, and she was invited to lunch at the Nevilles' on Sunday before returning to London.

'That way Julie can get an early night – it's still early days for her,' Sylvia said.

Jamie was next to go, bidding a fond farewell to his aunt.

'I'll have to say see you when I see you,' he said. 'And, Julie – what can I say?' He bent down and kissed her cheek, and she smiled up at him. 'The best of luck to you and the boy,' he said. 'Take care of my godson. Olivia, I hope we meet again sometime.'

Julie went home with the Nevilles, with a promise that

Sarah would dine with them on Sunday lunchtime before returning to town. Sarah sat up talking to Ada for some time until she went in to make sure Miss Farquarson was comfortable in her downstairs bedroom. It was quite late when Ada came to bed, and by that time the air raid warning had gone.

On the night of the tenth of May, London suffered what was to be its last major night attack of the war. Over five hundred bombers attacked the capital, enemy bombers making two thousand sorties. The following week it was to be Birmingham's turn, but on the night of the tenth, seven hundred tons of explosives were dropped on the capital together with tens of thousands of incendiaries. Nearly fifteen hundred people were killed and seven hundred acres of the city were devasted. They heard them going over in Andover, a heavy thunderous drone, a fearful ominous sound.

One of them, a Luftwaffe bomber pilot from Stettin, knew that he was losing height. Either his engine was failing or he had been hit. Turning sharply to the left, he dropped his load, taking no chances, in order to make his way home to remuster. The last bomb dropped in the garden of the house in Flag Walk, making a huge crater. The roofs of the three other houses caved in, walls were demolished, bricks flew, beams, plaster and dust were everywhere.

Sarah's first thought was to thank God Julie and the baby weren't here before she kicked aside some rubble to make her way to the next room where she found Ada sitting on the floor, surrounded by debris. She hauled her to her feet – 'Come on, Mrs Garrett' – and led the way down the stairs, which was hazardous since there were no banister rails and the steps were covered with ceiling plaster and splintered wood. Sarah led Ada outside to the garden then went back inside. The hall was a shambles with planks of wood across it and in front of the doors blocking her way, but she heaved at them with all her strength until they dropped away. 'Miss Farquarson, Miss Farquarson.' But there was no reply.

Pushing and pulling at great lenghts of plaster-coated timber, Sarah thrust them to each side and staggered into the room, her nightie torn until she was almost naked. In the corner, she could make out the wheelchair. The bed had been flattened. On the floor lay Miss Farquarson, almost unrecognisable with her face bleeding, her hair undone, her legs crumpled under her like a rag doll.

With a sob, Sarah tried to move her but she was so heavy. She was alive, Sarah was sure. Presently she heard her moan.

'It's all right,' Sarah said, 'it's all right – we'll get you out.'

She could hear fire engines and ambulances in the distance coming nearer as she inched Miss Farquarson towards the open window where jagged glass hung from the window frames. She would never get her out through the door across all that smashed timber. She would have to go through the window and take it gently.

She was practically exhausted when in the half light outside in the garden she saw Ada hurrying towards her. 'They're coming – the ambulances. Oh, be careful, Sarah!' But she pressed on, tugging and pulling, terrified that the ceiling would fall down and kill them both. She had got Miss Farquarson's head and shoulders as far as the window and was just heaving her through with Ada's help when she heard the sound of men – they would help. Her strength giving out, she collapsed on top of Miss Farquarson and heard Ada cry out: 'Sarah – oh, Sarah!'

When she came to she was on a stretcher being carried into an ambulance. Then Ada was sitting opposite her, showing concern.

'Sarah?'

'Miss Farquarson,' she whispered.

'She's going to be all right – thanks to you.'

Sarah couldn't hear anything, it was a dream. She only knew she was terribly tired and ached all over. She wanted to feel her face but her hand was so weak and suddenly she didn't care . . .

It was Sunday morning, and after an horrific night Giles Meredith took the first train out of Bath that was running and made his way back to London. He had heard the early news and knew of the blitz there. He couldn't wait to get back and see if Sarah was safe. He reached the capital mid-morning, his heart sinking as he walked through the darkened streets. There was the stench of burning rubble and chaos everywhere: water running from burst mains, smoke from damaged houses, gaping holes and gaps in once proud streets. He began to run, seeing horrific signs of the night's holocaust as he made his way to Charles Street with one object in mind – he had to find Sarah. He would go back and do what he could to help later, but now . . .

He reached Grosvenor Square and walked down Charles Street. Thank God she was safe! There was no sign of devastation here. Walking down the deserted street, he looked in surprise at number twenty-three which was boarded up. He walked up the steps and peered through the letter box. Why, the place was empty. No one lived there. He stood for a moment. Was it possible she had been lying about that, too? Where was she?

He sat down on the front step in despair, his injured leg aching from strain, before getting up again and continuing on his way. And now he was really worried. He spent the rest of the morning trying to contact someone at the studios who could give him the information he wanted. By midday he had his answer.

He walked swiftly through rubble-strewn streets and found Gaynor Street. This was more like it – a hostel for girls. He walked up the steps and rang the bell. A woman came to the door.

'I'm looking for Miss Lowman,' he said. 'Sarah Lowman. I believe she is staying here?'

'Yes, she is, but she's away for the weekend,' the woman answered.

'Do you know where she has gone?'

'I'm sorry, I don't.'

Giles walked back home, relieved that at least she was out of town. There were no newspapers, and he put the radio on to learn that not only had London been subjected to its severest raid, but that random bombs had been dropped over most of the Southern counties.

He took a deep breath. There was nothing more he could do. And she wasn't worth it, that was only too clear. All those lies! She was unable even to tell the simple truth. And to what purpose?

He had been on a wild goose chase looking for a girl who didn't really exist. She was just a figment of his imagination, not to be confused with a girl called Sarah Lowman who lied her way through life and had led him such a dance.

Who knew, for instance, where she was now? And with whom?

He made himself a strong cup of coffee and afterwards left the flat, anxious to do what he could to help.

Sarah woke up on Sunday morning – in a hospital bed, much to her surprise. For the moment she couldn't recall anything, but then her aching limbs and a splitting headache brought it all back to her. The bomb . . . Miss Farquarson. She eased herself up on her pillow and looked at the mound in the next bed. There she was, the old lady, recognisable despite a bandaged head. Her legs were in a cage but she was smiling, if somewhat ruefully.

'Ah, you're awake then. I owe my life to you, young lady.'

'Are you all right?' Sarah asked. 'Golly, your poor head . . . and your legs.'

'Yes, both broken – and I could have done without that. Still, at least it might make me forget my arthritis!' And she gave a weak smile. 'You are a very brave girl.'

Sarah blushed, and was saved from replying by the entry of a nurse.

'Ah, there you are, dear. You're awake – how are you feeling?'

'Stiff,' Sarah said, 'but I'm all right. Can I get up?'

'Doctor's doing his rounds, he'll be here in a moment,' the little nurse said, her round rosy face like an apple, black curls escaping from her probationer's headscarf, a Devonian accent very pronounced.

'You mustn't get up too quickly,' Miss Farquarson said. 'I know you are young, but you went through a lot last night.'

'I have to get back to work tomorrow,' Sarah said. 'Do you know if Julie and the baby . . .'

'My dear, they're fine,' Miss Farquarson said. 'Mrs Garrett has already been in this morning to see us, but they gave you something to make you sleep.'

'Oh, so that's why I feel peculiar.' Sarah made an attempt at a smile.

And then everything happened at once. The doctor came, and after examining her suggested she should stay in bed for a day or two, but on Sarah's insisting that she must get back to London, he allowed her to go home if someone could come and fetch her.

Julie came down for her in the little Austin Swallow and burst into tears when she saw her.

'What are you crying for?'

'I don't know,' Julie sniffed. 'You were so brave, saving Miss Farquarson. Mam said – '

'Oh, it was nothing,' Sarah said. 'I do it all the time.'

She said goodbye to Miss Farquarson and wished her well, promising to come down and see her again.

'You must spend a few days with me and visit my lovely garden in the summer.'

They all made a great fuss of her at the Nevilles' cottage, and she sat by Julie's bed as she nursed the baby.

'What does it feel like?' she asked curiously.

'Feeding him?' Julie said. 'Wonderful. You can hold him when I've finished. Burp him.' She looked down at his tiny hand gripping her finger.

'Burp him? What's that?'

'Hold him over your shoulder to get the wind up.'

'Oh.'

Sarah had a fleeting moment of envy as she watched the baby suckling, then pushed it aside. She was not ready for that yet. Then she imagined herself and Giles Meredith looking down at their firstborn. Now you are being ridiculous, she told herself.

'What will Miss Farquarson and your mother do?' she asked presently. 'The house must have been severely damaged.'

'It was,' Julie said. 'Miss Farquarson will be in hospital for some time, I expect, then she'll probably go into a nursing home. I expect they'll patch up part of the house for Mam to live in temporarily. It will all work out – there are lots of people in the same boat.'

Still rather shaken by her ordeal, Sarah boarded the

London train at Andover, despite entreaties by everyone to stay for a few days' rest. But she wouldn't hear of it.

'Don't fuss,' she said to Julie, quite crossly.

'Now you take care in London. I don't want anything to happen to Andrew's godmother – she's a very important lady.'

'Don't worry,' Sarah said, waving from the window of a train that was packed with troops.

She sat down and almost immediately took out her powder compact, eyeing her face in the mirror. Not too bad – she looked pale, but that was understandable. Things might have been worse – she might have been killed by that terrible bomb. She would wash her hair as soon as she got home. She clicked the lid of the case and sat back, not unaware that most of the young men standing ten deep in the carriage and the corridor outside were looking at her. She crossed her legs elegantly and took out a book. There was a wolf whistle from outside in the corridor.

Everything was all right, she thought, feeling much more shaken up than she actually looked.

She went to bed early and slept like a log, waking early and making her way to the station after a hurried breakfast. She wondered if Giles was back from Bath, but he was not in the studio where she was working. He might be in any of the others. At lunchtime she made her way to the canteen, having been delayed past her usual time, and saw Giles sitting over in the corner, a book proped up on the table.

She was delighted to see him and hurried over with her tray, standing by the table. 'May I?'

His face brightened, then the smile faded.

'Oh – Sarah.'

'I hoped I'd find you here,' she said, sitting down. 'I've had such a weekend! You won't believe . . .'

He went on eating as she began her story. 'I went down to see this friend of mine who had a baby son – to the christening actually. You know her husband is missing? He was a Spitfire pilot.' She buttered her roll carefully. 'Dream of a house – Georgian, with a lovely garden running down to the river.' And at this he looked up and stared at her, putting his knife and fork down.

'Anyway – ' she broke off a bit of roll, and put it in her mouth. 'We were bombed. The house is a wreck.'

'But you were all saved?' Giles said, staring at her.

Sarah stopped, the fork halfway to her mouth, realising something was wrong.

'I said, you were all saved? No harm was done?'

'It certainly was,' she said hotly. 'We were thrown out of our beds, the roof caved in, the walls came down . . .'

He rested his chin on his hand.

'Go on,' he said. 'No, don't tell me – I can guess. Some members of the royal family were there, and you saved their lives.'

Sarah looked straight at him, conscious now that he was being cruelly sarcastic. She put down her fork, her face flaming. He had found out about all her lies.

'There was a bomb, honestly,' she said. 'I woke up in hospital yesterday morning.'

She did look pale, he thought, and there was a blue bruise by the side of her right eye. He had a momentary doubt but brushed it aside.

'Do you know where I woke up?' he asked coldly.

She shook her head miserably. 'At number twenty-three Charles Street, Mayfair,' he said. 'I rushed there because that's where I thought you were. You didn't think to tell me you lived in a hostel in Gaynor Street where I also called – because I was worried about you, fool that I was.'

Her blue eyes looked wretched.

'I am sure your landed gentry family in Scotland must be awfully worried about you – poor little rich girl!' he said. 'And I don't suppose you've ever been on a stage in your life.'

'I have!' she said vigorously. 'I was with the Midlands Rep.'

'Oh' he said, folding his napkin. 'I beg your pardon, I must have misheard you. I thought you said the Birmingham Rep.'

He sat still, looking at her for what seemed like minutes.

'I know I do tell awful lies,' she said. 'I don't mean to – they're harmless really.'

'Is that what they are?' he sold coldly. 'Well, you could have fooled me.'

'I get carried away – it's imagination, really.'

'Is it?' he said. 'So you're still hoodwinking yourself. You are quite simply a liar, Sarah Lowman, and I can't stand liars.'

He got up and pushed his chair under the table, not looking at her again. She sat on alone for a long time then pushed her uneaten lunch away from her. He was right – she was a liar. She thought guiltily about him limping all the way to Charles Street – wherever that was – and her face flamed again.

Well, she hadn't been lying about the bomb, that had been real enough – and he hadn't believed her! Some joke. She didn't care if she never saw him again.

A week later she heard that he had gone to Canada on location to make a film for the Crown Film Unit. So that was that, she thought. Now she had better get on with her life.

She had made many friends while working at the studios, an assortment of people: make up artists, wardrobe ladies, props assistants, and there was always plenty of laughter and joking around the sets when the film was not actually under production.

She learned about having an agent, the best casting office to go to, what the chances were of getting a part – short of sleeping with the director. The life she had embarked on was precarious to say the least and even more so in wartime, but the camaraderie around the studios more than made up for that. The money was good, when it came, but the problem was there were not enough jobs to go round.

It was Dottie Lang, a studio hairdresser, who told her that a small part was going in a film about to be made about a family in wartime England. Owing to the sudden illness of the girl who was going to play the part, they were looking for a substitute – the daughter who was in love with a suspected spy.

Right up her street, Sarah thought.

'You could do it standing on your head, darling,' Dottie said. 'And you can but try. Here, give this chap a ring.' And she handed Sarah a telephone number. 'Tell him Dottie sent you.'

It was who you know. Petronella was right, Sarah decided. She promptly applied for the part, and got it.

So here she was, with a few weeks' work in hand, and she had arrived – well, made a start. Wouldn't Giles approve of her now?

She wished he was around so that she could tell him.

Chapter Twenty-seven

It was the end of July and baby Andrew was three months old, a bright, happy baby, with a covering of reddish hair, his mother's dark eyes, and a strong look of his father about him. Life at the Nevilles' cottage revolved around him; everyone adored him.

The terrible barrage from the German bombers had abated, they had something better to do now with the invasion of Russia, and people sat back to enjoy what was probably a brief respite for who knew what would happen next?

On one of these pleasant days Julie announced her intention of going over to Denham to see William and Pandora Anderson. 'I want them to see Andrew,' she said.

Ada didn't like the idea at all. It was a long way in the car, and you never knew what might happen, but it seemed a shame to stop the girl doing something she wanted to do.

She herself was living at Flag Walk where emergency repairs had been done to the house, enabling her to stay there, while Miss Farquarson was still in a nursing home.

'You will come with me, Mam?' Ada brightened. 'Oh, well, that would be nice.'

'You could do with a break, and I know you'll love the Andersons' garden – it really is quite beautiful. We have enough petrol because I don't use the car very much.'

So they set off after Andrew's feed, nappies packed together emergency supplies, sandwiches and drinks in case they got lost, identity cards and blankets – it was quite an adventure.

'We mustn't forget the map,' Julie said. 'With no signs anywhere – still, it's only this side. After we get through London, I know the way – it's a straight run down the Western Avenue.' She had telephoned Pandora who was delighted at the idea and suggested that they had lunch.

'Do we have to cross London?' Ada asked, looking worried.

'It's a long way round if we don't – and think how you will enjoy seeing the old landmarks again.'

Ada had to admit to herself that she was getting quite excited at the prospect. They had led such quiet lives since the raids had started and the birth of little Andrew.

Julie drove carefully, thrilled with doing something different for a change, while Ada sat beside her in the passenger seat, Andrew in her arms, looking about her with interest, becoming more and more horrified at the damage she saw in South London.

'I can't believe it!' she cried. 'It's worse than anything I imagined.'

By midday they had reached the outskirts, and stopped on a common to change the baby and give him a feed.

Then on again until by almost one o'clock they were in Denham and making their way through the lanes to the Anderson's home.

Julie felt a lump in her throat and unexpectedly her eyes filled with tears. She hadn't realised she would feel like this. She pulled into the drive, swallowing hard, as Ada threw her a sidelong glance. Oh, they shouldn't have come . . .

But now two people emerged – the Andersons. William looking quite aged, Pandora at his side in a flowing robe of cerise silk, her hair in a black chignon, looking quite theatrical in her heavy make up.

Ada was shocked. She didn't know where to look first – at the glorious garden, ablaze with colour, or the exotic bird of paradise who stood at William's side. They came forward to greet her, smiles of welcome on their faces. Then there were hugs all round and introductions and Pandora insisted on holding the baby who opened his dark eyes and gave her a lovely smile.

William looked on approvingly, smiling at Julie.

'She'll think there's no flower in the garden to touch him,' he said, nodding towards Pandora who was making little sounds and clucking to the baby.

'Oh, my dear, he is simply beautiful – and so like Andrew.'

Inside the house, Ada was entranced. It was lovely, flowers everywhere and a strong smell of polish, she thought approvingly, although she could not imagine Pandora doing it in her wildest dreams. No wonder Julie had been happy here, it was like a little garden of Eden. The war seemed so far away.

They had a light lunch, and while William took Ada to see the gardens, Pandora stayed with Julie while she fed Andrew in the spare room.

'I was the eldest of eight,' she said, 'and I used to watch my mother feeding the little ones. Takes me back.'

She waited until Julie had finished feeding the little chap and changed him, then took him from her while she cleared away and washed her hands.

'He's a beautiful baby, Julie,' she said, looking down at him. 'No news of Andrew, I suppose?'

It was asked so casually it was almost callous, and Julie stood stock still.

'News? But you remember, Pandora, that he's missing? That day the padre came round . . .'

And now Pandora looked uncomfortable. 'Yes, I know, but I thought – '

'What? What do you mean? Pandora!' Julie was almost beside herself at the slightest prospect of hope.

Pandora handed the baby back to her and sat down abruptly in a chair. 'I'm sorry, Julie, I shouldn't – '

She laid Andrew down gently on the spare room bed then caught Pandora's hands in hers. 'Please, please, tell me if there is anything you know.'

Pandora swallowed. 'Well, you remember Binkie Simpson – he used to fly with Andrew, didn't he? He was shot down over Kent somewhere and lost an arm. He lives with his wife down the road in the village. and works at R.A.F. Uxbridge – ground staff.'

'Yes – yes!'

'One night we were talking and he said – he said – he thought Andrew had got away. He saw his plane diving towards the French coast and wondered – prayed – that he might have made it.'

'Oh!' And Julie sat down on the bed abruptly. The baby blinked and looked up at her. She picked him up, cuddling him. 'Oh, Pandora, if it were only true.'

'Julie, you mustn't . . .'

'Of course I must!' She was laughing now, almost hysterically, while Pandora, conscious of having started something, twisted her rings. Then she went downstairs to meet William who was coming in with Ada.

'William! William, I think I've done something awful.' And Ada raced upstairs to meet Julie emerging from the bedroom, a faraway look in her eyes.

'What is it?'

'Pandora will tell you. I won't be long – I'm just going round to see someone. Where is it, Pandora? In the village?' She handed the baby to her mother.

'Yes. In the row of cottages just past the church – it's called May Cottage.'

'Look after Andrew for me – I won't be long.' And they stared after her as they heard the little Austin Swallow start up.

Ada looked grim. 'Perhaps you wouldn't mind telling me what you told her?'

It sounded ridiculous when Pandora repeated it to Ada, who breathed heavily. How dare this woman build up Julie's hopes, just when . . .

'I know I ought not to have said anything, but it is true, Mrs Garrett – there was talk among the other pilots.'

'Just talk, I daresay. You'd have done better not to repeat it.' And Pandora bit her lip.

William took a pipe down from the rack and filled it. 'I am not sure, Mrs Garrett, that there may not be something in this story. Many of them got away, many of them are in France and Belgium.'

'But we don't know that Andrew is,' said Ada, her lip quivering. 'It's cruel to rake it all up again.'

Pandora went into the kitchen, and when she returned

with the tea tray they could hear the little car coming back. Twenty to three, Ada thought, looking at her watch. We should be away soon.

'Was anyone there?' Pandora asked.

'Only Margaret Simpson – I'd met her once before. Binkie is working but he's going to ring me this evening.' She turned to Ada. 'Oh, Mam, wouldn't it be wonderful . . .' She saw Ada's face.

'We'd love a cup of tea, Mrs Anderson, then we must get going.'

Julie kissed Pandora when she left and spoke softly. 'Don't mind Mam, she's only worried about me – but I'm all right, really. I'm glad you told me, even if . . .'

Pandora kissed her. 'Thank you for coming. And I think your baby is lovely.'

They were subdued on the drive home. Ada sat nursing Andrew, talking to him from time to time when he woke, and it was almost six when they arrived in Flag Walk after stopping to change him and feed him on the way.

'Oh, it's nice to be back!' Ada exclaimed.

When the telephone rang at eight o'clock, Julie ran to answer it.

'Yes – yes, Julie Garrett. Hallo, Binkie.'

When she came back she was wildly excited. 'Mam, Mam, Binkie says he saw the parachute open – there were three or four. Andrew could be a prisoner of war.'

Ada was near to tears and shook her head from side to side.

'Julie, you would have heard – you would know by now – it's nine months or more.'

Julie bit her lip. 'I know, but you can't stop me hoping, Mam.'

Ada got up and went over to her and held her tight, her heart bursting.

She wished with all her heart they had never gone to Denham.

It was the fourth of August, a day Andrew was to remember well for it was his father's birthday.

Now, on *HMS Vidette* which had sailed from Gibraltar

279

bound for Plymouth, he was on his way home. A fitting end, he decided, to the bizarre and sometimes hellish experiences of the past few months.

The thought of Julie and home had kept him going all through his trials and tribulations. He hoped with all his heart that she was safely back at home with her mother or his parents. He fingered his shaven head, bristly now with a half inch growth of fair hair, looked down at his hands, weatherbeaten and stained. Not much of a hero, he thought – but he was going home! Home! He was on a British ship, thank God.

When he had landed that day in France, near St Omer, he couldn't have foretold what the outcome would be, nor how long it would take to reach home again. He had buried his parachute and made his way through tall grass to a hut on some farmland where a young boy had stared at him then beckoned urgently to him to get inside. Once inside the boy told him to wait, that the Germans were not far away – and when it was dark he was to come up to the farmhouse where he would be given food and shelter for the night. By morning he knew that this was by no means the first time they had done this, as they kitted him out with a farmworker's clothes and maps. The maps were crude drawings of all the back lanes he would be able to use in order to avoid meeting German soldiers. He had decided then that he would make for Spain.

He sheltered for the next two nights in a safe house the address of which had been given to him by the family near St Omer, and there he was given a little money, a new set of clothes, and introduced to Guy Bulstrode, a British bomber pilot who had been there for a few days. They decided to leave together and make ultimately for Marseilles, hoping if they were stopped they would be accepted as French farmworkers.

They were given the address of a member of the local resistance who would take them as far as Abbeville where they would be given false identity papers. Once in Abbeville they decided to go it alone, deeming it safer to travel separately.

And then began the long haul south when he travelled by

night and holed up by day, keeping to the fields as much as possible. Villagers sent him to a château run by a French-woman known for her allied sympathies where he was well fed and supplied with new boots before setting out again. A priest who spoke to him on the road gave him his bicycle which he rode for the next fifty miles until he found it missing one morning after sleeping in a barn. He was relieved that the night's rest had amounted to no more than the theft. On one occasion a local man paid for and took him on a train journey as far south as Chauvigny where he crossed the demarcation line.

Then began the difficult journey to Toulouse, and another safe house where he stayed for a few days with feet that were blistered and sore, making for Luchon after this where he was told he would be safe.

Feeling uplifted, he had almost reached the town when he was stopped by gendarmes who queried his papers. After some doubt when he thought he would make it, they changed their minds and took him into custody. The next day he was sent to a concentration camp in a château at Ile Jourdain, here he found thirty other prisoners, all intent on escape, but there he had stayed until mid-November when they were sent to Gort St Jean at Marseilles.

Here, Andrew decided, he would stand a better chance of escaping on his own, and one afternoon, while exercising made a dash for it, hoping to find a ship sailing from Marseilles. It took him two days to reach the port. So far so good — until the ship was searched and he was found, together with two British soldiers, and put into prison on a charge of stowing away without a ticket.

He served two months there, an experience he would not like to repeat, and at the end of that time was released and with the little money that he had, bought a train ticket to Perpignan and a little food. The freedom that day tasted like honey as he stood halfway up the mountains looking down into neutral Spain where he imagined the worst of his journey would be over, for he knew there was a British Consul-General in Barcelona.

On the morning of the fourth day he had reached the slopes at the foot of the mountain and realised freedom was within his grasp. His hopes were rudely shattered by the arrival of two Spanish policeman who were armed and promptly arrested him and took him to Figueras. The next day he was taken to the Castello, a military barracks, where he was locked in a small room together with prisoners of other nationalities. They lived like animals, herded together. He shuddered now as he remembered it. No sanitation, not enough food to keep a cat alive, only dry bread and soup, and morale among the men was low to say the least. They began to wonder if it had all been worth it. Most of them had believed that once they got to Spain that would be an end to their troubles.

Andrew had insisted every day to the dour Spanish guards that he must see the consul, and when he finally did, was told that he would be sent to the concentration camp at Miranda del Ebro. Once there, he would be able to contact the British Embassy in Madrid who would arrange for his release.

Things seemed to be looking up until the day came for the journey to Miranda which he learned later was the most infamous concentration camp in Spain. It was run on POW lines. His head was shaved and the Spanish guards used rubber hoses to control dissidents.

He spent fifteen horrendous weeks in that place until quite suddenly one day was told he would be released.

When the Military Attache came by car to pick him up he could hardly believe it.

After a while, he was taken to Gibralter to await a ship to England – and here he was.

How much he owed to those wonderful friends he had made in France, the safe houses who had helped so many escapees.

He looked down at the ill-fitting suit which had been provided for him. He had lost so much weight, he was a mere shadow of the man he used to be. He hoped he would not be too much of a shock to Julie. She probably wouldn't recognise him . . .

When the ship docked, an escort was waiting to drive him to base camp for interrogation.

'How soon may I make a telephone call?' were almost his first words.

From the front room of the cottage, Julie saw the camouflaged transit van draw up outside the house. Staring hard, she saw a man get out and the driver close the door behind him and give a salute.

Her heart leapt upwards so that it seemed to choke her and she let out a scream. 'ANDREW!'

Flinging open the front door she stood there looking at him then positively leapt into his arms which went tightly round her.

When they finally let go of each other, Julie took his hand.

'Come and see your son,' she said.

Chapter Twenty-eight

Flying to Canada with his film unit on an army transport plane, Giles Meredith thought about Sarah Lowman. In fact, he found himself thinking about her more and more often as the days went by. A pair of blue eyes came between him and his work more than he liked.

Sarah, he decided, was a born writer. No doubt about it. When her imagination ran rife there was no holding her. She told a story, embroidered it, captured your interest – even though you knew it wasn't true. Wasn't that the mark of a writer?

He regretted now the things he had said to her. He had spoken from a mixture of relief at finding her and anger that he had been duped. Of course she wanted to be an actress, but once she had got that out of her system, she would write and let her imagination run away as far as it would. It was all in that little head of hers.

Now he felt only he wanted to take her in his arms as he had once before – he wanted her, ambition and all, for himself. But she would have to have her freedom – there would be no holding her otherwise. Could he be content with that?

There was a lurch as the plane hit an air pocket which brought him back to reality. Just get this film over, he thought. He could hardly wait to return to London.

When Sarah received the news of Andrew's homecoming, she could scarcely believe it. It was like a dream come true. Who would have imagined such a thing?

Sitting in the dressing room, taking off her make-up, she

thought about the last few weeks – how strange it had all been. Not a bit like the theatre. Boring, you could say really, although filming held a certain measure of excitement. With a live audience you reacted to them, giving more; you could assess how they were receiving you, and if they were liking it, then you yourself got better and better.

Well, it was all grist to the mill, she told herself, with a newfound wisdom born of experience. Now what? She had no work lined up for the next few weeks, but the hours spent at the studios were so long that she wouldn't mind a break. Apart from an offer of crowd work, there had been nothing.

Still, she had heard through the grapevine that they were to start Giles's film at the end of the month and there was that part she coveted . . . What were her chances? She still felt she would like to go along and see Sam Bloxburg. After all, if he didn't know who was going to be in the cast, who did?

Someone's favourite, she would bet.

Given this break, she might well have gone down to see Julie, but not now that Andrew had come home. And it really was necessary to look for some work. She had been lucky meeting Giles. Strange how she missed him – wanted his approval of what she had done. What would he think of her when he saw the rushes? The producer had liked her performance; everyone on the crew had complimented her.

She made up her mind quite suddenly. She would do it – now. There was no time like the present. She put on a coat and hurried out towards the office block. She showed her identity card to the man at the door, then walked along the corridor until she reached the great man's office. She tapped on the door; he bade her come in.

The first thing she saw was the enormous desk and the man sitting there, in a pale tweed weekend suit – a massive man with horn-rimmed glasses whose thick pebble lenses hid his eyes.

She stood with her back against the door until he beckoned her with a finger and she walked forward. His eyebrows lifted.

285

'I apologise for intruding on your valuable time, Mr Bloxburg – I am a friend of Giles Meredith.'

He gestured her to sit down. 'Did he sent you?' His voice was deep and slightly accented.

'Oh, no!' She was shocked. 'Of course not. But I heard you were to start filming soon, and having read the script . . .'

'You say you've read the script?'

'Yes, before Giles went to Canada.' That should show him she was being honest.

'And so?'

'I wanted to know if there was a chance that I might try for the part of Alice?'

'And what qualifications do you have, Miss – er?'

'Lowman – Sarah Lowman.'

She was disappointed that he made no note of it. 'Well, I've just finished today in Studio Two. I had the part of Sonia.'

'I see. What else?'

'I worked for a long time in repertory – stage shows.' It wouldn't do to exaggerate too much. Giles would only put him right.

'I see. And on that basis you think you should be given the chance of a part in my new film?'

'Yes, please, Mr Bloxburg.'

'Well, young lady,' he sat back in his chair, 'this is highly unorthodox – and we are strict as to rules, all film studios are. Presumably you are with a casting agency?'

'Yes. But sometimes . . .' And he almost gave the glimmer of a smile.

'You think you might do better on your own. Well, I admire your enterprise, and I'll tell you what I will do. I will arrange for a screen test tomorrow morning at nine – how will that suit you?'

'Oh, thank you, Mr Bloxburg. Thank you!'

He wrote something down on a slip of paper and handed it to her.

'Ask for Mark Simon – nine o'clock. Not a minute later, remember.'

'Yes, Mr Bloxburg.' And she hurried to the door.

286

'Oh, and Miss Lowman?'

She turned.

'Don't do this again. Not every producer is like me.' And he watched her go, shaking his head.

That evening when she arrived home at six o'clock, early for once, she found a telegram awaiting her on the hall table. It was from Scotland. She tore it open hurriedly, her colour fading as she read:

DAD IN FACTORY ACCIDENT STOP MOTHER STOP

Her heart was racing as she read it again. Was he badly hurt? He must be for her mother to have sent a telegram – oh, at least he wasn't dead! Her dad – it was ages since she had seen him! And they weren't on the telephone. How could she find out? She must go to him, right away.

The housekeeper emerged from her room. 'Ah, there you are, dear. Did you see – you got your telegram. Not bad news, I hope?'

'Yes, I'm afraid so,' Sarah said. 'My father – in Scotland. I have to go to him.' And she raced up the stairs.

She flung off her coat and read the telegram again. What sort of accident? He might be dreadfully badly hurt, mangled by machinery . . . Her imagination ran riot but now she became purposeful and threw some things into a small bag, nightgown and make up and toothbrush. She would take the overnight train and worry about it all on the way. Oh, please God, keep him safe. Dear Dad, it was only at a time like this that you realised – and she swallowed hard and stopped to think. Her film test, tomorrow. She sat down abruptly. What was an old film test? There would be others, hopefully. The main thing was to be on her way. But she must let them know.

She left a message for Mr Bloxburg that she had been called away unexpectedly to Scotland owing to an accident to her father. There, that would have to do. She was on her way.

The journey was long and she couldn't sleep for worrying, imagining all sorts of awful things. Funny how it took something like this to show you how fond you were of your

287

family. Trying to take her mind off it, she began to think about Giles and wondered what he was doing now. She found herself thinking about him quite a lot; his kindness, the way he had asked nothing of her – and all he had from her in return was a hurried journey to that place in Charles Street, limping all the way. She still blushed when she thought of it. She seemed to have grown up an awful lot lately. Why had she told all those yarns? She had always done it, even at school. Perhaps, she thought, one day, when he comes back, he will see me again. We can be friends.

The journey to Scotland finally passed, then the long extra journey to Inverness and the taxi to the street of tall dark buildings. She realised that she didn't know if her father was at home or in hospital.

And there was her mother, embracing her and crying.

'Sarah – Sarah! Oh, bless you, you came.'

And there was Valerie, suddenly grown taller. And the warm smell of home, despite its being in an alien place.

'Dad – where is he? How is he?'

'He's in hospital. It was a bomb – daylight raider – lots of them were hurt, one man killed, but your dad is going to be all right. He's had x-rays, they thought it might be internal injuries, but so far he has three broken ribs and a fractured shoulder blade. But you know your father – he never complains.'

'Can we go to see him?'

'Yes, outside visiting hours at the moment. It only happened yesterday.'

'Let's go,' Sarah said.

Armed with flowers, the three of them made their way up the grim hospital stairs and into the men's ward. Tom Lowman was lying in the fourth bed from the door. At the sight of Sarah his face lit up in a broad smile. 'Hello, Dad.' She leaned over and kissed him, the sight of that face from her childhood moving her as she had never thought possible.

'Hello, Sarah.' His voice sounded weak, and he was a mass of bandages. 'Fancy you coming all this way.'

'To see my dad? I should think so! Now what have you been doing with yourself?' she teased, and they sat on the

288

bench beside him while the nurse put a screen around his bed. 'Five minutes – he mustn't get excited.'

Through the window, Sarah could see a magnificent skyline, dark buildings etched against a vivid blue sky.

'Your mother will be pleased to see you,' he said, hoping that all the other occupants would notice his lovely daughter when she went out. It was a tonic to see her again, he had missed her more than he had ever admitted. It had never been the same since she left.

The few minutes flashed by, and they left with a promise to return the next day.

That night, lying on her camp bed next to Valerie, Sarah was awake long after her sister was asleep. What a long way off was her life in London and the film studios – it was another world. This was her family. You might not like having a working-class background, but it wouldn't change anything. You could get up and push yourself out of it but roots were roots. What must Giles have thought when she told him her family had a Scottish estate? Surely he hadn't really believed her . . .

On Monday morning Giles went straight to the studios, where he saw Sam Bloxburg and got down to business. At the end of the day, everything having been wound up, he prepared to leave.

'See you next week then, Sam,' he said. 'I've a few loose ends to clear up.'

'By the way, that little girl – what's her name?' Sam said. 'She came to see me.'

'Who was that?' Giles was idly putting papers in his briefcase.

'Sarah someone or other.'

Giles looked up. 'Not Sarah Lowman?'

'Yes, she came to see me.'

'Well, I'll be damned!' You had to hand it to her.

'I arranged for a film test on Saturday morning.'

'And have you seen it yet?'

'It didn't come off. She sent a letter of apology – her father had met with an accident and she couldn't make it.'

Another lie? Giles wondered. But she had missed a screen test . . .

So inside devious, pretty Sarah, a warm heart still beat.

He waited until mid-week, then on Wednesday evening walked round to Gaynor Street with a bouquet of red roses, hoping she had returned from Scotland.

The housekeeper rang Sarah's bell, and soon she came tripping down the stairs, as lovely as he rememberd her, fair hair like a halo around her pretty face, blue eyes looking into his as she reached the bottom stair where she stood stock still.

'Giles!'

'Hello, Sarah.' And he gave her the roses.

She looked down at them, buried her nose in them, then looked up at him.

'Thank you. I'm afraid I can't ask you up to my room – it isn't allowed.'

'That's all right. Shall we go for a walk?'

'Love to,' she said. 'Do you mind waiting while I put these in water and get a coat?'

He shook his head, smiling, and sat down in the hall chair.

He hadn't been wrong about her – just seeing her again was enough to convince him that he had fallen in love with her. How did she feel about him?

They fell into step as they walked, almost formal in their approach to each other.

'I missed you,' he said.

'I missed you, too,' she said. 'I thought after that day – '

'When I was so rude to you at the studio?'

'I deserved it,' she said. 'I really am sorry you had that walk.'

'Let's forget it,' he said. As they neared Hyde Park, he took her hand.

'How is your father?'

'How did you know?'

'I saw Sam Bloxburg.'

'Oh.' And she bit her lip. 'I expect you think that was an awful thing to do, too?'

290

'No, darling – and the sort of thing I would expect you to do. Anyway, how is he? Your father, I mean?'

'Recovering, I hope. He has three broken ribs and a fractured shoulder bone.'

'What happened?'

'A bomb fell on the factory where he works.' And he saw the pugnacious set of her chin.

Unable to help himself, he stopped on the long path leading to Kensington Gardens and kissed her soundly.

'Oh, Giles!'

They sat and talked by the Round Pond – about her family and her visit to Scotland. He told her aobut his trip to Canada.

'So what are your plans?' he said as they got up and began to retrace their steps. They strolled in the late evening sunshine, arm in arm as lovers have always done in London parks.

'Well, I had a call from the casting agency about a small part in a film being made at Ealing Studios – a French maid, not many lines. You know, Giles, I could do that easily. I had French grandmother and – '

He stopped dead in his tracks. 'Sarah!'

She laughed. 'I did! Well, a French step-grandmother. My grandfather married a Frenchwoman as his second wife.' And Giles laughed out loud, and bent and kissed her again.

'Anyway,' he said, walking on, 'I'm not sure about that. I'd like you for the part of Alice if Sam thinks you're O.K.'

'Giles! You wouldn't – I mean, would you? Oh, that would be wonderful!'

'Well, we'll see.'

'You know, it's quite true,' she said as they walked on. 'She was quite right – it's who you know.'

'Who is she?' Giles asked.

'Petronella. She said it's who you know not what you know. I think that's a shame at the end of the day. I'd like to think it's because I'm a good actress.'

'Oh, you're a good actress all right!' Giles laughed. 'No doubt about that.'

Sarah felt at peace with the world.

*   *   *

On the last day of April nineteen forty-two a great many strings had been pulled in order to celebrate young Andrew's first birthday in style.

The house in Flag Walk was completely restored, Miss Farquarson again in residence, and Ada happy as a sandboy to have her family round her. Andrew, once again in RAF uniform, had obtained a few hours' leave. His proud parents were beside him.

The lawns had had their first cut of the year, the tulips and wallflowers were ablaze with colour, while the cherry trees shed their pink and white blossom like confetti – a fitting contribution considering that the newlyweds, Giles and Sarah, had just appeared at the steps leading down into the garden. Giles was admiring Sarah's wedding gift from Miss Farquarson, a diamond and emerald brooch, which was also a thank you gift for Sarah's rescuing her on the night of the bomb.

'You must take care of her, young man,' she said. 'She saved my life.'

'Oh, I'll do that all right,' he promised.

Andrew, his arm around Julie's shoulders, watched with pride as their young son took a few faltering steps then sat down abruptly, his fat little legs encased in rompers, white doeskin boots freshly cleaned. His dark eyes with their long lashes surveyed the scene all around him. He guessed there was something going on, and hadn't he had some lovely presents? His reddish hair glinted in the sun as he crawled towards a daisy, a cheeky miss who had escaped the gardener's mower, and looked up, grinning at them all.

Julie squeezed Andrew's hand. 'I can hear a taxi,' she said. 'That'll be Olivia – and Jamie.' Only she knew that they were coming up together by train from Portsmouth. 'Don't say anything to Aunt Emily,' Olivia had written to her. 'Jamie and I met again, quite by chance in the town, and have seen quite a bit of each other. I don't want to say anything just yet – but I live in hopes!'

And now here they were together, Jamie dark-eyed and sun-burned, Olivia tall and elegant, her wonderful hair in a chignon on her swanlike neck. What a handsome couple they made.

'Olivia! Jamie!' Julie bent forward to receive their kisses.

'Is this him?' Jamie asked, his dark eyes on his godson. 'My word he's grown.' He had not been home since Christmas. 'And Aunt – you look wonderful!'

'Now come on, everyone,' Ada called from the terrace. She had been busy for two whole days, making the birthday cake and home made bread, which considering the shortage of food supplies was a miracle.

'What a perfect day!' Julie turned starry eyes to Andrew. 'I didn't know it was possible to be so happy.'

He bent his head to kiss her. Sometimes he couldn't believe he was really here.

Jean Chapman

The Bellmakers

Forced to take on her pedlar grandfather's tally round and sell stockings to save her family from starvation, Leah Dexter is unprepared for the abuse and prejudice she encounters travelling alone on the new railway. And when she arrives at the village of Soston just as brothers Ben and Nat are reclaiming the cursed Monk's Bell, the superstitious local folk take her appearance as an evil omen.

When Ben intervenes to save her he wins Leah's everlasting gratitude and heart. But prejudice, superstition and the unbridled lust of the squire's son still threaten the proud and beautiful pedlar girl and those she loves...

Mary Williams

The Bridge Between

From the moment she arrives in the tiny Cornish fishing village of Port Todric in 1904, Julia Kerr loves the place. Through the ups and downs of her own writing career and her marriage to a man who always puts his painting first, she draws strength and encouragement from the unchanging rhythm of village life.

Julia's daughter Sarah, while very different from her mother, shares the same passionate wilfulness. Will she break Julia's heart by continuing to estrange herself from her family after a quarrel? Or will their shared love for the village bring about a reconciliation?

A warm and realistic love story with a lovingly rendered Cornish background, *The Bridge Between* is a book to touch the heart.

Jan Webster

Tallie's War

Tallie Candlish is put upon by her clever sister Kate, a pupil teacher and suffragette, and by spoiled Belle, the family beauty. Wilfred Chappell, a young English schoolteacher lodging in their Lanarkshire home, is attracted by Tallie's diffident manner and quiet beauty. He encourages her to put herself first for once and follow her ambition to train as a nurse – and promptly finds himself wishing he hadn't.

While suffragette Kate discloses a vulnerability that takes him by surprise, Tallie reveals a strength and single-mindedness he has never suspected. But when war breaks out she needs every ounce of that strength to bring her through the horrors of nursing the war-wounded and the devastating news that Wilfred is missing, presumed dead ...

June Barraclough

Time Will Tell

Susan, Miriam, Lally and Gillian have grown up together in the
Yorkshire village of Eastcliff with their close friends Tom, Nick and
Gabriel. *Time Will Tell* is the story, told by Gillian, of the
intertwined adult lives of these seven very different friends. Will
anyone stay on in the village now? Will they all marry and have
children?

As their lives unfold it becomes clear that while some of them will
make their mark in the world, not all of them will find happiness.
Even far from Eastcliff, childhood events and attachments continue
to cast shadows over their lives until the friends come to see all their
pasts, including Gillian's own, in a new light.

Nina Lambert

A Place in the Sun

Carla de Luca has all the looks, talent and ambition an actress needs but so far the big break has passed her by. With her widowed mother and the family relying on her, she is forced to take temporary work as a saleswoman where she catches the eye of successful entrepreneur Jack Fitzgerald.

He offers her a job selling time-share apartments in his new Italian resort: fantastic commission, sea, sun – and eventually his heart. Regretfully, Carla turns him down. She has told Jack more about her past than she has ever confided in a man before but she dare not risk telling him everything ...

Further titles available from Woman's Weekly Fiction

While every effort is made to keep prices low, it is sometimes necessary to increase prices at short notice. Mandarin Paperbacks reserves the right to show new retail prices on covers which may differ from those previously advertised in the text or elsewhere.

The prices shown below were correct at the time of going to press.

All these books are available at your bookshop or newsagent, or can be ordered direct from the address below. Just tick the titles you want and fill in the form below.

Cash Sales Department, PO Box 5, Rushden, Northants NN10 6YX.
Fax: 0933 414000 : Phone 0933 414047.

Please send cheque, payable to 'Reed Book Services Ltd', or postal order for purchase price quoted and allow the following for postage and packing:

£1.00 for the first book: £1.50 for **two books or more per order.**

NAME (Block letters) ....

ADDRESS ....

.... Postcode...........................

☐ I enclose my remittance for £.......................

☐ I wish to pay by Access/Visa Card Number ☐☐☐☐☐☐☐☐☐☐☐☐☐☐☐☐

Expiry Date ☐☐☐☐

☐ If you do not wish your name to be used by other carefully selected organisations for promotional purposes please tick this box.

Signature ....
Please quote our reference: 3 503 500 C

Orders are normally dispatched within five working days, but please allow up to twenty days for delivery.

Registered office: Michelin House, 81 Fulham Road, London SW3 6RB

Registered in England. No. 1974080